Disreputable. Dangerous.

Wolf McCloud emerged from the barn and strode toward Julia, appearing every bit as malevolent as a dime-novel villain.

"Good morning, Miss Julia. You're looking especially lovely today."

She tensed. "Save your breath, McCloud. Your glib tongue does nothing for me."

"Ah, lovely Julia, you have no idea what my tongue could do for you."

In spite of the blush that prickled her neck, she looked at him. "You're so certain your shocking mouth will make a woman clasp her hands to her bosom and swoon. I find it in poor taste and not the least bit provocative."

His eyes danced with danger. "But you've used the words mouth . . . bosom . . . and taste . . . all in one sentence. Now who's being provocative?"

Her body betrayed her. "I won't give you the satisfaction of continuing this verbal sparring, McCloud."

"It's not verbal sparring, Miss Julia."

Before she could think otherwise, she asked, "What else would you call it?"

He gave her a lusty, smile. "Why, verbal intercourse. . . ."

Books by Jane Bonander

Dancing On Snowflakes
Wild Heart

Published by POCKET BOOKS

JANE BONANDER

WILD HEART

POCKET BOOKS

New York   London   Toronto   Sydney   Tokyo   Singapore

This book is a work of fiction. Names, characters, places and incidents are products of the author's imagination or are used fictitiously. Any resemblance to actual events or locales or persons, living or dead, is entirely coincidental.

An *Original* Publication of POCKET BOOKS

 POCKET BOOKS, a division of Simon & Schuster Inc.
1230 Avenue of the Americas, New York, NY 10020

ISBN: 0-671-52983-8

First Pocket Books printing October 1995

10 9 8 7 6 5 4 3 2 1

POCKET and colophon are registered trademarks of Simon & Schuster Inc.

Cover art by Jim Griffin

Printed in the U.S.A.

For my editor, Caroline Tolley

With special thanks to Don and Marsha Stewart, who live in the shadow of the Devil Mountain and have requested a story be set there; to Jack Harrison, Director of Outreach Docent for the Shadelands Museum, for his wonderful tour; and to Liv Harper, for getting me out of my painted corner. Again.

❧ Prologue ❧

Central California
1846

Wrapped in a blanket and buried alive.

Angus squatted next to the howling bairn, studying it. Thick, black hair grew low on its forehead. Eyebrows, dark as Satan's, were pinched together over eyes that were squeezed shut. Its mouth was open as it continued to wail, lips quivering over toothless gums.

Angus raised his eyes to the river, as if searching for the transgressor who had buried the babe and left it to die. He couldn't imagine a woman doing such a thing, not even here, in the devil's own wilderness.

When he'd first heard the bairn's cries, he'd thought it was an abandoned coyote pup. But as he'd drawn closer to the mound of Indian manzanitas, he knew he was wrong.

Angus unwrapped the babe. It was a boy. Pudgy arms and legs kicked free, flailing in the air. The length of the cord that had once supplied him with life lay slack against his belly. It was just beginning to shrivel. With one great breath, the bairn inhaled, then expelled a sound that came from deep within his lungs.

A harsh, scolding sound that undoubtedly condemned those who had put him there. An arrogant sound, to Angus's ears, coming from one so small.

The babe stopped crying when Angus touched him. He opened his eyes, which were a stormy blue, the color of the skies over Angus's Scottish homeland. Angus fingered the blanket, noting that it was not an Indian wrap. But the child was a half-blood, in spite of the color of his eyes.

Angus stood, hands on hips, and studied the boy. What in the devil would he do with a bairn? Baptiste, his trapping companion, would no doubt drive a stick through the child's heart and roast him for dinner, reminding Angus that they did not need another mouth to feed, especially one that could not feed itself.

But Baptiste's squaw might take pity on the squalling thing. After all, it was half Indian. He couldn't very well leave the boy by the river to die.

Stepping to his saddlebag, Angus pulled out a flask of whiskey and two sugar lumps, giving one to his mount. The other he wrapped inside his bandana and dripped whiskey over it. He returned to the bairn and, with clumsy hands, picked him up, resting him in the crook of his arm. The babe latched on to the sugar tit, and within moments was asleep.

Angus put him back on the blanket and wrapped him in it once again. "Aye, laddie," he whispered, "even in repose ye look angry with the world."

He wondered at a woman who could dispose of her flesh and blood like animal scat. He glanced toward the north, toward John Sutter's adobe-walled fortress of New Helvetia, and wondered if perhaps the woman had come from there. A servant, maybe. Someone who wouldn't be examined too closely as her time for birthing came.

He got to his feet and returned his gaze to the boy. Again, thoughts of what he'd do with such a handful troubled him greatly. Dare he keep him? Raise him as his own? Could he, Angus McCloud, be a father? Aye, as odd as it might sound to others, he could imagine such a thing. The thought was not distasteful to him.

There were many times when he yearned for some of the softness that had been in his early life, back in Scotland. When he tried very hard, he could transform bird song into music, and envision his sweet mother playing Mozart on her tinny piano.

He was still a stranger in this rough, harsh land, but he desperately clung to his memories lest he become as callous and vulgar as Baptiste.

Returning to his saddlebag, he removed the wooden box that held his beaver castoreum, then scooped out a handful of mud, depositing it on the grass near the water's edge. He put a small portion of the yellow gummy castoreum from the beaver's gland on the mud, hoping to lure a beaver to his trap, then returned the box to its place.

He picked up the bairn again, and, anticipating the vile, howling protest from Baptiste's tongue, he nevertheless swung himself and the bairn into the saddle and headed for their cabin in the woods.

❧ 1 ❧

In the shadow
of the Devil Mountain
October 1872, California

*D*isreputable. *Dangerous.*

Those were the words that had come to Julia's mind weeks before, when she'd first glimpsed the new man her father had hired. Now, as Wolf McCloud disappeared into the barn, those words rang in her ears again.

It had been a mistake to employ him, but her father wouldn't have believed her even if she had expressed her misgivings to him. She couldn't claim that the man didn't work. He was the best man they'd ever hired. It was all those other things about him that bothered her every waking minute. Who was she kidding? He'd even begun to invade her dreams.

She glanced at baby Marymae, who kicked happily on a blanket nearby, then leaned on her hoe, unable to get the man out of her mind. Disreputable. Dangerous. Even that very first day, she'd read him like one reads a book.

Inky hair to his shoulders and dark, dusky skin that hinted at his Indian blood. Cheekbones sharp enough

4

to cut glass. The flash of white teeth behind a cocky smile. His blue eyes, rimmed in brown, hinted at an impulsiveness that wasn't safe to trust. When he sat astride his stallion, arrogant and bold, his hips and thighs moved rhythmically, suggestively, with the horse's gait. The name ... Wolf ... was fitting in its texture, for it conjured up further wariness in those wise enough to sense it.

Yes, she'd read him like a book. Unfortunately, it was not the kind of book a decent young woman should read, although Josette devoured them like berries and sweet cream. If they had been fattening, her sister would be enormous.

Wolf McCloud emerged from the barn and strode toward Julia, appearing every bit as malevolent as a dime-novel villain. Her pulse quickened and she lowered her head, hiding her face beneath the brim of her father's battered hat. She hacked away at the dirt around her pole beans with a vengeance.

"Well, good morning, Miss Julia."

Lord, even the sound of his voice was indecent, sending tattletale shivers over her flesh. "Good morning." Her answer was abrupt.

"You're looking especially lovely today. Not many women could wear that getup and still look like a woman."

She tensed against his mockery, knowing full well how she looked in her father's old woolen trousers and oversized shirt.

"Save your breath, Mr. McCloud. Your glib tongue does nothing for me." She wasn't as easily bamboozled as her sister. Josette fawned and preened around him like a fool. Sadly, that was her normal behavior around *all* men.

"Ah, lovely Julia, you have no idea what my tongue could do for you."

The innuendo sent a rush of blood to Julia's cheeks, and her heart pounded foolishly. She wondered again, for the umpteenth time, why he'd been hired. She also wondered why she didn't report his insolence to her father.

"And please," he added, his voice smooth as whiskey, "as long as our tongues have become so intimate, why don't you call me Wolf?"

In spite of the blush that prickled her neck, she stopped working and looked up, catching the smile that tugged at his lean, sensuous lips. Wolf, indeed. A preposterous name for any man but this one.

"Why, I've made you blush." He sounded pleased.

"Don't flatter yourself. I know your kind well, Mr. McCloud. You're certain your shocking mouth will make a woman clasp her hands to her bosom and swoon. I find it in poor taste and, much as you'd like to think so, not the least bit provocative."

"I see." He studied her, his face thoughtful but his eyes dancing with danger. "But you've used the words mouth ... bosom ... and taste ... all in one sentence, Miss Julia. *Now* who's being provocative?"

Her traitorous nipples tightened beneath her shirt. It was the way he'd drawn the words out, that's all. She had no control over her body, but she certainly had control of her own mind. With the hoe gripped in her fists, she dug fiercely at the dirt. "I will not give you the satisfaction of continuing this ridiculous verbal sparring, Mr. McCloud. I have work to do. I'm sure you do, too."

He leaned close and pulled the brim of her hat up so he could look at her. "But it's not verbal sparring, Miss Julia."

"Well, please entertain me with your vast knowledge of words, Mr. McCloud. What else would you call it?"

He gave her a lusty, sin-filled smile. "Why, verbal intercourse, naturally."

She felt the words as though they were fingers, stroking the fires of her latent desires. With the utmost effort, she bent to her task again, more to keep him from seeing the effect his words had on her than anything else. She knew that beneath her prim exterior was a darker side. A side that was drawn to the danger this man exuded. *A side I will keep hidden until I take my last breath on this earth, so help me God.*

Marymae let out a baleful cry, jerking Julia out of her foolish musings. She dropped the hoe and hurried to the blanket, lifting the baby into her arms. When she turned, Mr. McCloud was still standing on the other side of the garden.

"Pretty baby. A girl, right?"

Julia looked into Marymae's big, blue eyes, a trait both she and Josette shared. Now, at two and a half months of age, her fair hair had golden highlights, like Josette's rather than Julia's own, which reminded her more of wheat than of a precious metal. "Yes, she is pretty. But surely, Mr. McCloud, you didn't come over here just to accost me with words or admire the baby. What do you want?"

His eyes always held a hint of something besides the mockery that was always there. She refused to look too deeply, for she might see it—that elusive, unspoken invitation that she'd met up with before in another man, and had foolishly answered.

He pulled his bandanna off and wiped his face, then snaked the cloth inside his shirt collar and wiped his neck. The shirt gaped, exposing a hard, bare chest, sleek with sweat. Julia's mouth went dry.

"Is your sister around?"

Her spine stiffened automatically, and she put Marymae on the blanket. Her conversations with men always came around to Josette. "She's in the house." Probably reading one of those dreadful novels, Julia thought, her lips pursing. Josette was always in love with the idea of being in love, and those novels fed her foolish fantasies.

"Ah. Do I detect a note of disapproval? Or maybe it's jealousy. You want me all to yourself, is that it?"

"Don't be a fool. If it were up to me—" She stopped, warmth flooding her. If it were up to her, she'd fire buckshot into his retreating behind.

"If it were up to you—what, Miss Julia? What would you do with me?"

Never in her life had she met a man as bold and outrageous as this one. His very existence made her life miserable. He was a threat to her sanity, even if he only invaded her mind . . . and her dreams.

"What I would do with you is against the law, Mr. McCloud."

He tugged playfully at the brim of her hat and smiled that smile again. "Sounds . . . provocative." How glibly he threw her word back into her face! "Would I enjoy it?"

"I doubt it." She gave him a secret smile of her own. "But I would."

He threw his head back and laughed, a sound that sent her blood racing again. "I'm sorry we have to stop this verbal intimacy, Miss Julia, but I *am* looking for your sister. She has requested my services this morning, and your father approves."

Oddly, he often sounded so . . . civilized, as if there

were another man imprisoned inside this one, screaming to get out. She pursed her lips again, cursing her
thoughts. It was only her imagination; he was what he
appeared to be and nothing more.

McCloud studied her. "But I can see that you don't
approve, Miss Julia."

"You can bet I don't, Mr. McCloud. I can think of
many things you could be doing rather than entertaining my sister."

"Like, entertaining you?"

She nearly snorted. "It'll be a cold day in hell before that happens."

She returned to the garden and bent to her task
again, grateful her face was hidden beneath her
floppy-brimmed hat. She couldn't understand why
Papa gave Josette permission to take the ranch hands
away from important work just to ferry her about. He
didn't seem to realize that Josette needed protection
from men like Wolf McCloud. Not that it would do
any good; Josette always found a way to disregard
propriety and do what she pleased.

"Anyway, Josette has work to do," she lied. "I'd
rather you didn't disrupt her routine."

"And, her routine would be . . ." He paused, waiting
for her to explain. Even without looking at him she
noted the skepticism in his voice.

"Her routine is none of your concern, Mr. McCloud.
Just take my word for it."

Behind her, she heard the door open. Josette's tin-
kling voice followed. "Good morning, Mr. McCloud.
Were you looking for me?"

As usual, Josette sounded cheerful and ready to face
the world, so long as the world revolved around her.

Julia continued working on the garden, gripping the
hoe handle hard as she attacked the dirt around the

squash. Josette invited the advances of men, pirouetting and dancing for them. Julia drove them away, thrusting and parrying her tongue like the sharp blades of a shiv. She hadn't always been that way. She'd been a much softer woman once—before Marymae's father swaggered into their lives. Sometimes she wanted to blame Josette for everything, but Josette was exactly what she and Papa had made her: frivolous, selfish, and unconcerned with anyone's needs but her own.

"Yes, ma'am. You wanted me to drive you to that patch of gooseberries, remember?"

Julia felt a stab of anger. Gooseberries, indeed. Lord only knew what they would do when they got there.

"Oh, piffle, Mr. McCloud, don't call me ma'am. Save that word for Julia. Call me Josette. Please." She gave him a dimpled smile. "I've even brought a basket for the berries. See?"

Julia turned to watch her sister, whose innocent beauty went no deeper than the skin. At times like this, when she desperately wanted to see Josette's flaws, she could find none. On the outside, Josette was lovely. Even in her plain blue calico, she was a vision. Her golden hair caught the sunlight, causing her to appear utterly angelic. Which was not possible, given Josette's weakness for men.

Julia sighed, dropped the hoe between the rows of squash and went to pick up Marymae, who was fussing again. It was time for her nap, which was the perfect excuse to escape into the house. Julia couldn't stop what she certain would happen, anyway. Not this time. But she sure as hell could prevent it from happening again. She would see to Mr. McCloud's termination when her father came in for lunch.

"Why don't you and the baby join us, Miss Julia?"

The invitation came as such a surprise, she almost choked on her tongue. "Don't be ridiculous. I don't have time to—"

"Oh, poor Julia never lets herself have any fun," Josette interrupted. "She never learned how."

The resentment that Julia was usually able to suppress flooded her, and she felt a sick knot of anger unravel in her chest. Flinging her sister a veiled look of hostility, she answered, "Marymae must be fed, then put down for a nap. I hardly have time to go gallivanting around the countryside, looking for *gooseberries.*"

"Another time, then, Miss Julia."

Although she didn't hear any sarcasm in his words, Julia refused to look at him, for she knew she'd see it in his eyes. That, or gratitude that she wouldn't be intruding on their little twosome.

"Josette," she called, "be back before lunch."

"Oh." Josette's delicate hand flew to her mouth. "Lunch. I should have thought to have Julia pack us one, Mr. McCloud."

Julia rested Marymae against her shoulder and rolled her eyes to the heavens as she walked to the house. It would never dawn on Josette that if she wanted to go on a picnic, she could pack the lunch herself. Julia wanted to blame Papa for her sister's behavior, but she knew she had to take part of the responsibility for it herself.

"I'm afraid I have work to do this afternoon, Miss Josette," McCloud said. "I can't be gone too long."

"Oh, pooh," Josette answered, making a moue. "I'd hoped we could spend the day together."

Wolf McCloud actually chuckled. "As entertaining

as that sounds, Miss Josette, I wasn't hired to be your escort."

Julia paused on the porch, taking her time, hoping to catch the rest of the conversation. She knew exactly what would happen if her sister and that . . . that rakehell spent too much time together. She was afraid it might already be too late.

"Oh, but Papa would let you spend the day with me if I asked him," she said, her voice sweetly seductive.

Julia could stand it no longer. "Josette!" She turned and glared at her sister. "Mr. McCloud has to drive a load of walnuts into Walnut Hill this afternoon. He is *not* here as your personal companion."

Josette bit down on her lower lip and gave Julia one of her practiced looks of injury. She even had tears in her eyes. "Don't shout at me, Julia, dearest. Please, don't shout."

Julia took a deep breath and shook her head. "Just . . . just don't be gone too long, all right?" She eagerly escaped into the house to prepare lunch for Marymae.

But once inside, she crossed to the window and watched the buggy move away, Josette clinging possessively to Wolf McCloud's hair-dusted forearm. Her stomach pitched downward, and she knew her worries were well founded.

She moved quietly around the kitchen, mulling over how she would approach Papa about her fears. She didn't think she was jealous or selfish. In spite of what had happened between her and Josette, she considered herself quite generous.

But if Papa allowed Wolf McCloud to stay, Julia was certain that in nine months, perhaps even less, she would have another baby to care for. And that one wouldn't be hers, either.

*　　*　　*

"Papa, Mr. McCloud is a dangerous kind of man to have around." Julia had met her father at the washstand on the back stoop when he'd come in for lunch. She wanted to speak with him before Josette returned.

"Well, dang it, Julia. He's a good worker. I hate to have to let him go. He's the best man I've ever hired."

"Hired hands are more plentiful than you think." She wasn't nearly as certain as she sounded.

"I think you got him all wrong, honey. He's not—"

"Papa," she interrupted, "if we don't let him go, we'll go through hell again when Josette has to face another birthing."

Her father frowned and shook his head. "I think you're wrong about him, Julia."

"Papa." Her voice was stern, brooking no nonsense. "What'll I tell him?"

"Oh, I don't know." She tried to quell her impatience. "Does it matter? Papa, something has to be done. I don't know what." She'd thought of trying to get Josette to use measures to keep from getting pregnant, but that was like telling her it was all right to do . . . what she did. Julia felt tears of frustration sting her eyes. "We've got to do something, Papa. Things just can't continue this way. She's . . . she's becoming a tramp."

Julia watched the emotions flick over her father's face, knowing he was trying to find the solution himself. She should have been angry with him for the way he pampered and protected Josette. At times she was, but she was to blame, too. And she'd never really fought with Papa before. His life was hard enough. Instead, she'd stood by and watched her sister become a pretty, but useless, appendage to the family.

Josette had Papa wrapped around her little finger. It had been that way ever since their mother died. He could deny her nothing, but in doing so, he'd led her to believe that the only things that were important were her own selfish needs. Heaven forbid that she should have any responsibilities, Julia thought peevishly.

"Don't defame your sister, Julia."

"*Defame* her? Papa, she does that well enough all by herself. She doesn't need my help. Have you forgotten about Marymae?"

He cleared his throat and wiped his hands and face on a towel. "Nobody knows about that but the three of us—"

"Oh, Papa. Surely you don't believe that no one *knows* what happened?"

His frown was filled with more sorrow than anger. "Why, nobody's said nothin' to me."

Julia forced down her impatience. "Just where do you suppose they think the baby came from? That she just fell from the sky? That the stork dropped her on the way to someone else's house?"

"Now, no need gettin' sarcastic," he answered with a weary sigh.

Julia pressed her fingers against her eyes. "Papa, we don't live in the middle of nowhere. People notice things like brand-new babies."

"Yeah, I suppose they do. I'm just glad no one's asked me about it. I wouldn't know what to tell them."

"The truth might be nice." She was unable to curb her sharp tongue.

"Oh, but to have people think my little Josie—"

"You'd rather they thought Marymae was mine?" She was incredulous, but shouldn't have been surprised.

"Well, dang it, Julia, even *I* sometimes forget that the baby is Josie's. You act like the child's ma."

"It was either that or watch her starve to death right before my eyes." Even though she'd come to love Marymae as her own, her resentment toward her flighty sister welled up within her again.

Her father walked to the edge of the stoop. Julia knew his face would be filled with longing as he gazed out over the vast acreage that used to be rife with wheat and now lay fallow.

"After your ma died, we moved here to get a fresh start. It's been ten years, eight of 'em growin' and sellin' more wheat than we thought possible. Now look at what we got. We got nothin', Julia. Nothin'." He massaged his neck with gnarled fingers.

Julia didn't answer; she didn't have to. She knew his thoughts. Knew he was remembering the torrential downpours they'd endured three and four years before, which ruined the grain, and on the heels of the rain had come two years of drought. They hadn't recovered. She wondered if they ever would.

"I've tried to do right by you girls. Guess I shoulda married again. It wasn't fair to either of you to grow up without a ma. Why, just look at the two of you. You're all but worn-out doin' all of the work around here. And Josie . . ." He sighed. "Josie needs a firmer hand than mine. When the trouble started, I should've sent her to your aunt Mattie in San Francisco like she wanted me to. Maybe she could've done something for Josie, but I don't see how. Mattie was a wild one, too."

Julia was surprised he even mentioned his younger sister's name. He usually only referred to her as "as the wild one," because she hadn't followed the conventional path of marriage and babies. At forty-five,

Mattie Larson ran a successful boardinghouse in San Francisco. Julia had no doubt that Josette would have been a different person if Mattie had been around, for the adult Mattie stood for no nonsense from anyone. And Josette was absolutely filled to the brim with nonsense. But Papa had refused Mattie's help from the very beginning, probably because they had never seen eye to eye on anything. "Aunt Mattie would have made mincemeat out of Josette and you know it."

"Yeah, well, maybe that's what she needed, honey. You both needed a ma, but I just couldn't bring myself to marry again. Just couldn't replace your ma in my heart. At least Mattie would've been a woman for the both of you to look up to."

Julia was close to tears whenever her father exposed his fears and his broken heart. "Oh, Papa," she said, coming up behind him and hugging him around the waist. Shock raced through her when she felt how thin he was. He'd had less stamina lately, too. Poor Papa. He was wearing out. "You've done a fine job. Josie and I love you very much."

He snuffled a skeptical laugh. "Yeah. I done a mighty fine job, ain't I? Got me one daughter who can't get enough of men, and the other who can't stand the sight of them. Not to mention that I've got me a grandchild, but no son-in-law."

He ran his fingers through his thick, gray hair and lowered his head. "Who's gonna run this place after I'm gone?" He laughed bitterly. "Who am I kidding? If things go on like this, there ain't gonna be a place left to run."

Julia clung to her father. The very idea that one day he'd be gone made her stomach cave in. She didn't like to think about it. She wished he wouldn't mention it. His mood had been so low recently, she'd become worried about him.

But she felt frustration, too. Basically, she'd been running the ranch for years. She'd done everything but keep the books, and knew she could have done that, too, but her father refused to let her. Before they lost the wheat, she'd been responsible for hiring the threshing crews and seeing that the grain got to Martinez, where it was loaded onto the ships bound for Europe. Now, all they had left were a few walnut trees and more fruit trees than they knew what to do with. And . . . a folder full of unpaid bills.

If they'd been the only fruit growers in the area, perhaps they could have sold enough to make a go of the ranch, but many grew fruit because it was such an effortless crop. But it was delicate, too. If shipped too far, it would spoil. If picked too early, it wouldn't ripen. Daily she fought her panic that the time would come when they'd be forced to leave. It would kill Papa. He seemed to be dying some each day, as it was.

They could no longer afford to keep help. Papa had wanted at least one good permanent hand, and he'd hoped it would be Wolf McCloud. If Julia knew nothing else, she knew it shouldn't be him, no matter how hard he worked. She felt threatened by his presence, and she *would* get rid of him.

She gave her father a final squeeze, then led him into the house. "Let's not worry about that now, Papa. Something will happen. It always does," she suggested. "Come to the table. Your lunch is ready."

When he sat down, she put a piece of leftover quail pie and a dish of peach sauce, which was his favorite, in front of him, hoping to stimulate his appetite. He'd been eating so poorly of late.

Her heart ached for him. Until recently, she hadn't

thought much about his loneliness and personal heart-break. Children rarely think about their parents' problems, for they're so wrapped up in their own lives. Like Josette. But Julia saw herself in him, could almost envision herself sitting at the table twenty years from now, alone, but hopefully not lonely, but she couldn't be sure. That thought spawned another.

"Papa, I haven't seen the Henleys lately." Meredith Henley and her son Serge, whom she'd once tried to marry off to Julia, usually came by on a weekly basis.

"They went back East. Left Frank Barnes in charge," he answered, toying with his pie.

The mere sound of Frank Barnes's name made Julia flush with humiliation and anger. "I don't know why they had to hire him, anyway. He should have been run out of town."

"Just because he went and got your sister pregnant don't mean he ain't a good hand, Julia."

Oh, Julia thought, if that were the *only* reason she despised him. She would never forget how he'd pretended to court her, and all the while was sleeping with Josette. He was pond scum. Buffalo chips. Hog slop. And she was glad he was gone.

"Serge and Meredith will be gone a few months," her father offered, interrupting her thoughts.

Julia vividly remembered the day Meredith had tried to convince Papa that a marriage between her and Serge was essential. She knew Meredith wanted their land, for it backed up against the creek. Not exactly a union made in heaven.

But recently Papa hadn't seemed interested in pursuing that. He'd even been reluctant to visit much with Meredith, which surprised Julia, for they had been close friends for many years. At one time she'd even thought perhaps Papa would ask Meredith to marry him. But Meredith was too strong a woman for her dear, sweet Papa. She would have flattened him like a herd of wild horses.

Unlike sweet, unthreatening Serge. Julia was happy her father hadn't pursued the marriage thing, for though she wanted to save the ranch, she didn't want to marry someone to do it, not even Serge.

Watching Papa now, so frail and sick, brought a fresh stab of guilt. She was being selfish. "Papa, if marrying Serge would make things better—"

"No!"

Julia's relief was overshadowed by her surprise at the look of fury that crossed her father's face. "But—"

"Don't bring it up again. I won't have ..." He paused, his fork clenched in his fist. "I don't want my girls to marry just to save the ranch."

"But, Papa, I would—"

"I know you would, Julia, honey. That's the sin of it. I know you'd do anything to save my hide, but I won't let you waste your life. It's too hard on a woman out here. If she don't marry for love, she ain't got a life at all."

"You and Mama didn't marry for love," she reminded him.

"But we grew to love each other, honey. That's the difference."

"Well, but how do you know Serge and I—"

He actually laughed. "Serge? Tarnation, Julia, you're more of a man than he is."

Julia felt no insult; she knew what he meant. Serge was the most complaisant man she'd ever known. Not like Wolf McCloud. Or Frank Barnes. But she wouldn't dredge all that up again. She was faced with it far too often as it was. Daily, in fact, whenever she looked into Marymae's sweet face.

"I guess I might reconsider such a thing if Serge were a different kind of man."

Julia gave him a puzzled frown. "What do you mean, different?"

"You don't know, do ya?" His smile was sad, cheerless, as he plunged his fork into the quail pie. He ate with little enthusiasm.

Julia reached across the table and stroked the back of his hand. "All I know is that I would do anything you asked if it meant saving the ranch." But she was grateful he wouldn't make her marry against her will.

"I know, Julia, I know. And I love you for it."

As she sat across the table from her father, she knew something troubled him besides his fallow land and his daughters. He'd brooded long hours at his desk, poring over maps and papers and books. And his appetite was nearly gone. Yet when she questioned him, he would not take her into his confidence.

She rose and cleared the table, carrying the dirty dishes to the dishpan. As she poured hot water from the teakettle over them, she looked out the window, toward the small corral next to the barn that her father had built for the horses. Mr. McCloud's black Arab warm-blood pranced inside the enclosure, appearing frisky and anxious for a run. Their two geldings, Ole and Lars, stayed toward the back, avoiding him like cowards avoid a bully.

Julia loved horses, and had been dismayed when so few people rode them in the valley, using them instead to draw buggies or pull wagons and buckboards. She had a feeling it was because most of the settlers had come from the plains and hadn't become accustomed to riding horseback out here, where the land was rolling with hills.

But Julia had. And now, what she wanted most was to give both her and McCloud's stallion a bit of exercise. Papa kept McCloud so busy, he didn't have a chance to ride his horse. Completely ignoring the scolding voice that reminded her it wasn't up to her to rectify that problem, she checked on the baby, then dug into the bin for a few small apples. She hurried from the house, slowing her steps as she reached the corral.

Stepping on the lower rung of the fence, she hung over the top and studied the animal. How perfect he was! Beautiful as a statue. Yet she'd watched him run, graceful as a gazelle, the brawny pockets of muscle beneath his sleek hide rippling with power.

"Here, boy," she urged, extending her hand. What had McCloud called him? Baptiste? "Come, Baptiste," she crooned. The animal came toward her, his nostrils flaring slightly and his majestic head bobbing. He approached her hand, the bristly hairs around his muzzle tickling her palm as he took the apple from her. He whickered and nudged her hand with his nose when he finished his treat. She inhaled, loving the smell of horseflesh as she rubbed his forehead.

"You're a wild thing, aren't you?" she whispered, watching him paw at the ground.

She went into the barn, retrieved McCloud's curb bit and split-ear headstall, then entered the corral through the side door. She fed each of the geldings an apple, then spoke softly as she moved toward the other horse.

"Whoa, Baptiste." Surprisingly, he stood quietly while she worked the bit into his mouth, then slipped the stall over his ears. Perhaps he was as eager for a run as she. The saddle, which straddled the fence, would be something else entirely, for it looked heavy.

She lifted it off the fence, groaning under the weight. By sheer strength of will, she flung it across Baptiste's back and cinched it, pulling it as tightly as she could.

She mounted him, flinging her leg over his back and settling in the saddle. He quivered in anticipation beneath her, and her heart responded in kind.

They left the corral and raced past the walnut grove, down the hill toward the peach and apricot trees, then beyond, through the fallow wheat field and into the open meadow. Grass, dried and golden, crunched beneath them as Baptiste's hooves thundered across the hard-packed earth.

Wind stung Julia's face, bringing tears to her eyes. Her hair came loose, whipping wildly around her head. She tugged on the reins, slowly bringing Baptiste to a stop. He pranced in place briefly, then lowered his head and fed on the grass.

Shading her eyes, Julia squinted toward the mountain. She loved it. Compared to other ranges, the summit of Devil Mountain was not high, but to her it was majestic. At this time of year the grassy slopes were a tawny gold, speckled with thick green clusters of oaks, pines, and laurels. In the spring, lupine and meadow daisies swept into the valley and over the bluffs, their purple and yellow beauty robbing Julia of breath. In the winter there was snow capping the higher peaks, but it didn't usually stay. When they'd first built the house, she'd made sure her and Josette's bedroom faced it. Not that Josette had cared, but Julia had.

When Baptiste raised his head, she flicked the reins on the side of his neck, coaxing him to turn, and they galloped toward home again. She wanted to get back before McCloud returned with Josette.

But when they drew up in front of the barn, Julia's stomach dropped, for McCloud and Josette sat in the buggy, watching her. Sally, their Morgan mare, whinnied and tossed her head, her reddish mane flying.

Baptiste snorted and sidestepped, his neck curved high and his nostrils flared.

"Whoa, boy," she whispered, pulling on the reins.

"Julia! What on earth are you doing?"

Josette's tone was more one of mortified disbelief than of scolding.

"I took Baptiste for a little run." She couldn't meet McCloud's gaze, but she knew it was on her. She felt a hot blush sneak into her face, for she'd been wrong to take the animal out without asking.

"Oh, Mr. McCloud," Josette said around a pretty frown. "What a dreadful way to end such a perfectly *lovely* morning. Seeing Julia riding around like a man is *such* an embarrassment. Nevertheless," she added, able to change moods arbitrarily, "thank you so very much for a wonderful time."

She threw Julia a hooded look, then stretched across the seat and kissed the bastard, full on the mouth.

Julia fumed, and she kept her gaze on Josette as her sister stepped from the buggy. Josette accepted the basket of berries that McCloud handed her, then tossed him a flirty little good-bye wave.

"Julia, I think I'd like jam. Do I have enough here for you to make some?"

Julia ignored her, and Josette shrugged her dainty shoulders and went into the house.

Julia dismounted and found Wolf McCloud so close she could see the brown rim around his stormy blue eyes. A pulse throbbed at his temple. There was careless black stubble over his cheeks and chin. Every time he clenched his teeth, a muscle flexed in his jaw. There was no hint of a smile in his eyes or around his mouth. She'd never seen him so utterly and completely restrained.

Handing him Baptiste's reins, she pulled her gaze away and unhitched Sally from the buggy.

While he fed and groomed Baptiste in the corral, Julia cared for Sally in the barn, away from the other horses, especially the virile Baptiste. They couldn't afford a foal next year. They'd probably just wind up selling it, along with everything else, if things didn't get better.

Finishing in the barn, Julia stepped outside to where McCloud was currying Baptiste. Finally, she could stay quiet no longer.

"I want you to stay away from Josette."

He uttered an indelicate snort. "Only if you'll stay away from my horse."

Her face reddened again. Point well taken. "I regret taking him out without your permission." That she should have to apologize to *him* was almost more than she could bear.

"Well, I don't regret taking your sister out for a ride, ma'am. Sorry I can't accommodate you."

His voice was tight with emotion, but his audacious answer was not unexpected. "You will if you want to keep your job, Mr. McCloud."

Despite the fact that his gaze was on her, she climbed the corral fence instead of going out through the gate. As she walked stiffly to the house, she realized that whether he stayed away from Josette or not made no difference. He was as good as gone.

"But Papa!" Josette wailed. "That's not fair. Julia's just jealous because he pays attention to me and not her. It's *always* that way with her! She's the one who made Frank leave, too, and now she's doing it again."

Julia was in the dark pantry, lifting cream from the fresh milk with her tin skimmer and pouring it into the butter churn. Years ago she'd tried to give the job to Josette, but her sister had had no patience then, and she had none now.

Josette's petulant cries awakened Marymae, who had been asleep beside the stove, and she began to cry. Julia laid the skimmer on the shelf that held the canned fruit sauce, left the pantry and plucked the baby from her cradle, cuddling her close. She wouldn't be comforted, for she continued to belt out long, mournful sobs.

Josette frowned and pressed her hands over her ears. "Can't you keep her quiet, Julia? What's the matter with her, anyway?"

Julia rocked Marymae back and forth in her arms, wanting desperately to smack her sister across the mouth. "Your caterwauling woke her, and she'd mad. And wet. And hungry. For heaven's sake, Josette, she's just a baby. Sometimes I wonder what *your* excuse is."

"Papa," she wailed again. "Don't let her talk to me that way."

"Now, Julia, don't be too hard on your sister. You know how delicate she is."

Julia felt the beginnings of a pounding headache at the base of her neck and between her eyes.

"Yes, Julia. You have no right to be mad. *I* had that baby, not you. *I* went through the worst agony in my life having her. I almost died. I *wanted* to die, it hurt so much. Be nice, Julia. Can't you just be nice, dearest?" she ended, attempting to pacify her sister by sweetening her words.

Julia felt the tension increase in her neck as she put Marymae on the table and changed her diaper. It did no good to lose her temper. Neither her father nor her sister understood why she was angry. Neither of them realized that she might have weaknesses, too, even though she never allowed them to show.

"All right, Josette, I'm sorry. But about Wolf McCloud, I'm only thinking of you. I just don't want a repeat of what you went through with Marymae."

Josette pouted but said nothing, convincing Julia that her fears were well-founded.

"It hasn't already happened, has it?"

"That's none of your business. Papa," she whined, turning toward their father, "tell her that's none of her business."

He sat at the table, his twisted fingers pressed against his eyes. "Tarnation, Josie, I like Mr. McCloud as much as you, but you gotta be careful around men. You can't let 'em all have what they want. Men take advantage of sweet, innocent girls like you."

"But he'll marry me, Papa. I just know it."

Julia gasped, unable to believe a word of it. Men like Wolf McCloud didn't marry women, they merely deflowered them. "Has he asked you to marry him?"

Josette's pout deepened. "Well, no. But ... but he might."

Julia felt a rage so deep, she thought she might fly apart. She crossed to the pantry, took a bottle of milk from the cooler and returned to Josette, thrusting both it and Marymae at her. "Here," she snapped. "Feed your daughter."

Josette hesitantly took the baby and the bottle. "What are you going to do?"

Julia stormed to the door. "I'm going to do what

should have been done in the first place. I'm going to get rid of Wolf McCloud."

With long, purposeful strides, she reached the barn door and flung it open. "Mr. McCloud?"

Ready for a fight, itching to send him packing, she was disappointed when she met with silence. She walked past Sally's stall, rounding the corner to the door that led to the corral. Pushing open the top half of the door, she peered outside.

"Mr. McCloud?" she called again, her anger turning to disappointment when she saw there were only two horses in the enclosure. She spun around and went to the corner of the barn where she knew McCloud had slept. Her heart thumped anxiously. There wasn't a trace of him anywhere—except a note with her father's name on it hanging from the nail where McCloud had hung his hat.

Julia pulled the note off, carried it to the door and opened it, moving it into the waning afternoon light.

Amos—I'm sorry to leave you without help, but I thought it best if I found other employment. I can be reached by sending word to John Sutter. Regards, W. A. McCloud

Julia crumpled the paper and stuffed it into her pocket. *Damn.* She'd wanted the luxury of firing him.

❧ 2 ❧

In the woods on the
American River, California
January 1873

He'd had his first whore when he was thirteen. Her name was Rose, and she'd been old enough to be his mother—if he'd had one. He often wondered if that was why he remembered her name yet couldn't remember any of the others. And there had been many others. Most younger by years than Rose, and all of them prettier by any man's standards. But at thirteen he'd been certain that any woman who could give such pleasure was not only beautiful, but talented as hell.

And he'd never forgotten that Rose hadn't made fun of him. He'd been too nervous to tell her to simply call him "Wolf," and when she'd asked him his name, he'd responded, nervous and horny as a goat, "Wolf-gang Amadeus Morning Cloud, ma'am."

"That's quite a moniker." She'd given him a suggestive smile.

"You aren't gonna make fun of it, are you?" His voice had cracked, and he'd felt stupid.

"Make fun?" she'd said. "Honey, how'n the hell

can I make fun of a name I can't even pronounce? Come over here, boy."

With hesitant steps he'd made his way to her. When she cupped his groin, his turgid young root had nearly exploded.

"Names is the *last* thing we think about in this place." She then proceeded to give him his first taste of heaven.

Before his trip to Rose—a gift from the bawdy Baptiste—his earliest memories had been of rejection. Even though he'd been literally yanked from the jaws of death, he felt abandoned by both of the worlds responsible for his life.

Now, in his twenty-sixth year, not much had changed. Early on, it had been because of his color. He could have been a cherub, and he would have been rebuffed by the world around him. As he grew older, dismissal came because of his attitude. It still did.

Deep inside, there were times when he wanted to change. But he usually sloughed them off, becoming whatever those he dealt with expected him to be. It was easier than proving himself to be something else.

He wasn't even sure to which tribe he belonged. He resembled none of the half-bloods he'd met in California; he'd never felt a part of their world. And even though he had no proof as to whether his mother was Indian or white, Angus had assured him that few squaws would abandon a child so savagely, no matter how it was conceived. He didn't know whether or not it was true, but he'd clung to that statement all of his life.

Armed with this pseudo truth, he imagined that the

woman who bore him had been raped by a Pawnee or a Cheyenne on her trip across the prairie. Even so, anger pooled around his heart when he thought of her.

In his mind, she was like a shape shifter. Because he never knew her, she could be Rose one day, or any number of other prostitutes who serviced the miners in Sacramento City the next. Or maybe the woman who cooked at the camp along the river, or the one who took in laundry. Whoever she was, to him she was always white, and his father was not. He'd never envisioned it being the other way around.

He didn't hate all white women because of what she'd done to him. He only hated her. No matter how many times he told himself it no longer mattered, he could not shrug off the intense feelings of hostility that continued to stir in his gut when he allowed himself to think about her. He desperately wanted resolution. It wouldn't come.

When he was young, he'd wanted memories of a nourishing mother, rocking him to sleep, holding him against her warm bosom, singing him sweet songs. Instead, to her his life had been worth no more than animal shit, kicked over with straw and buried in the dirt.

Tossed in a grave to die, ye were. Angus had been honest with him, never coating the truth with honey-filled words. Yet Wolf had searched for her everywhere. He'd learned of a serving woman who had given birth while working for Sutter and mysteriously returned to her chores without the child. She'd led Wolf to the place where she'd buried the dead baby. The small grave was covered with grass and weeds, but the headstone was a crude cross and there was a name carved on it.

Then there was the preacher's wife, ostracized from

the community because she'd been taken by the Indians, although released unharmed a few months later. Living in a shack on the edge of town with a tolerant sister, she told Wolf, in a droning monotone, she'd had a half-blood child, but it had been a girl. And her husband, a man of the cloth who supposedly worshiped a forgiving God, ordered the child killed and refused to take his wife back.

And although Wolf didn't feel he belonged to a California tribe, he found an Indian woman who had lived with a settler for a time and had given birth to his child. The young man was nearly Wolf's age, but he was alive and well, living in the village with the rest of his people.

Finding the woman who bore him had become an obsession Wolf couldn't shrug off. An addiction he couldn't kick. And after years of searching, he'd finally turned to the lists of settlers who had come overland in covered wagons, venturing west before the discovery of gold at Sutter's Creek. He found her among them. Don't ask him how he knew; he just knew. It was at that moment that he realized he had a sixth sense about his mother.

He wondered if she ever had any premonitions or intuitions about him. Nightmares, hopefully. But in truth, she probably didn't even think about him. After all, he hadn't been important enough to save.

In the meantime, one thing had not changed. He didn't feel welcome in the world, for he was neither Indian nor white, yet the blood of both coursed through his veins.

The blaze in the fireplace crackled and hissed, and rain buffeted the cabin, clamoring at the windows, seeping in around the frames. Wolf sat in Angus's old chair near the fireplace, his feet wrapped in warm wool stockings and propped up on a battered footstool, his boots drying by the fire.

Once again he looked down at the letter he'd picked up at John Sutter's post, noting the November date and the troubled message.

Mr. McCloud,
I have a proposition for you. I ain't a well man.
When you get this, please contact my lawyer, Earl
Williams, in Martinez. He'll get in touch with me
and find us a place to meet.

Amos Larson's squiggly signature was shaky at the bottom of the page.

Wolf folded the letter and tapped it against his chin. As he studied the fire, he wondered what Amos wanted from him. He'd liked the old man. They'd had many intense discussions; Wolf sensed that Amos was dying. He'd felt terrible leaving him the way he did, but he could predict what would have happened if he'd stayed. Josette Larson was a tease, pure and simple. It didn't matter that she'd acted sweet and innocent; she'd known what she wanted, and she'd wanted him.

He snorted a soft laugh. Christ, that sounded arrogant, didn't it? But hell, she wasn't even subtle about it. She had heat in her drawers, that one. And the way she'd talked about her sister had put him off as well. He was far from the most innocent man in the state, but even he knew that when a person spoke ill of someone, they were often trying to cover up something in their own life.

The vision of Amos's older daughter shoved its way into his head, and he uttered another indelicate snort.

That was one rancher's daughter who hid none of her feelings. She'd wanted him out of their lives in no uncertain terms, and had been about as receptive to him as a tree stump. She intrigued him. She was the kind of woman a man like him didn't dare dream about, because there wasn't a chance in hell he could have her.

But dream of her he did. She was a complex package of contradictions. Light eyes that brimmed with intelligence and wit, when they weren't snapping with anger, and a full, lush mouth most whores he knew would kill for. A back so ramrod straight, he thought she might have a poker for a spine, and an ass that jiggled as sweetly as jelly on a plate. A stubborn, tenacious chin, and a neck as smooth and white as swan's down. Contradictions.

Hell. It was a waste of time to think about her. If he could have been another kind of man, he'd have wanted a woman like Miss Julia. A woman who was pretty enough, but whose beauty went deeper than the surface. A woman who would work hard beside him, be faithful, have his children ... Tension gathered in his groin at the thought of bedding a woman like that. He often wondered what had happened to her baby's father. Oddly, in the two weeks he'd been on the ranch, no one had ever talked about him.

Bedding Miss Julia ... He let out a whoosh of air. The idea made him reel. He'd never had a woman like that. A woman who hadn't been used by many others. But there was a passion in her, he'd seen it in her eyes. And obviously she'd experienced such passion once, anyway. The baby was proof of that.

She wasn't one of those simpering, mewling women who teased a man one minute, then cried foul the next. The way she dressed said as much.

Men's breeches ... that suggestively hugged rounded hips, shapely thighs, and a sweet ass. Oversized shirts ... that didn't hide the firm, loose breasts beneath. A big, floppy-brimmed hat ... that couldn't conceal thick, honey-wheat hair that cried out to be loosened from the pins that held it.

Like the day she'd returned from exercising his horse, her hair windblown and curling to below her shoulders. The sight had made him angry, not because she'd taken his mount out without asking, but because for the first time since he'd arrived, he actually had stirrings of desire. And he never allowed himself to desire a woman like that. A woman beyond his reach. A woman who looked upon him like he was something she'd picked up in the barnyard on the bottom of her shoe.

It had been almost a relief to leave. Almost. He'd hated leaving Amos. He remembered the day he'd come across him, doubled over, clutching his stomach. Yeah, something was wrong.

Baptiste's new bride was in what passed for a kitchen, and he could smell the fry bread she'd recently retrieved from the fire. He sensed her approach, but had heard nothing. Suddenly she appeared before him, bearing a plate of fry bread drenched in honey.

"You want?" She shoved it toward him, her eyes downcast and her face expressionless.

Wolf took the plate and studied the young Miwok woman. She was pretty by Indian standards. Soft, round face, narrow eyes, the barest hint of a flattening where her nostrils met her cheeks. And she was plump. Sturdy, actually, something he knew Baptiste looked for in a woman. She was barely twenty, yet she was the old buzzard's fourth wife. He'd outlive God.

The fry bread was warm. He took a bite, his mouth

watering around it. As he munched the tasty, chewy bread, he thought about all of the years he'd spent in this cabin. It was odd, he mused, that even though he'd been raised here with two of Baptiste's women, his nurturing had come from Angus. It was from Angus that he'd learned to read and write, to appreciate music, and had learned the principles of being a gentleman. He rarely practiced what Angus had preached. Angus had exuded sensitivity, assuring Wolf that all men had a sensitive side. As yet, Wolf hadn't discovered his. For all he knew, he didn't have one.

What he'd learned from Baptiste had been far more useful. More *practical.* He'd learned how to survive in a hostile world. He'd learned that money could buy pleasures, not only women, but good whiskey and excellent cigars. He'd been hedonistic, thanks to Baptiste.

The door opened and Baptiste stepped inside, shaking himself like a hound, sending sprays of water everywhere. His laughter boomed in the quiet room.

"Seen that devil of a stallion that bears my name hitched in the lean-to. Never could understand why you named him after me, Wolfgang."

Wolf couldn't suppress a smile. "I want him to have a long life filled with memorable conquests, Baptiste. Who better to name him after than you?"

Baptiste roared with laughter again. He always filled a room. His jocularity and booming voice made up for his small, wiry stature.

"What brings you home this time, after so many months of absence, *mon ami?*"

Wolf shrugged. "Just wanted to see you, you old reprobate."

Baptiste's eyes twinkled, but he shook his finger at

him. "You came to look at my new squaw. Shame on you. Go find one of your own."

A smile cracked Wolf's mouth. "No, but congratulations, anyway."

"Woman! *Mon chou!*" he bellowed.

Obediently, with her head lowered, she appeared before him and helped him off with his wet jacket. Baptiste flung himself into his chair, took his pipe off the overturned crate that passed for a table, and filled the bowl with tobacco. The woman hung his jacket by the fire, then returned to remove his boots.

Wolf shook his head. Only Baptiste could use an endearment like "my cabbage" and make it sound like a threat. At any rate, she was well trained. It amazed him that a man like Baptiste, with his enormous carnal appetites and his disregard for anything by mouth but raw meat, alcohol, tobacco, and fry bread soaked in grease, could outlive a man as pure in heart and soul as Angus McCloud.

"Well, Wolfgang," Baptiste began between puffs on his pipe. "What have you been doing with yourself?"

Wolf hadn't been home since they'd buried Angus, almost a year ago to the day. "I've been working."

"What? You already spent all of St. Angus's money?"

Wolf ignored the sarcasm. He'd been amazed that Baptiste and Angus had been friends for so many years, considering how different they were. When Angus died, everything he owned had been left to Wolf. Not a small fortune, but Wolf had been shocked that Angus had money at all. Now, Wolf couldn't decide what to do with it. Foolish as it was, he couldn't spend it on cigars and whores. Angus wouldn't approve. God, but he was getting soft.

"No, I haven't spent it. I've been working at the

Cumberland." Which was the truth. He'd worked in the coal mines on the northern slopes of Devil Mountain before and after his little tryst at the Larson ranch.

Baptiste spat in disgust. "Coal. The whole damned world is falling apart. I yearn for the old days. The days when McCloud and I owned the mountains. And the river. And the beaver." His voice was deceptively hard, but there was sadness in his eyes.

Wolf rose, stuffing Amos Larson's letter into his pocket. "Those days are gone, Baptiste. The sooner you realize that, the better."

Baptiste swore. "I don't have to. I ain't going to be around long enough to care, *mon ami*."

Wolf walked to the window and stared out into the stormy afternoon. The oaks stood stalwart against the rain, but the boughs of the fir trees that flanked the cabin waved frantically, tossing and twisting in the wind. "You'll outlive us all, you old roué."

"Where are you going, and when?"

"Martinez." It had been a quick decision. Wolf was curious to know why Amos wanted him to see his lawyer. "And soon."

"To a woman, no?" Baptiste's voice was sly.

Wolf turned from the window. "Is that all you think about?"

With a casual shrug, Baptiste threw his rough, callused hands into the air. "What else is there? If I quit thinking about women, and no longer want one in my bed, I will die."

Wolf chuckled in spite of himself. "Is that what's keeping you alive?"

His sly smile widened. *"Oui.* Why do you think ol' Angus died so young, *mon ami?* He lived too pure a life."

Wolf nodded, feeling a twinge of sadness. He missed Angus more than he cared to admit. Angus had been a father to him. Wolf knew what kind of man he himself was, and knew that without Angus, he'd have been even less.

Turning to the window once more, he stared outside and thought about the trip to Martinez. The rain had not subsided. But he would leave at first light, whether it was storming or not. If he kept to the grassy knolls above the river, he could be there by late tomorrow afternoon.

To Wolf's surprise, Amos had greeted him with a warm embrace. Now, as they sat in front of the fire in Earl Williams's law office, Wolf could see that Amos's health had declined even further.

"I'm dying, McCloud." Amos gazed into the fire, his features bleak and bony.

Wolf didn't know what to say, so he simply waited. He had an old aching in his gut, similar to the one he'd had when he lost Angus.

"I should have died weeks ago, but I couldn't leave this earth until I knew my Julia had some peace."

Wolf shifted in his chair. "What do you want of me, Amos?"

Amos continued to study the flames. "Remember that piece of land you took a shine to? Over there, at the bend in the creek?"

"I remember," Wolf replied. It had been a place to which he could escape, and he had. The next ranch, perhaps a mile away, had also been visible. It was the one he'd taken an interest in. The one where he hoped to find the woman that had left him to die.

"I'll sell it to you cheap, on one condition." His voice was soft, yet filled with dignity.

Wolf felt a thrill of excitement but controlled it. "What's your condition, Amos?"

"That you stay on after I'm gone and act as Julia's foreman."

Wolf felt a shiver of dread inch up his spine. He wondered how long he'd be there before the strident daughter with the lush mouth drove a stake through his heart. Or before the one with the hot drawers smothered him.

He flung himself out of his chair and strode to the window. "Oh, no you don't, old man."

"McCloud, you're a lot like I was when I was a pup," Amos mused.

As Wolf studied the Martinez harbor, where empty three-masted ships bobbed lightly atop the water, he thought about his life, about the sins he'd committed against humanity and himself. He thought of the orders he'd taken from the Army superiors that had caused countless innocent lives to be lost—all in the name of progress. He recalled the command that had meant robbing land from unsuspecting Indians and giving it to white settlers who didn't need it but wanted it just the same—all in the name of progress. He thought of the supplies that were meant for the Indians, and how he'd known they were being sold to the whites for next to nothing, leaving the Indian people to starve over the harsh winter—all in the name of progress. And he thought of the innumerable children who had died because of his actions. Their deaths were a constant heavy weight on his heart.

He'd known demons and devils and every shade of hell imaginable. Most men had no idea what he felt in his soul. More times than not, he wasn't even sure he had one, for how could any man, whether he had

Indian blood or not, be a party to what was done to the unsuspecting Indians of California?

"I'm nothing like you, Amos."

Amos was quiet for a moment, then said, "Don't sell yourself short, McCloud. I've seen the man you pretend to be." He paused. "I've also seen the man you try so hard to hide."

Wolf smirked. "Am I that easy to read, old man?"

Amos ignored the question, asking one of his own instead. "Doesn't my offer appeal to you?"

Wolf turned from the window. "The part that appeals to me is overshadowed by the part that doesn't."

"And which part doesn't?"

Wolf took a deep breath, expelling it slowly. "Amos, your daughter Josette is—"

"I knew what you're going to say, McCloud. I know what she is. She—" He pressed an old bandanna to his mouth and coughed, deep sounds that seemed to rob him of strength. When he finished, he sank deeper into the chair, his head against the back, his eyes closed.

"She's gone, McCloud."

Wolf heard the old man's defeated tone. "Gone?"

"Up and run off with some Gypsy fellow." He shook his head. "Julia was right. I pampered Josie somethin' awful."

"So Miss Julia is there alone?" He didn't know how he felt, but a ripple of excitement returned.

"Yep, and after I'm gone, she'll need help." His gaze was rheumy as it landed on Wolf. "And I want it to come from you."

Wolf knew Miss Julia well enough to know she wouldn't take this lightly.

"If I agree to this, Amos, we'll have to draw up a paper or something. Miss Julia—"

"I know, I know," he interrupted. "Julia thinks you're like the last foreman I hired. Don't worry. Earl has drawn up the papers." His twisted fingers shook as he picked at his trousers. "Julia's a hard worker, McCloud. *Too* hard. I've come to depend on her. And because she never once complained, I dumped all the work on her that should have been shared between her and her sister. She's had a few hard knocks in her life, but she's got a good heart."

Again Wolf presumed the reference was to Miss Julia's baby, but he didn't ask. "She's not going to like it, Amos."

Amos sighed, a sound so forlorn, Wolf felt a twinge of fear. "She'll come around. And when she does, she'll need the help. We got bills to pay, McCloud. I ain't got a clue how to make good on them, but I got a feelin' you do. We talked about it, remember?"

Wolf felt Amos's gaze on him, and when he returned it, he was stunned by the feverish glaze in the old man's eyes. "About drying the fruit?"

Amos simply nodded. "It'll work. I never thought of it. The wheat was my whole life; the fruit was just . . . there. Always too much, rotting on the ground . . ."

Wolf wanted that piece of land, even if it meant butting heads with the haughty Miss Julia. Yet he wasn't convinced. "Are you sure this will work, Amos?"

"It's got to. The bills ain't the only problem, McCloud. My land butts up against the creek. I've got the only private land that does. Someone wants it. There's plenty of ranchers hereabouts that would do just about anything to get it. The water is way down, McCloud. Even with the drought, it shouldn't be that low. Something's wrong, but I ain't got the strength to find out what it is." He paused, and again Wolf felt his feverish gaze. "You do."

Wolf studied the fire. He wanted that piece of land. It's what Angus would want him to do, and for some reason, even though Angus was dead, Wolf knew he would approve. "Let me take a look at those papers, Amos."

Amos smiled and visibly relaxed. He appeared serene as he pulled them from his pocket and handed them to Wolf.

Wolf studied them and signed his name at the bottom, handing them back to Amos as he stepped away.

"You keep a copy for yourself, McCloud. Will you be comin' back with me now?"

"I'd like to go to Sacramento and get my inheritance, Amos. Close out my account there." He extended his hand, which Amos took. Despite his weak appearance, Amos had a strong grip. "I'll be back in a few days."

Amos smiled, his leathery skin wrinkling like a raisin. "I promise I won't die till you get there, McCloud."

Wolf felt that twinge in his gut. He almost wanted to embrace Amos again, but knew he was being foolish.

A robust fire erupted in the fireplace, yet Julia rubbed her arms, hoping to drive away the chill. Except for the sound of the storm, everything was silent. The pendulum on the grandfather clock ticked slowly, rhythmically, and she found herself waiting for it to strike, just to hear some noise. It was so quiet without Papa stirring about . . .

Tears stung her eyes and she pressed her lips together to keep them from quivering. She couldn't believe he was gone. There was a gaping hole in her heart, and the ragged edges of pain continued to cut at her like shards of broken glass.

The clock chimed, making her jump. So often she'd dreamed of this kind of silence, hungered for it, if only for a few moments. The reality was far less appealing, especially when it went on for days, and could be expected to continue forever. As it did now.

She went into her bedroom and undressed in the dark, tempted to crawl into her cold bed and escape into sleep. But she couldn't. Or wouldn't. But sometimes when she thought about the future, a sense of panic rose within her so strong, she felt she might lose her mind.

Her pulse would race, and she could scarcely catch her breath. Her thoughts would blur and she was unable to concentrate on the most mindless task. She would feel as though she were drowning, but just before she went down for the last time, succumbing to the bliss of escape, she would remember Marymae. And the ranch. And her father's desperate dreams. And she knew she had to face reality even though thoughts of escape tempted her.

She shrugged into her flannel robe, belting it snugly around her waist, then picked up the dish that held the squat candle and went into the kitchen. She lit the candle, then swung the light back and forth over the containers of food that had been left by the neighbors. Pies. Cakes. Smoked pork. Pickled cucumbers. She put the candle on top of the pie safe, then began filling the safe with the extra food that didn't fit onto the pantry shelves. More food than she could ever eat before it spoiled.

It was wasteful, but she understood that people had to do something in troubled times, and they usually did what they did best. Even if it meant cooking and baking enough food for a harvest crew.

Just as she slid the last pie into the safe, she heard a knock at the door. Frowning, she picked up the candle, stepped into the other room and glanced at the clock. Eight-thirty. Who in the world would be out on such a nasty night?

She went to the door and opened it a crack, then flung it wider, clinging to the knob when she saw who it was. Oddly enough, she *had* thought about him lately. It hadn't been intentional; he was there again, invading her daydreams as well as those she wrestled with at night.

"What are you doing here?"

"I heard about your father. I'm sorry."

His response was so unexpected, she merely stood and stared at him. The candle flickered and sputtered against the force of the wind, sending his face into devilish planes of light and shadow.

"What? No sarcastic remarks, Mr. McCloud?" His gaze was on her, and she shivered.

"Despite what you think of me, ma'am, I don't find death a subject for levity."

Cold, wet fingers of wind reached through her robe and nightgown, sending gooseflesh over her skin. "Come in," she offered, stepping away from the door.

He came inside, firmly closing the door behind him, then wiped his boots on the mat.

"What happened?"

His concern was surprising and caught her off guard. She pulled the lapels of her robe together and went to the fire in an attempt to dispel the chill that had invaded the house, and her bones. After warming her hands, she turned up the kerosene lamp on the mantel.

"How did you hear?"

He took off his hat and raked his fingers through his hair. "A person hears things," was all he said.

"He went . . . he went hunting up on the mountain. He took Sally. He rode her now and then, just so she wouldn't forget—" She pressed her fingers to her mouth, unable to continue, for the knot of tears in her throat threatened to choke her.

She swallowed and took a shaky breath. "When Sally came back alone, I was frantic. She's a sweet mare. I rode her, giving her lead, and she took me right to him." She closed her eyes against the picture of her father lying in a pool of blood, part of his head blown off. "He must have tripped. The gun went off." The possibility that his state of mind had propelled him to take his own life was painful, but not unrealistic. She didn't want to think about that and refused to verbalize it.

Her knees felt weak, and she grabbed the back of a chair.

Suddenly McCloud was there beside her, his arm around her shoulders. She desperately wanted to turn to him, to allow herself to soften and be soothed by him. A touch—even his—would have been welcome.

"Will you be all right?"

She shrugged him off and turned away, angry that he affected her at all. "Of *course* I won't be all right, Mr. McCloud. My father is dead. How would you feel if you were in my shoes?"

He said nothing, but took a turn around the room, stopping in front of the photograph of her and Josette that had been taken the summer before. "And your sister?"

So, Julia thought, trying to push away the foolish hurt, he finally got around to that. She turned, wanting to be sure her distress wouldn't show. "You've made the trip for nothing, Mr. McCloud. She left."

He turned swiftly, his expression unreadable. "She's really gone? You don't expect her back?"

She tried to smile, but knew she failed. "For all I know, she could come back any time. Does that make you feel better?"

Returning his gaze to their picture, he said nothing for a long time. Julia sensed his disillusionment. When it came to men and their feelings for her sister, Julia knew she always came in a poor second.

"I'm sorry you're here alone, ma'am. I would think something like this would bring the two of you closer."

Julia wanted to tell him that ever since Frank Barnes had played one sister against the other, things had not been good between her and Josette, but it would serve no purpose other than to make her sound peevish and churlish. "Josette is better off away from here."

"And you're left to deal with everything?"

"Don't sound so surprised." She tried not to sound bitter. "Josette wasn't very helpful even when she was here."

"I guess what surprises me is that she hasn't come back to help you now, considering—"

"She probably doesn't know, Mr. McCloud. But I'm not sure she'd come back even if she found out."

His jacket was dripping water onto the floor. She had to either tell him to leave or ask him to stay. Her mind had been made up before she moved toward him.

"Here," she said, "give me your jacket. I'll hang it by the fire. Did you take care of your horse?"

"Afraid not. He's hitched up outside."

She moved away, toward the fire. "Take care of

him, then come inside. I'll fix you some coffee and something to eat. Lord knows I have enough food," she added with a wry twist of her mouth.

When he left, she took the candle, hurried into her room and checked herself in the mirror. Dark smudges lay beneath the thin skin under her eyes, announcing her grief and her inability to sleep. Her face was pale, her lips cracked and dry. Her hair was whisked back into a loose braid. Except for her eyes, which looked too big and too dark to be hers, she was completely void of color.

She sucked in a resigned breath and went into the kitchen. Nothing could be done about her appearance now, and what did it matter? If he had come because of Josette, then he would leave. If he had come because he truly wanted to help, then he would stay. But did she want him to?

❧ 3 ❧

Wolf hung his jacket by the fire, then stepped into the kitchen. Heat radiated from a cast-iron stove that sat against the wall, and a kerosene lamp on the table fanned light into the room.

"There's warm water in the basin on the back stoop," she offered.

He went outside onto the small porch, rolled up his sleeves and washed, wondering when he'd had warm water last, and realizing he couldn't remember.

As he wiped his hands and face, he mulled over Miss Julia's reaction to him being there. It worried him that Amos hadn't told her of their agreement, and Wolf was sure he hadn't, for she would not be so accommodating if he had. He also remembered the talk when he'd stopped in Martinez on his way back from Sacramento.

Earl Williams had given him two envelopes, neither of which he looked at. One, he assumed, was his and Amos's agreement, and the other was for Miss Julia. Earl had suggested that Amos, depressed over his illness and his bills, had killed himself. Wolf didn't believe it. He didn't think it was an accident, either. Many things had been bothering the old man. Possibly his concern that someone wanted his land was well-founded. That was another reason Wolf intended to stay. He wanted to discover whether or not Amos's suspicions had been justified. Justified enough to warrant fearing for his life.

But Miss Julia had to be told of their agreement. He didn't have a clue as to how to go about it. It was the first time in his life he felt like a coward.

Returning inside, he found a plate of cold chicken on the table, along with hard-cooked eggs, cucumber pickles, and bread. A piece of pie nearly filled another plate. It was a feast, and even though his mouth watered, his stomach rebelled. He was actually afraid of this woman.

As he ate, he watched her, shifting his gaze to the side when she looked at him. She was different tonight, the death of her father notwithstanding. There wasn't that hard, angry edge she'd used with him before. And would no doubt use again, once she found out what her father had done to her.

The sight of her in her nightclothes stirred something inside him. She was a slim woman, sweetly curved where it counted. He wondered what she looked like beneath the layers of flannel. Skin, smooth and creamy everywhere, if the skin at her neck was any indication. A tiny waist. High, firm breasts—with pale, pink nipples, he mused. Long, shapely legs, tightly muscled, strong enough to grip the sides of Baptiste's black belly—or his own thighs. Hadn't he wondered about that the day she'd taken the stallion out for a run? And at the juncture of her thighs, a thatch of thick, wheat-colored hair ...

He looked at his plate and mouthed an oath, for thinking of her body did wild things to his own. A lot of good it would do him. Once she heard his news, his hide wouldn't be worth a loose shithouse brick in a wind storm.

"I ... I suppose you'll be moving on." Her voice disrupted his troubled thoughts.

He took a slurp of coffee and washed down the mouthful of pie, then stopped eating and waited. He had to tell her. Oh, God, he had to tell her! *Well, life's been good, Wolf, old man. Pity it has to end.*

He cleared his throat. "Miss Julia—"

"No," she interrupted, waving her hand at him. "Wait. I know I've never given you any reason to stay. I was less than hospitable, and my attitude toward you was inexcusable."

She wouldn't look at him, keeping her gaze on her lap. "Things are pretty bad around here, Mr. McCloud. I mean, since the drought, we no longer have a cash crop. Only a few walnut trees and too many fruit trees. There's little money coming in ... Oh, who am I kidding? There's *no* money coming in."

Her vulnerability surprised him. And touched him. He didn't know how to deal with it.

"Well, aren't you going to say anything?" Suddenly her voice held the peevishness he'd come to expect from her. It made him more comfortable.

"You want me to stay and work for you for nothing, is that it?" *Tell her, fool.*

She lifted a skeptical, tawny eyebrow. "I should have known better than to ask."

"Then you *are* asking me to stay." His gaze dropped to her hands, which were spread on top of the table, noting that her nails were short but well cared for. He also saw how roughened and callused her hands were.

A queer feeling of pity dug into his gut, and he remembered how she'd worked this place as hard as any man.

"Surely you wouldn't. Especially if I can't pay you."

"Then you *aren't* asking me to stay." She was proud and strong, and he didn't deserve her or anything she had to offer—willingly or otherwise. He should forget the whole idea. Amos obviously hadn't gotten around to telling her what they'd agreed to do.

She uttered an exasperated sigh, pursing her lips the way she did when she was annoyed. "I know I'll live to regret it, but yes. At least think about it. No one else has anyone to spare, so I guess you're it. But why you'd be willing, I'll never know, especially since Josette isn't here."

Her stern demeanor made him smile. "How can I refuse such an enthusiastic offer?"

"Don't get cocky, Mr. McCloud. I can just as easily change my mind."

He forced a smile. *And you will, pretty Julia. You will.*

"You can sleep in the barn," she snapped. "There should be a dry spot in there somewhere, if not with the horses, then maybe with the pigs."

The tight muscles in his neck loosened up as soon as she began to sound like herself. "Miss Julia, I know you don't raise pigs. Don't go getting my hopes up, you hear?"

"You *know* what I mean. Sleep anywhere you please, just don't expect to sleep in the house." Her cheeks were pink.

"Well, now, you make it sound mighty appealing. I think that a barn is just the right place to have a friendly toss in the hay, but it's no fun alone." He stood and curled his thumbs around his belt loops. "Care to join me?"

She marched to the fireplace, her sweet ass jiggling a tad beneath her robe. If anyone had ever asked him, he'd have said he was an ass man. Breasts were nice, hell, every man liked breasts, but he rarely focused on them. He enjoyed watching a woman walk away from him in her nightclothes, her ass twitching and wiggling ever so slightly, just as Miss Julia's was now. It was like an open invitation to touch. Well, he thought, his mouth twisting with scorn, maybe not this time, and not with this woman.

She yanked his jacket off the hook and threw it to him. "Good night, Mr. McCloud."

He shrugged into it and crossed to the door, turning toward her before he opened it. "By the way, don't get any ideas about getting me up too early. I wouldn't want you to catch me wearing nothing but a smile." He watched her eyes widen in horror, then added, "Good night, Miss Julia."

All the way to the barn, he wondered if he had a death wish and hadn't known about it. Now, he had to prolong his agony until morning. It would have been so much wiser to take care of things tonight. In some ways, he was thinking of her. By delaying the news, only one of them would be robbed of sleep.

Julia slammed the door and sagged against it, her heart beating wildly against her rib cage. Lord, what had she been thinking? He personified every disgusting example of manhood on the face of the earth. She *knew* that. She'd known it from the first moment she'd laid eyes on him. He was brash, indecent, cocky, disreputable, and, yes, dangerous. Even so, he waltzed in, acted deceptively human for one lousy hour, and she'd forgotten everything she'd hated about him in the first place.

Lightning flashed in the sky, followed by a hard crack of thunder. The rain continued to hammer the windows. She welcomed it. Maybe it would drive him away. The barn roof leaked; she doubted there was a square foot anywhere that didn't have a hole in it.

No man with an ounce of civilized blood would stay more than one night in a cold, leaky, mouse-infested barn.

She was feeling pretty good about everything as she turned out lamps and closed up for the night. It wasn't until she'd checked on Marymae and crawled into her own bed that she realized Wolf McCloud's blood was probably as wild and uncivilized as his stallion's.

The rooster woke Julia. She hadn't been asleep very long. She'd lain in bed for hours, listening as Marymae sucked contentedly on her thumb, thinking about Wolf McCloud. As she slid from the bed, she knew there was no way on earth she could let him stay, no matter how much she needed the help. That he was incorrigible was a fact. She would deal with it. That she responded to him on some visceral level was something she could not deal with, nor did she have any intention of trying.

She went to the window and looked outside, noting that the storm had blown on, leaving the air wet and clean. The sky was clear and so blue it looked like something out of a painting. Her gaze moved toward the barn, and she saw no movement whatsoever. She narrowed her eyes, drawing on her anger toward him and the ease with which he was able to embarrass her.

The slug would probably sleep until noon, she thought. *In nothing but a smile.*

In spite of herself, she started to imagine him that way, comparing his long, hard lines to those of his stallion's, then rolled her eyes and cursed. A war was going on inside her. There wasn't a person who knew her who would believe that beneath her prim, aloof exterior lay a heart thirsting for danger. Fortunately, she'd been able to control it before, and she could now, too. Lord help her, if there was ever a time for control, it was now.

She pulled off her nightgown, shivering in the cold room, and dressed while Marymae gurgled and cooed, kicking her legs against the sides of her bunting.

She gazed down at the child. Five months. It had been over five months since Josette's birthing shrieks and screams riddled the air. If every woman carried on as Josette had, surely the population of the world would be lessened considerably, for not one of them would choose to go through it again. Josette had sounded as though she were being skinned alive.

Julia wasn't unaware of the pain of childbirth. She'd heard other women talking about it often enough. Even now, when she was so angry with her sister she wanted to throttle her, she felt a rush of pity for her. Poor, poor Josette, whose life had been made easy, but for whom no one and nothing could relieve the pain of delivering a child.

Marymae looked up at her and gave her a wide, dimpled, smile. She'd been surprisingly sweet-tempered, in spite of the fact that she was teething. All of Julia's anxiety fled when she looked at the babe.

"Good morning, love," she murmured. "You're such a good girl." She picked her up, cuddling her close, ignoring the fact that Marymae had grabbed her braid and tugged.

After changing her, Julia carried her into the

kitchen and fastened her into the special seat her father had made. She left Marymae to play with a string of beads while she fired up the stove, put on a pot of coffee, and made some oatmeal.

She was mixing hotcake batter when she heard Wolf McCloud outside. Thinking he was going to enter, she waited. When he didn't, she went to the back door, looking out the small window. Her heart fluttered when she saw him.

In spite of the cold, he'd taken off his shirt. The rounded muscles in his chest and the straplike muscles under his arms bunched against his brown skin as he forked hay into the corral for the horses. He stopped, leaned on the pitchfork and looked at the house. Julia moved away from the door, yet allowed herself the luxury of memorizing each and every ridge in his hard, flat stomach. Sunlight glanced off his sleek, sweaty skin.

She'd never touched a man anywhere but his hands and face. Wolf McCloud looked smooth and hard, as if he were a living statue with muscles of stone, covered with the finest quality of flesh.

It was just unfortunate, she thought, dredging up her anger, that his perfect body had to be the vessel for such a depraved, degenerate soul.

He rested the pitchfork against the barn wall, picked up a bucket, and strode to the horse trough, where he filled it with water. She watched as he carried the bucket to the overturned crate used as a washstand by the help during harvest, and sloshed water over his face and chest. She shivered, knowing the water was cold.

He turned away briefly, exposing his back, and Julia gasped, shrinking from the window. He'd been lashed. She took a deep, shaky breath and peered out the window again. He stood there, gazing at the barn, his back to her. There was barely an area of his skin that hadn't been carved by the angry end of a whip. Though the marks did not look new, Julia felt a thrust of sympathetic pain.

When he put his shirt on over his wet skin and started toward the house, Julia scurried into the kitchen, her face warm and her heart thumping hard. There was so much she didn't know about him.

In spite of wishing it were so, she knew he wasn't a slugabed. She wasn't surprised to find him up and working. It didn't matter. There were other chores to do, chores that he probably wasn't aware of. Feeding the horses had been just one of them.

She heard his footsteps on the stoop again, then he knocked. Moving to the door, she held it while he stepped inside. His hair was wet; he smelled like fresh air. Although it was cold outside, his body exuded a warmth that made Julia breathless. The memory of his arm around her shoulders the night before bloomed in her mind, and her labored breathing continued. She looked away, down past the healthy bulge in his jeans to the safety of his knees. She realized then that he was carrying the pails.

"What have you been doing?" she asked, raising her eyes to his.

His lopsided smile tunneled into her chest, further shortening her breath. "What does it look like?"

"You . . . you've done the milking and gathered the eggs?" Her heart sank, for she'd hoped he hadn't been that industrious.

"And fed the chickens and the horses. Anything I've missed?" There was a sarcastic quality in his voice, as though he'd read her thoughts.

She turned away and went into the kitchen, anxious

to busy herself with breakfast. She pulled out a slab of ham left for her by one of the neighbors and dropped it into a skillet. It hissed, sending steam into the air.

"Those are my chores. You didn't have to do them." She didn't want to be grateful. She wanted a reason to send him packing.

He followed her into the kitchen, stopping to watch Marymae. "I figure I should earn my keep. What other reason would there be for keeping me on?"

She didn't know whether it was excitement or disappointment that filled her stomach. Both emotions affected her by making her a bit nauseous. "Then . . . then, you'll be staying?"

"Isn't that what you asked me to do last night?" He took a cup off the table and poured himself coffee. "It sounded pretty clear to me."

"That was before—" She stopped, reluctant to admit how he affected her. She wasn't even willing to admit that to herself—at least not out loud.

"Before I got your hackles up?" he finished, a wicked grin flashing across his face.

She felt herself flush as she turned the meat. "Don't be foolish."

"You mean it didn't bother you when I told you I slept in only a smile?"

She flipped the first batch of griddle cakes, knowing her blush had deepened because her face felt hot and her ears burned.

"I guess I have to learn that you're more comfortable when you're insulting me." She spooned oatmeal into a dish and poured fresh cream into it.

"Is that what you think I'm doing? Insulting you?" Moving so he could see her, he studied her over the rim of his coffee cup.

She stirred Marymae's cereal, making sure it was soupy and just lukewarm. "Well, isn't it?"

An odd look crinkled the corners of his eyes and his lips hardened. He moved toward her, and she took a step back, threatened not only by him, but by her own feelings.

"Maybe I think you need to loosen up a little, Miss Julia. For a widow woman, you're as tight as the spring on a watch."

"W-Widow woman?" Julia couldn't stop her astonished response.

A brief look of surprise crossed his face as well, but he recovered. "You are a widow, aren't you?"

She swallowed the lump in her throat, attempting to compose herself. "What I am is no concern of yours, Mr. McCloud. From now on, I'm your boss, and that's all you need to know."

She watched him out of the corner of her eye, and could almost see the wheels turning in his head. Marymae's parentage had obviously never been explained to him, and oddly, he hadn't heard any of the rumors she knew were rampant in every community from Ygnacio to Martinez.

With a quick, nervous motion she flipped the griddle cakes onto a platter and plunked it onto the table. She knew that explaining Marymae would make Josette look bad, but she just didn't feel like going into the whole, sordid story, even though it would exonerate her.

"What happened to the other two hands who were here before?"

Julia pulled Marymae to the table and tested the milky oatmeal on her tongue before feeding it to the baby. "They both disappeared the day after Papa died. I'll never understand why, unless it was because Papa died on the mountain and they somehow felt threatened. They're afraid of the mountain, you know. Bad medicine, or something."

"They're not afraid of it. It's not an evil presence, Miss Julia, it's a sacred one. They worship it."

She stopped feeding Marymae, who let out a wail of displeasure. "I didn't know that." She knew he was a breed, even though he looked like no other she'd ever seen. "Are they ... is that what you believe, too?"

He gave her a dry smile. "It wasn't part of my religion."

"What was?" She watched him eat, suddenly wanting to know something about him.

His smile turned bitter. "Nothing much."

"What ... what tribe was your ... is your ..."

He noted her discomfort with a shake of his head. "I have no idea."

She frowned. He appeared more white in manner than Indian. "You were raised by whites."

"I was."

He'd turned taciturn on her. She picked up the carving knife and sliced the ham. "Do you know anything—"

"Miss Julia." Wolf could put it off no longer. "I have some papers for you. I should have given them to you last night, but ..." Expelling a heavy sigh, he pulled the two envelopes from his pocket and slid them across the table to her.

"I suppose there should be some way to introduce this, but damned if I know what it is." He cleared his throat, anticipation flooding him. He wasn't accustomed to feeling so powerless.

She looked at the envelopes, then up at him. "What is this?"

He held out his hand. "Pass the knife, please, I'll finish carving."

At this point it was better for him to have a weapon than her.

With an impatient movement she handed him the knife, then pulled one of the envelopes toward her. She glanced at the upper left corner, then at McCloud. "From Papa's lawyer? How did you get it?"

He sighed again, and put the carving knife beside his plate. "You'll know soon enough."

She pulled out the papers and opened them. "Papa's will," she said.

Wolf frowned. "His will?"

She nodded and scanned the first two pages, her expression thoughtful and sad. Abruptly, her entire demeanor changed. "What? *What?*" She raised her head, her face chalky white and filled with disbelief.

"Is something wrong?" He hadn't known about the will, hadn't known Amos had one.

She shook her head. "No. *No.* He can't mean this. He *can't.*" She swallowed repeatedly, then added, "Papa wouldn't do this to me. He promised me he wouldn't make me get married just to save the land. He *promised.*"

Married? What in the hell was she talking about? "Here," he said, reaching for the paper, "let me—"

She pulled the will out of his reach and stood, shoving the chair back until it toppled over and hit the floor. The baby cried out, but she was ignored.

Julia swung around, nailing Wolf with a glare meant to kill. "And to *you* of all people," she hissed.

Wolf couldn't have been any more surprised if she'd hit him over the head with a board. He raised his hands to fend her off. "I don't know anything about marriage, Miss Julia. I agreed to buy a piece of land and stay on as your foreman. I don't—"

She swiped at her cheeks, and he realized she was crying. He felt helpless and stupid. He took his and Amos's agreement from his shirt pocket and put it on the table.

"Here. Read this. This is all I know about."

She inched back toward the table, swung the paper around and looked at it. "What's this?"

"It's the agreement I had with your father. It's the only one I know about, Miss Julia. Let me see the will."

She flung it at him, then turned away, crossing her arms over her chest. Wolf read the will with mounting surprise. It was dated after he'd seen Amos. In essence, it forced Julia to marry him if she wanted to keep the ranch. And it forced him to agree, or he wouldn't get the land. If either refused, the ranch would go to the creditors.

"Why, that sly old dog," he muttered, appreciating the cleverness of the ploy, if not the ploy itself.

"Why would he do this?" she asked no one in particular.

"Maybe it's explained in the other letter," he offered.

Glaring at him again, she grabbed the other envelope off the table. "I suppose you know what's in this one, too."

"No. And as I told you, I didn't know what was in the other one, either." For some reason, he no longer wanted to rile her.

She read, tears of anger streaming down her cheeks, dripping off her chin onto the paper. Wolf sympathized with her. He couldn't understand why Amos had done such a thing. What in hell would have made Amos think he would agree to it?

When she finished, she let out a wail of anguish, crushed the letter into a ball and tossed it onto the table. It bounced, landing on the floor beside him.

She ran from the room. Seconds later he heard a door slam, and he was alone in the kitchen with the baby, who was crying as well, her fingers periodically jammed into her mouth.

He picked up the crumbled paper off the floor and put it on the table, not wanting to know what was written on it. He had too much to consider, himself. Strangely, it was all unreal to him. Marriage to Miss Julia? It wouldn't happen. Something could be done to avoid it. He could ...

Wolf scratched his chin, a feeling of unease tunneling into his stomach. He could loan her the money he'd gotten from Angus to keep her creditors at bay. Yes, he could. But did he want to? Hell, the money wasn't the issue. She could have the money, for all he cared.

But a new feeling grew in his chest, like a seedling taking root. This was his chance to do something with his life. And he was selfish enough to want to take it.

Hoping to distance himself from the sound of the bawling baby, he started to leave. He gave her one final look, and she stopped crying. She continued to hiccough and suck loudly on her fingers, all the while staring at him with those big blue eyes.

"Ah, hell," he muttered. He headed for the back door, then stopped when the baby let out another wail. With a shake of his head, he returned to the table and picked up the oatmeal. He'd never been able to stand the sound of a crying female—no matter what her age.

*   *   *

Someone had once told Julia she had a photographic memory; the ability to see words in her mind. Recalling the letter now, this was the first time she'd felt it was a curse rather than a blessing. Her father's words burned into her brain. Some of them actually making her head hurt.

Julia, dearest daughter,
  I know you think I've betrayed you. Wolf McCloud's inheritance will save the ranch for you. Without marriage, my pretty Julia, I fear he won't take my words seriously. I know how you think you feel about him, honey, but give him a chance. I would never do anything in the world to hurt you. Please remember that.
  For your old Papa.

Now, she stood at the window, ignoring the tears that continued to track down her cheeks. Why had he done this? He'd certainly not been in his right mind. But she knew with a wilting certainty that of all her father's failings, a weak mind hadn't been one of them. He may have been troubled and ill, but he wasn't insane.

Marymae's voice filtered through her pain, and she gasped. Lord help her, she'd left the baby with that ... that ... that *man*.

Scrambling to the door, she flung it open and rushed to the kitchen, where she stopped short. Wolf McCloud had straddled a kitchen chair and was diligently feeding Marymae her oatmeal.

✦ 4 ✦

The tranquility was deceptive as the three of them headed toward Martinez. They'd hitched the geldings to the buggy, leaving Sally and Baptiste behind—well separated from each other.

Marymae was good in the buggy; it rocked her to sleep. Julia's mind whirled with thoughts of getting rid of McCloud. She had insisted they see Mr. Williams. Surely something could be done about the ridiculous contents of her father's will. McCloud was quiet as well. Julia sensed a tension in him that wasn't usually there.

She smoothed one hand over her flower-sprigged dark blue calico, wondering if McCloud had even noticed that she wore a dress. As far as she could remember, it was the first time she'd had one on in his presence. That he hadn't made any comment one way or the other made her angry, but she didn't know why it should bother her at all.

"McCloud, if you have an inheritance, which it appears you have, then you can buy any property you want. Surely you'd want something more valuable than that piece of land Papa offered you."

Julia hugged Marymae to her, feeling a mounting sense of panic. There *had* to be a way out of this preposterous situation. For two days she'd stewed and fretted while McCloud stayed out of her way, attempting to patch the holes in the barn roof.

"I don't know." His voice was deceptively thoughtful. "I'm kind of partial to that piece of land."

"If you're trying to annoy me, McCloud, you're succeeding." She heard him chuckle. It would be so like him to make light of this whole issue.

They were silent again, Julia's mind awhirl with thoughts of doing something dastardly to him.

"You realize, Miss Julia, that if we don't marry, you'll lose your land. And, if I remember anything about your father, he didn't want the bank to take the ranch."

Julia clenched her teeth. Blackmail. He was using her emotions to blackmail her. "I'll find some investors."

"To invest in what, Miss Julia?"

She frowned. He *would* remind her of that. "There must be a way out of this, and I intend to find it."

The muddy state of the roads had made the trip longer than usual, and by the time they arrived at Earl Williams's office, it was two o'clock in the afternoon.

After arguing and pleading with Mr. Williams for more than an hour, Julia felt drained.

"There's no way out, Miss Larson," the lawyer said. "It was your father's wish." He tossed a nervous glance at McCloud, who stood at the back of the room.

Julia knew she was beaten. What else could she do?

"All right." Marriage didn't have to mean anything. And theirs wouldn't.

"Mr. Young, at the end of the hall, is a justice of the peace. Would you like me to get him?"

Julia's heart leaped into her throat. "Here? Now?" Lord, she wasn't ready. She swung her gaze to the door, where McCloud stood, stoic as a statue, more reserved than she'd ever seen him before.

"Are you ready for this charade, McCloud?" Why in the name of heaven had she asked him? He was probably chomping at the bit to get his hands on her land. And that was all he wanted. She felt a horrible sense of hurt and couldn't understand why.

"I'm ready." His answer was short, abrupt.

The ceremony was brief. Mr. Young, a short, fat man with a shiny bald head sporting a few well-spaced strands of long hair, pronounced them man and wife. "You may kiss the bride," he ordered, his smile wide.

Julia had never felt so ill. She wanted to scream. Cry. Curse her father for forcing her to marry a man she not only didn't love, but one who, in all likelihood, had probably already slept with her sister.

But that was swept away when she felt McCloud's fingers on her chin, nudging her face to his. A tingling began where he'd touched her, spreading into her chest, then to her stomach. She swallowed and looked up at him, hypnotized by his haunting eyes, surprised she saw no humor there. No mirth. No sarcasm.

His mouth descended slowly, and she automatically closed her eyes when his lips, warm and dry, touched hers. He pressed lightly, taking such gentle nibbles that Julia found herself reaching and stretching for something more.

It was over all too quickly. She opened her eyes, noting that his held the wicked light she'd seen so many times before. Feeling the fool, she moved away, huffing dramatically as she straightened her skirt. "I think we could have dispensed with that, Mr. Young."

The justice of the peace cleared his throat, then asked them to sign the marriage certificate, before he scurried back to his own office.

"Now," Mr. Williams said, his demeanor changed. "You must come home with me. Helga would never forgive me if she couldn't make your visit comfortable."

Julia felt swamped by everything. "Oh, we couldn't. We should get back to the ranch." But they didn't have to. She'd arranged for a neighbor to look in on the animals just in case they couldn't get back in time to feed them.

"But look," he replied, nodding toward the window. "Another storm has blown in. You'll have to stay the night anyway. Better with us than at the hotel, don't you think so?"

No, I don't think so. She looked at McCloud, whose face gave her no hint as to what he was feeling. Marymae began to fuss, prompting Julia to dig into her reticule and pull out a bottle.

Grateful for a reason to sit, she sank into a chair by the window and fed the baby, then turned to study the street. Rain fell again, swaying the sycamore branches, rattling the windowpanes. Her heart sank. They *couldn't* leave for home, no matter how much she wanted to.

"Maybe we should stay at the hotel." But what would they use for money, unless McCloud had some on him? The thought lost its appeal, for she didn't want to be beholden to him for more than she already was.

"Nonsense! You'll all come home with me." Mr. Williams had shrugged into his coat. "We'll have a celebration. Helga will be beside herself. Finally someone to coddle and fuss over." He tossed Julia a wide, winking smile. "Josh is getting too old for her to baby; as boys grow up, they tend to push their poor mothers away."

"Yes," she said, trying to respond. "I hear boys are like that." The muscles around her mouth refused to go into a smile, so she gave up trying. "Well," she said around a heavy sigh, "your offer is very gracious, Mr. Williams." She turned to the man whose name she would now share, but with whom she would share nothing else. "Is that all right with you, McCloud?"

As they followed him out the door, McCloud touched her arm, guiding her from the room. "I think it's a fine idea."

Julia forced herself not to recoil, not in disgust, but in pure frustration. Sometimes he acted so deceptively civilized, it frightened her.

Mr. Williams gave them the directions to his home before leaving the building. Julia and McCloud waited downstairs for the boy from the livery to bring the buggy around. She felt stiff and tense. "Don't expect this marriage to be anything more than a business arrangement, McCloud."

"Do you really think that's what Amos would want?"

His answer surprised her so, she shot him a swift glance. "I doubt that Papa expected me to share your bed," she snapped. "Thank heavens *that* option wasn't in the will as well."

"Too bad it wasn't." His cocky, sin-filled grin was back, and she knew he wasn't serious. She couldn't decide if she was pleased or disappointed.

Helga Williams was an incurable romantic, even after fifteen years of marriage. At any other time, Julia would have found this charming. Now, however, she found it exasperating. She'd deftly taken over Mary-mae's care and hustled the "newlyweds" off to the spare bedroom to "rest" before dinner.

Julia stood by the door, her nervous fingers wrinkling her skirt. "She doesn't know the circumstances. I'm sorry."

McCloud was at the window, watching the storm. "I'm sure you are."

At least he knew where she stood. Now it was her turn to understand him. "Why did you do this, McCloud? What could you possibly gain?"

He turned, giving her his handsome, wild, profile. "Appears I've gained a ranch, doesn't it?"

Anger tightened in the pit of her stomach. She swung away from the door and clutched the edge of the dry sink, her knuckles white. "Papa must have been crazy to think this would work."

"He wasn't crazy and you know it."

"But why would he do this to me?" She pressed her fist against her mouth, furious with herself for letting her feelings show and with Papa for betraying her, then dying before she could find out why.

"Maybe we should just make the best of it, Miss Julia, and not try to analyze it to death."

"No!" She made her way to the bed and sat, her head in her hands. "It's an impossible situation, McCloud. I don't want you and you don't want me. How can we possibly make the best of *that*?"

He continued to study the storm beyond the window. "Amos's will was as much of a surprise to me as to you. I was prepared to become your foreman for a small plot of land of my own." He raked his fingers through his thick, black hair; it fell to his shoulders again. "We can work it out that way, if you want.

I'll build a place of my own on the land at the edge of the property. I'll work as your foreman. You can have my money to pay your bills, or at least make a dent in them."

Julia's stomach quivered, again with unexplainable nausea. Disappointment? Excitement? Lord, she had no idea. "And the sham of a marriage?"

He shrugged. "According to the will, it can't be undone. But as you suggested, we'll just live our separate lives, if that's what you want."

"Of *course* that's what I want." Wasn't it? She didn't want to live with this man, no matter how inexplicably she was drawn to him on some baser level. But she had to learn to keep her thoughts and feelings to herself. This wasn't his doing any more than it was hers. He surely felt as trapped as she did, perhaps more so. Oddly, that thought hurt.

She felt a tiny bite of shame for her blatant behavior. "You ... you can take your meals with me, if you'd like."

For the first time since they'd stepped into the room, he turned from the window. His expression surprised her, for it was neither sarcastic nor insulting. "And where would you like me to sleep, Miss Julia?"

The question caused her stomach to dip, and there was an odd tingling between her legs. If only he'd had that wicked gleam in his eye, she would have told him to go to hell and sleep there, but he didn't. She didn't want him near her for many reasons, but in spite of everything, she wanted to be fair.

"Until you've built your cabin, McCloud, you can ..." She paused, unsure of her offer. "You can stay in Papa's bedroom." She swallowed hard, waiting for his barbarous response.

"I'd appreciate that, Miss Julia."

Again, his civility tossed her off balance. She cleared the nervous tickle in her throat, suddenly remembering their kiss after the ceremony. "About ... about tonight, McCloud ..."

As if planned, their gazes went to the bed, then to each other.

"Don't worry about it," he urged. "I'll take the floor."

Every muscle in Julia's body was so tight she was afraid they would twist into knots beneath her skin. And she was beginning to feel a headache coming on. Never in her life had she felt so awkward.

There was a knock at the door, breaking the tension in the room. "Julia?"

Letting out a shuddering breath, she went to the door and opened it. Helga Williams, almost as wide as she was tall, stood before her, a smile showing the gap between her front teeth.

"Oh, that baby," she gushed. "Such a good girl. And so pretty, too."

Julia relaxed. "I hope she hasn't given you any trouble, Helga."

Helga swept into the room, surprisingly agile for a woman of her size. "Not at all. I love babies. Wish I could have had more of my own, but God knows best, I guess. My Joshua is not a baby anymore." She held out the garment that hung over her arm. "Here," she said. "You'll need clothes to sleep in tonight." She stepped closer. "It's a little something I've saved over the years for special occasions." She gave Julia a conspiratorial wink.

Julia took the gown and robe, feeling a wash of color in her cheeks. "Thank you, Helga. That was very thoughtful of you." She didn't have to wear the gown;

Helga would never know. But did she really want to sleep in her clothes?

Helga walked to the door. "Dinner will be in an hour, you two. And we have champagne!"

Wolf sat across the table, watching Julia. Her color was high. She'd had too much champagne. She was also nervous, which was probably why she'd had too much to drink. Not so surprisingly, she appeared softer and more vulnerable. He'd trade his soul to the devil to kiss her delicious mouth again. Once, in the company of a lawyer and a justice of the peace, only stimulated his appetite for more. And each time their gazes locked, he saw interest where there had never been interest before. Again he knew it was the liquor, but it was an appealing concept, nevertheless.

"So, Mr. McCloud," Earl Williams began, turning toward him from his place at the head of the table. "What plans do you have for the ranch?"

Wolf toyed with the stem of his wineglass. "I have some ideas, sir."

Julia sat up straight, appearing surprised, and far too animated. "You do?"

He gave her a lopsided grin. "I do."

"What are you going to do?" She didn't sound hostile, which she would have been had she been sober.

"I'm going to pick all that fruit and—"

"Oh, posh, McCloud. We've tried that," Julia interjected. "It rots before we can even sell it."

She was quite appealing this way, all uninhibited. "I'm going to dry it."

"Dry it?" Earl Williams asked, surprised.

"Yes," he answered, leaning toward him. "I've drawn plans for drying racks using chicken wire and gauze. If the fruit is dried, we can ship it as far away as Boston. Or even Europe."

Julia sat back in her chair and expelled a huge, inebriated sigh. "Well. I'll be. That just might work, McCloud."

"I'm glad you approve, Miss Julia." He took a sip of champagne, then smiled at her over the rim of his glass. She smiled back, a becoming stain blooming on her cheeks.

He had a strange yearning in his gut, one that wished she would always be this receptive to him. But regrettably, he knew that come morning, things would be back the way they'd been before, and would undoubtedly be forever.

She yawned, covering her mouth at the last minute, expelling a hiccough at the end. "Oh, my," she said on a small giggle. "I think it's time for me to go to bed. Funny, though, I feel awfully good for being so sleepy."

Wolf hid his smile with his hand. She was crocked.

"Well," said Helga, "I'm keeping the baby in the crib in our room tonight, dear." She gave Wolf a sly grin. "Can't have a baby in the room on your wedding night."

"Hmmm?" Julia yawned again, her eyes at half-mast.

"The baby will be fine, dear, you just run along now."

Wolf took Julia's arm, surprised when she leaned against him.

"You taking me up to bed?" She looked at him, her eyes a languid shade of blue.

"I'm taking you to bed," he repeated, leading her toward the stairs.

Julia turned in his arms and peered over his shoulder. " 'Night, all!"

She continued to lean against him as they took the stairs to their room. He liked her there. She fit perfectly, especially all soft and pliable from the champagne.

Once inside their room, she whirled away, spinning in the center of the room. When she faltered, he caught her.

"Oh, heavens." She uttered another giggle. "I guess I won't do that again. For some reason, the floor is slanted."

"You've had too much champagne," he said with a smile.

She stood in front of him, swaying a bit. Punching her finger into his chest, she answered, "Don't be silly. I'm just feeling *really* good, that's all."

She walked her fingers to his neck, then to the back of his head, into his hair. His scalp prickled at her touch. A thickness gathered in his groin. "Your hair is the color of ink. I saw that the first time you rode in on Baptiste. You looked like you belonged together. Both so ... so wild ... and dark ... and dangerous."

"What else did you see, Miss Julia?" He wanted to remember everything about this night, because he knew he'd never see her like this again.

She sighed, hiccoughing again. "Oops," she said, grinning openly, her smile transforming her features from merely pretty to beautiful. "Well, lemmesee." She pinched at her lips. "Let me see," she repeated, saying the words distinctly. "Your face," she began, touching his cheekbones. "I kinda like it. Everyone thinks I'm a prude, you know. They don't understand that there's this part of me, deep down inside, that wants ..."

There was a sultriness about her that tied his gut into knots. "That wants ... what, Miss Julia?"

She stared up at him, her eyes filled with warmth and heat and desire. He ached for this to be the real her, but for him, it would never be.

She ran one hand along his shoulder to his arm. "I like your shoulders. Big and strong. But," she said, her gaze turning sad, "you've got scars on your back. I saw them." Tears gathered in her eyes. "I'm sorry someone beat you. Who beat you, Wolf?"

He caught a tear with his finger, then gently pressed his thumbs beneath her eyes. His name on her tongue was like nectar. He savored it, knowing that at any other time she wouldn't have said it. "Lady, you are drunk."

She whirled away, her mood changing again as she picked up the nightgown that lay on the bed. "Gotta get ready for bed." She stared at him, still swaying slightly. "Turn, turn, turn," she ordered, twirling her finger at him.

Wolf crossed to the window and looked out into the black, bleak night. There was a fierce aching in his gut, a yearning for the kind of life that had eluded him. He looked up, noting for the first time that she was reflected in the glass. Decency told him to close his eyes; necessity made him a voyeur.

She stepped out of her dress, sending it sprawling with an uninhibited kick. She looked pretty today, all gussied up in a fine dress to get married. He preferred her in trousers, for then he could watch her sweet ass move. But the dress was nice; she had a tiny waist and her breasts were outlined subtly behind the snug bodice.

Her undergarments were unadorned, like she was, yet so unlike her right now. He told himself he would watch only until her breasts sprang free of the garment that held them, but when it happened, he couldn't turn away or shut his eyes.

They were perfect. Firm and round, with nipples so pale he could barely detect them. When attempting to untie her petticoat, she swayed, reaching out to the bedpost to catch herself. Her breasts shook, the nipples tightened hard by the cool air of the room.

With a shuddering breath, Wolf lowered his head and closed his eyes, his hands balling into fists on either side of the window. He'd never seen nipples that fair, or breasts that firm, for that matter. Every woman he'd ever bedded had dark nipples and dark hair—everywhere. His new wife's wouldn't be. The thought of finding out sent waves of hunger nipping at his groin.

"McCloud?" she said, quiet laughter making her voice shake.

He took another breath and turned. She stood in front of him, holding the nightgown out by the seams. It was white with wide pink stripes ... and the size of a circus tent.

"Do you think she expected both of us to wear this?" She laughed again, her cheeks brightly stained. She slipped it on over her head, allowing him a view of her breasts again. His mouth went dry until she had the gown on, then he, too, had to laugh.

She was drowning in a sea of fabric as she struggled with her drawers, kicking them out from beneath the folds of the gown. She unpinned her hair, running her fingers through the wheat-colored mass as it fell to her shoulders.

"You could see me in the window, couldn't you?" She didn't sound strident or angry.

"Why would you think that?" He wanted to bury his face in her hair, against her neck ... her breasts.

She gave him a saucy, champagne-filled grin. "Because I can see myself in it now."

He turned from her, feeling ashamed. "A gentleman wouldn't take advantage."

She came around in front of him, a dreamy expression on her face. "When you act like a gentleman, it confuses me," she responded, touching his chest with her hand.

He swallowed hard, hoping to kill the desire that stirred in his loins. "Go to bed, Miss Julia." His voice was husky. Harsh.

Her eyes continued to have a dreamy look. "I keep thinking about our kiss, McCloud. I think I'd like another."

"You're still drunk. You don't mean what you're saying."

She leaned into him, her breasts pressed against his chest. "Try me."

If he'd been any kind of gentleman, he would have refused. He couldn't. He drove his fingers into her hair, cradling the back of her head with his hands, and drew her forward.

The moment their lips touched, something exploded inside him. Maybe it was the tiny whimper of pleasure that she made, maybe it was his own violent need for her, he didn't know. He didn't care.

He slanted his mouth over hers, nudging her lips with his tongue. When she opened for him, he ventured inside, liquefying the kiss, raping her tongue with tender strokes. In spite of the champagne, she tasted sweet and exotic, her mouth quivering like a virgin's against his.

His hands left her head and roamed her back, over the gentle swell of her ass. He was hard as a rock behind the buttons of his fly, and the sting of hunger surged through him like fire.

She emitted a long, breathy sigh, then went limp against him. Catching her up in his arms, he studied her slack features. Her harlot's mouth, with lips pink and sweet. The tiny, turned-up nose of a flirt, which she surely was not. Finely shaped tawny eyebrows over eyes that had thick, dark-edged lashes. Skin as soft as the petals of a flower.

But she'd passed out. If she was lucky, she wouldn't remember anything in the morning. He, on the other hand, would remember all of it for the rest of his life.

❧ 5 ❧

A herd of wild horses galloped through Julia's head, crashing against her skull. She moaned as she rose up off the pillow, feeling a hard rush of nausea. Pulling in a deep, slow breath, she put her head down, swallowing repeatedly.

She rolled slowly onto her back, opening her eyes a crack, scanning the room. It was empty. *Thank you, God.* She didn't remember much about the night before, but something told her she didn't want to.

She rarely, if ever, drank. The last time she'd sipped any alcohol at all had been a few years ago at Christmas when Papa had whipped up a batch of grog for the neighbors. She'd awakened with a headache that had threatened to push her eyes out, and she'd vowed never to imbibe again.

Temperance might well be a virtue, but the last few days would have driven a saint to drink, she thought. And yesterday. Oh, yes, yesterday had been the most potent potable of all. Imagine having to marry a man she abhorred! She didn't understand Papa's reasoning.

It was no wonder she'd downed champagne as if it had been water.

Rolling to her side and facing the door, she curled into a ball, pressing her hands against her stomach as she thought about her nervousness the evening before. She hadn't even recalled drinking more than two glasses, but she must have. She'd been jumpy as a cat, wondering how she and McCloud could possibly get through the night in the same room without her killing him for trying to ... what? Had she expected him to attempt seduction? She didn't think that even *he* was that big a fool.

The last thing she remembered was— Her stomach took a dive. Oh, God! He'd kissed her. How had she let that happen? Surely she'd fought him. She must have. Touching her mouth, she felt the slightest bit of chafing around it. She traced her lips. Had he put his tongue in her mouth? She shivered. Lord, yes. She remembered that well enough. Oddly, she didn't feel revulsion. She should have, because he was nothing but a despicable rogue. No decent woman should feel the thrill she'd felt when he'd kissed her.

The door opened and McCloud entered with a cloth-covered tray. "Good morning, dear wife." His evil grin was in place. "And how are you feeling this morning? Got a bit of a headache?"

"I feel just fine," she lied, giving him a suspicious eye.

He put the tray on the stand by the bed and whipped off the cover. The smell of coffee and something rather sweet floated toward her, and surprisingly, it didn't cause her stomach to heave.

"Quite a night we had, wasn't it? I know *I'll* never forget it." He fussed with the contents on the tray like an overzealous servant.

Rolling over again, she brought the covers to her chin. Her head continued to pound, and though she was no longer quite so nauseated, there was a nervous sensation in her stomach. "What are you talking about?"

He poured coffee into a china cup from a silver coffee server. "What? You don't remember? Look at the other pillow, Miss Julia."

Julia rose up off the bed and looked at the pillow next to her. The case was wrinkled and there was a dent in it, indicating—

She turned, gasping as her headache quickened. "You said you'd sleep on the floor, you ... you worm," she hissed.

"Oh, I would have." He held the dainty cup and saucer as though he used one every day.

The coffee smelled delicious, and Julia scooted to sit, positioning the pillows behind her before she took the coffee from him.

"But you took pity on me, insisting I share the bed." He gave her a look of mock injury. "Now, don't tell me you don't remember?"

She didn't answer him. Her look of fury was answer enough.

"Why, Miss Julia, I'm crushed. I certainly thought my prowess was memorable. That's what I've been told," he added with a wicked grin.

Julia mentally tested the area between her legs. She was smart enough to know she'd have felt different down there if they'd actually done something. He was purposely needling her, the wretch.

She donned a calm air and sipped her coffee. "Obviously your prowess is highly overrated," she answered, giving him a dry smile.

He threw his head back and laughed, the sound

tunneling into her heart. "That's what I like about you, Miss Julia. You're never at a loss for words."

She studied him, the straight white teeth, the laughing eyes, the complete and total male aura about him. Her insides quivered, signaling danger. "That was a dirty trick, McCloud."

His smile faded and his eyes became warm. "Last night you called me Wolf."

Something fluttered in her chest. "No," she argued, "I probably called you *a* wolf."

He laughed again, then offered her a buttered scone. She took it. Though their fingers barely touched, Julia felt a jolt all the way to her toes.

She wondered where he *had* slept, and felt a stab of remorse. Her guilt was assuaged when she realized that he'd slept in their barn for the nights previous to coming to Martinez. Surely one night on the floor, in a fine house was many steps up for this wild-hearted man.

"I don't want to rush you," he began, watching her eat, "but we should start back as soon as possible. I'd hate to run into another storm."

An odd feeling spread through her. She'd left her home a single woman. She was returning as a wife.

The ride back to the ranch had been short, probably because both Julia and Marymae had slept most of the way. They had swaddled the baby in blankets and put her in a handmade basket on the floor of the buggy. Julia had every intention of staying awake, but her headache had persisted, and she, too, found relief in sleep. When she awoke, she felt McCloud's forearm resting on her shoulder. She was curled up on the seat, her cheek on his hard thighs. She felt the bulge at his groin on the back of her head.

She sat up, cursing herself when her head throbbed anew. "You shouldn't have let me fall asleep," she scolded.

"I don't think I could have prevented it. Did you know you snore?"

"Don't try to rile me, McCloud, I'm not in the mood." She massaged her throbbing temples, willing the day away, for she knew tomorrow she would feel like her old self again. She pressed her hands against the small of her back, hoping to ease the ache that had gathered there while she slept.

The ranch was in sight, and it sent a rush of anticipation through her. Nothing would be the same again. Ever. She couldn't decide how she felt, for the nervous sensation in her stomach was, as always, either expectation or frustration.

As she scanned the property, she knew that something was different. Her pulse accelerated. "McCloud, someone's there."

McCloud shaded his eyes, squinting into the distance. "There are two horses tied up outside the corral." He turned toward her. "Recognize them?"

She shook her head, her anticipation growing. "They're Morgans, aren't they? Besides Sally, there isn't another Morgan in the valley."

McCloud inched the rifle from beneath the seat and rested it across his knees. He must have felt her gaze, for he turned toward her again. "Insurance," he murmured. "I'm going to stop behind the brush and sneak in. Here," he added, handling her the reins.

She took them, drawing them in her fists, relieved when the geldings lowered their heads and grazed.

"Can you use this?"

She looked at the rifle and swallowed hard. "Of course I can. But . . . but what will you use?"

He pulled out a knife that could down a cougar. Giving her a lopsided grin, he said, "I'm more comfortable with this."

Without a sound he moved toward the ranch. Julia felt oddly comforted until he was out of sight, then she gripped the rifle stock. A quick look at the buggy floor assured her that Marymae was still asleep.

A wet breeze kicked up, rustling the brush, causing her heart to lurch in her chest. She straightened, clutching the rifle when she heard voices beyond the bushes. Then there was laughter.

McCloud rounded the brush, smiling like a fool, accompanied by two others. One was a man, as tall as McCloud but broader and thicker through the chest and shoulders. Had he not been laughing, Julia would have shuddered, for his forehead was scarred and his face was forbidding.

The other was a boy on the brink of manhood, his tawny hair shining in the sun.

Julia watched McCloud approach, stunned at his genial expression. Clearly, these two were his friends.

"Miss Julia," he announced, gripping both the boy and the man by the shoulders, "I want you to meet our culprits."

The man came forward, drawing the boy with him. "Nathan Wolfe, ma'am. This is my son, Jackson. I'm sorry we alarmed you. We heard McCloud was here and thought we'd stop by on our way back from San Francisco." He smiled, his eyes warm. "Had no idea we'd get to meet his new bride."

Julia stiffened. He'd told them about the marriage? But why? He hadn't wanted it any more than she had, and they'd agreed to go their separate ways, do their separate things. She forced herself to stay calm. "I hope you haven't been waiting long."

"Just long enough for Jackson, here, to work up a powerful hunger," he said, cuffing the boy's ear.

The boy blushed. "Aw, Pa. Ma says you say it's me who's starvin' when it's you. She says you've got two hollow legs and a bottomless pit for a stomach."

The gentle repartee worked its magic on Julia just as Marymae let out a squeal. "Well, then, what are we doing here?" She lifted Marymae up off the floor. "Seems there's more than one mouth to feed."

Leaping onto the seat beside her, McCloud took the reins and let the team pick its way through the brush to the ranch. McCloud's friends took the shortcut to the house.

Julia turned on McCloud when they were out of sight. "You told them we were married?"

He had a startled expression on his face. "We are, aren't we?"

She let out an exasperated sigh. "Of course. But I thought we were going to ... to ..."

"Pretend otherwise?"

She didn't know how to feel. "Yes."

"Sorry." He didn't sound the least bit so. "It sort of slipped out before I had a chance to think about it."

The nervous agitation in her stomach boiled like lye water on wash day. "I guess we'll just have to make the best of it. At least they won't be staying long." When he didn't agree, she glanced at him. "They won't, will they?"

"Nate's horse threw a shoe. I ..." He ran his fingers through his hair. "I told them that as long as it was already late, they could stay the night."

Julia's hand flew to her throat. "The *night?*" She thought of the room that she'd so generously told McCloud he could occupy. "And where do you propose they sleep?"

The buggy had stopped in front of the barn. While she waited for him to give her some reasonable answer, she glanced at the corral. The question faded from her mind when she saw both Baptiste and Sally there. Her gaze found McCloud's.

"What happened? Why are they in there, together?" Her voice came out little more than a whisper.

"When Nate and Jackson rode up, they noticed the half-door kicked in."

"Kicked in? How?" Her heart was thrumming.

"Baptiste," he answered.

Clarification wasn't necessary. They both knew what this might mean. "Do you think . . ." She took a shaky breath. "Do you think it happened?"

He didn't answer her. Instead he unhitched the team and led the geldings into the barn.

Clutching Marymae to her, she scrambled out of the buggy, not even waiting for him to help her down. She hurried after him. "Well? Do you?"

"Whether I think it happened or not isn't important, Miss Julia. We'll know in six months or so."

Julia didn't know where to vent her anger. She went to the corral and studied her mare, then glared at Baptiste. It would be just like McCloud's lusty stallion to get her sweet Sally pregnant.

The mere idea sent gooseflesh over her skin, and an odd heaviness gathered between her legs. Shaking her head, she walked to the house, knowing that she had to prepare herself to face strangers who presumed her own life was far, far different than it was.

Julia cleared the table, intensely aware of Nathan Wolfe's gaze on her. She would never have believed she'd welcome McCloud's presence, but when he left to check the stock, taking the young boy, Jackson, with him, she wished he'd stayed.

She poured hot water over the dishes in the dishpan, then added cold water and shaved soap. She was surprised when Mr. Wolfe appeared at her side with the dish towel.

He caught her look. "It's a tradition at our house. Sometimes it's the only time Susannah—that's my wife—and I get to talk."

Giving him a weak smile, she dug into the dishpan and scrubbed the dishes.

"Have you known McCloud long?" She wondered if he found it odd that she didn't use her husband's first name.

"Long enough. I owe him a life."

A life. Not *my* life. She had to smile. "That's an odd way of putting it, Mr. Wolfe."

He took the platter she offered, wiped it and placed it on the table. "Not so odd. I thought Jackson was dead. He brought him back to me."

A strange feeling rippled through Julia's body. "He did?"

"My first wife—Jackson's mother—was killed by an explosion near a mine. It was assumed that Jackson was dead as well, but we never found his body."

Julia digested this news, sensing the man's emotions. "And McCloud found him?"

Nathan Wolfe nodded. "He'd been with the Army when they'd set the explosives."

Another bit of news about her husband she hadn't known. "He was in the Army?"

"You didn't know that?"

She attacked the dishes with vigor. "No. He didn't mention it to me."

"Well," Nathan added, "he did scouting for them.

The commanding officer told him that the official report would read that they'd been killed by Indians. The man was covering his carelessness at not canvassing the area better before he set off the explosion. As you can imagine," he continued, "that didn't sit well with McCloud."

No, she couldn't imagine. He made it sound as though McCloud was a man of scruples. Nathan Wolfe obviously knew something about her new husband that she did not. On the other hand, she thought with a twist of her mouth, perhaps *she* knew the real Wolf McCloud.

"Years later he'd heard of a white boy living with an Indian tribe on the north coast. He discovered it was Jackson."

"And they let McCloud take him?"

The man smiled. Again, as before, it transformed his features. "He wasn't a prisoner. They'd found him wandering in the woods near the cave after the explosion. They gave him a home when he would have died."

"And you've remarried?"

His smile widened and his eyes filled with such tenderness, Julia had to look away.

"I have. Susannah and I each brought a son to the marriage. Corey is almost nine years old. We have two daughters, Miranda and Caroline."

Julia sensed the love and pride in his voice and still couldn't look at him. Somehow, knowing that others loved so fiercely made her heart ache, for her marriage was such an imitation of what a marriage should be. But never would be.

She was in the process of removing the dishpan when he took it from her and walked toward the back door. "How did you and McCloud meet?"

When he returned with the empty dishpan, she attempted to ignore his question, hoping he'd forgotten he asked. He hadn't.

"You and McCloud," he said. "How did you meet?"

"He ... um ... He worked for my father, here on the ranch. But please, Mr. Wolfe," she added, "tell me more about him. He's very reticent when it comes to talking about himself. For instance, how did he get those scars on his back?"

Nathan Wolfe glanced away. "Some of them are from a grizzly."

Her heart leaped into her throat. "A bear attacked him?"

"That's the story he tells."

Julia thought about it. "You said *some* of his scars came from the grizzly. What about the others?"

Nathan Wolfe's probing gaze made Julia uncomfortable. It was as if he knew far more about her situation with McCloud than he'd let on.

"He has a lot of secrets, ma'am, but he's a good man. He's had a hard life."

Julia wiped off the flowered oilcloth on the table, then cleaned the counter space in an attempt to appear nonchalant. "A hard life? Really, Mr. Wolfe, haven't we all?"

"McCloud's has been harder than most. Consider the plight of half-bloods. They don't belong in either world."

Julia stopped working. "I hadn't thought about it that way."

"Most of us don't. I admit I didn't until I met McCloud. At our first meeting he had a chip on his shoulder the size of a redwood." Nathan Wolfe laughed. "Cockiest bas—" He coughed. "Pardon me, ma'am. Cockiest man I'd ever met."

At least that hadn't changed. "Do you know anything about his childhood?"

Nathan poured himself a cup of coffee. "Not much. He's pretty tight-lipped about that." His gaze was thoughtful as he stirred in cream. "I *do* know he was raised in the wilderness by a couple of rough trappers and probably a squaw or two."

Julia went to the table and sat, clutching her hands in her lap. Unable to imagine being raised that way, she felt an insane ache in the pit of her stomach for the child McCloud had been. And the kind of life that molded him into what he had become.

Nathan Wolfe gave her an amused smile. "You don't know much about your husband, do you?"

Julia lowered her head. "No. We only got married yesterday."

"And here we are, horning in on you." His voice was soft, understanding. "I'm sorry, I—"

"No, please. Tell me more about him." McCloud's voice on the back stoop halted their conversation.

He and the boy entered, and his gaze locked with hers. She gave him a tremulous smile.

"So," she said, getting to her feet, "everything all right outside?"

"Everything's quiet." McCloud went to the stove and poured himself a cup of coffee. "Jackson, here, thinks Sally's going to foal early next winter."

Julia's pulse jumped. "Really, Jackson? How can you be so sure?"

He gave her a shy shrug and looked at the floor. "Just a guess, but sometimes I can tell these things. Isn't that right, Pa?"

His father nodded. "He's predicted both of our foals

months before it was evident that the mares were pregnant. They were winter births, too."

"I see." She gave her apron a nervous twist. "I should check on the baby. And see that your room is ready."

"Mind if I come along, Miss Julia?" Jackson was at her side. "I'm kinda tired. Bed sounds good to me."

"No, not at all." She was anxious to leave the two men behind.

Wolf followed her with his eyes until she was gone, then took a seat across from Nathan at the table. He avoided his friend's gaze.

"What brings you this way, Nate?"

"I had some papers to sign in San Francisco."

Wolf toyed with his coffee cup. "How's Susannah?"

Nate grinned, his eyes warm. "She couldn't be better."

"How did you know I was here?"

"I didn't. Not until Jackson and I had stopped in Martinez. We were at a chop house this morning having breakfast, and shared a table with a lawyer named Williams."

Wolf couldn't suppress a chuckle. "How in the hell did *my* name come up?"

"We got to talking about available ranch land. He said something about a deceased client whose land might have been up for sale if the old man hadn't established "the breed" into his will."

This time Wolf laughed out loud. "Whatever made you think it was me?"

"I didn't. I was just curious, so asked if he could give me the name of the breed." His grin was one of cunning. "Imagine my surprise. Lots of interesting questions, McCloud."

Wolf caught the smile in the words. "And I have no doubt you're anxious to ask them."

Nate gave him a quiet laugh. "I guess my first question would be—how in the hell did this happen?"

"It's a long story."

"Are you happy?"

Wolf's laugh was caustic. "Happy? That's not the word I'd use."

"And why's that?"

"Because my *wife* would sooner plunge a knife through my heart than be forced to play the loving bride." His disappointment puzzled him.

Nate leaned against the chair and steepled his fingers on his chest. "Interesting. Care to elaborate?"

Wolf left the table, went to the desk in the other room and returned with a copy of Amos's will. He retrieved a bottle of whiskey and two glasses from the dark pantry, then plunked the will, the glasses, and the whiskey on the table. "Here," he offered, pushing the will toward Nate. "Read page three." He poured them each a healthy shot of liquor.

Nate read the page, his expression one of shocked surprise. He downed his drink. "The old man forced you to marry his daughter? Wasn't there any way out of it?"

Wolf swallowed his whiskey and gave Nate a wry smile. "Believe me, my new wife tried."

"Care to tell me what led up to all of this?"

Wolf poured himself another shot of whiskey, but didn't drink it. "I was hired on last fall, during harvest. The old man and I got along well. He confided in me, was relieved to be able to talk to someone about the things that worried him. The ranch hasn't made a dime since the drought, and he knew he'd lose it to the bank if he didn't think up another crop."

He lowered the flame in the lamp, then threw down the whiskey, gritting his teeth as it burned his throat.

"Something else was on his mind, too. Something about the river, and the fact that the water level was down way too far in spite of the drought. But before he could elaborate, I ... felt the need to break off our association."

Nate frowned. "Why?"

Wolf gave him a sick grin. "Miss Julia has a very determined younger sister."

Nate leaned forward, his elbows on the table. "And ... ?"

"And she wouldn't leave me alone."

Nate guffawed, then clamped his hand over his mouth. "And that was a *problem* for you?"

"I know, I know. But she—"

"She was ugly?" Nate finished for him.

"Hell, no," Wolf exclaimed. "She was a real beauty."

Nate leaned back and studied Wolf. "Was?"

"Yeah. I left because Miss Julia suspected that something was going on between her sister and me." Wolf rubbed the back of his neck. "I hated to leave Amos, but under the circumstances, I didn't feel I had a choice."

"So, what brought you back?"

"Amos wrote and made me an offer. Said he'd sell me the land I wanted if I stayed on as foreman. We'd talked about a new crop, drying the fruit and shipping it to the East and Europe. I guess he thought it was the best chance he had to keep the place. And Miss Josette had run off with another man, so Miss Julia would be alone after Amos died."

Wolf shoved the bottle toward Nate. "Amos was sick. Had the wasting disease, I think. The whole idea of staying on here sounded like a good thing, but I told him he had to tell Miss Julia, because I knew she wouldn't believe he'd suggested the whole idea if it came from me."

Nate shook his head. "And you wound up marrying her?"

"The sly old dog changed his will after we'd drawn up the other agreement. Then he was ... then he died."

"From the disease?"

"No. It appeared that he'd either had an accident or killed himself. The official record states that it was an accident. I think Miss Julia suspects suicide, but she's never mentioned it out loud. I have a problem with that."

"Hey," Nate said, spreading his hands on the table. "It wouldn't be the first time someone had taken his own life because of a disease. He could have been depressed, he—"

"It might have been tongue in cheek, but he promised me he wouldn't die before I got here, and then he did. I think he had help."

"Why?"

Wolf shook his head. "Just a feeling, but I've been studying the river. I think his intuition was right. Someone is diverting the water away from the normal flow."

"And he was killed over that?"

"C'mon, Nate. Water's in short supply. No one's recovered from the drought."

They sat in comfortable silence, the sputtering of the flame in the lamp the only noise in the room.

"How do you feel about becoming a rancher?"

Wolf traced the pattern on the oilcloth with his index finger. "I don't know yet. I *do* know that for the first time in my life, I have something I can call mine, and I'll be damned if I'll let go of it easily."

There was a long, quiet pause. "Was she ever married?"

Wolf wasn't entirely surprised by the question. "I have no idea, but I don't think so. No one, not even old Amos, ever mentioned it. It's an odd thing to keep secret, don't you think?"

Nate raised his eyebrows. "And who fathered the baby?"

"Your guess is as good as mine." The presence of the baby had never bothered Wolf. The mere fact that Julia had had an indiscretion at least once in her life was comforting, for it meant she was human. He'd never been comfortable around virgins, anyway. He wasn't even sure he'd ever met one.

Nate gave him a slow, sympathetic smile. "I'll bet Jackson and I took your bed, didn't we?"

Wolf ran his fingers through his hair, then massaged his neck. "Yeah, and if you were any kind of friend, you'd sleep in the barn."

Nate's eyes filled with humor. "And let you get out of your predicament? Not a chance."

"As long as you know the situation, *I* might just as well sleep in the barn." He took another swig of whiskey, then turned to leave. "Turn out the lamp before you go to bed." He walked toward Julia's bedroom.

"Hey," Nate called after him, laughter in his tone. "The barn is in the other direction."

Wolf couldn't stay angry. "Go to hell, and free up my bed." Nate's laughter was still in his head as he opened the door to Julia's bedroom. He just wanted to look at her. He'd hoped she was asleep so he could. She wasn't.

She glanced up at him as he walked toward the bed, the lamplight casting a hazy shadow over the room. "Are they ... has he gone to bed?"

"He's on his way." She was beautiful. Her silvery braid rested over her shoulder, and she looked all soft and warm, cuddled in the bedding. He wanted to hold her. Crawl in beside her and pull her against him. Touch her in places a husband was allowed to touch a wife, soft, warm places that swelled with desire. He wanted to cup her womanhood, feel the heat expanding her flesh. The insides of her thighs would be like satin, and the cleft of her would be wet, aching for his mouth ... his tongue ... his root. He wanted her to shiver with anticipation, and cry out with joy at her release. He would trade every experience he'd ever had with a woman for one night with his wife. He was one hell of a dreamer.

"McCloud," she began, her eyebrows pinched into a frown as she shattered his erotic reverie. "I know this whole situation isn't really your fault. I'm sorry if I snapped at you earlier. I mean, what else could you have told your friend? After all, it *is* the truth. We are married, even though it's not what either of us would have chosen to do."

He bit back a smile. She wasn't very good at apologies. "I know, and I'll—"

"You can sleep here." She lay in the bed as stiff as a board, looking straight ahead. He swore she held her breath.

"Here?" Thinking about it was one thing, but an invitation to her bed with her in it was something he'd only imagined.

She drew in a sigh and flipped the covers back on the other side. "You can ... you can sleep with me. Just *sleep,* mind you."

Although it wasn't what he'd dreamed of, it was an invitation nonetheless. He had no idea what had changed her mind, but he knew it wasn't because she'd changed her feelings for him. God almighty, he wanted to sleep with her. But not if what she felt was duty. And the rigid way she lay in the bed plus the look on her face had "duty" written all over it.

He felt a mixture of emotions, angry with himself for feeling anything at all, and disappointed that there would be no passion, spontaneous or otherwise, in this union.

"You don't have to do that, Miss Julia. I'm content to sleep in the living room." Her sense of duty had all but extinguished his desire, and he turned and walked toward the door.

"You mean you're rejecting my offer?" There was an odd cracking in her voice, which Wolf assumed was relief.

He sensed she'd welcome his barbed tongue. In truth, he didn't know how else to answer her without letting her see more of him than he wanted her to.

"Not so much the offer, Miss Julia, as the possibility of getting frostbite in your bed."

He left the bedroom, not anxious to see her reaction. He didn't doubt for a minute that she'd look like a prisoner given a stay of execution.

❖ 6 ❖

During the night, the warm, wet air from the marsh-lands rose to meet the cold night air, and tule fog had blanketed the ground, intensifying Julia's morose mood. If the presence of guests hadn't forced her to make breakfast, she might have stayed in her room until noon, just to avoid McCloud. As it was, having his friends around kept her from taking her father's will and holding it over a hot flame, or tossing it into the blazing fireplace.

Nathan Wolfe left when the fog lifted, promising to return with his wife. Julia hoped it wouldn't be too soon, for she knew she hadn't even been able to fool this man; how could she convince another woman that her marriage was anything but a sham?

McCloud had loaded up the wagon with wood and went to his precious corner of land to begin building his cabin. Julia hoped he was a fast worker; a finished cabin couldn't come soon enough for her.

She forced her hands not to shake as she pieced together quilt squares. What a fool she'd been! Softening toward that buffoon because of a sad story about his childhood that probably wasn't even true. No doubt he and his friend had cooked up the tale together, hoping it would get just the reaction from her that it had.

And to have him *reject* her. Her hands stilled and she studied the rough edges of the clinker brick fireplace. That had hurt more than she'd never admit to anyone. It shouldn't have surprised her. After all, she wasn't Josette, and he obviously hadn't forgotten that fact.

It wasn't as if she'd expected him to *do* anything last night. She'd just offered him a warm place to sleep. However, she wasn't fool enough to ignore the fanciful picture of having him in bed beside her. A big, hard, warm body. She had no idea how it would feel, but she'd been willing to give it a try. Obviously, he'd rather sleep in the barn under a leaky roof and on a bed of straw than be anywhere *near* her.

Frostbite, indeed. Forcing down her hurt, she clutched the quilt top, her fingers automatically making the small, neat stitches needed to keep the pieces together. She'd give him frostbite, all right. More than he ever in his wildest dreams bargained for.

She had no idea how long she'd worked, but when the afternoon sun slanted through the window onto the floor beside her, she knew it was time to wake Marymae from her nap and start supper.

Hearing noises outside, she went to the window. She expelled a gasp of surprise and hurried to the door, flinging it open and stepping out onto the porch.

"Serge!" Her heart lifted at the sight of him, and she gave him an eager wave.

He dismounted and came toward her, his arms outstretched. She went into them with ease. "When did you get back? I've missed you, you old shoe." She returned his hug.

He pulled away and studied her, his thickly lashed dark eyes cautious. "I can't leave you for a minute, can I?"

Julia's heart dipped. "What do you mean?"

"I go away for a few months, and when I come home, you've got a husband," he scolded.

She felt the involuntary blush stain her cheeks. "Oh. Oh, that. I'm sorry, Serge, I—"

"I'm disappointed, Julia. I thought it would be you and me."

Sensing that he was serious, she gave him a wan smile. "So did I."

He continued to hold her. "Then what happened?"

She examined his handsome features. He had his mother's looks. Wavy blue-black hair and flawless skin. His cheeks always held a hint of color, which gave him a boyish look, one he'd never lost as he grew into manhood. She was angry that she felt no spark, no sense of heat, nothing.

"Oh, it was Papa." She gasped, remembering that he'd been gone. "He's dead, Serge. Did you know?"

He gave her a consoling sigh. "I heard. That's why I came right over." He hugged her again. "I'm so sorry, Julia, honey. So sorry. Now," he added, "what's this foolishness about Amos being responsible for your marriage?"

She accepted the embrace, for it had been the first she'd had since Papa had died. She refused to count the one McCloud had tried to give her the night he arrived. After all, an embrace was something one returned, and she hadn't returned his. "In his will, he *ordered* me to marry his last ranch hand, Wolf McCloud."

He stroked her hair. "Oh, poor lamb. What prompted that? Had he gone around the bend?"

She smiled into his shoulder. "Don't think I didn't wonder, but Papa's lawyer assured me he was as sane as any man." She wanted Serge to understand. "I tried to get out of it, but the will was binding."

He pulled her close again. "Poor, poor, honey lamb."

As she clung to him, she had the absurd feeling that she was going to fall apart. Tears stung her eyes and the aching void in her stomach, the one she'd fended off since her papa's death, came back full force, and she began to cry.

He patted her back. "There, there. Let it out."

It wasn't the embrace she wanted, but she was grateful, just the same. "Oh, Serge," she said between sobs, "I hate to even consider it, but I think Papa killed himself."

He continued to rub her back. "That isn't what I heard, Julia. Word is that it was an accident."

"I know, I know. But he'd been so depressed about the ranch, and Josette running off. He wasn't well, Serge. He'd gotten thin and frail; he was so sick."

"Don't worry yourself like this, Julia, honey. I'm here now. I'll make things better."

There was a noise behind her, and she turned—and stared into the dark, dangerous eyes of her husband. A tremor ran through her, an involuntary thing that sent shivers along her spine. He stood before them, removing his work gloves with all the grace of a gentleman removing a pair of white gloves in a San Francisco drawing room.

"If anyone's going to make things better for my wife, it'll be me." There was a tightness to his jaw that Julia found fascinating.

Serge didn't appear to want to let her go, so she extricated herself from his embrace.

"Serge, this is Wolf McCloud. "My ... my husband." She dug into her apron pocket, fished out her handkerchief and dabbed at her eyes before facing the man she'd married.

"Serge Henley is a very old and dear friend, McCloud." She'd emphasized "old" and "dear," hoping to somehow pacify her husband, but she didn't understand why she would want to, or even why she would have to.

Neither man made an attempt to shake hands. Serge's expression was closed. McCloud's appeared stormy. It was almost as if he actually *cared* that someone else was holding his wife, which was ludicrous, of course.

McCloud went to the pump and poured himself a dipper of water. Julia watched him drink, captivated by the water that tracked both sides of his mouth, dripping off his chin onto his shirt. When he finished, he said, "You have business here, Mr. Henley?"

Serge approached him, his chest puffed out. "I don't need to have business to see Julia. She and I have been friends for years. I don't need your approval to be here, Mr. McCloud."

Julia watched as an odd change came over her husband. One side of his mouth lifted into a smile, and his eyes became expressively clear.

"No. I can see that you don't, Mr. Henley. Please. Come by as often as you like. I'm sorry if I appeared rude, but I'm new at being a husband, and I get just a bit crazy when I see my wife in some stranger's arms."

Julia noted that Serge's stunned expression certainly mirrored her own.

Serge removed his hat and stepped from one foot

to the other. "I will, Mr. McCloud. Make no mistake about that." He turned to Julia. "I've got to get back, Julia, honey. Mother is expecting me." As he mounted his horse he threw McCloud a threatening glance. "If you ever need anything, just let me know, Julia."

"I will. Thanks for stopping by." She waved as he rode away. When he was gone, she turned on McCloud.

"Just what was that all about?"

He wiped his chin with his sleeve. "What was what all about?"

"You know very well what I mean, McCloud." She couldn't understand her anger. He'd turned civil; for that she should have been grateful. But truth to tell, she'd preferred the possessiveness he'd exhibited when he first saw her in Serge's arms. Suddenly it was clear to her: he hadn't found Serge the least bit threatening. The clarity made her emotions tumble around inside her. She'd wanted him to be jealous, but of course he wasn't. He'd even invited Serge back again.

He shook his head. "Tsk tsk, Miss Julia. You shouldn't think so much."

"What do you mean?"

"I can almost see the wheels turning in your head." A small smile tugged at his lips.

She walked toward the house and he followed. "So I think. So what? Are you that unfamiliar with women who do?"

He chuckled as he fell into step beside her. "I have to say I find it a refreshing change from most women I know."

Whores and nitwits like Josette, she thought, but didn't say.

He held the door for her, and she walked through, grazing his chest with her arm. It tingled, and she found it difficult to breathe. Damn! Why couldn't she feel those things with Serge?

McCloud washed up on the stoop, then came into the kitchen. "So, I gather this Henley fellow was a paramour of yours?"

She went into the dark pantry and retrieved some potatoes, slamming the door harder than was necessary on her way out. "And if he was?"

McCloud laughed. He actually laughed!

"I don't think it's funny, McCloud," she said, fuming inside. "You might not find me all that desirable, but believe it or not, other men do." Which was an absurd exaggeration.

He stopped laughing, but his smile lingered. "You would never have married Serge Henley, Miss Julia, and if you had, you'd have been miserable."

She rounded on him, her fists on her hips. "And what makes you say that?"

He studied her, still smiling. "Because Serge Henley isn't the marrying kind."

She turned away and started peeling potatoes. "What a stupid thing to say," she scoffed.

"You've never noticed anything peculiar about him?"

This conversation was ridiculous. "Certainly not. Serge is the most kind, gentle man in the world."

"And unthreatening, Miss Julia. Don't forget unthreatening."

That was exactly the word she'd used to describe Serge herself, in a conversation she'd had with her papa before he died. "Yes. He's unthreatening. What of it?"

"Your Serge Henley is a queer bird, Miss Julia."

She clutched the potato in her fist. "A what?"

"He's light in the heels. A Nancy-boy."

Julia frowned and shook her head. "You aren't making any sense, McCloud."

"Serge Henley doesn't like women, Julia." He paused then added, "He likes men."

Julia turned and hurled the potato at him. "How *dare* you imply such a thing!"

McCloud caught the wet, slippery vegetable as though he'd been expecting it. "Don't get your knickers in a knot, Julia. It wasn't meant as an insult."

"Oh, it wasn't? How does one take something like that? As a *compliment?*"

He hefted the potato, tossing it into the air and catching it. "It was just an observation." He threw the potato at her, and she caught it, fumbling to keep it from hitting the floor. Oh, but she wanted to fling the thing at his head!

"How dare you say something like that about Serge. And . . . and what makes you such an expert, anyway?"

She turned and began peeling another potato. In her haste and her anger, she sliced her thumb with the potato peeler. Sucking in a breath, she dropped the potato into the sink and clutched her hand.

He was beside her immediately. She tried to pull away, but he took her hand firmly in his and pressed the cut together. As angry as she was with him, his touch still unnerved her.

Taking a dipper of water from the pail on the counter, he poured it into a dish and forced her hand into it. "I didn't mean to make you lose your concentration."

His nearness was a bane to her sanity. "You made me angry, that's all. What makes you an expert on such things, anyway?" she repeated.

"I've upset you. I thought you might know." He continued to hold her hand in the water.

"Me? How in the name of heaven would *I* know?"

"I thought you might have guessed." His fingers were massaging hers, and it was very disconcerting.

"Oddly enough," she said, her voice laced with sarcasm, "I'm not in the habit of wondering about a person's inclinations. It's not one of those things I give much thought to." She had, however, had brief questions about Serge's lack of interest in her sexually, but had shoved them into the attic of her mind.

"Oh, I don't think that's true, Miss Julia. A clever girl like you? I'll just bet you wondered why he never took you out behind the barn to have his way with you."

What was he, a mind reader? "What you think is of no interest to me. And Serge is too much of a gentleman to try such coarse things. Break the word up, McCloud. He's a gentle man. Something you can't comprehend." She tried to sound blasé, but noted the tremor in her voice.

"I think," he went on, ignoring her barb, "that when Serge Henley kissed you, you felt nothing."

"Serge's kisses are none of your concern, McCloud."

"And all the coaxing in the world," he went on, as if she hadn't even spoken, "even from you, wouldn't get Serge Henley to make a serious pass at you."

His shoulder was pressed against hers at the sink, and she felt the tattletale quivering low in her belly. "You're inferring again that I'm not desirable, McCloud. It's unkind of you to keep hammering away on that point. I may not be pretty, like Josette—"

He turned her toward him and reached into her apron pocket. His hand grazed her stomach, and she gasped and pulled away. "What are you doing?"

"Searching for your handkerchief." His eyes danced.

She took a deep breath, expelling it slowly. "You might have asked me for it."

"I wanted to find it myself," he said, his smile devilish.

With a fierce scowl, she gave him the linen square. He pulled her hand from the water and wiped it. Before she knew what was happening, he'd brought her hand to his mouth and turned it over, kissing her palm. The touch of his lips on her skin was like water drops on a skillet, and she gasped, attempting to pull away. He held her hand and wrapped her thumb.

"Did Serge's kisses make you respond like that?" His voice was a husky whisper.

"That's none of your business." Her voice shook.

He drew closer. "Oh, I think it is. After all, you *are* my wife, legal and binding."

She willed her legs to hold her, but an aching weakness tunneled into her belly, scooting from the place between her legs, down the insides of her thighs to her knees. She wanted to pull away, truly she did, but she didn't have the strength. "That doesn't mean anything, McCloud, and you know it."

She gazed up at him, studying the tiny lines that fanned out from the edges of his eyes, the clearness of his light brown skin, the slight stubble on his cheeks and chin.

"It *will* mean something, Miss Julia." He pressed another kiss on her palm. "Make no mistake about that."

A confusing tumble of emotions spun inside her head, leaving her fuzzy as well as aroused. She'd always been able to control her head, if not her heart. She was beginning to wonder if that was true anymore.

"Did Serge's kisses make you feel like this?" His

mouth came down on hers, pressing hard, demanding entrance.

She made a sound in her throat, intending for it to be a sound of resistance, but when it came out, she wasn't sure. She wanted to fight him, but ...

She opened her mouth and accepted his tongue. Sounds of pleasure oozed from her, for never had she experienced such excitement, such elation. The firmness of the kiss changed, and became a subtle seduction, coaxing from her a response she'd never known she possessed. He nibbled, he licked, his tongue touched hers, his breath was hot; it made her weak.

He pulled her tighter, grinding against her, briefly grazing the sides of her breasts with his thumbs. Her nipples hardened even though they hadn't been touched.

She was drowning in sensations. Flinging her arms around his neck, she returned his kisses, melting against him, aching with a hunger new to her.

He raised his head. "That's my girl. There's passion in you, Miss Julia. I knew there was passion in you."

She could feel him, long and hard, against her abdomen. Her own senses were awash with lingering desire, and she rested her head on his chest, listening to the thundering of his heart. A tiny thrill passed through her; he had not been unmoved by the kiss.

"Miss Julia?"

She raised her head. "Yes?"

He nodded toward the bedroom, and her heart zinged into her throat. He wanted her! He wanted to bed her! Oh God, oh God, oh God.

"The baby."

"Wh-What?"

"The baby is crying," he said.

Julia shook her head, hearing Marymae's wail for

the first time. She stumbled backward, anxious to get away. "Oh. Of course. The baby." Her limbs trembled, her heart clubbed her ribs.

As she made her way to the bedroom, she wondered how she was going to survive having him around. It was one thing to know he was out there, somewhere, building a cabin on her property. It was quite another to realize that until it was ready, he would sleep under her roof, mere feet from her own bedroom.

"You saw him? This ... this man who married Julia?" His mother accepted the healthy shot of brandy he handed her.

"I saw him, Mother." Serge poured himself a drink.

She straightened her purple velvet skirt, then lifted her chin high and put her arm on the back of the settee, as if posing for a portrait. "And?"

He shrugged, feeling uncomfortable when his mother interrogated him. "And, what?"

"And what's he like?"

Serge frowned. "I'm not sure."

"What's that supposed to mean?" she asked, her voice strident.

"I don't know, Mother. He ... he appears to be a very nice man, actually."

She made an exasperated sound in her throat. "We should never have gone back East. All of this happened because we weren't here."

Serge fiddled with his glass. "I guess we just weren't supposed to have that land, Mother."

"Oh for God's sake, Serge, must you act like such a ... a castrated fool?"

The derogatory reference to his masculinity hit him like a slap across the face. Not that it was the first time. She enjoyed putting him down, reminding him that he wasn't the son she'd either expected or deserved. He gritted his teeth, knowing that one day he'd prove to her that he could be what she wanted.

"Mother, I don't know what else to say. We were gone when Amos died. We—"

"Yes, we were, Serge. But you returned before I did," she reminded him.

"Mother! Are you suggesting that *I* had something to do with the poor man's death?"

"I should hope not. There are other ways to curry my favor." She held out her empty snifter toward him. After he poured her another brandy, she continued castigating him.

"I do so hate it when you simper and whine like a weak woman. And *now* what are we going to do? I want that land, Serge. How am I going to get it if you don't marry Julia?"

He often wondered how he could love his mother and hate her at the same time. He was certain that on some level, hate was there, often stronger than love. But he also knew that he would do anything in the world she asked him to, on the chance that she could forgive him for being what he was, and not what she wanted him to be.

He hadn't forgotten what he'd learned on their trip East. She thought she held all the cards, but he had an ace up his sleeve. He suddenly realized he was learning to play by her rules, for now they were equal: he had a weapon. He'd discovered her dirty little secret.

❧ 7 ❧

Julia had trouble sleeping. Visions of McCloud kissing her wouldn't leave her alone. On top of that, she'd only remembered her vow to give him frostbite long after she'd responded to that kiss. She'd had no will of her own once he touched her. It was a terrifying realization.

Rolling onto her side, she looked out the window, into the night. Tule fog had not blocked out the moon, for it shone through, casting eerie shadows off the trees.

Try as she might to concentrate on something else, she found McCloud creeping back into her thoughts. She had no idea how she would deal with it, for the longer they were together, the more often she thought about him.

She couldn't hate him for forcing her to at least think about seeing Serge as he saw him. He could very well be right.

If Serge *was* that way, it in no way lessened her feelings for him, for they were friends. Even if

McCloud was right about him, that friendship wouldn't change. And McCloud didn't sneer and belittle Serge's affliction—if indeed he had one—as other men would have. Frank Barnes, for one, she thought.

No, McCloud was nothing like Frank Barnes. Her father had known that. She hadn't. Or had she purposely painted McCloud with a dark brush because of her embarrassing attraction to him? She rose up onto her elbow and punched her pillow, hoping to find some comfort in the bed and finally get some sleep.

She was just dozing off when a cry pierced the darkness, bringing her bolt upright.

McCloud. She scooted from the bed. With shaky fingers she lit the lamp and hurried from her room, her heart in her throat. She flung open his bedroom door and stepped cautiously inside.

"McCloud?" She inched forward, the lamp lighting the way. He was sitting on the edge of the bed, his head in his hands. Her pulse raced. "McCloud? Are you all right?"

He raised his head, his expression bleak. "I'm fine. Go back to bed."

As she drew closer, she saw that he was bathed in sweat. "What is it? What's wrong? Are you ill?"

"No, I'm not ill." His voice was laced with impatience. "Go back to bed."

Ignoring his order, she grabbed a towel off the bar by the dry sink and sat down beside him. He flinched when she dried off his back, but he didn't move away.

"You'll catch cold like this." She felt the grooved scars on his back and something inside her hurt, as if she'd been attacked herself.

Gripping her arm, he pushed her away. "Julia, get out of here."

Never before had he sounded so fierce. And rarely

had he not prefaced her name with "Miss." "But McCloud, you're—"

"Julia." His voice threatened.

Her gaze moved over his naked chest to the pillow on his lap, and down over his bare legs and feet. Remembering how he slept, she swallowed hard, understanding. Peering up at him through the veil of her lashes, she noticed his hardened features.

"You're right, Julia," he said, as if reading her mind, "but tonight I'm not even wearing a smile. Now, go back to bed. Please, damnit, before I . . ."

Her eyes grew wide and her heart almost sprang free from her chest. "Before you what?"

He swore again. "Julia, *please* get out of here."

Feeling light-headed, she rose. As she floated toward the door, she turned for one last look. Her lamp cast just enough light for her to see how dark he was. His bare calves were tight and well-muscled. The only men's legs she'd ever seen in her life were her father's thin, hairless white ones. McCloud's were brown and hair-dusted. His were beautiful. The urge to tell him so was so strong, she almost said so aloud, but thought better of it. She wasn't sure she could speak of it, anyway.

"Good night, McCloud. I hope you can get some sleep." She closed the door and slipped away to her own room. But once in her bed, sleep further eluded her, for the vision of McCloud's nudity beneath the pillow he'd held over his lap wouldn't go away. Despite her inability to conjure up a picture of what he would look like, she felt a throbbing between her thighs.

So, what are you going to do about it? Do? she wondered. Why, nothing, of course. She rolled to her side, their conversation in the kitchen before he'd kissed her coming back to haunt her. Seduce her.

You are my wife, legal and binding.

That doesn't mean anything, McCloud, and you know it.

It will *mean something, Miss Julia, make no mistake about that.*

Whatever did he mean? That he meant to make their marriage real? Closing her eyes, she turned her face into her pillow, her breath coming in shaky gasps. The words were clear. Stirrings of the kiss returned, furrowing deep, flooding her with hope-mingled dread. She wondered if his words had been a threat. Or a promise.

Wolf groped for his jeans and slipped into them, knowing he wasn't going to get any more sleep. He hadn't had that particular nightmare for months, that suffocating, choking feeling of being buried alive.

Shaking away the residual feeling of panic, he buttoned his jeans, put on a shirt, and left the bedroom. In the darkness he made his way into the kitchen, where he lit a squat candle and placed it on the table. Leftover coffee sat in a small pot over the reservoir attached to the stove, and he discovered it was warm. He took a cup from the shelf near the pie safe and poured himself some, then sat down at the table, his thoughts turning to Serge Henley.

He smiled, though if someone were to have seen him do so, they would have seen the cynicism in it. Serge Henley. His half brother. All of his life he'd had an instinct that had not been nurtured, but had remained strong, nevertheless. The moment he'd come across Meredith Columbo's name on that list of people who had crossed the prairie with the Hardin party, an odd sensation had played over his skin. He'd been looking at those lists of settlers for months, not knowing just what he expected to find. He saw her name and he knew. Somehow, he knew.

Then, when he discovered a notation in an old Sacramento newspaper, listing her marriage to Gordon Henley, his skin had prickled again. And today, when he'd met Serge Henley face-to-face, he felt the same damned reaction.

Through all of this there was another sensation, one he hoped would be satisfied once he met his mother. It was an unfinished feeling, a feeling of being only half a person. He could never describe it to anyone else. It wouldn't make sense. It didn't even make any sense to him.

His gaze wandered over the dimly lit kitchen, coming to rest on Julia's apron, which hung over the back of the chair next to him. He picked it off and pulled it to his face, inhaling the scent that lingered. Through the superficial cooking smells, he detected her scent. It burrowed into his chest with all the reality of an arrow dipped in an aphrodisiac.

As a boy, he'd learned to discern between those things that were Angus's and those that were Baptiste's by the scent of each man. It was one gift he'd honed, and now he was glad. He knew that if he were thrown blindfolded into a room filled with women, he could find Julia in an instant.

Even now, with just the apron in front of him, he not only felt desire, but a strange sense of peace. Permanence. He swore, wondering what she'd do if she knew how she affected him. Having her sit beside him in her nightgown, knowing she was naked beneath, had nearly been his undoing. He wanted her. He wondered if he'd ever have her.

*   *   *

Serge dug out Grandmama Rosa's journal, which he'd discovered in her attic on his recent trip back East. They'd packed her up and moved her out to live with them; he didn't understand why. Meredith appeared to hate her own mother. He lifted an eyebrow. Perhaps hating one's mother ran in the family.

Turning to the page he wanted, and careful not to destroy the fragile paper, he read again the passage that had stunned him. His grandmother's beautiful script, in Italian, leaped out at him. He knew enough Italian to translate and understand.

In essence, she'd written of their stop in Dakota Territory, and Meredith's rape by a savage. And the difficult birth when they arrived in California. And her own agony when Meredith ordered her to get rid of— the words were hard to translate. The closest word he could come to was "evidence."

He closed the book, his fingers stroking the battered edges. His mother had ordered Grandmama to get rid of the child. How? He found pleasure in the knowledge that his mother had such a terrible secret. It was almost arousing, made more exciting by the fact that she didn't know he knew. But what frustrated him was that nowhere in the journal was there a mention of how the bastard was "gotten rid of."

He closed the book and stared into the fire. Boy or girl? When he'd first learned of it, he had wondered where his half sibling was, then realized there was a slim chance at best that the savage was alive. A white woman who spawned a savage's brat never kept it. Never wanted it.

Closing his eyes, he tried to remember his own father. He'd been seven years old when the man had died. The only memories of Gordon Henley that came to mind were bland ones, overshadowed by his mother's domineering presence. Of course, he'd been rich. Had he known his wife's secret? Serge doubted it. Queen Meredith only allowed people to know what she wanted them to know, he thought with a disparaging look of scorn.

Again the secret aroused him. He rose from his chair by the fire, put the journal into its secret hiding place, and left his bedroom in search of some satisfying company.

The morning was cold. Shivering as she stepped from the bed, Julia crossed to the window. Although it was dark, she knew there would be frost on the grass and the rooftops. She glanced at the barn, noting the faint glimmer of light coming from the stalls where they kept the milk cows. McCloud was up.

Pressing her forehead against the cold glass pane, she closed her eyes and let the images from the night before frolic through her mind. Again, the kiss, and her childish assumption that he wanted to bed her when he'd nodded toward the bedroom door. What had she been thinking, anyway? She smirked, a snide salute to her foolish innocence. She'd been so awash with feelings, she hadn't been thinking at all. That's what happened when he touched her.

There was no help for it. Just imagining his mouth on hers made her all tingly again. She hugged herself, drinking in the mental and physical sensations his embrace created. How odd it was to be kissed that way. Touched that way. Exciting, but odd. In her youthful daydreams, she'd wondered about such things. In private, of course. Never had she shared her dreams with Josette, for Josette would have laughed at her. After all, who would want to kiss her when Josette was available? So she'd kept her daydreams to herself even then, presenting a picture of coldness. Aloofness. But she'd been a private dreamer, a discreet romantic in a life that was anything but. It was not until Frank Barnes that she even began to think such things could happen to her. Even then, when she knew he hadn't meant a word he'd said, she'd wanted to believe his fiery declarations of love.

Marymae made a gurgling sound, drawing Julia to the cradle. "What's to happen to me, sweetheart?" she asked as she lifted the child into her arms. "Am I going to fall head over heels, only to find I've once again discovered hell instead of the raptures of heaven?"

But even now she knew that her feelings for McCloud were stronger by far than any feelings she'd had for Frank Barnes. That made it worse, for when she was tossed aside, it would hurt just that much more.

She muttered a mild oath, scolding herself for letting her thoughts race like wildfire. She changed Marymae's diaper and dressed her. "Wouldn't McCloud cluck his tongue at me now?" she said softly. "All this thinking could give me a headache." She kissed Marymae on the cheek. "I can't afford to suffer from one of those wretched things."

She dressed and went to the kitchen, stopping in the doorway when she found McCloud building a fire in the stove. She stood and watched him, remembering the terrible scars on his back and shoulders and how they'd affected her. She felt a physical pain when she thought about them.

He turned when the baby began to babble. "Good morning, Miss Julia."

She made an impatient sound as she tied Marymae into her seat with a dish towel. "Honestly, McCloud,

I think you can dispense with the formality. 'Julia' will do."

He started making a fresh pot of coffee. "I can't do that."

She studied him, surprised. "Why not?"

"I'm not ready." He turned, and there was an odd gleam in his eyes.

She put her fists on her hips. "You called me 'Julia' last night," she reminded him.

"That was different."

"Why?"

"I was angry."

One hand went to her throat. "At me?"

He shook his head. "No. At myself."

"But why? I—"

"I don't want to talk about it, Miss Julia."

It was like he'd shut off his emotions. She decided it was best not to probe further. "When do you think you'll be ready to dispense with the formalities, McCloud?" She didn't know why it mattered, but it did.

His gaze lingered on her, moving over her breasts, her waist, her hips. "I'll know."

There was a quivering in her chest. "I see." She didn't.

"In the meantime," he said with a lopsided grin, "don't you think you should call me Wolf?"

"No, I don't think so."

"And why not?" he asked.

She smiled a secret smile of her own. Every instinct she had warned her that once she did that, all of her defenses would come crumbling down. "I'm not ready, either." And may never be, she vowed.

She prepared Marymae's oatmeal, sensing McCloud's gaze behind her. It was almost a physical thing, and it shook her resolve further. He sat at the table while she fed the baby.

"Tell me," she began. "Were you actually attacked by a grizzly?"

He gave her a nonchalant shrug. "What of it?"

Her jaw dropped. "What *of* it? Good heavens, McCloud, you could have been killed."

He gave her a heart-stopping smile. "Would you have missed me?"

Shoving away her feelings of breathlessness, she scoffed, "I wouldn't even have known you. And why do you always have to play the fool? I don't believe for a minute that you actually take that sort of thing lightly."

He studied her for a long, quiet moment. "Maybe it's easier to deal with that way."

Julia stirred the oatmeal, hearing the unspoken emotion in his voice. She was beginning to understand this man. She didn't know him very well, but she knew without being told that there was much, much more to her husband than met the eye. That thought sent a fresh batch of feelings scampering over her flesh.

"How are you coming on your cabin?" She was beginning to wish he wouldn't finish it. She could get used to having him in the house.

"The shell should be done in a few weeks." His gaze was still on her. "Once I get the roof on, I can sleep out there."

She wasn't expecting the disappointment that washed over her. "That soon?"

He grinned at her over the rim of his coffee cup. "I'm a fast worker."

She had no doubt about that as she raised a cynical eyebrow in his direction. "You're also incorrigible."

"What did I say?" he asked, giving her a look of innocence.

"It's never *what* you say, McCloud, it's how you *say* it."

He chuckled. "I believe you're actually accusing me of innuendo."

She couldn't stop her own smile. "Sometimes I think you invented it."

His smile turned warm. "You bring out the best in me, Miss Julia."

They studied each other, Julia's heart filling with unspoken tenderness and confusion. Unable to cope with her feelings, she turned and continued feeding Marymae her cereal.

After breakfast, when he was gone, Julia felt a foolish sense of loss, even though she knew he'd be back before supper.

Wolf pulled Baptiste to a stop on the rise overlooking the Henley spread. An unexpected wash of fear spread through him. He cursed his weakness, but decided that the anxiety would keep him sharp.

As he made his way to the house, he studied the ranch. Exceptionally well maintained. No lack of money here, he thought, remembering Julia's unfortunate circumstances.

A mob of barking dogs assaulted him, coming at him from all directions. Baptiste reared, whinnying.

Someone stepped outside from the barn and shouted a command. The dogs backed off but continued to bark.

Wolf walked Baptiste to the barn, where the man stood studying him. Wolf returned the perusal. The man was blond and cruelly muscled, with a permanent snarl smeared across his face. Wolf disliked him on sight.

"You want somethin', breed?"

Wolf hid a caustic smile. Some men used the term 'breed' matter-of-factly, having grown up with it. Others, like this one, used it as one would use an insult. "I'd like to see Meredith Henley."

His snarl turned to a hateful grin. His teeth were white and strong, the front two chipped. He had an arrogance about him that Wolf found humorous, but he kept it to himself.

He gave Wolf a suggestive leer. "I'll just bet you would. You got an appointment?"

"She'll see me." *Ass wipe.*

He snickered. "She don't look kindly on breeds. She ain't apt to waste her time with you."

"Mr. McCloud!" Serge stood on the wide, closed-in porch.

Wolf gave the hired man a final smirk of his own, then met Serge at the steps. He dismounted, tying Baptiste's reins around the post.

"Mr. McCloud," Serge repeated. "What can I do for you?"

"I'd like to see your mother." Wolf's heart pounded like a callow youth's.

Serge appeared surprised. "Mother? Why?"

At that moment a handsome woman stepped out behind Serge. The harshness of her black dress in no way diminished her beauty. Her jet-black hair was pulled back from her face, and her skin was white and youthful. He didn't know what he'd expected, but it wasn't this. His senses came alive with such force, he was surprised they didn't leap onto his skin, like gooseflesh.

She looked at Wolf, color draining from her face.

He was surprised she could get any paler. "Oh, my God," she whispered, clinging to Serge's arm.

He turned, grabbing his mother at the waist. "Mother? What is it? What's wrong?"

So, Wolf thought, his heart hammering, she felt it, too.

She straightened, moving away from her son, appearing to pull herself together. "Show the man into the study, Serge."

"Yes, Mother," Serge said with a puzzled frown.

She gazed past Wolf, her eyes narrowing. "And tell Mr. Barnes to quit gawking like a mindless idiot and get back to work." She disappeared into the house.

"You heard her, Frank," Serge shouted, his voice filled with false bravado.

Wolf followed his half brother into the house, drawing in a quiet breath at the opulent furnishings. A sick feeling, textured with layers of apprehension, spread through him. He finally began to react. All these years, he'd wondered how any woman could do to a child what she'd done to him. He understood why she hadn't wanted him. That happened often enough to half-blood babies. But to be tossed away like worthless trash. That he didn't understand.

"What's this about, Mr. McCloud?" Serge opened a heavy, oak door and stepped into the room, motioning for Wolf to enter. "Ranch business? If it's ranch business, maybe you should talk to me. I'm more aware of what's going on than Mother—"

"It's not ranch business, Serge."

Serge puffed out his chest—a gesture Wolf was beginning to learn Serge used when he felt threatened. "Well, if—"

"Leave us, Serge." Meredith Henley entered and waited for her son to leave.

"Mother," he said, putting up hopeless resistance.

She sighed, as if accustomed to his bouts with attempted domination. "I'll call you if I need you, dear."

Serge eyed Wolf suspiciously, but obeyed. He slammed the door as he left, as if establishing his pique.

She turned to Wolf, appearing calm, but Wolf noted the pulse that vibrated at her throat. He wondered if she noticed his. She was a handsome woman. She lived up to every fanciful daydream he'd ever had about her. Until she opened her mouth.

"So. My past has caught up with me."

Wolf lowered his gaze, examining the expensive carpet. Christ. What had he expected? That she'd weep and wail, begging his forgiveness for what she'd done to him? Draw him to her bosom and smother him with sweet, motherly kisses? God, but he was such an ass.

He found it difficult to look at her, but he forced himself to do so. "You know who I am." It was a statement. Flat. Void of childish hopes and dreams.

Her smile was anything but warm. "I can't deny it." She studied him as one studies a bull, examining him for flaws, and if finding them, anxious to have him destroyed. "You've inherited the curse as well."

Curse it was, but he feigned ignorance. "Curse?"

Another smile, equally as cold. "Don't play ignorant with me, breed. I've left no tracks. It's that damned extra sense that brought you here." She went to the sideboard and poured herself a brandy. "It's unfortunate that I didn't have it the night I was raped by—" She threw Wolf a look of fury that would have bubbled paint.

"Serge doesn't have it," Wolf offered.

She uttered a sharp laugh. "Serge doesn't have a lot of things."

He wanted the upper hand. "So I've noticed."

She turned on him. "Whatever he is, he's my son and my heir. If you've come to extort money—"

"I don't want your money," Wolf said, angry that she'd suggest it, but not surprised.

"Then what *do* you want?"

Wolf marveled at her complete sense of disinterest in him as a person. He also was surprised that it didn't hurt more. "I wanted to see the woman who could bury a child alive."

Her reaction wasn't what he'd expected. "Oh. You're *that* one."

Wolf felt a frisson of excitement. "Which one is that?"

Her trenchant smile returned. "My my. That extra sense of yours doesn't tell you everything, does it?"

"Explain it to me." Wolf felt mounting alarm.

"You're a twin, breed. Can you believe it?" She spat a mild curse, washing it down with brandy. "I didn't want *one* of you, and God saw fit to give me two."

8

Wolf finally understood the unfinished feeling he'd had for so many years. A cautious eagerness crept up inside him.

"What happened to the other child?"

She turned from him and crossed to the window, her black skirt swishing on the carpet. "I don't know and I don't care. For all I know, he—"

"I don't believe you," he interrupted, trying to hold his temper in check.

She snorted a caustic laugh. "I don't give a damn what you believe."

"Did you bury him, too, hoping he'd suffocate? Hoping maybe he'd be dragged from the grave and eaten by coyotes?" His sudden burst of emotion angered him and he turned away, cursing his weakness.

"I don't expect you to understand." Her voice was surprisingly soft.

Her sudden vulnerability had no impact on him. "I think you know what happened to him."

She turned from the window and gave him a gla-

126

cial stare. "He could be dead. Just as I'd hoped you were."

"Ah, a mother's instinct is such a tender thing," he said, lacing his voice with sarcasm.

"My instinct was to survive."

"At the expense of not one child, but two," he chided, almost under his breath.

"Yes." Her answer sounded like an angry hiss. "At the expense of two savages. Two little black-haired, dark-skinned heathens who howled like spawns of the devil."

He studied her angry stance, measuring his own feelings against hers. "You know," he began conversationally, "it's not the abandonment that has bothered me. I can understand that. It's how you did it that will puzzle me until the day I die." He waited a beat. "If I'm fool enough to allow it to eat at me that long."

She gave him a crisp smile. "Something tells me you won't."

Wolf vowed to make sure she was right. "He's not dead. If he were, I wouldn't feel the way I do."

"Ah, yes," she said, giving him an odd smirk. "That damned curse again."

"Well?"

She turned away. "To be honest, I don't want to know where he is. I don't need the two of you coming at me, exposing my shame to the world." She gave him her profile. "And trying to blackmail me because of it."

Wolf wasn't surprised by her attitude, but he was surprised that he'd expected it. "I said I didn't want anything from you, and I meant it."

Rounding on him, she spat, "Then why did you come here? Why didn't you just leave it be? If I'd wanted anything to do with you, I wouldn't have—"

"Buried me alive?" he finished.

She composed herself quickly. "How did you survive, anyway?"

"I was found by a trapper."

She expelled a dry, humorless laugh. "Wouldn't you know. I asked my own mother to get rid of you, and she couldn't even do that right." Even though it was not yet noon, she poured herself a second brandy. "Why have you come?"

"As I said, I wanted to see the woman who could do it. Who had so little respect for human life that she could want her own flesh and blood dead." He laughed, but it sounded harsh even to his ears. "As I grew up, a part of me wanted to believe that I'd been taken from you. That you had nothing to do with what happened to me. That you mourned my loss. That you continued to look for me." He muttered a curse. "Childish musings from the mind of a lonely young boy.

"Instead," he added, his voice laced with irony, "I find it was *you* who ordered my demise. Left me to die, no more important to you than a pile of maggot-infested garbage."

She raised her perfectly shaped black eyebrows. "It surprises me when one of your kind makes anything of himself. Of course, in your case, you married into it. It's not as though you've worked for it."

Ignoring the insult, he asked, "And just who are my kind?"

Her face clouded and her eyes became expressionless, closing down from the inside. "One tribe of savages is the same as another. We were in Dakota Territory when it happened." She stared into space, her thoughts miles away and years in the past. She took a deep breath, as if erasing that past from her mind.

"Now, I want you to leave before I have someone drag you away. If I hear that you've mentioned this visit to anyone, I'll have you hung by your thumbs."

Wolf walked to the door, turning toward her before opening it. "No need for threats. Now that we've met, I don't think I'd care to admit to anyone that we're related."

Her look of surprise was the response he'd hoped for. Giving her a brief nod, he left, feeling a strange sense of release. And relief.

Meredith returned to the window and watched him go. A nightmare. This was a nightmare! There hadn't been a hint of either of them surviving all these years. She'd often thought about the other one, the one her mother had sold. That's the one she'd feared, for the possibility of him tracking her down might have been remote, but it was real. But *this* one. He wasn't supposed to live. She'd wanted them both dead. They hadn't meant anything to her because she hadn't wanted them to. She remembered how she howled in pain at their birth. The memory of their robust, squalling screams as they erupted from her body often woke her at night as well. Lusty little savages, they were.

She took a swig of brandy, relishing the sting. If only she'd been able to convince her mother that both of them had been better off dead. For their sake as well as hers. She remembered the man whose seed had been planted in her womb. He'd been tall and strong and wild. He'd come with his men to trade with the wagon train. They'd come in peace, yet she had seen the dangerous look in his eyes, and she'd wanted some danger. Some excitement in her dull, monotonous life. God almighty, what a rebel she'd been. Then he'd raped her. . . .

Rape? A cynical smile curved her mouth. No, she'd been a willing partner. And in spite of her attempts to forget what happened those years ago, she couldn't. Maybe it was because she didn't want to. After all, it was the only excitement she'd ever had. In her entire dreary life.

But now, at least one handsome half-blood from the scurrilous union had found her. He could ruin her. If word got out, her credibility in the community would be blown away like silt in the wind. Something had to be done.

The door opened behind her.

"Mother?"

She didn't turn. "What is it, Serge?"

"Grandmama is asking for you."

Meredith felt a swell of impatience. It had been one thing to talk about bringing her mother back to live with them. Having her here was quite another. The old woman was too keen for her own good. It was all Meredith could do to convince everyone else that her mother was getting senile, for her memory about the day she had given birth was sharper in the old woman's mind than what she'd had for breakfast that very morning.

"She was at the window when the breed left," he stated.

Meredith's impatience turned to alarm. Keeping it hidden, she asked, "So, she got out of bed."

"She said she knew who he was."

Meredith turned, hoping her expression was guarded. "That's ridiculous. She's not in her right mind most of the time, Serge, and you know it."

He strolled over to the cupboard and poured himself a brandy. "Yes, I know. But don't you find it odd?" He took a sip of his drink, then asked, "What was Julia's husband doing here, Mother? Why did he want to talk to you?"

She turned away again, unable to hide her alarm. Surely Serge didn't know anything. It was her imagination and her conscience, dredging up images that weren't there. "He just came by to introduce himself. Nothing more."

"Ummm. I see. Quite civilized for a breed, wouldn't you say?"

Meredith didn't answer, but something deep inside her told her that this half-blood son that she'd tried to abandon was, indeed, very, very civilized. She also knew without a doubt that he was very, very dangerous—to her and to everything she'd worked for.

"Do you want me to ... arrange for an accident, Mother?"

She jerked her gaze to Serge's, noting his devious smirk. "I will not be a party to any serious wrongdoing, Serge."

He gave her a lazy smile. "Wrongdoing is all right, then, as long as it's not serious?"

"You know what I mean. Don't ... do anything rash." Her heart pumped hard and she felt a bite of excitement.

"Not even if it means getting rid of him?"

She had difficulty breathing. "We are not murderers, son."

He laughed, sounding almost sinister. This was a side to her son that she'd never seen before.

"Murder? Heavens no, Mother. It'll just be a small accident. A warning, if you will."

Meredith felt a nibble of shame at even contemplating what Serge suggested. "You know who he is, don't you?"

He merely smiled at her. "I've watched him since the day we returned with Grandmama. At that time, I only knew that he'd taken what you wanted me to have. Nothing else, Mother. But I know his routine."

He hadn't answered her question outright, and she was glad. If the words were not spoken, Serge could not be blamed for his actions. "I do not want him killed, Serge." But in the secret recesses of her heart, she knew that wasn't true.

On a whim, Julia wrapped Marymae in a heavy bunting, hooked up Sally to the buggy, and drove out to see how McCloud was doing on the cabin. She'd taken special pains to wear dresses ever since her wedding day, not only because it was appropriate, but because she wanted to look nice for McCloud. It was foolish, really, because she didn't think he would notice no matter what she wore.

But she was anxious to see the cabin. Out of curiosity, she told herself as her leg touched the basket filled with lunch. But deep down she wanted to see him, for something else had been on her mind, and she didn't know how to handle it. His words about her role as his wife just wouldn't leave her in peace.

Leaning on a stack of wood, he watched her approach. When the buggy stopped beside him, he reached into it and lifted out the lunch basket. "Slumming?" he asked with a slight smile.

"Don't be silly. I wanted to see how you were coming along."

He stood back and surveyed the cabin, which actually had begun to look like one. "Like I said, it should be finished in a few weeks. If it doesn't rain."

She was beside him, sharing his pride in his meticulous handiwork. "There could be more rain," she reminded him. "It's only February."

Small talk. Uncomfortable small talk. She pulled her arms inside her cape and hugged herself to get warm. The wind was cold. He noticed her discomfort.

"You should have worn something warmer. Here," he added, pulling her toward the cabin. "Let's eat inside. It won't be warm, but it will keep the wind out."

"Wait. Let me get the baby." She hurried to the buggy, lifted Marymae out and joined him inside. He'd spread a blanket on the wood plank floor and had begun to unpack their lunch.

Keeping the dish towel around the coffeepot, he poured her a cup. She wrapped her hands around it, watching the steam waft into the cold air as he unpacked the rest of their lunch.

He made a sound of approval. "Fried chicken. To what do I owe this honor?"

She shrugged. "It's not that special." Since the day before, when he'd kissed her with such passion in the kitchen, and when she'd sat beside him on his bed, she knew that she wanted more from this marriage. No one could have been more surprised, for she'd been so certain she despised him. But she didn't know how to tell him what she wanted. His words haunted her, making tattletale promises of a marriage with all its trappings, but she was afraid of being rejected, just as she'd been when she invited him to sleep in her bed. Of course, maybe he didn't expect to stay around that long. That thought made her stomach sink.

"McCloud?"

Leaning casually against a column, devouring a chicken leg, he appeared content. A feeling of hope blossomed in her chest.

"Yeah?"

"McCloud," she began, "I have to know your intentions." She held her breath.

A wily smile curled his lips. "A breed's intentions are never honorable, didn't you know that?"

She expelled an exasperated sigh. "Why do you do this? Can't you be serious for just once?"

"What makes you think I'm not serious?" He wiped his mouth on a napkin.

"Because you don't even know what I'm talking about." She burrowed through the basket for the bread she'd packed.

"All right, I'll be serious, but first I have to know what you're trying to say."

The moment of needing to know the truth had passed. "Never mind. It's no longer important."

He reached down and gave her braid a playful tug. "Come on, Miss Julia, tell me what's whirling around in that pretty head."

Pretty head? Her pulse raced at the words, but she swatted at him anyway, pretending they didn't matter. "Don't try to honeyfuggle me, Wolf McCloud. I'm not pretty, and we both know it."

His eyes softened, but he said nothing.

She waited for him to contradict her. He didn't, and she felt a rush of disappointment. "It's too late anyway. I don't care anymore. What you do with your life is of no concern to me."

She dug deeper into the basket, and he ran his forefinger under her arm, along her rib cage. She yelped, clamping her arm to her side.

"You're ticklish," he said with an evil grin.

"I am not," she countered. "You just startled me, that's all."

His fingers touched her again, and she sucked in a

breath, unable to keep from releasing a nervous laugh. She swatted at him, this time hitting his chest. "You just stop that, McCloud."

"Is it just there? Or are you ticklish here, too." He sat down beside her and grabbed her calf, running his fingers over her stocking at the back of her knee.

She whooped and convulsed on the blanket, automatically writhing away from the tickling motion. "Stop it! Oh," she moaned between bouts of sharp laughter, *"please* stop it, you ... you worm!"

His hand stopped, but he didn't pull it away. It cupped her knee, then slid to the upper part of her calf. His eyes never left her.

They stared at one another, Julia's heart hammering, her pulse trembling, her heart almost exploding with emotion. She tried to speak, but her mouth was dry. Swallowing hard, she warned, "You should take your hand off my leg."

He didn't smile, but his eyes were warm. "Yes, no doubt I should. That doesn't mean I will."

She had trouble breathing, and what breath she had shook. "Why would you want to touch my leg?"

He continued to stroke her calf. "There are other parts I'd rather touch, but you'd ram your heel into a very special part of my body if I did."

It was a game, and she'd never played it before. But the lure was strong. "What else would you touch? If you could? I mean, if ... if I let you?"

He smiled, his strong teeth white against his tanned skin. "It wouldn't be gentlemanly to say."

She couldn't prevent a laugh. "Since when has that ever stopped you?"

His fingers moved higher, just to the top of her knee, inside her thigh. The place between her legs tingled and felt swollen. It throbbed like a heartbeat.

"I love women, Miss Julia. Ever since—" He stopped, giving her a lazy grin. "Ever since I was old enough to know there was a difference between us."

A rich stew of emotions swirled inside her, both good and bad. She'd never liked being compared to other women, but her curiosity got the best of her. "What things do men like? What do you like?"

His fingers moved higher, and she had the urge to spread her legs. Instead she trapped his hand between her knees. He gave her a wicked grin. "Thanks," he said. "It's nice and warm up there."

Giving him a stern look, she reached under her skirt and removed his hand. "Are you going to answer me or not?"

He leaned on his elbow and studied her. "Why are you so interested, Miss Julia?"

"Because I don't know men very well. And since you *are* my legal husband, I thought perhaps I could get a straight answer out of you." Marymae was awake. Julia found her bottle and lifted the child into her arms, avoiding McCloud's gaze. "I guess I was wrong."

"I'm an ass man, myself."

She gasped. "McCloud!"

"Well, hell. You asked."

"Yes, but I didn't expect you to ... to—"

"You expected me to use flowery language, maybe? Like, 'Ahh, Miss Julia, I love your lips and your eyes. I want to drown myself in them, and in you. Your hair reminds me of wheat, ripe to be mown. I want to bury my face in it.' Is that what you wanted to hear?"

She flushed, angry with herself and with him. She didn't know what she'd expected, but it wasn't such a bold statement about a woman's backside. "I'm sorry I asked."

"No, you're not."

"I am, too!"

He took her ankle, rubbing the bone with his thumb. A jolt sped up her leg, settling in her pelvis, and she couldn't suppress a shudder.

"You want to know what I like?"

She put Marymae on her shoulder and rubbed her back to burp her. "I don't think I even care anymore, but I suppose if you're going to tell me, I'll have to listen."

He continued to caress her ankle. "What do *you* think men like?"

She inhaled, snorting in the process. "That's obvious. Men seem to find a woman's ... um ... bosom, fascinating." She felt herself blush. This was not a topic she should be speaking of with a man, even if he *was* her husband.

He chuckled. "It's because we don't have anything like it."

She understood that. "But everyone has a backside, McCloud. What's so fascinating about them?"

"You've never seen yourself from behind. You filled out your father's trousers far better than he did, Miss Julia."

Her blush deepened, spreading into her neck. "But what's to see? I mean—"

"Would you slap me if I said you have the best set of 'walkaways' I've ever seen?"

She fiddled with the edge of her cape, trying to appear casual amidst her tumultuous feelings. She was beginning to believe that he actually found her attractive. It was a hard thing to accept after so many years of thinking she wasn't. "Walkaways?"

"You know what I mean, Miss Julia. I love to watch you walk away."

She studied her lap, a blush creeping into her cheeks. "Oh. I see."

"And then do you know what I like?"

"No, but I'm sure you'll tell me."

His mouth lifted into a half smile. "I like to say to her, 'Take off your drawers, sweetheart. Get naked under all those petticoats. Ache for me. You'll like it, I promise—' "

"McCloud!" Her face and neck were so hot she was afraid steam was shooting out around her collar.

"I love a woman's ass," he said, not the least bit apologetically. "What can I say?"

She blew air onto her face, hoping to cool it. "You should be ashamed of yourself. These are things a gentleman wouldn't talk about."

He continued to stroke her ankle. "Not even to his wife?"

"Not if he had any respect for her," she argued.

"I don't believe that. I think a husband should be able to excite his wife any way that works. And words can be damned exciting."

She jabbed at his hand with her other foot, but couldn't dislodge his fingers. "And what makes you think I find this talk the least bit exciting?"

He grinned again, exposing his white teeth. "The same things that get a man horny excite a woman, Miss Julia. Any woman honest with herself would admit that."

She tried for an icy glare, but knew her eyes were shiny with emotion. "If you'll please tell me what I can do to make my *bottom* less interesting, I'd appreciate it."

His mouth curled into a full smile. "The more you think about it and try to stop the natural motion, the more I'll enjoy it."

"You are incorrigible." And he was. He was also a very sexual, sensual man. She swallowed, hoping to quell the hunger that rose up inside her. She knew nothing about men and women, and he knew everything. How in the world could she ever hope to keep him?

"But I'm honest, Miss Julia. I was raised by two very different men. Angus was educated in the finer things. He taught me to read and write, to appreciate music and knowledge. Baptiste—"

"Like your stallion?"

He nodded. "Baptiste is French Canadian. He's a lover of the flesh." He grinned. "He taught me to appreciate *carnal* knowledge."

In spite of where this was leading, Julia was fascinated. It was the first time she'd had any insight at all into McCloud's past. "This Angus. Where is he?"

McCloud looked away. "He died last year."

"I'm sorry. But Baptiste. He's alive?"

McCloud nodded. "He's living with his fourth wife."

Julia gaped. "Fourth?"

"Yep. He's the one who taught me to appreciate a woman's *derriere*. He'd say, 'Wolfgang—' "

"Wolfgang?" she interrupted. "Your name is Wolfgang?"

He gave her an impatient nod. "Now, do you want to hear the rest of this or not?"

She just stared at him. Her mouth was open, and she knew it. "I'd never have believed your name was Wolfgang. You seem so very much like a 'Wolf.' I thought that the moment I saw you. But Wolfgang ..." She shook her head, puzzled. "It's so European. Wolfgang McCloud," she said, rolling the sound around on her tongue. "So unusual."

"That's not my full name."

When Marymae squirmed, turning away from the bottle, Julia put her on the blanket. The baby rolled onto her stomach then over again until she hit McCloud's leg.

"Are you going to tell me what it is?" Julia persisted.

"What's it worth to you?"

"I just want to know, McCloud. It isn't worth anything to me," she lied. Her curiosity was bubbling over, nearly coming out her ears.

"I'll make a wager with you."

"I don't gamble." She pulled the blanket over Marymae, who was falling asleep again.

"I'll tell you my full name if you'll let me kiss you."

Her stomach fluttered. "I'm not sure I want to know that badly."

His fingers were on her calf again, working their way to her thigh. "Oh, I think you do."

A cornucopia of dangerous desires careened through her. "All right." The words came out a husky whisper. "Just stop what you're doing, McCloud."

"It could get better," he promised, moving his fingers higher.

"No," she said quickly. "I'll let you kiss me. Just stop . . . what you're doing." *Before I get in too deep.* When he removed his hand, she swore she could feel his fingers on her skin.

He was beside her, his hands at her shoulders, turning her toward him. "McCloud," she said, putting her hand on his chest. "Your name first."

His mouth came toward hers. "Wolfgang," he said before touching her. He nibbled at her lips and she responded, opening for him.

"Amadeus," he added, pressing his mouth to hers and kissing her gently. She put her hand on his shoulder, running her fingers down his strong arm. His hand came to her breast, and when he touched her nipple, she gasped, lost in wild, wanton sensation.

"Morning Cloud," he finished, delving into her mouth with his accomplished tongue.

She made anxious, eager sounds in her throat, pulling his tongue in farther, then thrusting it with her own. His hands cupped her face as he devoured her mouth, and out of innocence and eagerness, she took one of them and returned it to her breast.

Desire stirred in her belly like a fireplace blaze with flames licking lower. The heat there was uncontrollable, a burning urgency she hadn't known before, but one she wanted to experience.

His mouth left hers and he pulled her onto his lap, holding her there. Her breath quickened, and she couldn't get enough air into her lungs. She needed something—something more—and she sensed she would get it when his hand snaked beneath her skirt again.

Yearning made her weak. Her heart hammered and she began to shake with desire. His fingers took a slow, lingering path up the inside of her calf, past her knee to her thigh. She inched her legs apart, pressing her face into his neck, knowing she was being reckless. The feelings were new, extraordinary, filled with equal doses of pleasure and pain. Wanting and regret.

The place between her legs tingled, and when his fingers met the tops of her stockings, lingering on her bare flesh, the tingle became an ache. She fought for breath now, taking in deep swallows of air to fill her lungs. Yet when his fingers touched her *there,* at the place that ached and burned and screamed to be touched, she clamped her knees together.

"No, no." She pushed his hand away. "I can't. I *can't.*"

She flung herself off his lap, pressing her thighs together to rid herself of the pleasure-filled agony of his touch.

"It's all right to feel those things, Julia."

She felt tears sting her eyes. Devastated and embarrassed that she'd let him go so far, she croaked, "It's not all right. It's *not.*"

She swiped at her tears, then threw their lunch into the basket, anxious to get away. "We've bothered you long enough. You'll never finish the cabin at this rate." She was back in control.

"Julia."

He didn't preface her name with "Miss." She wondered why. When he touched her arm, she yanked it away. "Don't say anything, McCloud, please. Don't embarrass me further. I feel terrible enough as it is."

"You asked me what my intentions were," he reminded her.

She put her hands to her ears. "Please. If you have any feelings for me, don't say another word. Just never mind. Forget I asked. It was a foolish thing to do. I don't know what I was thinking, for heaven's sake."

She hauled the sleeping Marymae into her arms and stood, refusing to face him. "If you'll bring the basket, I think the baby and I are ready to leave you in peace."

His touch confused her as he helped her into the buggy. "Will you be working late?" she asked.

"I'll be back before dark," he promised.

Later that afternoon, Julia unpinned the last dry diaper from the line and dropped it into the basket. She heard McCloud ride up behind her and, remembering what had happened earlier, felt color creep into her cheeks.

She turned, prepared to set aside her feelings of embarrassment and discovered the stallion standing alone, pawing at the ground.

"McCloud?" She felt a bite of concern as she ran toward the barn. She called his name again; there was no answer.

She left the barn; the stallion stood outside. He snorted and whinnied, tossing his majestic head.

The picture of Sally returning without her father was painted in Julia's memory, and she felt a cold chill sidle up her backbone.

She glanced at the porch, where Marymae gurgled and babbled in the sunshine. She couldn't leave the baby here while she searched for McCloud. But she knew something was wrong, for Baptiste would never come back without his rider, unless the rider was in trouble.

She stood in the yard, her mind whirling with pictures of McCloud in trouble, and she knew she had to do something. Looking down at her apron, she lifted the corners and tested them for strength. Could she? Would it work as a carrier for the baby?

"Nothing ventured, nothing gained, old girl," she chastised herself, and went to get Marymae off the porch.

From deep inside the cave, Wolf had heard the deafening rush of rubble, rock, and earth as it plunged downward, entombing him.

He had no idea how long he'd been in there; panic had set in when darkness descended upon him, as he knew it would. Every day, as he returned to the ranch after working on his cabin, he rode past these caves, and every day they drew him, like whiskey draws an alcoholic. But until today, he hadn't been tempted to test his fears. Fears instilled in him years ago, when he'd been scouting for the Army and had tried to stop the soldiers from murdering innocent women and their children.

His back tingled, as if it, too, remembered, for they'd whipped him into unconsciousness for defying their orders. And when he'd awakened, he smelled the death around him. Tangy, metallic blood had oozed into his mouth, and when he clawed at the dirt, his fingers found the limbs of the dead that had been buried with him.

Closing his eyes to block out the blackness, he fought the panic in his chest. Sudden, violent memories exploded in his mind, and the cloying smell of death-warm bodies permeated his nostrils, coating his lungs, closing his throat.

A cacophony of noises erupted in his ears: the sounds of weeping, shrieking women and frantic, screaming children ... the explosive gunfire ... the whipping sound of the lash as it landed on his back ... Then, the dead-calm silence of the aftermath.

The calf, which he'd crawled into the cave to rescue, wailed, thrusting Wolf forward into the present. He sucked in another hungry breath of air, forcing down his fear.

He'd thought the calf had been caught somehow and couldn't escape. On further investigation, he found a rope tied to the calf's ankle. Panic ripped at him like a spur. His pulse leaped as he traced it to a root that extended into the cave. A trap. It had been a trap. For him? But why? And by whom?

Wolf untied the calf, then dug his way through the debris, pushing dirt and small rocks to either side, forcing down his anxiety. This was a message. As he scooped away the dirt, he knew there was only one person to whom he was a threat, and she'd already warned him that she wanted him gone.

Hearing someone outside the cave, he stopped digging.

"McCloud?"

He welcomed the sound of Julia's voice, although it bordered on panic.

"In here!" He heard her digging at the earth.

"Are you all right?"

"Oh, fine and dandy." He pushed at the dirt, spitting it out of his mouth, brushing it from his eyes until he finally saw daylight. He shoved the bawling calf out ahead of him, then slithered into the fresh air himself.

"Oh, my gracious, McCloud." Her face was pinched with concern. "How did this happen?"

He wasn't about to tell her his suspicions. "Damned if I know. I was riding home, and heard the calf bawling from the cave. Somehow it had gotten caught in there."

Frowning, Julia studied the rocks and dirt, then shifted her gaze higher, to the source of the slide. "Seems strange that it could have just tumbled down all by itself."

"I've seen it happen before," he lied.

She bent and stroked the bawling calf, looking for a mark. "Whose is it, do you know?"

"Too young to be branded. Who knows?" He knew, all right.

The baby, wrapped in what appeared to be Julia's apron, began to fuss on the grass. Julia picked her up and held her close. "When Baptiste came back without you, the only thing I could think of was that day Sally came back without Papa." She briefly closed her eyes, then gave him a steady look. "I was frightened, McCloud."

He touched her cheek, marveling at the softness of her skin. "I'm fine." Grinning, he added, "And better now that I know you care."

She made an exasperated sound. "I don't know why you have to make light of things."

"What's not to make light of? So part of the hill came down. So what? I could have disturbed something when I went inside. The calf is fine and I'm fine. Don't make it out to be more than it is."

He didn't need her worrying about him, and because she was the woman she was, he knew she would. But until he found out why this happened, he didn't want her to suspect anything.

They ate supper in silence, and Julia was relieved when it was time to prepare for bed. Something was bothering McCloud, of that she was certain. Oh, he'd been his convivial self all the way back from the accident, but she sensed a tension beneath the banter.

After putting Marymae down, she slipped back into the kitchen to set the yeasty dough so she could bake bread in the morning.

She felt, rather than heard, McCloud behind her. It was odd, for her senses went crazy whenever he was near. It was like nothing she'd experienced before.

"There's nothing you can help me with, McCloud. I'm nearly done here," she said, tossing the words over her shoulder.

"This afternoon you wanted to know my intentions."

She stopped working and her heart took a dip in her chest. "I had no right to ask you that." She covered the yeast starter with a warm cloth, then put it on the ledge at the back of the stove.

"You had every right. Considering the terms of the will—"

"I know you think you were tricked into this marriage, McCloud. Even *I* can't understand why Papa would have done such a thing. I can imagine how you must feel." She didn't dare face him; it was easier to talk about this with her back to him.

He was so quiet, she thought he'd left. When she turned, he was leaning against the doorjamb, studying her with his earthy, dark-lashed eyes. As usual, the look made her pulse jump.

"I've done a lot of things I'm not proud of, Julia, things that would make you recoil and run from me in terror." He glanced at the floor, his thumbs hooked into his belt loops. "Why Amos did this to you, I'll never know. Personally, I think you deserve more. But I'm here for you for as long as you need me. If—" He cleared his throat, avoiding her gaze. "If, at some time, you find someone else—"

"This is a marriage, McCloud, not merely a partnership. Marriages aren't dissolved because two people don't . . . love each other." She felt sick to her stomach, because she didn't know what he was trying to say.

"That's right." His face was void of expression. "I just don't want you to feel trapped."

Me? What about you? She couldn't believe how much she wanted this marriage to work. And in order for it to work, she'd have to trust him as much as she was beginning to love him. She wasn't sure that was possible.

"If I ever feel trapped, McCloud, you'll be the first to know." It was a statement of bravado, to assure him that she didn't care any more for the situation than he did.

She turned out the lamp, casting the room into darkness, except for the flashes of lightning that stabbed through the window.

"Good night." She walked past him toward the bedroom, knowing that if anyone was going to feel trapped by this marriage, it would be him.

❋ 9 ❋

Julia tossed and turned. With McCloud in the house, insomnia was becoming a ritual. She thought about him constantly. Every day she woke and found him there brought fresh wonder to her soul. Feeling the pull of sleep, she was just drifting off when something awakened her. Frowning, she sat up, listening for the noise again. Lightning flashed and a shard of thunder exploded in the distance, but she'd slept through storms before.

She listened harder, this time hearing the horses. They were kicking up a fuss. She left the bed and went to the window, a cold drenching of fear racing through her when she saw the yellow and red flames that shot into the air from the barn.

Fumbling for her work boots, she found them at the end of the bed and shoved her bare feet into them. She grabbed her robe as she ran out of the bedroom, bumping into McCloud in the hall.

"There's a fire, McCloud! The barn is on fire!"

"I know." He gripped her arm as he hurried toward the door. "You'd better stay here."

"I will not. I can't," she argued, her voice rising as fear gorged her chest. "We have to get the animals out. Oh, God!" A wrenching sob tore from her throat as she followed McCloud outside, trying to keep pace with him.

Despite the dampness in the air, the fire crackled and roared, devouring the wood. It raced up one side to the roof, brightening as it went, showering myriad tiny glimmering spurts that exploded into masses of solid flame, licking hungrily at the black night sky.

Julia grabbed the hem of her robe and covered her nose and mouth, trying in vain to keep the smoke out of her throat. She heard Sally whinnying from inside the barn, and her heart plunged in her chest.

"Sally!" she shrieked, lurching toward the barn door.

McCloud hauled her back. "Open the corral gate, Julia! I'll get Sally." He yanked at the wide barn door. Plumes of smoke spewed out around it, erupting in wild abandon when he got the door open. He staggered, coughing.

"McCloud!" She ran to help him, but he motioned her away.

"Get that damned corral gate open, Julia!"

She obeyed, stumbling to the corral, pulling the door open so the horses could get out.

She ran into the enclosure and smacked Lars on the rump. He sprinted away, Baptiste at his heels. Ole, more timid, needed coaxing. Julia grabbed an old rope bit off the post and flung it over his head. He balked.

"Damn you, Ole, *move!*"

Grabbing a fistful of his mane, she tried to pull herself onto his back. It wasn't possible without a leg up. She went in front of him and yanked on the rope again, tugging at him until he reared, pulling the rope from Julia's grasp as he galloped through the gate to safety.

Julia's eyes stung from the smoke, causing tears to stream down her cheeks. She swiped at them with her fingers, then the sleeve of her robe as she stumbled from the corral.

She ran to the barn door, which looked like the mouth to hell, for dark smoke and flames ebbed and surged in the opening. "McCloud!"

He staggered out, his handkerchief over his mouth. She caught him before he fell to his knees, coughing. "I'm all right." He coughed again, as if dredging up the putrid smoke from his lungs, then turned toward the barn.

Julia clung to his arm. "Where are you going?"

"It's Sally. She's still in there." Even though he was shouting, she could barely hear him over the noise of the fire. Frantic light from the flames illuminated him, and she saw that his face was bathed in sweat and dirt.

Julia cringed from the intense heat and the crashing noise of timber splintering, popping, and cracking around her. "But, you can't—"

"I have to!" He wrenched free.

Suddenly his safety was most important to her. "McCloud! It's not worth your life!"

Once again, he was inside the inferno.

A flicker of light caught her eye, and she gasped, catching sight of a flame as it leaped from the roof and onto a small pile of dried wood near the chicken coop. She ran, pulling off her robe as she stumbled over the uneven ground. Angry sparks burst into flame, and she took her robe in both hands and beat at the fire until there was nothing left but charred wood.

Exhausted, she wiped her forehead with the back of her hand, then turned toward the seldom-used paddock her father had built well away from the barn. The stallion and her geldings were there, and her milk cows and the calf were feeding on a patch of winter wildflowers that grew near the house. But Sally still wasn't there.

Julia ran toward the barn. Heat and smoke attacked her eyes and throat but she pressed on, mindless of her own discomfort. She had to save Sally. Her precious mare! She was almost to the door when McCloud staggered out again and grabbed her.

"Let me go!" She fought him, trying to pull away from him.

The barn shuddered beneath the weight of the flames. A thundering roar billowed out from the inferno. In a heartbeat, the roof collapsed, sending flames and sparks exploding into the night sky.

Julia recoiled, allowing McCloud to hold her fast. "It's too late, Julia."

Her mouth quivered and her eyes filled again, and she felt a wrenching, aching tightness in her chest. The final shrill, high-pitched scream from her mare as the flames engulfed her sent Julia against McCloud's chest. Clinging to him, she pinched her eyes shut, dying inside, suffering with despair at the loss of her mare.

"Oh, McCloud." She pressed close to him, inhaling the smoky smell while her tears dampened his shirt. "She's gone. My poor, poor Sally." She continued to weep.

He put his hand on the back of her head, drawing her to him.

Snaking her arms around his waist, she wept as thoughts of the loss invaded her quiet dreams. Both Papa and the barn he'd built were gone. And now,

Sally was gone, too. There would be no foal come next winter. There was nothing.

"I'm sorry, Julia. I'm sorry I couldn't save her. She was a good mare."

Julia felt a fresh flood of tears. "Don't blame yourself, McCloud. It's not your fault." And she meant it. If she'd had to make a choice between McCloud and Sally, this is the one she would have made. Still, she sobbed, the pain of her loss twisting inside her like bailing wire. Wiping her eyes, she turned, and they watched the barn burn together.

"What do you suppose happened?" she asked, wiping her face with her fingers. "Lightning?"

He rubbed her arm, warming her. "Sure. It could have been lightning."

"Oh, God, I just hate to stand here, doing nothing while the barn burns to the ground." She took a shaky breath. "I remember how proud Papa was when he'd finished building it." She pressed her lips together, knowing she was going to cry again.

"Go inside, Julia. There's nothing you can do. There's nothing either of us can do. The other animals will be fine. In the morning, we can think about rebuilding."

She gave him a caustic laugh that ended in a sob. "With what? Wishes and dreams?"

He held her close as they turned away from the dwindling fire. "I've got some money."

"But, McCloud," she argued, "that's yours. It was enough that you put a dent in my bills. You shouldn't have to—"

"Don't worry about it. Right now, the money is the last thing we should be concerned about."

It was a cryptic statement, but Julia was too drained to dwell on it. Grateful he was with her, she put her arm around his waist and her head against his shoulder as they walked toward the house.

Once in the kitchen, she lit the lamp. She felt a bubble of laughter in spite of her anguish as the light flickered over him. It was the second time in a day that he looked like he'd wallowed in a pig pen. "You're a mess."

He grinned, exposing white teeth that appeared that much whiter because of his black, soot-smudged face. "You're not dressed for a trip to church, yourself."

She glanced down, remembering that she'd left her charred robe at the site of the smaller fire. Her nightgown was streaked with dirt and soot. Her hands were filthy, her bare legs cold. The smell of smoke permeated the room.

Drawing her gaze to his again, she saw that his shirt was torn, one sleeve hanging in shreds. There was a singed circle on the fabric above his left shoulder blade. She touched it. "You could have been burned." The thought of it brought a knot to her throat.

His fingers moved to her braid, which hung over her shoulder. "You, too."

With a shaky sigh, she stepped away from him. "I was going to suggest coffee, but—" She gave him a sad, wry smile. "I think we both need a bath." Realizing the inference, she gasped and pressed her fingers to her lips.

His eyes were warm, his smile slow and lazy. "Any other time, and I'd take you up on that, Julia, but not tonight."

She blushed, unable to conjure up a picture of the two of them in a tub of water together. "Aren't you ever serious, McCloud?"

"Who says I'm not serious?" His lopsided grin and the mischief in his eyes told her he was. He took the pail off the counter and walked to the door. "I'll get you more water and bring in the tub."

She took a step toward him. "McCloud?"

He turned, his eyes intent as he studied her from across the room.

"Do you want me to save some warm water for you?"

He shook his head, his gaze lingering. "Don't worry about me, Julia. I'll clean up outside."

After bringing her water and the tub, he went into his bedroom, returning with clean clothes and a towel. The clothes were slung over his arm, the towel around his neck. He was bare to the waist.

Julia's stomach was clenching nervously. "Where will you be?"

"I'm going to check on the stock, then I'll wash up at the pump."

She noted his amused smile. "What's so funny?"

"Don't worry, dear wife," he said, the words sounding strangely endearing as he walked toward the door, "I'll give you plenty of time to finish."

Warmth flooded her face as she poured a teakettle of hot water into the cold that was in the oblong tin tub. "I wasn't worried about that," she lied.

His smile was filled with the same heat that warmed his eyes. "You should be." He closed the door behind him.

Pressing her hands over her beating heart, Julia went to the window and watched him walk toward the paddock. When she was certain he wasn't going to double back, she hurried to the table, lit the squat candle and turned out the lamp, which gave off more light. She put the candle on the floor by the tub, unbraided her hair, and pulled off her boots and her filthy nightgown. Shivering in the cold room, she stepped into the tub, sinking into the warm water. She couldn't stay long; he could return any time.

She washed her face and hair, then wrapped a towel around her head and leaned against the rim of the tub. The towel acted as a pillow, and she felt a weary lethargy sweep over her. Shaking herself to stay awake, she scrubbed her hands and feet. It wasn't possible to fall asleep in the tub, anyway. It was far too small. Oh, but the water felt so good. She huddled deeper into the warmth, vowing to enjoy the water only until it got uncomfortably cool.

Wolf stepped inside. The room was dark except for the candle Julia had left on the floor beside the tub. He wondered why she hadn't put it on the table. He crossed to the tub, intending to carry it out and empty it, preferably somewhere near the smoldering rubble of the barn. He stopped short and his throat locked. She was asleep, her head wrapped in a towel. His gut tightened, for the rest of her was not wrapped in anything at all.

He spun away, rubbing his hand over his face, cursing the wild beating of his heart. He stared into the darkness, the faint light of the candle allowing him to see her out of the corner of his eye.

Wake her, fool. He swallowed a derisive laugh. Yeah, that was the answer. He could see it now. *Oh, Julia. Wake up, dear wife. Don't look so stunned,* ma bichette. *I didn't look at your succulent, upthrusting breasts with the sweet, pink nipples. And I didn't even notice your long, silky legs, one bent slightly to give me a view of the patch of golden hair between your thighs.*

Hell. He wiped the beads of sweat off his forehead, then pressed the cloth against his eyes. Slinging the towel over his shoulder, he felt a rush of relief when he noticed that she slept on. She didn't even have to know he'd been there.

He went into the living room and added wood to the fire, building a powerful blaze that heated the room. As he studied the fire, he knew he couldn't leave her in the tub. He'd go out the front door and come in through the back, making enough noise to wake a drugged mule.

Julia woke, disoriented. She knocked her knee on the side of the tub and cringed as the cold water splashed over her bare stomach. Drenched in goose bumps, she shivered, rose, and stepped from the tub. As she reached for the towel that hung over the chair, she heard the door open. She grabbed the towel, holding it in front of her like a shield, her heart hammering and her knees quaking.

McCloud entered the room and stopped, appearing as surprised as she was.

She stepped from one foot to the other, her body wet as she shivered behind the towel. "You could have knocked," she scolded. Thank heavens she'd at least had time to grab the towel.

He swaggered toward her, and though it was too dark to see his face, she knew without asking that the worm was smiling.

"What? And miss all this?"

The smile in his voice was proof enough. She attempted to dry herself without revealing any more of her body than was already exposed. "Get out of here and let me dry off, McCloud, I'm freezing to death."

"If you hadn't fallen asleep in the tub, this wouldn't have happened."

She gasped. "You—" He'd *seen* her!

He stopped in front of her, close enough to touch.

His chest was brown and hard, the muscles well-defined. He radiated a heat that drowned her senses. "Want me to wipe your back?" And his voice was silky and seductive.

"You *peeked!*" She lashed out at him, but he caught her hand.

Gripping her fingers, he brought them to his mouth and stared into her eyes, holding her gaze. "You fell asleep," he reminded her, his breath falling hot against the soft surface of her fingers.

She felt drugged. Hypnotized. He pressed her palm to his lips, grazing it with his tongue, making gestures with it that suggested something indecent, for her nether regions tingled, the response rousingly naughty.

She swallowed hard, wrenching her gaze away. "Let me go." She was breathless and anxious, and her knees felt like raw bread dough.

He moved her hand to his throat, down over his chest to just below his left nipple. His skin was smooth, drawn tight over the potent brawn. Her lips were level with his neck, and she saw the pulse at the base. She doubted it was pounding as erratically as her own.

"Can you feel it?" he asked, his question rife with primitive suggestion.

"Feel what?" The words came out on a breath that even she had trouble hearing.

He rubbed her hand in a circle around his nipple. "The beating of my heart, dear wife."

She tried to pull away, but he wouldn't let go. "Everyone has a heartbeat, McCloud."

He pressed harder, and she did, indeed, feel his heart drumming in his chest. "But mine beats for you," he murmured.

She yanked her hand away. "That's nonsense." But

it was a thought that warmed her clear to her toes. "Now, go away, McCloud, and let me finish drying off before I freeze my—"

He gave her a suggestive grin. "Before you freeze your pretty ass?"

"You are depraved, McCloud." She meant it, too, even though she was aroused by the crude word.

He gave her an innocent look. "Depraved and deprived."

His meaning wasn't lost on her. "I'm glad you agree, now get *out.*"

He grinned. "There's a fire in the fireplace. You'd better not go to bed wet and slippery." He tugged lightly at the towel, then sauntered out of the room with all the arrogance of a rooster in a henhouse.

Her body throbbed. Blast him! Why did a perfectly innocent string of words have to come out sounding like a seduction? She wrapped the towel around her and waited to hear his bedroom door close, then scurried into her room, checked on the baby, and pulled on a clean nightgown.

It wasn't until she was brushing her hair in front of the fire that she remembered he'd found her asleep in the tub. No doubt he'd stood there, gawking like a fool. Her body betrayed her, sending tingly messages up between her thighs.

She stopped brushing, rose from the sofa and walked toward her room. She hoped that's how he'd reacted, for if he'd stood there and compared her to all the women he'd had in his lifetime, she thought, she'd come up lacking.

Wolf sat at the kitchen table with a glass of whiskey, ignoring the coffee on the stove behind him. He kept his gaze on the window, eyeing the remnants of the barn, now a smoky heap of rubble. Lightning? He was skeptical. It was possible, but how likely?

He shook his head and stood, sneering at his suspicious mind. He went to the window and stared out at the wreckage, his thoughts turning to Julia and the loss of the mare. Her reaction had affected him like nothing he'd experienced before. He felt compassion. Sympathy. A rush of tenderness so foreign to him, he cursed out loud. Never had he felt so deeply for someone else. Never.

Life was so damned unfair. It hadn't been that long since Amos died, and now this. And losing a healthy, pregnant mare was like throwing money into the fire. He was sure Julia hadn't thought about the financial loss, but he had. Hell, it was his first thought.

Hearing a noise behind him, he turned. "Julia. What's wrong?"

She was shaking. "I c-can't get warm, M-McCloud." Her teeth chattered.

He went to her and folded her against his chest, inhaling the clean smell of her hair. "Come on. You'll never get warm out here." He brought her with him to the table, where he blew out the candle, then walked her to the bedroom.

"Crawl back into bed, Julia." He flipped the covers back for her.

"W-Won't do any good." Her teeth still chattered. "McCloud?"

He urged her into bed. "What?"

"I know you don't w-want to, b-but ... would you crawl in with me? Just to get me warm?"

Something pinched his heart, leaving him open and vulnerable, unable to think of a quick, snappy retort. "In bed? With you?"

"Just to warm me up. Please?"

He stood staring down at her, unable to form words or thoughts, knowing that nothing coherent would come out of his mouth even if he tried.

"Please?"

His feet were rooted to the floor.

Huffing an impatient sigh, she slammed her fist on the bedding. "For heaven's sake, McCloud. I'm not asking you to jump off a cliff, I just want to get warm."

Expelling a deep breath, he sat on the edge of the bed and removed his boots. He couldn't do this. Lie next to Julia and do nothing? Feel nothing? Christ . . .

The moment he crawled in beside her, she backed up against him, her sweet, lovely ass innocently nestling his groin.

"Put your arm around me," she ordered.

"You're pretty damned bossy," he muttered, forcing an edge to his voice to cover his mounting hunger.

She grabbed his arm and pulled it around her. "You knew that the day we met."

That he did. And he hoped to hell she never changed. He drew her closer, purposely avoiding her breasts. He was stiff with anxiety, unable to relax. God, the feel of her. The smell of her.

Remember, you dumb shit, you're here to warm her up. Nothing else. If he repeated those words often enough, he might force his body to believe them. The voice of reason, ringing with quiet irony, also told him he'd get an elbow to the ribs or a knee to the groin if he tried anything else.

Shivering, she snuggled closer. He mouthed a curse.

"McCloud?"

"Yeah?" He heard the first drops of rain against the windowpane and felt a sense of relief. Rain would snuff out the smoldering wood.

"This isn't easy for me to say, but I'm glad you were with me tonight. If I'd been alone, *all* the animals would have been lost. Thank you."

He had no doubt that thanking him was one of the hardest things she'd ever done. "You're welcome, Julia. Now try to get some sleep."

She shifted, her nipple grazing his arm. The nub tightened, pressing at the fabric of her gown, sending a heavy bite of desire into his groin as hunger rose up within him. He stifled a groan. She relaxed, and soon her breath came deep and steady. He envied her. He knew he wasn't going to get any sleep this night.

Julia woke to find Wolf gone and Marymae asleep beside her. She didn't want to soften toward him, but if he continued to do things like this, she might in spite of her good intentions. She smiled down at the babe. As if sensing Julia was awake, Marymae turned toward her. Julia kissed her hair, then stretched under the covers, remembering her bold request the night before. Had she expected him to try to seduce her? She smirked. Had she wanted him to? A better question was, what would she have done if he'd tried?

She inhaled, then let her breath out slowly. She was a prize ninny, that's what she was. No matter how suggestive his talk, he wasn't so swept away with lust for her that he couldn't control himself, even when he was in the same bed. That surely said a lot for her appeal, didn't it? She snorted a disparaging laugh and slid from the bed.

She was carefully piling her hair into a chignon when Marymae woke and began to fuss. Julia examined herself in her mirror, actually liking the way she looked in her soft blue dress. She decided she had a decent figure, in spite of the fact that she didn't have a full bosom. She pinched her cheeks, amazed that she even cared about her appearance. She never had before. Not for Serge, and certainly not for that bastard Frank Barnes.

"Only for you, Wolf McCloud," she said under her breath, then rolled her eyes at such nonsense. She changed and dressed the baby, then took a deep breath and went into the kitchen. McCloud stood over the stove, stirring what smelled like oatmeal.

"You can cook?"

He turned, giving her a lazy, indifferent once-over before going back to his chore. Any look from McCloud sent shivers over her flesh, indifferent or not. She knew he was remembering the night before, no doubt trying to recall just what she'd looked like in the tub. If that was the case, she certainly wasn't very memorable, she thought, her mouth twisting into a dry smile.

"I get by. I've even mixed up griddle-cake batter."

Her heart continued to patter out a swift, unwanted tattoo. "Is it lumpy?"

He chuckled, a warm sound that sent her heart racing. "Is Baptiste a black stallion?"

Hearing Julia's warm laughter behind him, Wolf felt the hollow ache of loneliness yawn inside him. All night he'd lain awake, wondering what it would be like to have her love. She no longer felt revulsion for him, he knew that. But everything he was stemmed from the circumstances of his birth. That he'd been not merely a bastard, but a throwaway baby. Unwanted. Unloved. Add to that, not feeling welcome in either world, and he'd been on a downhill slide to nowhere most of his life.

All of the wild living he'd done had been because his mother hadn't wanted him. Deep down he knew it was an excuse to continue to live that way. Maybe he was afraid he couldn't change, even if he wanted to. No amount of lecturing from Angus had been able to alter what he felt inside. Wolf sensed that he alone could change what was there.

He'd whored around, drank to excess, and lived a bawdy life, because it was expected of someone like him.

Meeting his mother face-to-face had helped him put much of his despair behind him. What she'd done to him had made her unworthy in his eyes. He was sorry he'd wasted so many years punishing himself for something over which he had no control. But there was still a part of him that felt unclean. Especially to a woman like Julia. She didn't know him yet. But eventually she'd find out. It didn't matter how often he tried to convince himself that he was just like everyone else. He wasn't, and he knew it.

If Julia got too close, he'd hurt her. Because when someone got close, they saw inside him, to the vast emptiness of his soul.

God, but he wanted her. And not just her body. She touched a place deep inside him that no one else had. Ever. He didn't want to mess up what he could have with Julia. Maybe, if he worked hard, she would care for him enough so that what he'd been in the past wouldn't matter. He could only hope.

He finished breakfast and rushed through the chores, setting the milk and eggs on the stoop. With a backward glance at the house, he went to the paddock, saddled his stallion, and rode out toward his precious piece of land.

Dawn was painting the sky lavender when he reached his cabin. Stunned surprise tore through him when he saw what was left of it. The cabin, like the barn, was only a pile of charred rubble.

He rode back to the ranch, his mind whirling. Lightning? Striking both structures? A grim smile tugged at the corners of his mouth. Unlikely.

After yesterday, he knew better than to ask himself who was responsible. His conversation with Amos before he died, regarding the water and the land, erupted in his mind like volcanic ash. His suspicions about Amos's accidental death loomed, too. Did Meredith Henley have something to do with Amos's death? Maybe her need to get rid of him, a son who'd survived, was more complicated than just wanting him gone. Perhaps she wanted Amos's land as well.

Wolf knew he had much to learn, but until he understood what was happening, he couldn't involve Julia. No sense troubling her until he was certain there was something to worry about.

❧ 10 ❧

That night after dinner, Julia found McCloud at her father's desk by the fireplace, going through his papers. She stood in the doorway, holding a cup of coffee, and watched him. The way he turned his head, cocking it slightly to one side, reminded her of her father, and how he sat in that same chair, pondering a new problem—or an old one, for they'd had many. An emotion that went deeper than sadness tugged at her.

McCloud dove his fingers through his inky hair, an absurd gesture, for it fell forward again. He looked up, saw her standing there and grinned. Another emotion shuddered through her. Smiling back, she found herself thinking about the night before, surprised at the disappointment she felt. She thought she'd be grateful he wasn't interested in her as a woman. Oh, he teased and he flirted, but that was just how he was. He probably teased and flirted with toothless old crones, too. Although, she thought, her heart thrumming, she doubted he kissed them, at least not the way he'd kissed her.

"Is that for me?"

Startled by the sound of his voice, she shook herself, remembering that she held the coffee. "Yes, of course." She crossed to the desk and put the cup beside the stack of papers. "What are you doing?"

He was studying a map of the fan-shaped valley that indicated ranch borders and ownership. Standing at his shoulder, she resisted the urge to touch his hair.

"I thought it might be a good idea if I finally familiarized myself with things." He traced the stream, then stopped. "I also want to pay some more on your bills. You don't mind, do you?"

"Oh, McCloud, you shouldn't have to—"

"It benefits me as well as you, Julia. With the bills paid, we can start fresh."

She wanted to ask if he had enough money, but decided not to open that can of worms. She'd have been a fool not to be grateful, but it was so hard to tell him so. Ever since their marriage, she found herself relying on his strength, and it made her angry. She'd always been strong; she didn't want to become an appendage.

"Your land backs up to the creek. It's the only private land that does."

She allowed her gaze to follow the line of the creek as it meandered through land she knew was rocky and harsh, land incapable of growing any suitable crop.

"Papa was lucky. The ranch next to ours became available just after we moved here. I remember the trouble he had when he bought it. His bid was the first one in, but there were others who coveted it."

McCloud studied the map. "Like who?"

"Everyone who wanted access to the river. Burnham's, Henley's, Crawford's . . ."

"Do all three own ranches here?"

"Yes. Burnham's and Crawford's are run by their sons. Meredith Henley has run her spread ever since her husband died." She laughed. "Knowing her, she ran it when he was alive, too. Why do you ask?" She rubbed his shoulders—something she'd done for her father when he'd been working at the desk too long. Suddenly realizing how intimate the action was, she stopped, letting her hands fall to her sides.

"Don't stop," he ordered, though his voice was soft.

She swallowed and resumed her massage, startled at how tight he was.

"And these other ranchers need water?"

She pressed her thumbs along his spine, unable to find the bone for the muscle. "Of course. Who doesn't?" His muscles refused to loosen up. "McCloud? What's wrong?"

He didn't answer her for a long time, then said, "It's nothing for you to worry about, Julia."

She stopped probing his back. "Is that anything like, 'Don't worry your pretty little head about it'?" She went to the side of the desk and glared at him. "Don't treat me like this, McCloud. I'm not one of the vacant, empty-headed women you're accustomed to. If there's something wrong, then you'd better tell me, or I'll ... I'll ..."

"You'll what?"

His grin, suddenly so boyish, was like a gift. Her anger fizzled like a shrinking balloon. She wanted to trace his mouth with her fingers. Swallowing hard, she threatened, "I'll think of something awful to do to you."

He took her hand, bringing her closer, pulling her onto his lap. She felt a wealth of emotions stirring inside her, but tried to pull away from the intimacy.

"Do you want to know what I'm thinking, Julia?" His eyes were solemn; she found no hint of mischief.

She sat on his lap, feeling stiff, uncomfortable, and foolish. "Yes. I want to know." But she was apprehensive. The serious side of McCloud frightened her, for it meant there was substance to him. It meant he was a man worth loving, worth having. It frightened her because she knew how easy it would be for him to leave. And by that time her love would be too deep to forget, and the hole he'd leave in her life could never be filled by someone else.

"I'm thinking that Amos's death was no accident."

Her heart sank, aching on its way down. "He didn't kill himself, McCloud. He didn't." Anger swelled within her even though she'd had that same thought.

"No, I don't think he killed himself."

"Then what are you saying?" She wasn't sure she wanted to know.

"I think he was killed by someone else."

Stunned, she studied him, again finding no hint of mischief in his dark-rimmed gaze. "You think someone killed Papa? But why?"

He stroked her hair, removing the pins that held her braid in place at the back of her head. The chignon tumbled over her shoulder, and he threaded his fingers through it, loosening it. The familiar gesture wasn't lost on her, but it continued to puzzle her.

"When I saw him last, he was worried about something. He wouldn't tell me what it was, but he couldn't hide the fact that something was gnawing at him."

He spread her hair over her shoulder, then combed his fingers through it. She could feel it snag on the rough edges of his calluses. The tenderness of his touch troubled her concentration.

"And ... and you don't know what it was?"

He shook his head, his eyes searching. "He did say something, though."

"What?" she asked, barely above a whisper, for his fingers were now at the back of her head, massaging her neck.

"He promised he wouldn't die until I got here. Amos didn't appear to me like a man who wouldn't keep his promise." He waited a heartbeat. "Unless he had no control over it."

Thinking about her father's death so quickly on the heels of Sally's demise brought fresh tears into Julia's throat. She fought her instincts to push herself off his lap, and settled against McCloud's chest, her head resting on his shoulder.

"He's gone, no matter how he died." She uttered a heavy, quaking sigh. She hadn't allowed herself to think about the rest of her life, void of her father's gentle, soft-spoken voice. His presence. She pressed her fingers over her mouth.

"Oh, McCloud," she said, fighting tears, "I don't think I've ever missed him more than I do right now. Why would someone want him dead? He was just a harmless old man. He didn't have any enemies."

He stroked her hair again; it was a soothing motion. When he embraced her, she pressed her face against his neck, breathing in his primitive, masculine scent.

As they sat together, Julia knew she was falling deeply in love with her husband. The coarse Romeo he'd been when he'd first arrived was there, for he exhibited that side of himself often. But this McCloud that held her now was one she feared. Not because she didn't trust him, but because she didn't trust herself. That she could love him frightened her, for she had no confidence in his ability to be faithful, much less love her back. Or stay, for that matter.

Suddenly he stood, with her in his arms.

"McCloud, put me down," she scolded, clinging to him.

"It's time for bed, Julia."

She pushed at his chest, but he held her fast. "Don't act like a fool. I'm capable of getting to bed on my own two feet."

Again he gave her that boyish grin. It was white and sudden, making him look impossibly sweet. "How well I know it."

Her chest flooded with apprehension as they moved toward the bedroom while visions of the night before played havoc with her thoughts.

But once in her room, he dumped her onto the bed, then crossed to the door. She knew better than to voice her foolish disappointment. "Good night, McCloud."

Turning before he left the room, he gave her a heart-stopping smile. "Sweet dreams, Julia."

She made a face at his retreating back. Sweet dreams, indeed. She undressed, yanking her clothes off, tossing them onto the chair by her bed. What did she have to do, anyway? Seduce him?

With a soft, indelicate snort, she considered his reaction. Another rejection, no doubt. She'd never been one to give up on something, but she'd also never had any faith in her ability to attract a man. Living with Josette had reinforced that. But Josette wasn't here, and by bloody darn, she was determined to take advantage of it.

As she buttoned her nightgown to her chin, a quivering sensation attacked her stomach. She wouldn't take advantage tonight. Not wouldn't, but . . . couldn't. But as she slid beneath the covers, memories of the night before inundated her. It was too bad she didn't have an excuse to go to him. Too bad he didn't have another nightmare. This time she wouldn't leave him.

As determined as she was, she wasn't brazen enough to approach him. Not without reason, and *wanting* him just wasn't reason enough to face another rejection. She rose onto her elbow and punched her pillow. Hard. She flopped back onto the bed.

And why not? Why was she afraid of another rejection? She was sick and tired of having a union that was more like a friendship than a marriage. She had nothing to lose. She'd lost her pride. Nothing else mattered. And a man like McCloud wouldn't turn down an offer to make their marriage real. He was a lusty, sensual man, and if she didn't offer herself, he'd go elsewhere, and Lord knows, she didn't want that. It would be the ultimate shame, as far as she was concerned. That she was willing to go to him proved to her that she feared his straying to find intimacy elsewhere more than she feared the intimacy itself.

Flinging the covers aside, she slid from the bed and crossed to the door, going over the sensible reasons why McCloud should accept her into his bed. She left her room, anxious to present her proposal to him before she lost her nerve.

She hesitated at his door, then stepped inside, not wanting to give him time to prepare. The room was dark; she couldn't even distinguish the bed.

"McCloud?"

There was rustling of the bedding. "What kept you?" His voice was huskier than usual.

She felt a wash of confusion. "What do you mean?"

"I expected you in here earlier."

He was laughing at her; she heard it in his voice. Her stomach churned. "Then why didn't you come to me?"

"Because I knew you'd come to me."

There was a smile in his voice, the arrogant bastard.

"Tell me what you want, Julia."

She took a deep breath, expelling it slowly. Why not? Her dignity was in shreds anyway. "It's nothing serious. I just want you to sleep with me." She held her breath, biting back a groan at how stupid and inane she sounded.

He let out a whoosh of breath of his own. "Julia—"

"I know, I know," she interrupted, anxious to voice his opinions for him before he had a chance to do it himself. "It's not what you want, McCloud, but it's foolish not to at least—well, sleep together. I mean, I'm offering myself, and believe me, it isn't an easy thing to do." And it wasn't. It was the hardest thing she'd ever had to do, but . . .

"I decided the worst thing you could do would be to reject me, and since I've survived your rejections in the past, I can do so again. I—"

"Julia, I just don't want you to be sorry, that's all." He no longer sounded amused.

She made a face in the darkness. It was clever of him to rest the whole thing back on her shoulders as a way of wiggling out from under the burden of her request.

"The ranch is half yours, McCloud. I should think that at the very least you would want an heir." The idea of producing one with him made her ache in places that she'd only learned existed in her own body since McCloud came into her life.

There was a long, significant pause, during which time Julia considered turning on her heels and racing back to her room. But she was no coward. Whatever his decision, she would learn to live with it.

"You want me to make love to you so I can have an heir?"

She heard the caution in his voice. If that was the only way she could have him, then, yes. "I would think you'd want that, too."

He didn't say anything, but she knew he would. She'd learned he was a master of the pregnant pause.

"What about Marymae? She's your heir."

Julia was getting impatient, and her feet were cold. "Marymae has nothing to do with it," she snapped.

He cursed in the darkness. "Are you *sure* you want this?"

She answered with a mild curse of her own. "If I wasn't sure, I wouldn't have thrown my dignity to the wind and come in here, begging."

"I just want—"

"McCloud," she interjected, "you have the most resourceful way of dissolving a mood. Do you want me or don't you? I'm getting cold." She was not only impatient, but insecure as well. He'd seen to that.

He chuckled, and she heard him flip the covers back. "Only you could make an offer like that sounds like an order. Get in here."

Ignoring his comment, for to dwell on it would have caused her to run, she hurried to the bed.

His body, warm beneath the bedding, radiated animal heat. Closing her eyes, she bit back a sigh when he brought her to him. She put one foot on his calf.

"Youch! Your feet are as cold as a witch's—"

She snuggled closer, ignoring his reaction. "A witch's . . . what?"

"A witch's bosom," he finished lamely.

"I don't think that's what you were going to say, McCloud." She hoped she wasn't purring, but she wasn't sure. His body was warm and hard. He smelled brazenly masculine, a scent that caused her to tremble with innocent desire. She was flirting with danger, and she knew it. But somehow she felt brave, too, and realized it was because it was dark. She didn't have to look into those potently playful eyes ... and he couldn't see that she wasn't the perfect woman. She wrinkled her nose. He'd discovered that last night when she'd fallen asleep in the tub.

"Say what you mean, McCloud, don't mince words because of me. I won't break," she chattered on, her voice filled with nervous anticipation. "I'm strong for a woman. I won the woman's woodchopping event at the fair last year, and—"

"Are you always so talkative in bed?"

She forced herself to snake her arms around him, knowing it was a bold gesture. Her fingers touched his mutilated back and she felt the telltale ache for what he'd gone through, wondering if she'd ever get used to it.

"I have no idea." She hoped her voice was light. "Now, tell me what you were going to say. My feet are colder than a witch's what?"

"It'll sound crude."

She pressed her nose into his neck, rubbing her lips back and forth on his skin, fighting the urge to bite him—gently, of course. Strange, this desire to eat him. "Since when has that ever stopped you?"

"I'm going to regret that verbal intercourse we exchanged earlier, aren't I?"

"Oh, go ahead, McCloud. Be crude. I won't melt."

"If you say so." He took a breath, expelling it against her hair. "Your feet are colder than a witch's tit."

She felt a shameless, exciting nibble of arousal at the uncouth word. "Hmmm," she murmured, trying to sound casual. "So men actually call them that." She tucked the toes of one cold foot between his calves, ignoring his sharp intake of breath.

"Call what what?"

She moved her toes back and forth over his hard, hairy leg. "What you said."

She felt him smile against her forehead."I want you to say it, Julia."

What a silly request! Enticing, though."Why?"

"Because a little crude talk is exciting foreplay," he explained, one hand stroking her back.

She was already feeling heat between her legs. "I didn't think men liked that, McCloud."

"You mean foreplay?" His hand dipped low over her buttocks, then over her hips and her waist.

She was having trouble breathing. "Yes."

"Some men do." His thumbs brushed the side of her breasts.

"And do you?" Lord, was that her voice, so breathy and insipid?

He nuzzled her ear, making a satisfied sound in his throat. "I like foreplay, Julia. Now say the word."

Her nipples hardened even though he hadn't touched them. "Which word is that?"

His thumb grazed her nipple as he cupped her breast. "*That* word, Julia. I want you to use it in a sentence."

She almost lost control; her thoughts became drugged with a hunger she'd never known. "Who would have thought I'd get a lesson in grammar instead of seduction." Her words came out shaky and unsure.

He tilted her chin up and kissed her, nibbling at her lips, taking his time as his hot breath mingled with hers. "A lesson in lovemaking, Julia. Come on," he urged, "say it."

"Who's being talkative in bed now, McCloud?" She hoped he didn't hear the uncertainty in her words. "I thought men only wanted to do one thing." How brave that sounded!

His mouth hovered over hers, his tongue extended. Gathering her courage, she touched it with her own, feeling deep stirrings of desire.

"They do," he whispered, planting deep, wet kisses on her lips. "It's just how we get there that's different. Use the word, Julia."

She hadn't imagined this sweet, provocative love play. She wanted to scoff but found it titillating. "Oh, I can't do—"

"I'll help you," he offered, kissing her neck. "Repeat after me. 'Wolf, please, *please,* kiss my titties.' "

Her nervous giggle was caught up in a gasp when he continued to fondle her breasts. "I can't—"

"Think about my mouth on your nipple, Julia. Think of how it will feel for me to tug on it gently with my teeth," he added, biting down on her earlobe. "Imagine how it'll feel when I wet it with my tongue and pull it into my mouth."

Her nipples were hard as pebbles, and she swore her breasts actually swelled at the sound of his words. "Mc—"

"Wolf," he corrected. As he slid the buttons from the buttonholes on her gown, he pushed his bare knee between her legs.

Something low in her belly tightened, and she had the urge to straddle him, like she'd straddled tree trunks as a girl. Giving in to her hunger, she enclosed his knee between her thighs, sucking in a breath at the contact. He continued to touch her breasts. Releasing a long sigh, she knew she could get used to this.

"Come on," he urged her again, rubbing his thigh against her.

She squirmed under the new wealth of sensations, arching her back. On the verge of begging, she whispered, "Wolf . . . please, *please,* kiss my . . . my titties."

He obliged, cupping one in his hands and making love to it. Everything inside her came alive, swelling, aching, itching for something more. Gripping his hair, she pulled him closer, urging him to devour her breast while she rode his thigh.

She began to shake. There was a need building up inside her, a simmering heat that threatened to send her out of control.

His mouth returned to hers. "Repeat after me, Julia. 'Take my nightgown off, Wolf.' "

Words were no longer necessary. She helped him rid herself of her gown, then flung herself against him, noticing for the first time how hard he was. Her own hunger made her feel hot and swollen, too.

He pressed her onto her back and touched the place of fire between her thighs. She spread for him, making mingled sounds of need and contentment in her throat as he stroked her. All too soon he stopped.

She tossed her head from side to side on the pillow. "McCloud?" Was that mewling sound her voice?

Suddenly she felt his mouth on her stomach, inching lower. His hair caressed her skin while his tongue dipped into her navel.

She shuddered, her breath coming in shaky gasps. "McCloud, what are you doing?"

He moved lower, his hands gently drawing her legs apart. Desire, thick as warm honey, swelled through her as he nudged her with his thumbs, making sultry circular movements on her mound. Every nerve she had was centered there, alive there, screaming to be touched. Her heart raced with shock when she felt his breath there, and she tried to wrench away.

"No! Oh, McCloud, not there," she wailed, anxious for his touch but fearing it, too.

He gentled her by caressing her thighs, his fingers moving up toward that place again, stroking it, searching for something she didn't understand. She knew when he found it, for she felt a hot spurt of hunger there, and couldn't stop the sounds that escaped from her throat.

"Ah, Julia, Julia," he said, his voice lust-husky. "Just one kiss there. Just one."

She squeezed her eyes shut and braced herself, for somehow she knew what he was going to do.

He kissed her mound, then dragged his tongue over the folds of her flesh. The exquisite sensation caused her to clamp her thighs together, momentarily trapping his head down there. And he continued to make love to her with his tongue.

Suddenly afraid of the sensation that was building up inside her, she grabbed his hair and pushed him away. "No more, McCloud. Please, no more," she croaked on a shaky breath.

Then she felt his shaft nudging her. Gripping fistfuls of bedding, she lifted herself toward him, gasping in surprise when he entered her. He drove deep, and she released a cry of alarm as a burning pain shattered her desire.

He stopped, spitting out a curse. "Julia?"

She heard the puzzled question in his voice. Wrapping her legs around him to keep him from leaving, she pleaded, "Don't stop, McCloud. Please, don't you dare stop."

Gathering her close, he drove deep. She wanted to get back what she'd lost when he'd broken through her virginity, but it wouldn't come. His breathing became harsh and his thrusts more insistent, until he stiffened over her. She caressed his back, learning the depth and width of each scar, making them her own, wishing she could have absorbed his pain.

He released her and flopped onto his back. "Christ, Julia. You were a virgin." His voice was accusatory.

"I never said I wasn't." He felt far away even though he was right next to her.

"What about the baby?"

She released a sigh. She didn't want to talk about Josette, not right after McCloud had made love to her. It might get him to comparing, and she didn't want to think about that, either. "Do we have to talk about this now?"

"Can you think of a better time?" He sounded exasperated, and if he was, it was with her.

She snuggled next to him, hoping to distract him. "Any time but now, McCloud."

He turned, taking her into his arms. "I didn't satisfy you. I think we should try again."

With shy fingers she caressed his smooth chest, loving the way his hard muscles bunched beneath her touch. "I don't mean to sound ignorant, but what else can you do?"

His hand moved over her abdomen, to the cleft below. "First I'll make you come with my fingers."

She sucked in a breath and spread her legs, eager for him to touch her, disappointed when he didn't.

He rolled away from her and lit the lamp by the bed. She squinted into the light as he got out of bed. "Where are you going?"

"Stay there. Don't go away." As he crossed to the

door, she studied his firm, hard buttocks. A shudder of pleasure tightened her throat. He was right about bottoms. His was perfect. The muscles in each cheek clenched as he walked away, and she realized that he had the same cocky, impudent stride dressed or naked.

Feeling chilled, she brought the covers to her chin while she waited for him to return. She turned to her side and pulled his pillow to her face, inhaling the smell of him on the pillow slip. A knot of apprehension formed in her chest, one that warned her not to get too used to these pleasures.

He returned with the teakettle. As he approached the bed, she gazed at him, swallowing hard when she saw what he looked like down there, where his thick bush of black hair grew. He wasn't stiff and hard, but slung low and impressive in size. She bit back a self-critical smile. As if she had anything to compare it with.

"What are you going to do with that?" She nodded toward the teakettle.

"You'll see." He poured hot water into the porcelain bowl on the dry sink, then added cold until he appeared satisfied with the temperature. After placing the bowl on the bedside table, he dipped a washcloth into it, then sat on the bed and pulled the bedding down. The cold air hit her, and she shivered.

"Spread your legs," he said, his voice almost a caress.

Suddenly understanding his objective, she tensed. "Oh, no. You aren't going to do *that.*"

He bent over her, his hair caught behind each ear. If ever he looked dangerous and disreputable, it was now. "I want to." He lowered his head, his lips grazing her stomach.

She nearly catapulted off the bed. "McCloud!" She

pushed him away, only to feel his lips lower, below her navel. "McCloud!" Feeling his breath on her mound, she gasped, her breath shaking as the feeling she'd experienced before he'd entered her returned.

Once again he kissed her there, just where her thatch of hair started, and she nearly flew apart. "Oh God, oh God, oh God!" She tugged at his hair. "Stop it. Please, stop."

Raising his head, he gazed at her, his eyes dark. "Are you sure?"

Was she? Lord, no. She wasn't sure about anything anymore. "It's ... I ..." How could she tell him that having his mouth there pushed her out of control? "I'm not ready for it."

"Then let me wash you, Julia."

Swallowing hard, she obeyed, allowing him to dab at the folds of her swollen flesh. She felt the stirrings of desire again. Had she not, she would have been uncomfortable and embarrassed at being tended so. But the warm water felt so good, and his touch so intimate.

He removed the cloth and she saw the bloodstains before he rinsed them away in the water. He touched the cloth to her again, dabbing further, dipping deeper. She couldn't suppress a shudder of pleasure.

"You're hair down here is the color of sunshine," he mused, stroking her. "And your skin is pink and ripe beneath it."

She felt like a wanton, her legs spread akimbo while this man so boldly washed away the remnants of her virginity. Curious, she asked, "Have you had many women, McCloud?"

"Does it matter?" He returned the bowl and the cloth to the dry sink, then came back to the bed.

She had no answer. Not one she wanted to voice,

anyway. Still unable to get the picture of McCloud and Josette from her mind, she scolded herself. He would never admit he'd had a liaison with her sister, and at this point, she didn't want to know.

She felt strange, lying naked in bed with this man. She also found it strangely exciting, but the night air was cold, and she reached for the covers.

He stopped her. "I want to look at you, Julia."

Something blossomed in her chest. "But I'm cold."

He bent and kissed her turgid nipples, laving them with his tongue. "I'll heat you up."

She didn't doubt it a bit, she thought, biting down on her bottom lip.

He raised himself onto his elbow again, his eyes dark and filled with heat.

"You're skin is so pale." He moved his fingers over skin that was as smooth as satin, as rich as velvet. Never had he seen such perfection. Such purity. "I've never seen anyone with hair this color." He ran one finger over her golden triangle, relishing her sharp intake of breath.

"McCloud, how can I be so hot when I'm so cold?"

Emotion swelled within him. He'd never had a virgin. Never known one, for that matter. He'd never thought he wanted one. Baptiste had warned him that they were trouble. Hell.

He wanted to satisfy Julia. He wanted to bed her again. And again. He just didn't want to feel any emotion stronger than selfish, animal need.

"Spread your legs, Julia."

She complied, but asked, "Why can't we do this under the covers?"

"Because I want to watch you." He rubbed her cleft, discovering how she was made, finding her tiny bud as hard and intense as his own shaft.

She spread them farther, but he noticed she kept her eyes shut. "That's my girl, Julia," he whispered. "You're getting wet and slippery." Moistness flooded his fingers. He noted her ecstasy, her flushed cheeks, her mouth, open slightly as she breathed. "I like touching you this way. Do you like it?"

She nodded, her eyes closed.

"Talk to me. Tell me, Julia." He moved his finger over the slick, wet skin, nudging the essence of her with his finger, a motion that made her grip the bedding and buck on the bed.

Her sounds of pleasure aroused him. He wanted to be inside her again. "Come on, sweetheart, tell me what you like."

"I've never—" She gasped, bucking on the bed again. Her breathing shuddered and deepened through her sweet mouth, and she rolled her head from side to side. Then she clutched at him, pulling him toward her, then shoving him away, unsure of what she wanted.

Two fingers, then three, delved into her, and he felt her open for him, her hunger at its peak. Then she came, trapping his fingers inside her, bucking wildly, crying out his name.

He grabbed the covers, pulling them over both of them as he entered her. "Hang on, sweetheart," he ordered. "We're going for one hell of a ride."

He wanted to watch her come again, but his own hunger was rampant, and he only heard her cry of completion as it mingled with his own.

Julia slid from McCloud's embrace, which had slackened in sleep. Finding her nightgown in a rumpled heap on the floor, she put it on, then turned for one last look at her husband. She gazed at his dark beauty, swallowing the sob that threatened to burst from her throat. He'd made love to her both tenderly and fiercely, but she wondered if he could ever feel for her what she felt for him.

She caught her reflection in the mirror over the vanity, and her heart sank like a stone. Though her cheeks had a rosy glow, she was a bland and colorless woman. Bending toward the lamp, she turned it out, then made her way to the door. Above all, she must remember, too, that she'd been the aggressor. If she hadn't come begging, he wouldn't have made love to her.

Wolf waited until she'd gone, then rolled onto his back, bracing his neck with his hands. He closed his eyes, searching for some reason not to care for her. From the beginning he'd told himself not to screw up the opportunity for the kind of life others so effortlessly had.

He and Julia had settled into a comfortable existence together. He'd known she was honorable. In the last few days he'd also discovered that her prickly nature covered a warm, caring woman who didn't shrink from tragedy, but faced it. Worked at his side to try to prevent it. Grieved at loss when it happened. She didn't faint or swoon. She didn't pass the blame.

And she'd come to his bed. His initial delight had been tempered by her pragmatic reason for being there; even so, he couldn't have turned her away.

But she'd been a virgin.

He pressed the heels of his hands against his eyes. Emotion tightened his throat, sending an exquisite feeling of possession through him. No, he didn't want to mess up this new life, this rescue from a life that had led to nowhere. But he also couldn't let her know how much he was beginning to care. Things were too tenuous. Yes, she'd come to his bed. But only because she thought he wanted an heir.

Everything they were had been forced upon them. He was beginning to feel grateful, but he wasn't sure that deep down Julia would ever forgive her father for forcing her into a life she had not chosen.

❖ 11 ❖

Julia was up before dawn. Even so, McCloud had beat her, for she saw the lantern flickering outside, in the makeshift corral where they kept the milk cows and the little calf.

She scrambled some eggs, cutting up leftover ham into them before pouring them into the skillet. The smell of cinnamon and sugar hung in the air as coffee cake baked in the oven.

The back door opened, and she found herself twisting her apron hem, waiting for McCloud to enter. When he stepped into the room, she broke into a cold, heart-hammering sweat. She felt skittish, light-headed, anxious. Her thighs tingled. Had she actually slept with this dangerous, wild-hearted man? Every part of her body told her she had, for she had so much energy, she felt like skipping around the room.

Knowing he could see the longing in her eyes, she turned away.

"Why did you leave my bed last night, Julia?"

She even reacted differently to the sound of his

voice this morning. The way he said her name, drawing it out, softening it, like he truly enjoyed saying it.

"I'm used to sleeping in my own bed." *And staying would have given you the idea that I care, McCloud, and I can't let you see how much I care.*

"I woke up around two o'clock, cold, alone, and damned horny."

She grimaced at his crude words. So much for dreams of romance. She should have known better, but last night he'd been so perfect. She should have known it was too good to last. Scolding herself, she continued preparing breakfast, embarrassed anger surfacing. "Surely you know how to please yourself, McCloud."

"Not as good as you could do it," he volleyed.

Heat flooded her cheeks. What a fool she'd been to even mention it!

"I didn't hurt you last night, did I?"

Her heart began to thump. "What's this, McCloud? Actual concern?"

"Well," he drawled, "you might not come to my bed again, demanding that I sleep with you, if you think it will hurt."

Mortified, she busied herself with breakfast. "Oh, don't worry. I'll only be back if I don't get pregnant." God, why was there such an ache in her chest?

"Then I can only hope you'll be back. Again and again."

She should have been accustomed to his teasing, but she wasn't. Not after last night. Not after the tenderness he'd shown her and the passion he'd brought out in her. She pulled the coffee cake from the oven, cut it into squares and put it on the table. "I guess a backhanded compliment is better than none."

Neither spoke as the silence stretched taut between them.

"Tell me about Marymae."

She felt a gentle tug at her heart. "Why do you care about Marymae?"

He shrugged, appearing only mildly interested. "I'm curious to know if it was the Immaculate Conception."

She snorted a response. "Of course not. Marymae is Josette's baby."

He shook his head, a cynical smile spreading across his face. "Now, why doesn't that surprise me?"

"I don't know, McCloud, why doesn't it?" She scooped the eggs into a bowl and placed them on the table beside the coffee cake, then motioned him to help himself.

"Who's the father?" He filled his plate, then took a bite of eggs.

She turned away again, remembering the rejection she'd suffered at the hands of Frank Barnes, who had successfully played one sister against the other. Remembering how he'd courted her in the afternoons, bringing her bunches of wildflowers, touching her elbow as they walked through the orchards. He'd even backed off, apologizing for being forward when he tried to kiss her. He was a crude man. Uneducated. But she'd forgiven him for that because he seemed to be trying hard to please her.

She thought something might come of their relationship, until that fateful night she made a trip to the barn and discovered Frank between Josette's thighs, pumping at her like a bull. Julia had been so sick to her stomach that she'd stumbled from the barn and vomited on the grass. His deceit still made her ill, but she felt fortunate, too. Fortunate that she hadn't allowed him to take advantage of her.

The worst part was that Josette had seen her. Julia would never forget the smug smile on her sister's lips. Nor would she forget the way Josette's legs circled Frank's back when she saw her watching.

"It isn't important, McCloud."

"No, I suppose it isn't."

She sat across from him, toying with her food as she watched him eat. She took a bite of eggs, wondering what he was thinking, knowing it was only fair to tell him everything. Almost everything. He didn't need to know about Frank and the humiliation he'd caused her.

"Is everyone in the valley aware of this, or am I the last to know?"

His hostile question surprised her, but it shouldn't have. No doubt it rankled that Josette had a child by another man. "What concern is that of yours?"

"Because you could have told me you were a virgin," he accused.

She swallowed the lump in her throat. His anger was so misplaced. Why hadn't she felt it last night? "You sound sorry."

He shoved his plate away. Leaning back in the chair, he studied her, his gaze raking her breasts. "Virgins are often more trouble than they're worth."

A hollow ache settled around her heart. "Even if the virgin is your wife?"

He took a drink of coffee, still observing her. "Sometimes."

She was the first to look away.

"Tell me," he began, "who knows about the baby?"

Why it mattered to him, she couldn't imagine. "I don't know who knows and who doesn't. Papa—" She took a breath and rubbed the back of her neck. She felt a headache coming on. "Papa was rather like an ostrich when it came to Josette. He didn't want to see her flaws. He pampered her." She expelled a disparaging laugh. "I did, too, I guess. It was just easier to do things myself than keep after her to do her share."

"That doesn't explain how she got pregnant, and how you got saddled with her child."

"She got pregnant the normal way, McCloud." She could have bitten her churlish tongue.

"How did you get saddled with the child?"

Julia cut her piece of coffee cake into a number of smaller pieces, then forced herself to eat one of them. "You make it sound like Marymae is a burden to me. She's not. I love her as much as if she were my own. And anyway, it's a long story."

There was silence, tense and dark. "I have nothing but time, Julia."

The memory of it all came back in a hard, painful rush. "It's very simple, really. If I hadn't, she would have died. She would have *died*, because Josette didn't give a damn."

Julia smoothed back the sides of her hair, uncertain that she even wanted to continue, yet unable to stop herself. "She didn't want her, McCloud. She didn't want anything to do with her. She tried to talk one of the hands into taking the baby and leaving her somewhere far enough away so she couldn't hear her cry. She wouldn't even have cared if Marymae had been given to strangers." Swallowing a sob, Julia felt the anguish as if it had been yesterday.

"She'd bribed one of the hands to—" She closed her eyes and shook her head. "That sweet, beautiful baby. So exquisite. Why would anyone in their right mind want to get rid of her? And how could something so perfect come from two such—"

She stopped, unwilling to put her thoughts into

words. She couldn't stand to think about what Josette had done, and she felt revulsion every time she thought about Frank Barnes. How could she speak of any of it?

"To what?" He appeared tense across from her. "She bribed one of the hands to do what, Julia?"

She took a shaky breath. "Suffice it to say that Josette would have gone to any lengths to avoid motherhood. She was angry when I intervened. I couldn't have lived with myself—" She stopped, to slow the rush of feelings. "I couldn't have lived with myself if I hadn't saved Marymae." She dabbed at the food left on her plate, surprised she'd eaten as much as she had, considering the hitch in her throat.

"It's odd," she said with a wistful sigh. "I never thought much about children. I didn't think I had any deep need to have one, or raise one for that matter." She smiled, remembering the warmth that had coated her insides the first time Marymae recognized her. "But the first time she smiled at me, I was smitten."

She laughed, embarrassed. "It sounds foolish to a man, McCloud, but I'd give my life for her, if need be."

She pressed her fingers against her mouth, sorry she'd bared her soul. But it had been building up inside her. Although she couldn't tell McCloud everything, she was sorry she'd allowed her feelings for Josette to show, exposing this angry, selfish side to her nature.

"I'm sorry," she apologized. "I'm sorry I went on so."

He studied her, his expression grim. "And I suppose if she came back with another child for you to care for, you'd take on that responsibility, too."

Something cold crept into Julia's chest. The inference was clear. It was possible that Josette had been carrying his child when she left. The bitter chance of

Josette showing up and disrupting her tenuous life with McCloud unsettled her stomach. "Is there any reason for me to believe she *will* return with another child, McCloud?"

He stood, pushing his chair back so hard it toppled to the floor. "How in the hell would I know?" He strode to the stove and poured himself more coffee.

How would he know, indeed. His angry reaction was answer enough. She closed her eyes. *Don't think about it.* She wouldn't let it bother her. She wanted this man for as long as he was willing to stay, no matter what he felt about her. Petty jealousy would drive him away. As much as it hurt to admit it, where he was concerned, she had not one shred of dignity left.

She massaged her neck, trying to ward off the impending headache. "I'm sorry, McCloud. I didn't mean to sound peevish. I'm getting a headache, that's all. It puts me out of sorts."

He turned from the stove, studying her. "And Amos let everyone believe the baby was yours?"

"Yes." She rotated her neck, hoping to release the tension in her muscles. "But I'm not so sure people didn't know the truth, anyway. After all, Josette was ... well," she said with a shrug, "Josette was the pretty one."

With a violent curse, he crossed to the back door. "Don't make yourself out to be so damned pitiful, Julia."

She sat up straight. "Pitiful? I don't mean to sound pitiful, McCloud, I—"

"Like hell you don't. How many years have you felt second best? How long did it take you to perfect this 'poor me' attitude?"

She stared at him, her mouth agape. "If that's the way I come across, I apologize. I—"

"And that's another thing. What have you got to apologize for? For your sister's loose morals?"

"In a way, yes."

"Why?" The question sounded like a curse.

"Because if Papa and I hadn't spoiled her, maybe she wouldn't have been that way." How many times had she thought of that? How often had she wondered what things would have been like if she and Josette had shared the work?

His gaze probed her, like he was examining her soul. "Quit apologizing for her, Julia."

"But she *is* different," she urged. "Surely *you* can't deny that she's pretty. Dear heavens, McCloud, I'm not blind. We may be sisters, but the resemblance ends there. I don't pretend to be anything but what I am. I'm plain. Josette is pretty. I'm prickly. She was and always will be a flirt. She has dimples when she smiles, and knows how they affect men."

Julia forced a smile. "See? I have no dimples. I don't know how to flirt. I'm just me."

His gaze probed her, and it was filled with such potency, she had to look away. Inside, there was a woman she'd never shown anyone. A woman with feelings and dreams. It was just hard for her to let them show. She couldn't be like Josette. Even Papa had known it was true. He'd nicknamed her sister his darling Josie. He'd never had one for her.

"It used to make me sad that I couldn't be more like her, then I'd scold myself and remember that I was the strong one. The dependable one. The capable one."

She felt a foolish pinch of self-pity and wiped at her eyes with the hem of her apron. "I'm sorry. This has nothing to do with you. When I start getting a headache, I get maudlin. Leave me alone before I embarrass myself further."

He stood in the doorway, his face emotionless. "I'm going in to Walnut Hill and order some lumber," he said, his voice flat. Before he left, he turned toward her.

"Who in the hell fed you such a line of bullshit, Julia?" Without waiting for an answer, he went out the back door, slamming it hard.

Pulling in a shaky breath, Julia folded her arms on the table and rested her head on them. Who, indeed? But it wasn't bullshit, as he'd put it. Not entirely. Oh, in subtle ways Josette had made her feel less feminine, less beautiful, but each time Julia glanced into a mirror, she could see that for herself. Perhaps she'd allowed it because it was easier to deal with than making herself attractive for a man. Maybe she was afraid where it would lead. Maybe she felt safer, convincing herself she was plain and unbeauteous. Maybe she'd been responsible for perpetuating the "bullshit" herself.

How foolish she'd been to go on before McCloud, extolling Josette's virtues. But the more she thought about it, the more she realized Josette and McCloud were very much alike. Both beautiful ... both outrageous flirts ... and both experienced in ways she'd never be. Maybe they *did* belong together.

But Josette wasn't here, Julia reminded herself as she stood and cleared the table, and she intended to make the most of it. She refused to be weak, even though loving McCloud threatened to make her feel that way, especially knowing he couldn't possibly love her back. And she refused to let thoughts of Josette ruin what she might have. She'd never given Josette that much power when she'd been here. To give it to her now, when she was absent, was absurd.

However, as she washed the breakfast dishes she wondered how long McCloud would stay. She wondered if he was placating her, maybe waiting around for Josette to return. She would look for signs of rest-lessness, for though the ranch bound them together, she feared nothing was stronger than a man's need to be free to make his own choices.

Wolf took the long way to town, traveling the bank of the river. Having learned what kind of woman Josette was months before, he wasn't surprised to learn that Marymae was her baby. He wasn't even surprised that she didn't want it, for it would have cramped her style. She was a lot like Meredith. Maybe worse. He didn't know either of them well, nor did he want to.

But Julia was another story. Not only did she take over the baby's care, but she treated her like her own. A knot in his chest threatened to squeeze his heart. She was the complete opposite of her sister ... and his mother. She was warm and loving, generous and, yes, noble. When he considered Julia, the word leaped into his mind.

She was more than he deserved, and everything he wanted. He didn't feel worthy of her affection, much less her love.

His eyes found the creek. It had rained recently, but very little water trickled over the stony bed. He reached a natural fork, noting that beyond it was a smaller one, leading toward land that was completely incapable of growing anything but chaparral. There had to be a way to discover who was diverting the water, even if it meant going over every inch of land.

He thought of his own small parcel, on which now stood the burned-out shell of his cabin. If the map was right, his land came to a V at the end of Julia's property. He kneed his mount away from the river and murmured a command. As he galloped toward Walnut Hill, Wolf knew he had to do something. If Amos had been right, and there was something to worry about, there was no one else to take up the gauntlet.

Julia dragged herself to Marymae's crib, the child's sharp cries hurting her ears. The left side of her head pounded and she felt sick to her stomach.

She lifted the baby from the crib and brought her to her shoulder, her eyes watering from the pain in her skull. Checking for fever, she pressed her lips to Marymae's forehead, shocked at how hot it was.

"It's all right, darling," she crooned. "I'll make it go away, I promise." She wished someone could get rid of *her* pain.

Forcing herself to move, Julia went into the kitchen. Marymae clung to her neck as she grappled with the dishpan. Light sparkles flickered on the edge of her vision, and she blinked hard, hoping they would disappear, knowing they wouldn't.

Marymae continued to cry, hiccoughing against Julia's neck as she poured a small amount of hot water into the dishpan. She followed it with cold, testing it until it was merely lukewarm, then put Marymae on the table to undress her.

Tears streamed down Julia's cheeks when she bent over, and she tried to ignore the pain that threatened to explode at her temple and behind her eye.

She lifted Marymae into her arms again, hushing her as she brought her to the dishpan. The child shrieked when the water touched her, and she fought, making her legs stiff. Julia massaged the baby's knees until they relaxed, then sat her in the water.

Julia cried, from her own pain as well as her sympathy for Marymae. "Oh, precious, I'm so sorry, but we have to get your fever down." As if explaining it to her would do any good, she thought with a lift of her brow. But as Marymae's cries became louder and deeper, Julia's head felt ready to splinter into pieces. She forced herself to bathe Marymae in the water, squeezing the wet cloth over her shoulders, under her arms, down her back and stomach.

Pressing her lips to Marymae's forehead again, she found it somewhat cooler. She lifted her from the dishpan and wrapped her in a towel, cuddling her close as she took her back to the bedroom.

After getting her to take some sugar water, she dressed her and put her into the crib. Once Marymae had cried herself to sleep, Julia collapsed across the bed. Too exhausted to even get up and prepare a potato poultice for her head, she lay there, trying to ignore the fact that her headache had spread its angry tentacles into the muscles of her back, arm, and hip.

She fell asleep. When she woke, Marymae was crying and McCloud was sitting on the edge of the bed. She scrambled to sit, gasping as the pain in her head intensified.

"Oh, McCloud," she said, trying to sound normal. "I must have fallen asleep. I'm sorry, I—"

"Damnit, Julia, quit apologizing! Are you all right?" He touched her forehead, as if testing for a fever.

"I'm fine," she lied, pushing his hand away. "The baby's fever must be up. I have to—" She tried to stand, but a wave of nausea attacked her, intensifying her headache. Pressing her apron to her mouth, she sat on the bed.

He turned her face to his. "What's wrong?"

She shook her head and swallowed as the nausea eased. "It's just a headache. I get them every now and then." She tried to stand again, but the pain was so intense it brought tears to her eyes.

McCloud's hands were at her bodice. "What are you doing?" She batted them away, confused.

"Get undressed, Julia. You're in no condition to do anything."

He continued to unbutton her dress, and she found she was too weak to fight him. "But the baby—"

"I'll take care of her." He helped her stand, then pulled her dress and petticoats down over her hips. "Get into bed."

She knew she shouldn't, but her headache had never been so intense. "I should get a cold cloth. Or a potato compress."

He swore—something she was getting used to. "Potatoes? You put *potatoes* on your head for a headache?"

Why was he so angry? "It works, McCloud. At least sometimes it does."

Marymae began to wail in earnest, her piercing cries like knives plunging into Julia's eardrums. She pressed her hands over her ears and pinched her eyes shut. "Oh, God, help her, McCloud. Put her in the dishpan ... lukewarm water ..."

He pushed her onto the bed and covered her. She couldn't relax, for even when he'd gone, taking Marymae with him, the baby's shrill cries jabbed at her eye like a thousand needle pricks.

Sometime later McCloud returned and helped her sit up. "Here," he ordered. "Drink this."

In too much pain to argue, she took what he offered, shuddering at the vile taste before falling back onto her pillow. Moments later she felt as though she were floating. And her headache began to subside.

The clock on the mantel in the other room chimed twice, waking Julia. Her mouth was dry; she was thirsty. She licked her lips and swallowed, cautiously opening her eyes. It was dark. She blinked, testing her head. It hurt, but not as much as it had before. And she was groggy; she could sleep another ten hours. But of course she wouldn't get that chance. She would soon need to be up to do her chores and care for the baby.

With slow determination she slid from the bed and lit the lamp, squinting at the brightness of the flame. She stood, swaying slightly, then crossed to the crib. It was empty. Feeling brief confusion, she pressed her fingers to her temples and weaved out of the room, groping the wall as she made her way down the short hallway to the living room. The blaze in the fireplace hurt her eyes, but she saw McCloud's head on the sofa pillow and moved closer.

In spite of her discomfort, she couldn't prevent a smile, followed by a sense of relief. He lay on the short sofa, his legs hanging over the end and Marymae curled in the crook of his arm. They were both sound asleep. Their argument at breakfast returned to haunt her, and she tried to push it away, because she didn't want to think about Josette.

Julia removed Marymae from McCloud's arms, then glanced at his face. Her pulse jumped. He was awake.

Loving the way he looked when he woke, all sultry and warm, she smiled at him as she lifted Marymae into her arms. "Did she refuse to go to sleep?"

His mouth lifted into a lazy, answering grin. "She's quite a determined young lady when she puts her mind to it."

Julia stood, mesmerized, studying the fine lines at the corners of his eyes and the brackets on either side of his mouth as he smiled at her. His beard stubble enhanced the aura of danger she'd been drawn to from the very beginning. She would never tire of him.

She felt a moment of dizziness. "I'll put her back to bed," she said, moving toward her room with Mary-mae in her arms.

"Julia?"

She stopped. "Yes?"

"You look damn good in your underwear. If you were feeling better, I'd help you out of it."

In spite of her headache, she felt a stab of desire as she recalled the night before. She gave him a shy glance over her shoulder. "If I felt better, I'd let you."

"How's your head?"

"Not too bad." She couldn't look at him lest he see the longing in her eyes. "I don't know what you gave me, but it's working."

"Go back to sleep. If you're not awake in the morning, I'll take care of the baby," he offered.

His kindness was like a toasty fire inside her. "Thank you, but I'm sure I'll be fine in the morning."

Julia woke. It was long past time to get up, for it was daylight. And the light didn't hurt her eyes. She sat up slowly, moving her head. Testing for pain. There was none.

She expelled a sigh of relief, left the bed and checked the crib. It was empty. Throwing her robe on over her undergarments, she hurried into the kitchen. It was empty, too.

McCloud. She ran through the living room into McCloud's bedroom, where his bed was made and what clothes he owned were folded carefully over a chair. She flew from his room, and as she passed the living room window, she stopped. McCloud was unloading lumber from the wagon, and—

Frowning, she rushed outside. "McCloud?"

He dropped the load he was carrying, turned and watched her approach. "Are you feeling any better?"

She just stared. "I feel fine. What's that contraption on your back?"

He clucked his tongue. "Did you hear that, Marymae? She called you a contraption."

Julia laughed. "Not the baby, McCloud, that . . . that *thing* you have her in."

He touched the wide straps that were attached to the carrier on his back in which Marymae sat, looking over his shoulder. She grinned and drooled, only her sweet face peeking out from inside her warm bunting.

"This," he explained, touching the straps that crossed his chest, "is the way Indian squaws carry their children. It frees their hands and arms so they can continue to work."

Shivering as a gust of wind tunneled beneath her robe, Julia hugged herself. "Very clever. No doubt some man invented it."

He unloaded more lumber from the wagon, depositing it on the stack near the burned-out shell of the barn. "You don't sound impressed."

She watched how effortlessly he worked, despite carrying the baby on his back. "Oh, I'm impressed. But it's just like a man to invent something that enables a woman to care for her child and do all her other chores at the same time."

He gave her a sly smile, his eyes twinkling. "Yes, we men are a devious lot."

She swallowed as her heart threatened to leap into her throat. Yes, she thought, aren't you, though? With McCloud so easily finding a place in her home as well as her heart, she kept forgetting the unanswered question between them. The question of him and Josette.

She felt an unwanted bite of jealousy. "I'll take Marymae inside now, McCloud. I don't think she should be out too long."

He unfastened the straps, put the carrier on the ground, and lifted Marymae out. Julia took her from him.

"Her fever is gone, Julia. She needed fresh air."

It angered her that he thought he knew more about raising children than she did. "Oh, a lot you know. Just how many babies have you cared for to glean such a vast knowledge, anyway?"

He studied her, his expression suddenly guarded. "I've buried a few, if that's any consolation." Turning away, he continued to stack wood.

Julia felt a catch in her throat. "You've buried them?" Softening toward him, she asked, "What happened?"

He unloaded the last of the lumber from his trip into town, then removed his gloves. "It's not something I'm proud of, Julia."

She rocked Marymae on her shoulder, anxious for him to continue. "You brought it up. What happened?"

He shook his head, slapping his dusty gloves against his long, hard thigh. "It was a long time ago. When I was scouting for the Army."

He pulled the empty wagon toward the lean-to. Julia followed him. "What children did you have to bury?"

Unleashing a long, ragged sigh, he stopped and looked at her. "Indian children, killed along with their mothers."

She gasped and swallowed the knot of emotion that clogged her throat. "Oh, my. How did they die?"

He was quiet for so long, Julia wasn't sure he would answer her. "We killed them."

She pressed her face into Marymae's blanket so he wouldn't hear her sound of anguish. When she felt she had some control, she raised her head and stared at him. "You? You killed them?"

As he shoved the wagon into place, Julia noticed how white his knuckles were. "I could just as well have. There was nothing I could have done to stop them."

"Nothing?" Her voice was but a breathy whisper.

"One man against an army stands no chance, Julia."

There was such pain in his eyes, she had to look away. "But you tried. I'm sure you tried." She hoped it was true.

"I tried," he said. "And got whipped for my efforts."

Her gaze flew to him again. "Your back?"

Giving her a terse nod, he walked away.

Julia followed him. "Tell me more, McCloud."

"I don't think you want to hear the rest of the story."

"I want to know."

When he turned, his eyes were shiny. "Because I tried to stop them from the slaughter, they whipped me until I was unconscious, then tossed me into the grave with the dead."

Julia clutched Marymae to her chest even tighter.

"When I came to, all I felt around me was death. After clawing my way out of the grave, I vowed never to find myself in small, dark places ever again."

She swallowed, then bit her lip so hard she drew blood. "The cave?"

"I have no idea how long I was there before you came for me. Something happens, and I go blank."

"I'm so sorry, McCloud," she whispered.

He gave her a grim smile, then turned away. "That's so like you, Julia. Apologizing for something you didn't even know about."

She turned away, too, tears threatening as she tucked Marymae closer and hurried toward the house. She didn't even wince as pebbles and twigs dug into her bare feet and wind funneled through the opening of her robe. Somehow, she knew that no matter what she'd gone through in her life, it wasn't enough to help her understand his.

Once inside, she put the baby on the kitchen table, unwrapped the blankets McCloud had covered her with, and examined her. Noting Marymae's rosy cheeks, she gave the baby a wry smile. "You enjoyed your little escapade this morning, didn't you, sweetheart?"

Marymae kicked and giggled, making gurgling sounds in her throat which erupted into bubbles that broke and dripped down the sides of her mouth.

Julia lifted her into her arms again and pressed her lips to the baby's forehead. It was cool. And her eyes didn't have that glassy look, as they did when she was fevered.

She pulled back and examined Marymae further. "What did he give you? You look like you haven't even been sick."

Marymae tugged at Julia's braid and babbled an answer.

She changed the baby and gave her a bottle, then put her down for a nap. Dressing quickly, Julia buttoned the bodice of her dress as she dashed toward the kitchen. The clock struck eleven. She'd slept for almost an additional ten hours.

As she prepared lunch, she felt a tug of pride at the

way McCloud had taken over Marymae's care. Even her father hadn't been that considerate when she'd been sick, not even offering to do anything for himself, much less anyone else.

She stopped slicing bread as McCloud's words, so filled with pain and shame, filled her head. His friend, Nathan Wolfe, had been right. McCloud had suffered more than any white man could, or any man at all should.

She stacked the bread on a plate and put it on the table. His sense of responsibility bothered her. Not that she didn't like it. It just bothered her. Never in her life had anyone cared for her while she was sick. Not since her mother had died. With each headache, she had dragged herself through her housework. Her cooking. The care of her father and sister and, most recently, Marymae.

When they had all been struck with the grippe, including her, she was the one who got up and tended to everyone else. When she'd sprained her ankle, Papa had fashioned a crutch for her so she could get around, but had not once offered to do her chores, or told Josette to help. That time when she, alone, had eaten berries Josette had picked, she had stomach cramps for two days. But no one had offered to do her work.

She bit back a sob. Why did McCloud act as if he cared? It was one thing to love him in spite of his faults. Quite another to discover that perhaps he didn't have as many as she'd thought.

Lost in a world of her own, she went to the dark pantry to get jam and butter. As she opened the door, she heard a faint hissing sound. Curious, she lit a squat candle and raised it toward the noise.

❧ 12 ❧

At the sound of her scream, Wolf had his hammer midair. It almost came down on his thumb. Flinging the hammer aside, he raced to the house. Julia stood in the corner by the stove, her face white and her hands over her mouth.

"What is it?" When he got no response, he felt a stab of panic. Gripping her shoulders, he shook her. "Julia? Damnit, what's wrong?"

She pointed past him, her eyes huge. "The ... pantry." Her voice shook.

Frowning, he turned toward the pantry door. She grabbed his arm.

"Be careful," she warned, her voice a conspiratorial whisper. "It's a rattlesnake. Coiled on top of the potatoes, I think."

Wolf reached for his knife as he moved toward the door. Sweat dripped down his back and his heart thumped hard. He had hoped he'd overcome his fear the day in the cave. But as he approached the pantry, he knew he hadn't.

He wiped his forehead with his sleeve and tried to push away the dark, painful memories. Sucking in a resigned breath, he stepped inside.

She'd dropped the candle, but fortunately, it had not fallen over. Shuttered, its light snaked into the dark space. He heard the noise.

Raising his knife, he aimed, ready to strike. Then he saw it. A bubble of laughter rumbled from his chest. Putting his knife in the leather sheath on his belt, he reached down and picked up the snake, ignoring the squiggling tail, and stepped out of the pantry.

Julia squeezed her eyes shut when he emerged, the snake wiggling from his fist. "Get it out! Get it out of here! Out! Out! Out!"

"Christ, Julia, it's only a garden snake."

Julia opened one squinty eye and watched him go out the back door. He returned without it. "Did you kill it?"

"A garden snake won't hurt you." A smile lingered on his lips.

She shook her head. "I don't care, McCloud. I *hate* snakes. I absolutely *hate* them!" She rubbed her arms with her hands. "And ... and are you sure it wasn't a rattlesnake? I heard the noise, McCloud. I heard it. I really did." She swallowed a shudder, remembering.

He went back into the pantry, returning with an old tin lard bucket. He shook it at her. "Beans, Julia."

Her mouth opened and she frowned. "What?"

"He disrupted a can of your dried beans."

She motioned toward the door. "Throw them out."

"The snake wasn't *in* the can."

"I don't care. As long as I know there was a reptile anywhere near my food, I won't use it. I'll starve first. I hate snakes. I loathe them." She swallowed another convulsive shudder.

"Snakes are beneficial, Julia. They're good for—"

"I don't care *what* they're good for. Don't you understand? I go crazy when I see one. I can't explain it. I just do. My heart pounds so hard I'm afraid it's going to break a rib. I can hardly breathe, I'm so frightened." He was no longer smiling. She noted the dark pantry entrance. "Oh, McCloud," she said with an understanding smile.

He shrugged, his own smile slight. "We're quite a pair, aren't we?"

Grateful he hadn't teased her, she said, "I was going to ask you to search the pantry to make sure there aren't any more of them lurking around. I don't suppose you would." She paused, giving him a hopeful look. "Would you?"

He rubbed his neck, then dragged his hand over his face. "Sure."

She turned and faced the counter. "Would you mind bringing some strawberry jam? I mean, if you can?" she called over her shoulder.

She heard a muffled curse. "Where in the hell is it?"

Frowning, she put down her knife, went to the door and stepped inside. It was dark, but to Julia it was both intimate and arousing. "It's right in front of you." She reached past him to grab the jam off the shelf. "Bring the butter, would you?"

He stood there, stock-still, tense as a wire.

"McCloud?" She pressed her fingers to her mouth. "Oh, McCloud." She winced, knowing what he was going through. "I'm so sorry."

He picked up the butter and gave her a gentle push out the door. "There you go, apologizing for something that isn't your fault. I have to get over this sooner or later."

She released a sympathetic sigh. "Yes. I should get

over my fear, too. But I don't plan on ferreting snakes in my pantry to do it."

He gave her a crooked smile. "I've heard it's best to tackle the problem head-on."

"Then I guess I'll never get over it." Her fear was real, but she sensed that McCloud's was more serious.

Later, after they'd finished lunch and Julia had put Marymae down for her afternoon nap, McCloud came looking for her.

"I want to show you something," he said, pulling her to her feet.

His hands were rough and warm, his grip firm. She liked it. Hastily putting her quilt squares down, she asked, "Is something wrong?"

He gave her a half smile. As usual, it made her insides mushy. "Not this time."

She followed him to the back door. "Are we going far?"

He gave her a suggestive leer. "How far do you want to go?"

She swatted at him. "I mean, should I wake the baby?"

He shook his head. "No need. This won't take long." He ushered her outside. Baptiste was tethered near the door.

Julia balked. "I hate to leave the baby here alone, McCloud."

"All right. Put her in the travel basket. I think I can handle both of you."

She hurried into the bedroom and lifted Marymae out of her crib and into the basket Helga Williams had given them, then covered her with a warm blanket. Julia was grateful the baby could sleep through anything.

Once on Baptiste's back, she clung to McCloud's waist. He held the basket in front of him. They rode south, toward the rocky slope of the mountain, stopping at a willow thicket. California oak, laurel, and chaparral grew in abundance around them.

He dismounted, put the basket on the ground and lifted his arms to help her down.

She went into them, feeling their strength. But instead of releasing her, he held her fast and studied her.

Her heart hammered. "What is it?"

One side of his mouth lifted. "I like having you out here in the middle of nowhere all to myself."

Her pulse fluttered. "You have me to yourself every day, McCloud. We live alone, remember?"

"Yeah." His smile widened and his eyes danced. "But this is different."

Like the lovesick fool she was, she had to ask. "Why?"

"Because nothing is more exciting than making love in wild, uncivilized places, Julia."

In spite of her desire for him, she thought back to the times he'd taken Josette out to "pick berries." Had they . . . ? She forced it from her mind. No sense borrowing misery. It usually came calling without being invited.

She lifted her skirt to avoid getting it snagged on the bristly undergrowth and followed McCloud down a cool, shady path. Under a group of pines stood the old, dilapidated outbuilding where she and Josette used to play house. But unlike before, it was sided with screen and barbed wire.

"I'd forgotten about the shed. Why is it covered that way?"

"You'll see." He went through a number of maneuvers to open the wire-clad door. Gripping Marymae's basket with one hand, he stepped inside, and Julia followed. It wasn't dark. The boards were so rotten, light seeped in everywhere. But it was warm and smelled sweet.

He put the basket in which Marymae slept by the door, lit one lamp, then another, until the room was bathed in light. His bedroll was unfurled along one wall. "Do you plan to sleep here?"

"Not if I can help it." There was a smile in his voice.

Julia scanned the shelves, bringing one hand to her chest as she sucked in a quiet breath. "What are you doing?"

"I'm drying fruit. Come here," he urged, taking her arm and tugging her around the small stove toward the back of the room.

There were layers upon layers of shelves covered with chicken wire and cheesecloth. Each layer held countless peaches and pears, all sliced, all beginning to dry.

"You really *are* doing this," she mused, remembering back to the night they'd stayed with Earl and Helga Williams. The night they'd gotten married. In spite of herself, she felt a tingle of delight. "When have you had time?"

"There's always time, Julia. I think this crop will be ready to sell by the end of the month. But," he added, "I can't continue to do this here. The bears can be troublesome. That's why I had to put barbed wire over the screen."

She picked up a piece of fruit and put it in her mouth, surprised at how sweet and chewy it was. "Have you a buyer?" Her mouth watered.

"MacMillan and Sons will buy the whole lot and ship it east."

Happiness and a frisson of hope burst through her.

She turned, throwing herself at him. "It's wonderful, McCloud. Wonderful."

His arms folded around her. "Am *I* wonderful, too?"

Happiness rose up inside her like dandelion fluff. "Maybe," she answered on a breath.

As they stood together, Julia felt the stirrings of desire. She raised her face to his and stroked his chest, then linked her arms over his shoulders. He lowered his head to her mouth, the force of it opening hers. The kiss was hot. Wet. Filled with indecent promise.

He broke the kiss. "Take off your drawers, Julia."

A dampness exploded between her legs, and she swallowed hard, relishing the feeling of hunger. But she'd never been subservient. She put her palm on the front of his shirt. "I beg your pardon?"

He grinned. "You heard me."

"Yes. I heard you." She returned his smile, feeling a sense of power. "You take off yours first."

"Only if you'll unbutton my jeans."

She stepped closer, her heart hammering and her knees quaking as she put tentative fingers on the fabric of his jeans. Sucking in a ragged breath, she felt him imprisoned there, long, turgid, and ready.

She reached her fingers inside, touching the satiny surface of him, and unbuttoned his fly. His breath was as shaky as her own, and her feeling of power grew. When he sprang free, she murmured her delight.

Forcing herself to step away, she ordered, "Take them off."

He did, stepping out of them and kicking them to the side. He was magnificent. The tail of his shirt hung open on either side of him, framing his thick root and black hair.

Julia swallowed the urge to purr.

"Do you want to touch it?"

The query was improper. Erotic. She was weak with hunger and found she could hardly stand. "Yes."

His grin was quick. "As soon as you take off your drawers."

She moved away and reached under her dress and petticoat for the tie. As her shaky fingers fumbled with the knot, she watched him shrug out of his shirt. He was, without a doubt, the most perfect man in the world.

"Did you have this planned?" She shook with desire.

His grin was hot enough to scald milk as he watched her. "Oh, yeah."

She untied her drawers and stepped out of them, kicking them so they landed on top of his jeans.

A smile quirked his mouth. "You've got too many clothes on."

"You promised I could touch you," she reminded him.

He drew her hand to his root and she gripped gently, amazed at the texture, for he was like rock encased in velvet. She moved the skin back and forth, eliciting a primitive groan from her husband. Her sense of power increased.

He pulled up her skirts and lifted her, coaxing her to bring her legs around his back. She felt him plunge into her, and she hung on and rode until desire exploded inside her.

He sank to the floor, bringing her with him without breaking contact. They sat together, neither speaking. Julia listened for sound from outside, but nothing penetrated their harsh, raspy breathing or the thundering of their hearts.

He hardened inside her. Placing a knee on either

side of him, she rose, then settled onto him, discovering the pleasure of control. His fingers found her cleft, and he nudged it with his thumbs, teaching her to ride. This time when she came, she cried out as spasm after spasm rocked her.

She slumped against him, and he fell backward, drawing her with him. She lay on top, feeling the pounding of his heart. His hand roamed her back, snaking under her dress, where he caressed her bottom.

"I want to see your beautiful ass, Julia."

His words, though crude, made her feel desirable. "Do you always get what you want?"

"I didn't want much until I met you."

He sounded so serious. "And now?"

"And now I want you."

Her pulse raced. She ran her palms over his shoulders, down his arms, letting her fingers find the sharp delineation of his muscles. "As simple as that?"

His hand continued to stroke her bottom. "No. It's not simple at all. It's complicated as hell."

She rose and studied him, her intuition warning her not to be glib. "What makes it complicated, McCloud?"

His eyes held hers. "You don't know anything about me, Julia. You don't—"

She pressed two fingers over his lips to quiet him. She didn't know what he wanted to say, but she was quite sure she didn't want to hear it. Not now.

"You wanted to see my ... bottom," she reminded him.

He gave her a lazy smile. "I'd be much obliged."

She pulled herself up and stared at him, lifting one quizzical eyebrow.

"Please." His eyes were hot.

With a shaky laugh, she rolled away, her desire for him returning. She would do anything he asked. Anything at all. She had a feeling he would do anything for her, too. But she had much to learn. She stood and unbuttoned her dress, pulling it down over her petticoat and stepping out of it.

"Now that thing you wear over your breasts." The order was soft, seductive.

"It's a camisole." She pulled on the tie at her waist then unbuttoned it slowly.

He grinned his bright, evil grin. "Women wear too damned many clothes," he said, his gaze locked with hers.

She got to the bottom button and hesitated.

"That's the way, Julia. Make me wait."

Lowering her gaze, she hid her look of confusion. It hadn't been her intention to seduce him. "McCloud—" she began.

"Take it off, Julia."

She pulled the two edges of the fabric together. "McCloud, my breasts aren't very big."

One corner of his mouth lifted. "I know how big they are, Julia. You were naked in my arms the night before last."

She gave him a nervous laugh. How could she forget? "Oh, of course. Then why would you want to see them again?"

His gaze was hot; it made her throb. "I can't get enough of you. The first time I saw your breasts, you were wearing your father's work shirt." He gave her a lazy grin. "I wanted in the worst way to see them, because they jiggled when you walked."

She studied the floor as heat spread into her face. "You're a naughty man, McCloud."

"And you love it, don't you?"

She drew her gaze to his, giving him a heated smile of her own. "Maybe."

"Come on, Julia, take it off. Don't you know by now that you're beautiful?"

She bit her lip to hide the catch in her throat, then let the camisole slide down her shoulders.

"They're perfect. You know what they say," he drawled.

She wanted to cover herself with her arms but didn't. "No, McCloud, what do *they* say?"

"More than a handful is wasted."

She was unable to curb her smile, or the pride that spread through her.

"Your petticoat is next."

Eager for him, she pulled the string that held it and let it fall to the floor. His sharp intake of breath gave her further courage. She turned around, showing him her bottom. Suddenly he was behind her, his hands caressing her.

She slumped against him, feeling the ache of desire as his hands fondled her breasts, her stomach, the place between her legs.

He murmured provocative, sin-filled words in her ear and drew her back onto the bedroll. They kissed, mouths open, tongues exploring. She was wild with need when he entered her, and pleasure exploded inside her. When she could form a thought, she hoped one day she could learn to please him as he'd pleased her. It was the only weapon she could think of that could possibly make him stay.

They rode back to the house, Marymae awake and squirming to be held.

Julia fidgeted as well. "I want my drawers,

McCloud." She felt odd riding horseback with a bare bottom.

"No. I don't want you to wear any for the rest of the day."

She made a face at his back.

"I saw that," he warned, reaching behind him to stroke her bare leg.

She swallowed a nervous laugh and pushed his hand away. "You did not." His hand returned—farther up this time—and touched her between the legs.

"McCloud!" She had to grab him to keep from falling off. "Behave yourself or you'll drop Marymae."

He gave her a put-upon sigh. "All right."

She wrapped her arms around him and stroked his chest.

"You can put your hands lower," he offered.

She smiled into his shoulder. "Don't get your heart set on it."

They rode in silence the rest of the way home. Julia didn't know what he was thinking, but all she could think about was how much she loved him.

While she prepared dinner, he came up behind her, lifted her skirt and put his hands on her bare bottom. She went forward, using the edge of the counter for support. One hand moved to the front and he dipped a finger inside. She leaned back, resting her head on his shoulder, letting her arousal grow.

"I hope there's a purpose to all this, McCloud." That she could speak in a complete sentence stunned her.

"Oh, I think you know my purpose."

Her knees gave way. Turning in his arms, she raised her face to his and clung to him, rubbing against him.

He gave her a quick, wet kiss then pulled away, his eyes filled with dark fire. "Not yet, wife."

She turned back to her chores. "Then stop *doing* that."

His hands roamed her bottom. "Stop doing what?"

Resting the top of her head on his chest, she murmured, *"That."*

"Don't you like it?"

"I'm drooling on your shirt, McCloud. Of course I like it."

He gave her an innocent look, but his eyes were hot as he touched her. "Oh, is all this down here for me?"

With effort, she laughed and pushed him away. "Get out of here while I fix dinner."

He brought his hand to her chin. "One kiss before I go."

She raised her face, her mouth eager for his. His tongue danced with hers. He nibbled at her lips. The kiss went deep. She would die if he didn't take her soon.

By bedtime she couldn't undress fast enough. He took her hand and pulled her to his room.

It was exciting to have him dressed while she was naked, but not very satisfying. "Do I get to watch you undress?"

"You ordered me to undress in front of you once today. Maybe this time you should undress me yourself."

With cautious anticipation, she unbuttoned his shirt. She knew nothing about seduction, only what he'd taught her. "I ... I really don't know what to do." Opening his shirt, she kissed his warm flesh, moving her lips over it.

"You're doing fine." He circled her nipples with his palms, sending a rush of desire into her pelvis.

She stilled his hands, stood on her tiptoes and kissed

his chin. "I can't do anything when you do that." She gave him a mischievous smile. "I'm afraid I'll have to ask you to keep your hands below your waist."

He behaved himself while she took off his shirt, even minded his manners when she kissed the hair-covered skin that circled his navel.

But as she unbuttoned his fly, his fingers found her warm, wet delta, and she inhaled sharply. "I told you to keep your hands to yourself." Her words came out on a rush of laughter.

He drew her to him. "No. You said to keep them below my waist." He touched her again. "See? They're below my waist."

"No, they're below *my* waist, you devil."

They laughed together as she hurried to undress him, but levity stopped when he stood before her, his root bobbing from the weight of his hunger.

"Look at me, Julia."

She wrenched her gaze from his groin to his face, her lips parting and her breath coming in erratic spurts.

"Your breasts are quivering."

Indeed they were. But she was shaking like that all over. She expelled an exasperated sigh. "How long are you going to draw this thing out?"

He smirked. "My thing is drawn out pretty far, wouldn't you say?"

She laughed, then bit her lip and studied him. She was aswim with desire. "If you don't do something, McCloud, I'll resort to—"

He led her to the bed. "You'll resort to what?"

She tumbled onto it, pulling him down with her. "I think you know what I mean."

He mouthed a breast and Julia arched toward him, gripping his hair, tugging him closer.

She wrapped her legs around him as he entered her. In a few short, rough thrusts, they both climaxed, screaming each other's name.

He made love to her again, this time slowly, and Julia knew she would love him until the day she took her last breath. It wasn't just because he'd awakened in her all the latent desires she'd known were buried there. There was another part of him that touched her equally as deeply. His charm. His teasing banter. His clever repartee. His innate goodness. And there was something else. Something she would occasionally see in his eyes when he didn't know she was watching. A haunted expression. A look of pain that went so deep, she wondered if he would ever express it. She loved that, too, and wanted in the worst way to be his confidante.

But that would mean he would have to love her as much as she loved him. And she didn't think that was possible. Not even under the best of circumstances could he ever love her as much as she loved him.

✴ 13 ✴

Julia woke and stretched. She opened her eyes and found McCloud on his elbow, studying her. Something near her heart burst like flower buds into bloom. Over the past weeks, she'd discovered how expressive his eyes were. Odd that she hadn't noticed before. But now, when she was so deeply in love, she knew every nuance of him. One of the things she loved most was that when she talked to him, he concentrated on her, making her feel like the most important person in the world. No man had ever done that, not even her father.

"Happy anniversary," McCloud said, his voice husky from sleep.

"Anniversary?" She stretched again, briefly glancing away, wondering if her eyes spoke of the love that was in her heart.

"We've been married a month."

As if he'd had to remind her. Two weeks ago they had first made love, and she savored every memory. She'd also not had her menses. She wasn't sure how she felt about that. She wanted McCloud's baby, but it could easily make him feel trapped, and she didn't want that.

She put her arm around his neck. "Has it been a month already?"

He smiled a warm, intimate smile. One that she loved. "With your help, I've almost got the skeleton of the barn done."

She frowned, upset that not one of their neighbors had come to help rebuild.

"I know what you're thinking, wife."

She gave him a wry smile. "You usually do."

He settled back on the bed, taking her with him. "When you married me, you married a man with baggage, Julia."

She gave him a quizzical look.

"Because I'm a breed," he explained.

Uttering a troubled sigh, she rested her head on his chest and listened to the beating of his heart. "And I was so sure that all my neighbors were my friends." She wrapped her arms around his neck.

He pulled her to him and kissed her. They made slow, lazy love.

Later, after McCloud had left to check on the fruit, she was sweeping the porch when she heard a rider approach. Shading her eyes, she felt a friendly warmth as Serge approached on his gray.

"Good morning!" Serge stopped and dismounted, tying the reins to the post.

"Good morning yourself. It's about time you came to see me." She swept the dust onto the grass.

"I just heard about the barn, Julia. I've been in San Francisco. If you want, I'll send Frank and a couple of other men over to help."

Her stomach pitched. "Frank Barnes?"

"I know how you feel about him, but like it or not, he's a capable carpenter. I can spare him and a few others off and on for a couple of weeks. Would that help you out?"

Julia swept the steps. She didn't want Frank Barnes on her land. She *didn't*. But they needed the help. "Yes. Thank you, Serge. I'm sure McCloud would appreciate that. Want some coffee? I have fresh coffee cake."

He gave her a brief smile, then furrowed his brow. "Sure. I'd like that."

Julia caught his expression. "What's wrong?"

He opened the door and she walked inside, resting the broom against the wall. "I've got some news. I don't think you're going to like it."

She went to the pie safe, brought out the plate with the coffee cake on it and put it on the table. After pouring him coffee, she sat down across from him.

"What is it?"

Serge sighed and sat back in his chair. "How's your marriage?"

She frowned. "That's an unusual question. It's fine." Couldn't be better, she thought, biting the insides of her cheeks to keep from grinning.

He muttered a curse. "That just makes what I have to say that much harder."

A sense of foreboding crept over her. "Then say it, Serge. If this has something to do with McCloud, I want to know." Didn't she?

"Did you know your husband has been trying to sell some of your land along the river?"

Julia stared at him, her happiness teetering like a rock on a cliff. "He's what?"

Around a mouthful of cake, Serge explained. "He's approached Jake Crawford with an offer." He pinched his brows together as he swallowed, then took a slurp of coffee. "I was hoping you knew about it, that maybe it was your idea since I know how—" He cleared his throat. "Since I know how bad things have been for you."

Julia's stomach tightened like a fist. Papa's will had specifically stated that none of the land should be sold piecemeal. McCloud knew that. "I can't believe it." She didn't want to believe it. There had to be an explanation, but for the life of her, she couldn't think of one.

Serge took her hand and squeezed it. "Julia, I didn't want to hurt you. Honest, honey, I wish you'd been aware. You're like a . . . a . . ."

"A sister to you?" she finished.

He nodded, a blush creeping into his cheeks. "I wouldn't have even mentioned it if I hadn't felt it was important. I just thought you should know what kind of man you married."

She pulled her hand out from under his, put it in her lap and began twisting at her apron. "But why would he do this without asking me?"

Serge looked uncomfortable. "How well do you really know him, Julia?"

She swallowed, unsure how to answer. It was possible that her first instincts about him had been right after all. Perhaps she was just a love-starved fool, anxious to believe the honeyed words of a dangerous stranger.

"Papa trusted him."

Serge took her hand again, this time clasping it with both of his. "Don't get angry with me, Julia, but your father was sick. I know you want to think differently, but his mind was failing toward the end. Why, Mother said that there were times they were together when he didn't even know who she was."

She frowned at him, unable to believe it. "I hadn't noticed anything like that."

He squeezed her fingers. "And why would you? He was your father. We always think of our parents as being strong and unchanging. We choose not to see their failings, Julia."

Studying the floor, she saw nothing but her father's dead body, half of his face gone from the force of the bullet. She shuddered. "McCloud thinks Papa was killed."

"What?" Serge cursed, then stood and walked around the table to where she sat, pulling her from her chair.

She went into his arms, grateful for his friendship. "He thinks Papa found out something about the water. That someone was diverting it from the river, and they killed him because of it."

He smoothed her hair. "That's ridiculous. Normally, Amos was the most level-headed man I'd ever known, Julia, honey. But at the end ..." He sighed. "At the end, when he was so sick, I don't think he knew what he was saying. Mother said that even when he was himself, he'd often be awfully distant with her, and that wasn't like Amos at all. You know how close they were."

Julia bit down on her lip until it hurt. Her father and Meredith had been friends. At one time. But in the months before his death, he'd seemed to want to distance himself from her. Was it because of his illness? It had to be. What else could it have been?

Serge drew back. "Who would want to harm such a kind, gentle old man?"

She took a shaky breath. "That's what I said when

McCloud brought it up. Why would he say those things, Serge?"

He touched her chin, tipped her face to his and gave her a sympathetic smile. "I don't know. You probably don't want to hear this either, but I hope it wasn't just to get his hands on the ranch."

She pushed him away, unwilling to let his words become planted in her mind. But it was too late. What *did* she know about her husband? She'd known Serge for ten years. She'd known McCloud for only a few months.

Once Serge had gone, Julia paced, trying to make sense of what she'd learned. Even though she'd known Serge forever, she didn't want to believe him. Not about this. Not about the man she'd fallen so deeply in love with. The man to whom her father had entrusted both his land and his eldest daughter.

By the time Marymae had awakened from her nap, Julia knew that she had to face McCloud. It wasn't her way to avoid the truth, even if it hurt. The trouble was, if McCloud was the no-good bastard she'd thought he was when she first met him, could she trust him to tell her the truth?

Wolf stepped into the kitchen, drawing the delicious smells of supper into his lungs. Julia had her back to him, at the stove. Her waist was small enough to span with his hands, and the swell of her hips enticed and aroused him. Dressed or naked, she was the most provocative woman he'd ever known. And she had a quick, lively mind. Qualities he'd admired from the beginning. If someone had told him a year ago that he would feel this way about a woman like Julia, he'd have pronounced them insane. Not because he wouldn't have been attracted, but because he wouldn't have had a chance.

He wasn't ready to call it love, even in the quiet recesses of his heart, but it was something special, and he didn't want to lose it.

He stole up behind her and kissed her neck. Startled, she dropped her spoon; it clattered to the floor.

"Oh! I didn't hear you come in." She fussed with her hair.

Wolf put his arms around her, placing one hand just above her left breast. He felt the bounding of her heart. "Does your heart beat for anyone special?" He bent and blew in her ear.

With a nervous laugh, she tried to push him away, but he turned her to him and kissed her, loving the way she tasted and smelled.

He raised his head. "You taste good enough to eat. Do I have time for a bite before supper?" He leered at her, wiggling his eyebrows.

She bent and picked up the spoon. "Not tonight, I'm afraid."

Frowning at her response, he tucked her to him and rested his chin on the top of her head. Hell, she didn't have to be in the mood just because he was. With Julia, he was randy as a goat all the time. "The fruit is ready to ship. I'm going to start packing it up tomorrow."

"Good. I'm glad."

She wasn't as pleased as he thought she'd be. He pulled back and examined her. "What's wrong? Do you have another headache?"

She turned away and wiped her hands on her apron. "Serge was here earlier."

A warning sounded, but he chose not to address it.

Serge's visit could mean a lot of things. "What was on his mind?"

She fidgeted with her apron strings. "He was sorry about the barn. He didn't know it had burned because he's been in San Francisco." She opened the pie safe and pulled out some buns. "He'll send some of his men to help you rebuild it."

"How generous of him," he mumbled, unable to dredge up the proper enthusiasm.

She plunked the plate of buns down on the table so hard, one bounced off and landed on the floor. "Well, I thought it was." Her eyes snapped with anger.

He picked up the bun and tossed it onto the counter. "What's wrong with you?"

Her courage appeared to waver, for she shook her head and moved toward the dark pantry. "Nothing."

He followed her, putting his hands on her shoulders. "Tell me what it is, Julia."

She paused, then raised her chin and stared at him. "Serge told me you're trying to sell off some of my land. You know that's not what Papa wanted."

So that was it. Of course, she knew only half the story. Why wasn't he surprised it was his half brother who had come to her, bearing the news? Wolf wanted to give her an explanation. He could tell she wanted that, too, for there was a beseeching look in her eyes. He rubbed the back of his neck and swore. He wasn't ready to tell her. He thought he'd have more time to work things out, but for now he only had his suspicions. "I see."

She began to pace. "Is it true?"

He inhaled, forcing air out between his lips. "What else did he say?"

She stopped, jamming her fists on her hips. "He

thinks your comment about Papa killing himself is ridiculous. So does his mother."

A slow burn crept into Wolf's chest. "And I suppose one brief talk with the Henleys and you're ready to believe them, rather than me."

Rounding on him, she announced, "Believe you? How can I believe you if you won't talk to me?" She pressed her palms to her temples. "I've known Serge a long, long time, McCloud. He's a good friend. Maybe even my best friend. And while I was growing up without a mother of my own, Meredith Henley tried her best to fill the void, and—"

His bark of laughter stopped her. "Meredith Henley a mother figure? Spare me, Julia."

She glared at him. "I'm surprised you know Meredith well enough to form an opinion one way or another."

Ah, yes. His mother was one more thing he hadn't told Julia about. He felt her slipping away, but now wasn't the time to explain how Meredith fit into his life. And he needed proof about the water before he could tell her anything. "I'm full of surprises."

"Yes." She came to him and put her hand on his chest, her eyes filled with uncertainty. "I'm beginning to understand that. But I can't dismiss the Henleys as if what they think doesn't count, McCloud. And you didn't answer my question. Did you approach Jake Crawford about buying some of my land?"

It upset him that she'd found out so quickly. By offering each of the ranchers a piece of prime riverfront property, he'd hoped to smoke out the person who was diverting the water. If someone wanted the land badly enough, they would jump at the chance to buy. Crawford had wanted it, all right, but he told Wolf he'd have to check with Julia first.

Wolf knew the rule: If you were a solid citizen and you were white, you didn't do business with breeds. He hadn't expected Crawford to run to Henley, but it didn't surprise him that Henley beat a path to Julia's door, just to announce her husband's apparent betrayal.

He wasn't sure if all of this would lead to Amos's killer, but he had a hunch it would. And his hunches were usually good. As for now, he only had suspicions. And they wouldn't sit well with his wife.

"And if I did?" He hated being abrupt with her when what he really wanted to do was hold her and tell her everything would be fine.

"Why would you do that without asking me?"

She was so crestfallen, he couldn't bear to look at her. He examined his boots. "Believe me, Julia, I had my reasons."

"Were you going to share them with me?"

"You wouldn't believe me."

"Try me, McCloud. Help me understand," she pleaded, close to tears. "I want to have faith in you, can't you see that? But how can I if you won't talk to me?"

He walked to the door, then stopped, knowing he had to say something, even if it hurt her. "If I tell you what I'm doing and why, you'll think I'm crazy."

A sprout of hope blossomed in Julia's chest. "Better that I think you're crazy than to think you're doing something deceitful behind my back."

McCloud expelled a shuddering sigh. "I don't have proof."

"Proof of what?"

"That someone is diverting the river water to their own land. That's why the level is so low."

She frowned. "Diverting the water? How?"

"I'm not sure yet. But I intend to find out."

She pressed her hands together and brought them to her lips. "How were you going to do this?"

"I had a hunch that if I offered each of the surrounding ranchers a piece of land that *was* on the river, I could discover who it was. I had no intentions of selling it, Julia. It was bait."

Julia digested his words. "Why didn't you come and tell me what you were going to do?"

"I didn't want to worry you." His gaze rested on her.

She swung away. "Don't treat me this way, McCloud. I'm perfectly capable of helping you make decisions about *our* land. I'd gladly have helped you trap the scofflaw."

"Even if it were Serge Henley?"

Surprised, she turned and stared at him. "Serge? Why, that's ridiculous. Whatever makes you think it's Serge?"

McCloud crossed to the window. "This is why I didn't say anything, Julia. I wanted to be certain of my facts before I mentioned it at all."

"But ... but *Serge?* I've known him for years and years, McCloud. He couldn't—" She saw him tense and understood what she was doing. All right. Let him suspect Serge. Let him suspect Meredith, for that matter. When the truth came out, he would be wrong. Until then, there was nothing she could do to convince him.

"What are you going to do now?"

He turned and came toward her, stopping in front of her, so close that she felt his body heat. It affected her the usual way, causing her knees to go weak and her heart to beat a frantic cadence in her chest. She wondered how something that felt so right could possibly be so very wrong.

"I'm not sure. But I'll tell you this much. Jake Crawford was interested in buying the land, but he told me flat out that he wouldn't consider it unless he talked with you first. That leads me to believe that he isn't the one responsible. But he also told your friend Serge pretty damned fast, Julia, and Serge was on your doorstep, heralding the news within hours of my conversation with Crawford."

She toyed with the buttons on his shirt, then smoothed her hand over his chest. "To me, that only means that Serge was concerned."

McCloud moved out of her reach, and her hand fell to her side. A wall was beginning to form between them, and until the situation with the land was settled, nothing could be done about it. He felt he was right, but she knew he was wrong.

"I know, Julia. I know." He went to the door that led to the rest of the house. "That's what makes this so damned hard to do."

She watched him leave, hating to see the rift growing between them, but unable to see any way to avoid it.

She massaged her head, hoping to ward off another headache. She guessed if there was any consolation at all, it was that he hadn't lied to her.

Wolf didn't sleep. He didn't even bother going to bed, for his conversation with Julia kept him awake. He'd hoped to have answers before she even heard what he was up to, but that had been a pipe dream. And he'd known what her reaction would be. In her heart, she thought he was wrong to suspect Serge Henley. But he knew he wasn't wrong. He knew Henley was involved one way or another.

Julia considered his half brother her best friend. Wolf clenched his fist, slamming it against his palm. He'd have the Nancy-boy's balls on a string before he'd let him hurt his wife. But once the truth was out, there would be no way to protect her from it.

And now he had to go back to Jake Crawford and eat crow. He needed an ally. If he explained to Crawford what he suspected, maybe he could elicit his help in catching the "scofflaw." He smiled. What a word. Leave it to his cerebral wife to come up with it.

Before dawn he went outside and did his chores, then hooked Baptiste to the wagon and headed out to get the fruit ready for shipping.

It was early afternoon when he finally returned, the wagon filled with crates of dried fruit. He could have left for Martinez from the shed, but felt Julia deserved to know how long he'd be gone. As he rode into the yard, he noticed a buggy in front of the house.

Curious, he walked over and peered inside. A face, old, frail, and encased in a fur hood, stared back at him. Her eyes lit up, and she smiled. "You're the breed," she said without preamble. Her voice had the whisper of dried leaves and held just a hint of an accent.

Wolf felt a tightening excitement in his chest. "Who are you?"

Her mouth lifted into a half smile, creating fragile lines in her papery skin. "You know who I am."

He knew. She was merely an older version of his mother, but her eyes were kinder. "Yes. I guess I do. Is Meredith in the house with Julia?"

"Does it worry you that she is?"

He raised an eyebrow. *"Should* it worry me?"

"Perhaps." She gave him a canny smile, one which caused her parchmentlike skin to crease into the mink trim of her hood. Her eyes were a piercing black, flashing youth and intelligence despite the wrinkles time had forced upon her. "I saw you the day you came to see Meredith. I watched you from the window."

"And you knew who I was?"

Her gaze didn't waver. "From the moment you rode in."

The curse, no doubt. Wolf glanced at the house. "How long have you been here?"

"Not long." She reached out and grabbed his arm with surprising strength in spite of fingers that were twisted from years of toil and joints swollen with arthritis. "You're the one I buried."

He expelled a quiet, humorless laugh. "But I didn't die. Disappointed?"

She leaned forward. "No, I'm glad." There was a conspiratorial gleam in her eyes.

"Where is he?"

"So, she told you about the other one." She grinned, wispy brackets appearing on either side of her mouth.

"Where is he?" he repeated, sensing that she had to know something.

She shook her head. "I do not know."

He felt a crushing disappointment. It must have showed, because she grinned and shook a crooked finger at him.

"But I remember the name of the man who took him."

Behind him, Wolf heard the door open.

"Mother!"

Wolf turned from the buggy as Meredith Henley

scurried down the steps. She swept past him and stepped into the seat beside her elderly mother. Meredith glared at him.

"Mother isn't in her right mind most of the time." Her voice had a hard, impersonal edge to it. "I wouldn't put much stock in anything she says."

The old woman's eyes sparkled with life and a hint of amusement

Not in her right mind, my ass. Wolf took her hand, shocked that it was merely skin and bone. His eyes held the question he didn't dare ask.

As Meredith prepared to drive off, the old woman bent close to the window. The buggy pulled away just as the woman whispered a name, the word caught up in the sound of creaking wheels and gravel.

But Wolf heard it, just the same. His excitement mounted. Fletcher. She'd said, "Fletcher."

He watched the buggy disappear, then turned toward the house. Julia stood at the window, dropping the curtain when she discovered he'd seen her.

There was a squeezing pain in the vicinity of his heart. He hadn't been the same since the day he'd first seen Julia, and he hadn't known why. Her inability to believe in him made it clear. He was beginning to care, and he wanted her trust. Hell, he'd *cared* from the beginning, otherwise he wouldn't have let Amos force him into a marriage he'd known Julia didn't want.

He'd never loved a woman. He wasn't even sure what that meant. All he knew was that the last two weeks of his life had been more than he'd ever hoped to have. He should be satisfied he'd had that much, he told himself, but the thought of losing Julia dug at him like a dull knife. He couldn't stand the idea of never hearing her sing to the baby, or never again watching her loving smile whenever she picked Mary-mae up and cuddled her close. She was an exemplary mother to a child who wasn't even hers. He could only imagine the kind of mother she'd be to children of her own.

A knot of longing twisted inside him, for he realized that marriage to Julia was only part of the pleasure he'd thought would be denied him. For her to bear his children was the other half of the pleasurable picture, and he wanted it all. Damn it to hell, he wanted it all.

The things she'd unconsciously done for his life went without saying. She'd given his life meaning. Purpose. Value. To never know those things again made him ache. To never hear her joyous cries of ecstasy when they made love sent waves of longing through him.

Yeah, he should be satisfied he had memories of those things. He wasn't. Before all hell had broken loose, she'd begun to care for him. Because of that, he would fight for her. He just didn't have the ammunition. Yet.

She stepped outside, a shawl around her shoulders. He saw something in her eyes—pain, hurt, something—before she glanced away. What had Meredith told her?

"I have to take the fruit to Martinez." They'd talked about making a trip out of it. She'd promised a picnic. He'd promised to make love to her under the trees. None of that would happen now. There would be no intimacy until this whole thing with the land and the river and her father's death was settled. He wondered how she would handle the truth.

She pulled her shawl closer and stepped to the edge of the porch. "Will you be back?"

What rubbish had Meredith filled her head with, anyway? "Is that what you want, Julia? Do you want me to leave?"

She closed her eyes and pinched her lips together. "I didn't say that."

"Then why did you ask?" His jaw was tight.

Releasing a shaky breath, she shook her head. "I don't know."

He smiled, knowing it was filled with contempt. "Did you think I'd sell the fruit and not come back? Is that it?" He shouldn't have been surprised. After a visit from Meredith Henley, it was a wonder Julia didn't carve out his heart with a butcher knife and feed it to the animals. A fire raged in his gut.

"No. I don't know." She was contrite. "Not really. I . . ." She caught her lower lip between her teeth and studied the steps. Suddenly she went inside, returning with a basket. "Here," she offered, handing it to him. "It should be enough to feed you the rest of the day."

He let the basket dangle from his fingers. "I'll be back in time for morning chores."

Nodding briefly, she turned to go. "I'm having dinner with Meredith tonight. As long as you won't be here, I might stay over until morning."

That wasn't good news. Another visit with Meredith Henley, and his wife could be lost to him forever. "Julia?"

She turned, her face filled with expectation. "Yes?"

"What did Meredith have to say?"

Her shoulders visibly slumped and she sighed. "She said you'd ask me that. That you'd want to know."

"What in the hell does that mean?"

Her eyes were filled with confusion, or so he wanted to believe. He didn't want to think it was disillusionment. "She said all of your energy is misguided and misdirected. And—" Julia ran her hand along the railing.

He nearly stopped breathing. "Yes?"

"Oh, McCloud," she said on a rapid breath, "I'm trying to be fair. I'm trying to be rational about this, but—"

"That's all I ask, Julia," he interrupted, unwilling to hear the rest of her thought. "That's all I ask."

She went inside and closed the door firmly behind her. To Wolf it felt like she was shutting him out of her life.

Julia watched him leave, a permanent ache stamped on her heart. Expelling a shaky sigh, she turned from the window and went to the settee in front of the fire. She sat, her feet curled under her, and studied the flames.

Meredith's words still rang in her ears. *Your man is trying to find answers where there aren't any, Julia. He's looking in the wrong places. Serge and I love you. We'd never do anything that would hurt you. We are your dearest friends in the world, Julia. We want you to be happy. How can you be happy with a man who goes off half-cocked, blaming your neighbors for something he might well have done himself?*

Was that McCloud? Going off half-cocked, as Meredith suggested? It didn't seem like him, but then, how well did she know him? She wanted to trust him. Perhaps he didn't love her, but things had been so perfect between them. Until now. Closing her eyes, she rested her head on the sofa back. It was hard to be sensible when Meredith was in charge.

Rising from the settee, she went into the bedroom to prepare for her visit to Meredith's. Julia had to delve deep into her wealth of pragmatism not to be swayed by Meredith's reasoning, for Meredith had no ax to grind. Although she knew that Meredith had once wanted her to marry Serge, they both knew that would never happen. They'd been friends and neighbors for a long time. Never had there been cause for her not to trust Meredith's judgment.

Weary, Julia regretted promising to join them for dinner. All she wanted to do was undress and curl up in front of the fire. *Snug in McCloud's arms.*

Shaking off visions of him, she went to change her clothes.

✶ 14 ✶

Julia hitched the geldings to the buggy and left for the Henleys while it was light. She'd packed a small valise with a few of her things and some changes for Marymae, knowing that they would stay the night. And McCloud had promised to be back before morning chores. Right now, she felt that was too soon. She wasn't ready to face him.

Just thinking of him brought about changes in her body. Not just physical changes, though she'd loved what they'd had together. And not just emotional changes, even though every part of her was rife with emotion when she thought about him.

She also wanted to defend him. But as she'd listened to Meredith and Serge, who told her that Wolf had no idea what he was doing, she found her defenses—for him and for herself—wavering. Both Meredith and Serge had an answer for everything, and on an intellectual level, they made perfect sense. While her intuition told her McCloud was not the man the Henleys said he was, her intellect began to convince her otherwise.

When she was alone, as she was now, and had no one to influence her reasoning, she thought about McCloud's explanation of what he was doing. She desperately wanted to trust him, but what he was thinking seemed too farfetched to her. Meredith made a convincing argument that McCloud was just out to take from her what he could, then leave.

Julia didn't want to accept that, but a niggle of doubt remained, nevertheless. In her mind she strived to be fair, because in her heart she loved him. McCloud had plumbed deeply into her emotions, and once they were tapped, her pragmatism disappeared. But from experience, she knew that the follies of the heart should never win out over the pragmatism of the mind. She'd long ago learned that it wasn't safe to trust those poignant, tender feelings.

Remembering how close they were to McCloud's cabin, Julia flicked the reins over the geldings, anxious to see how much progress he'd made on the building. An odd feeling of dread seeped through her as she approached it, for something wasn't right. She pulled the horses to a stop. In fact, something was dreadfully wrong.

Pressing her hand to her throat, she found her pulse thrumming heavily. "What happened?" she said aloud, her fingers moving to her mouth as she studied the burned-out shell.

The geldings jerked at the reins, and she pulled on them, making soothing sounds to gentle them. She left the buggy and walked to the rubble. With nervous fingers she reached out and touched the charred wood. It was dead and cold. The fire was old. Why hadn't he told her?

There was no reason to keep it a secret from her, unless he'd—

She pushed the remainder of the idea away.

Anxious to get to the Henleys, she hurried to the buggy, hoping to remove all thoughts of McCloud from her mind. But she knew that wasn't likely. Now and forever, whatever the outcome, McCloud would be in her head. And in her heart. Lord help her, but she was a stupid, stupid fool.

They were seated in Meredith's opulent study, having an excellent cup of after-dinner coffee. Julia wished she could appreciate the exotic aroma, but her thoughts were elsewhere.

Meredith returned after settling her mother down for the night. "I'm sorry, dear. Mother gets so quarrelsome when she hasn't had her medication." She uttered a hopeless sigh. "She's gone 'round the bend, I'm afraid."

Julia gave her a polite smile, but said nothing. She rather enjoyed Rosa Columbo. And she didn't believe for a minute the woman had lost her mind. She couldn't understand why Meredith kept harping on it.

"You were saying something about your breed's cabin."

Julia automatically bristled at the aspersion. "His name is McCloud, Meredith. Wolf McCloud."

Meredith raised her chin and pursed her lips. "Of course. It came out wrong, dear. I'm sorry. Anyway," she added, settling herself into the seat beside Julia, "what's this about his cabin?"

"I rode past it on my way here and discovered it had burned to the ground. It was nothing but rubble and ashes. And I don't think it just happened, either, because everything was cold."

Meredith poured a shot of brandy into her coffee

and made a "tsking" sound with her tongue. "That's a shame. A real shame."

"I suppose it could have been lightning," Julia suggested.

"But dear, you say it doesn't look recent."

Julia shook her head. "It isn't. And we haven't had a lightning storm since the night our barn was struck."

Meredith glanced at Serge, who had just entered the room. "I suppose it's conceivable that lightning could have struck his cabin, too."

"Yes." Julia gave her a slow nod. "But do you know how unlikely that is? And even so, why didn't he tell me about it? Why keep it a secret?"

Meredith took a long sip of her coffee, put her cup on the table in front of her, and gave Julia a sympathetic look. "Why, indeed."

She reached over and squeezed Julia's hand with her fingers, then clasped it. Meredith's hand was clammy. It gave Julia the shivers, but she didn't remove her own.

"I know you've been hearing some awfully negative things about your new husband, Julia, and most of them coming from Serge and me. But these things must be said. And since Serge doesn't want to hurt your feelings further, I guess it's up to me."

Julia tugged her hand out from under Meredith's and briefly closed her eyes, dreading what Meredith would say. She didn't have the energy to stop her.

"Isn't it feasible," Meredith began, "that he burned down the cabin himself? That the lightning striking the barn gave him the perfect opportunity to get rid of that awful shack he'd promised to live in?"

Julia's heartache intensified. That was exactly what she'd stopped herself from thinking when she saw the rubble. "But why? Why would he do such a thing?"

"Julia, my dear," Meredith said around an exaggerated sigh. "What an innocent you are in the ways of men."

Julia felt a kernel of anger coil inside her. "What do you mean?"

"Must I spell it out for you?" She reached for Julia's hand once more, but Julia put it in her lap. "I'm sorry if this is blunt, dear, but it's possible that he deliberately set fire to his own cabin, knowing he could blame it on lightning, in order to stay in the house." She paused, then added, "And in your bed."

Julia felt color stain her cheeks. She kept her eyes down, fussing with the pleats of her skirt with nervous fingers.

"So," Meredith said, her voice soft. "He *has* been in your bed."

"Mother!" Serge was on his feet, his hands balled into fists. "Must you be so crass?"

She glared at her son. "If I'm crass, as you so eloquently put it, it's only because I'm concerned about Julia. This ... this *breed* has filled her head with all sorts of ridiculous nonsense. He's a scoundrel. An opportunist. Why, that day he was here, he—"

"He came here? When?" Julia was alert, interested.

Meredith swept the question away with an impatient hand. "Weeks ago, dear. Weeks ago. Anyway—"

"But why?"

"That's of no consequence. What's more important is that he could have coerced Amos into putting him in the will. How do we know he didn't take a gun to Amos's head himself, just to get him out of the way, then come to you, offering to help after he killed him? Playing on your weakness and your grief? Breeds can be very deceptive and convincing when it comes to getting what they want."

Julia found it difficult to catch her breath, and her heart threatened to splinter in her chest. Tears, stark and painful, blurred her vision as McCloud's credibility was decimated right before her eyes.

She stood, amazed that her knees locked. "I can't listen to any more of this."

Meredith was at her side in an instant. "I'm so sorry, dear Julia, but these things had to be said." She drew her into her arms and gave her a reassuring hug. "I don't want you to think I'm trying to fill your head with all of this just because I've wanted you for a daughter-in-law for more years than I can remember."

Julia needed to leave Meredith's embrace, but had no strength to do so.

"I've dreamed of the empire we could have if we combined our lands," Meredith crooned. "We would own the valley. We would *rule* the valley." She drew back, studying Julia with a look of concern. "It's not too late, dear."

Julia tensed. "What do you mean?"

Meredith walked her to the door. "Just sleep on it, Julia. Remember *everything* I've said, and we'll talk more in the morning. Now, go up to bed. There's a mild sedative on the nightstand. I urge you to take it. It will help you sleep."

Julia dragged herself up the stairs, anxious to be alone. She tried not to let Meredith's words influence her. She wanted to be fair to McCloud, but what if what Meredith said *was* true? But if McCloud had killed her father, she thought, why would he say that Papa's death was anything but an accident? Even suggesting that Papa had been killed could point the finger at him. Why bother, when the sheriff himself had ruled it accidental?

She reached the dark landing, trying to comprehend everything she'd learned. As she rounded the banister on the way to her room, something moved in the shadows. Startled, she clasped her hand to her breast.

"Oh, Grandmama Rosa." Meredith's mother stepped out in front of her, looking like a whispery apparition in her long, white nightgown. "You startled me."

Rosa Columbo touched her arm. "Listen to your heart, girl."

Had the old woman read her mind? Julia wondered. "That's easier said than done, Grandmama."

Rosa Columbo pulled Julia farther into the darkness, toward her room. "They'll have you believe I'm crazy," she murmured on a harsh whisper. "My daughter can be very convincing. Just trust your heart, girl. No one else."

Then the old woman left her, disappearing into the gloomy depths of the upstairs like a wisp of smoke.

Confused, Julia stepped into her room, grateful a lamp was lit at the bedside. The flame flickered, sending macabre shadows over the walls and ceiling. Shivering, she rubbed her arms, feeling like the doomed heroine in some gloomy Gothic novel.

Trust your heart. Advice she longed to embrace. With a sigh weighted in frustration, she crossed to the crib and glanced down at Marymae, whose thumb was firmly planted in her mouth. Julia smoothed the baby's wispy golden hair off her temple and felt a brief tunneling of warmth in her stomach.

"Whatever happens, sweet girl," she whispered, "I'll always have you."

She undressed, turned out the lamp and crawled into bed. Unwilling to take the sedative Meredith had offered, she found herself wide awake, her mind hurling images at her so fast, she could almost feel them.

At the head of the pack was Meredith's admission that McCloud had been to see her. What reason would he have to call on Meredith? She wondered why he hadn't told her.

The window seat drew her. She rose and walked to it, curling up on the upholstered seat. Moonlight sifted in through the filmy curtains. She could see a flickering light inside the dark outline of the barn. Tensing, she drew closer to the window, pulling the curtains aside.

Cupping her hands on either side of her face, she peered into the night. Two horses were led from the barn; two riders mounted and walked the horses over the gravel, then kicked them into a gallop when they reached the grass.

Julia continued to study the darkness long after the riders were gone. She missed McCloud. She missed what they'd had together before all of this happened. She prayed McCloud would sort out what was happening and learn the truth so they could get on with their life together.

Wolf allowed Baptiste to pick his way over the uneven ground, trusting the black's judgment in the darkness over his own. They traveled near the river, for he heard the faint gurgling of water over the rocks. Having arrived at the ranch and found Julia gone, as she said she would be, he discovered he couldn't sleep. Knowing she was spending the evening with Meredith Henley had compounded his insomnia.

He needed to prove his point before Meredith succeeded in turning Julia against him for good. He'd taken a chance when he faced Crawford and admitted that the land was just bait for a trap. For all he knew, Crawford could have been as crooked as Henley. But after talking with him, Wolf knew he wasn't. Thank God for his instincts.

It had been a lot to ask of Julia—to trust him though he could not tell her anything. She wasn't a woman who trusted easily. He sensed that she'd had her trust tested before, and whoever tested it had broken it.

No doubt Meredith had further influenced Julia's feelings, preying on her emotions, dredging up memories of her father. It was even likely that Meredith tried to blame him for everything, Wolf thought. It would be easy to do. Julia had said it herself. He was the stranger among them.

Baptiste stopped and tensed. Wolf became alert as well. He reached down and stroked the mount's neck and listened. There were subtle sounds in the distance.

Wolf dismounted and tied the horse to the low-slung branch of an oak tree, then crept toward the noise.

Flattening himself behind a thicket of dense chaparral, he peered through the brush, squinting into the distance. He saw two men. There was only a half moon; he couldn't see who they were. He heard them talking, but wasn't close enough to hear what they said. But from the sounds brought to him on the night breeze, he knew what they were doing. A burst of excitement sent his blood racing.

Still on his stomach, he began to crawl, using the night and the dense brush as cover. Instinct took over, and he moved with the stealth of one born to it, sliding across rocks and prickly grass until he was within earshot.

Each man shoveled dirt from the trench, tossing it on the grass, spreading it to avoid a mound. So, Wolf thought, tensing. Amos had been right.

"How much farther do we have to dig this damned thing, and how many more do we have to start?"

Wolf recalled the voice, if not the name. He was one of Henley's men. The one with the light hair and chipped front teeth who had approached him as he'd ridden up that day. He never forgot a voice.

"Christ, Frank, we dig until I say we stop. Why do you question my orders?"

The brief lifting of Wolf's eyebrows was the only evidence of recognition. He wasn't surprised to discover his half brother behind this. But he wasn't sure if it was Serge's plan or if Serge, too, took orders from someone else—like his mother.

"It'd be a hell of a lot easier to do this in the daytime, Henley. We'd get done faster." The man cursed. "We've been at this since last fall, and you ain't paid me for none of it."

Serge stopped working, and in the faint moonlight Wolf could see him leaning on his shovel.

"I can't get my hands on the cash right now."

"That's what you said two months ago. I ain't a patient man, Henley."

"Well, learn some patience, damnit. And we can't do this during the day, you fool."

"I ain't no fool! Don't call me a fool!"

Serge cursed. "All right, so you aren't a fool."

Both men had stopped, and the night air was so quiet, Wolf could hear them breathing.

"Christ. This is damned hard work. It would've been easier to just marry the girl, Henley. Then the land that butted up against the river would've been yours for the taking and we wouldn't have to sneak around at night, digging these damned ditches."

Serge expelled a disparaging laugh. "Two things wrong with that, Frank. First, she up and married that half-breed crook while I was back East. It did my heart good to tell her he was trying to sell her land. Second—well, you know the second reason."

Frank Barnes snickered. "Hell, if it were me, I would've married her anyway. And if that sister would've stayed home, I'd have screwed her on the side."

Serge laughed again, an unpleasant sound. "You already did."

"How'd you know that?" Frank's voice held a threatening edge.

"Everybody knows, Frank. Everybody with any sense knows that baby belongs to you, even if the wrong woman is taking care of it."

Barnes spat out a curse. "I tried to do 'em both, but plain old Julia caught on quicker'n I thought she would."

Wolf tensed at the slur. He clenched his fist and dug it slowly into the ground, imagining it was Frank Barnes's face.

"That's the only thing I regret," Serge said as he started to dig.

"What's that?"

"That I had to do anything bad to Julia. But it couldn't be helped. After all, Amos had discovered the north ditch."

"That's another thing. I ain't been paid for that, either."

"And if you don't stop harping on it, you never will. Do you have any idea how easy it would be for me to turn you in for his murder?"

"But you ordered it!"

"Who are they going to believe, Frank? You or me? After all, *you* pulled the trigger. I wasn't even here."

Frank Barnes grumbled something Wolf couldn't hear, then, "I want my money, or else."

"Don't threaten me, Frank. You can't outsmart me and you know it. You'll get paid when I feel like paying you."

Wolf had heard enough. Discovery had been easy. Proving it would be another matter, and he couldn't do it alone.

As he rode into the yard, Crawford's hound bayed from the porch. A fluttering light was lit inside, and soon Crawford stepped outside.

"Who's there?"

"McCloud."

Crawford came toward him holding a lantern. His trousers were pulled hastily over his nightshirt, held up by one suspender. "What do you want? It's after midnight."

Wolf had been relieved he could trust Crawford, but knew the man was only being civil because of Julia. "I need your help."

"Couldn't it wait until morning?" The hound lumbered over and flopped down on Crawford's boot.

"By morning I want the trap to be set."

Crawford leaned closer. "Trap?"

Wolf nodded. "I know who'd been diverting the water, and how they're doing it."

Crawford headed for the barn. "Follow me. We can talk inside."

✦ 15 ✦

The saloon was half full of ranchers, and it wasn't even noon. Crawford had revealed that Frank Barnes was a regular morning customer. Wolf sat with his back to the wall; Crawford faced him. There was a shot glass and a bottle of whiskey on the table, but they each drank coffee.

"Are you sure this is going to work?" Crawford poured a shot of whiskey into his cup.

"It's got to. Did you talk to the sheriff before you came?"

Crawford nodded. "He'll wait for you to come for him."

"Thanks. I don't think he would have believed me."

Crawford took a slurp of his coffee. "I'd wondered why the water level was so low. Hell, I've been through worse droughts than this, and that river has never been so dry."

"Now you know why." Wolf tipped his hat and sat up as Frank Barnes sauntered through the door. "He just walked in."

He watched Barnes slide a coin across the bar and accept a drink, drawing his gaze away when Barnes scanned the room. He stopped at their table. Wolf leaned across to Crawford, pretending to listen as Crawford spoke.

"He's on his way over."

"Let's do it."

"I tell you, Crawford," Wolf began, raising his voice, "I can get you a real sweet deal on that land."

"Sweet deal, hell. It isn't worth half what you're asking for it."

Wolf acted incredulous. "It's on the river, you fool." He pretended not to notice Barnes, who stood nearby.

Crawford appeared thoughtful and scratched his chin. "I don't know. You're sure Julia knows what you're doing?"

Wolf slammed his fist on the table. "It's my land now. I can do what I want with it, and to hell with her." He scowled at Crawford and poured a shot of whiskey into his coffee. He could see Barnes out of the corner of his eye.

"What do you want, Barnes? We're making a deal here."

Frank Barnes snickered and took the empty chair, scooting it close. "For that piece of land by the river?"

Wolf rose halfway out of his chair. "Get the hell out of here. I'm not bargaining with you *or* your boss."

Crawford put his hand on Wolf's arm. "Settle down, McCloud." He turned to Barnes. "Is there something wrong with that piece of land, Frank?"

Barnes moved his chair closer to Crawford. "You was really gonna do business with this breed?"

Crawford expelled a heavy sigh. "I need water, Frank. Amos hogged that land all his life. Wouldn't even listen to an offer. If it's available, I'm going to buy it."

"Even if the old man's will said none of his land was to be sold?" Barnes asked.

Crawford took another slurp of his coffee as Barnes eyed the bottle on the table. He shoved the shot glass to him.

"Hey," Wolf snarled, reaching for the bottle. "I paid for that."

Crawford caught his arm. "Let him have a drink. By the way, McCloud, did you know about this will?"

"Yeah, I know about it. So what? Listen, I've got that sorry woman's bills to pay, plus a few debts of my own. If I don't get them paid off, you might as well kiss my ass good-bye." He sank low in the chair, crossed his arms over his chest and sulked.

Crawford tossed Barnes a private look and shrugged. "Are you sure Amos didn't want to sell that land?"

"I heard it from a good source, Mr. Crawford." Barnes was anxious to please the upstanding rancher, especially when it appeared Crawford was interested in what he had to say. He poured himself another shot of whiskey, downed it, then poured another, throwing that one down, too.

Wolf snorted. "From Julia's precious friend Serge, no doubt. I don't like him sniffing around my wife. Tell him that."

Barnes leaned toward Wolf. "Hey, I don't have to tell him nothin', breed."

Wolf rose up out of his chair again, pretending to weave. "Is that 'cause you and the Nancy-boy got something going?"

Barnes leaped to his feet, the chair clattering to the

floor behind him. They were glaring at each other when Crawford stepped between them.

"Settle down. Dammit, settle down. Frank, we *were* having a private conversation."

The men sat down again, and Barnes tossed back another whiskey. Wolf wondered how much it took to get him drunk.

"If you got money to buy land, you have money for some information, Mr. Crawford."

"Hey!" Wolf grabbed Frank's arm. "This is *my* deal, Barnes."

Barnes shrugged off Wolf's hand as if his touch were contaminated. He turned his back on him. "Well, Mr. Crawford?"

"What kind of information, Frank?"

He motioned over his shoulder. "Does he have to be here?"

"We're negotiating. He stays."

Frank moved close, as if doing so would shut Wolf out. "You can buy all the land along the river you want, Mr. Crawford. But you won't get the water."

Wolf, tensed, but kept quiet. He'd tipped his chair against the wall and closed his eyes, pretending to sleep.

"No?" Crawford looked surprised. "Why not?"

"We got a deal?"

Crawford leaned closer. "How do I know you'll tell me the truth, and not make up some cock-and-bull story?"

"Because if I tell you what I know, I'll need to leave town. And I don't want you sendin' someone after me."

Wolf listened carefully, while making occasional snoring sounds.

"How much do you want, Frank?"

"Five thousand dollars."

Crawford whistled. "That's a hell of a lot of money."

"What I got to say is worth every penny, Mr. Crawford."

"Why are you willing to sell me this information?"

"Because my current employer is an asshole. I done things for him I ain't proud of, but I done 'em anyways, 'cause he promised to pay me. Now he's tryin' to wiggle out of his obligation."

"All right, Frank. Shoot."

Wolf listened as Barnes spilled his guts about the trenches. Once he got going, it would have been hard to shut him up even if they'd wanted to. For an extra five thousand dollars, he pinned Amos Larson's death on Serge, not mentioning his own involvement, of course.

Wolf let the chair slam to the floor and pretended to come awake, startled. He yawned, rubbed his hands over his face and stood, weaving as he did so. "I gotta get me some fresh air." He stumbled from the saloon and went directly to the sheriff.

Julia stood at the window, watching Serge's men work on her barn, grateful Frank Barnes wasn't among them. McCloud was nowhere in sight. She hadn't seen him since yesterday afternoon, when he'd left with the fruit, but she knew he'd been there; the cows had been milked and the cream skimmed. There were also a few eggs in a small basket on the table.

She clutched her father's letter to her chest, the letter McCloud had brought with him that night he'd returned. She'd come across it while she searched for some old clothes to cut into quilt squares.

Pressing her forehead against the windowpane, she

closed her eyes and sighed. How could she have forgotten those words? Words that had angered her so then, gave her hope now, and also made her realize how much she missed the man who'd written them.

I know you think I've betrayed you ... I know how you think you feel about him, honey, but give him a chance. Deep down, he's a good man. I would never do anything in the world to hurt you. Please, please remember that.

The wrinkled, tearstained paper brought back memories of the morning she'd first read it. There was no way McCloud could have forced Papa to write that kind of letter.

After Meredith and Serge had continually tried to convince her that Papa had been sick in the head, she'd started to believe it herself. They were very persuasive. But Papa hadn't gone soft in the head. She may not have wanted to see that he was dying; it was far easier to rationalize and tell herself that he would get better. Toward the end, he was distant and depressed, but never once did he appear confused. And never had he displayed any bizarre behavior, at least none that she'd seen.

She missed him. Tears threatened, but she pushed them away. She'd had the urge to cry much too often lately. It wasn't like her at all. Scolding herself, she took a deep breath. She was being selfish. Papa was in a good place now. After so many years of separation, he was with Mama. And he wouldn't be old, or tired or sick. He'd be young and strong, like he was the day he and Mama had married.

A quivering smile spread her lips and she felt a weight off her chest. She could let it go. "Be happy for me, Papa," she whispered, looking at the sky.

"Things are far from perfect, but I love him. And you were right; McCloud is a good man."

She drew her gaze to the barn just as McCloud rode into the yard. Her heart raced, and she knew she had to go to him. Tell him she'd been wrong to let others influence her thinking. Beg him to forgive her for not believing in him. Not trusting him. She felt he pointed the finger of guilt at the wrong party, but the truth would come out soon, she was sure of it.

After checking on Marymae, she threw her wrapper on and went outside. Her eyes lifted to the mountain and the sloping hills that led up to it. Everything was awash with flowering mustard and orange poppies. Spring. She felt a pinch of excitement. Everything came alive in the spring, and she loved it.

As she rounded the side of the house, she noticed a buggy behind the hedgerow of fire-berry bushes that shielded the house from the north wind. She slowed her steps.

"You might just as well leave. Haven't you done enough damage around here?"

Recognizing Meredith's voice, Julia frowned and crept closer.

"Not half as much as you've done."

Julia's heart slid into her stomach. McCloud?

"Me? I've only tried to prevent her from making the mistake of believing you're here for her, instead of for yourself."

McCloud muttered an oath. "Oh, I know what you're trying to do. I've told you I'm no threat to your efforts for power. You've undermined yourself without any help from me."

"My, such a cryptic statement coming from someone on whom I could so very easily pin Amos Larson's death."

Julia's eyes widened and her hands flew to her mouth. Her heart was beating so loudly, she was surprised they couldn't hear it.

But her husband only chuckled. "What's the matter, Meredith? Did I come along and pluck the spinster from your clutches, ruining all your plans?"

Julia's heart dropped further and she felt nauseated. She ordered her feet to move, but they were rooted to the ground.

"Yes, if you must know, I had plans for her and Serge. I wanted—"

He interrupted her with a hoot of laughter. "I know what you wanted. And you would have done it, wouldn't you? You would have forever bound Julia to a man who could never love her the way a woman should be loved."

"And I suppose you can?"

Julia held her breath, waiting ... hoping.... The pause was her answer. And it hurt. But she wouldn't run away. That was for a woman with far more pride than she had at this moment. She stepped around the bush to face them.

Her husband's face showed genuine surprise. "Julia!"

"Yes, McCloud. I'd like to hear your answer, too."

He took her arm. "Fine. But first I want you to hear something else."

Meredith stood, tapping her foot with impatience. "He's going to try to convince you of something that isn't true, Julia. Remember, I've had your best interest at heart."

Julia's stomach tightened as she waited.

"I've been in Walnut Hill with Jake Crawford and the sheriff." McCloud's voice was stern.

Julia forgot about the answer she'd wanted. "The sheriff? Why?"

He put his arm around her waist and absently rubbed her hip. "Because I discovered who's diverting the water from the river."

She was unable to take her eyes off him. Whether he loved her or not didn't change her love for him. He was exactly the kind of man Papa assured her he was. "Who?" She had a funny feeling that she knew the answer.

"I think Meredith knows, don't you, Meredith?" His voice held an accusation.

Meredith appeared puzzled. "I have no idea what you're talking about."

"You're telling me you didn't know Serge was digging trenches from the river to your orchards?"

"Serge?" Julia couldn't believe it.

Meredith paled. "That's utter nonsense. I don't believe it."

McCloud opened his mouth as if to say something, then closed it. "I discovered him and Frank Barnes at one of the ditches last night. Quite by accident, mind you."

Meredith frowned, obviously shaken. "I don't believe you."

Julia remembered what she'd seen from the window seat. "I saw two men leaving your barn last night, Meredith. I didn't think much of it at the time, but now ..." she swung her gaze to McCloud. "It could have been Frank and Serge."

"This is insane." Meredith's voice was soft, shaky.

Julia felt sick to her stomach. "The sedative." Her gaze flew to Meredith. "If I'd taken it, I wouldn't have seen them leave the barn. Was that your intention?"

The woman's face showed true consternation. "Oh,

my dear. No. No! I only had Serge prepare it for you because it seemed you needed sleep."

Icy fingers played over Julia's spine. "Serge prepared it?"

Meredith's eyes filled with pain. "Yes, but he wouldn't have—" She squared her shoulders and glared at McCloud. "I don't believe a word of what you're implying," she said on a hiss of breath. "And no one else will, either. You're just a breed. *No* one in this valley will believe you over me. I wish you had died. You were *supposed* to die!"

Confused, Julia looked at her husband, whose jaw was tight and whose eyes were hard, then at Meredith. The woman appeared old, mean, and beaten.

"McCloud," Julia said on a whisper of breath, "what's she talking about?"

"Julia," he began, a small, tight smile creasing his mouth, "meet the woman who gave me life, then proceeded to try to take it from me by having me buried alive."

In her whole life Julia had never fainted. Never swooned. That suddenly changed.

Julia came awake slowly. She opened her eyes; McCloud sat beside her on the bed.

"How are you?" His face was filled with concern as he brushed a strand off her forehead.

"Marymae—" She attempted to sit up, but felt light-headed.

"She's right here." His eyes were soft. "I've had her on the bed. She's been pulling herself up on my arm."

Julia smiled, her love and confusion regarding this man drowning her. She focused on Marymae. "She's growing so fast."

"Julia." His tone spoke volumes.

She pulled in a rickety breath. "I'm listening."

"When Meredith Henley was fifteen years old, she was coming to California from the East Coast with her family. Their wagon train stopped to camp somewhere in Dakota Territory, and she claims to have been raped by an Indian. I'm the result of that rape."

She touched his hand, rubbing the tips of her fingers over the rough skin, resisting the urge to crawl into his arms. "Then it's true? Meredith is your mother?"

His hand tensed beneath hers. " 'Mother' is a loose term for what she is to me."

The image of another mother who had tried to dispose of an unwanted child sprouted like a poison mushroom in her mind. Again, he and Josette had more in common than she'd ever imagined.

The years Julia had turned to Meredith as a mother figure flooded into her mind. She'd anxiously taken Meredith's advice, because Meredith was the mother she missed so much. Even up to yesterday, she'd looked to Meredith for guidance. Her stomach churned.

"You said she tried to bury you alive."

"She did. But Angus McCloud found me before the coyotes did."

Horrified, Julia shuddered, unable to picture it. "How long have you known?" Her question was soft, but her heart drummed hard.

"If you mean, did I know who she was when I first came here, then yes. I've known who she was for over a year. I'd been combing through the records of families who had come to California in the forties before the gold rush." He paused and took a breath. "It's hard to explain, Julia, but we have this ... this odd sixth sense. When I came across her name on the list, I knew. I just knew."

Julia swallowed. "Then you came here looking for work, knowing that your mother lived just over the next ridge."

He gave her a short answering nod.

"Is that why you returned after Papa died?" She held his gaze, wanting to know. *Needing* to know. She wasn't certain she could handle another truth.

He broke eye contact. "Not entirely."

For a brief instant she felt a rush of hope. "Then why did you come back?"

Pulling in a ragged sigh, he got off the bed and went to the window. "Because I'd made Amos a promise."

Her stomach dropped. "To take care of his poor, pathetic, spinster daughter?"

McCloud raised his arms, framing the window with his hands. He was so big and strong. She wanted to go to him, put her arms around him and tell him she loved him.

"You may be poor, Julia, but you're hardly pathetic." There was almost a trace of humor in his voice.

"But I *am* a spinster, aren't I?"

"Not anymore." He gave her a brief smile over his shoulder. "I married you."

She twisted her hands in the folds of her skirt, berating herself for even dreaming that he might ever come to love her. "At least I can thank you for that, can't I?" She tried to sound frivolous.

"Julia." He turned and studied her.

Again her heart lifted in anticipation. "Yes?"

He shook his head and turned away. "There's no easy way to say this."

Dread coated her stomach. He was leaving. She'd known what they'd had was too good to last. It hurt anyway. "I find the best way to say something is to say it straight out, McCloud. Get it over with."

"Serge had your father killed."

She fell back on the pillows, struck speechless. He wasn't leaving? She shook her head to clear it. "Say that again?"

He returned to the bedside and sat. "You heard me tell Meredith I came upon Frank Barnes and Serge by accident last night." He drew the backs of his fingers over her cheek, sending shivers over her skin. "I couldn't sleep, not without you in my bed."

In a bold gesture, she brought his palm to her mouth and kissed it. "I didn't like sleeping alone much, either."

When she released his hand, he threaded his fingers through the fine hairs at her temple. "They were digging a trench, Julia. They were a good mile from the river near Henley land. It's one of many such ditches they've dug to change the course of the river."

"Serge was doing this?" At his nod, she added, "But what makes you think he killed Papa?" Serge was her dearest friend in the world. Wasn't he?

"He hired Frank Barnes to do it while he was back East with his mother. They talked of it last night."

"Did ..." She cleared her throat and swallowed. "Do you think Meredith had anything to do with it?"

"I thought she was the head of it, but now I don't know. Serge started changing the course of the river last fall. Amos was suspicious. I think maybe he stumbled across the ditches. When he approached Serge with his suspicions, Serge knew he had to do something. That's when he hired Barnes to do the job. And," he added, "made sure he was way across the country when it happened."

Julia shook her head and stared out the window,

sorrow pinching her heart. "I can't believe Serge would do such a thing, McCloud. I don't *want* to believe it."

"I'm sorry, Julia. I'm truly sorry."

Neither spoke. As far as Julia was concerned, Serge could just as well have plunged a knife into her heart. His betrayal went deep. And McCloud had been right all along.

She recalled what she'd seen on the way to Meredith's. "Why didn't you tell me your cabin had burned?"

"I didn't want to worry you. I wasn't even sure the barn had been struck by lightning, Julia. I'm still not, but it was unlikely both structures were hit. I was suspicious."

"Do you know what happened?"

"I have a pretty good idea."

"Serge?" The word came out on a whisper. At his nod, she asked, "Why?"

"I came along and ruined every plan he and his mother had for this valley, Julia. Not only that, I was a legitimate heir. Not one Meredith would recognize, but an heir just the same, and a threat to Serge."

"What will happen now?"

"Serge and Frank Barnes are in jail. I'm sure that's where Meredith went when she left here."

Julia dug into her apron pocket for her handkerchief and found her father's letter. She took it out and handed it to her husband. "I'm sorry I didn't trust you, McCloud. I let Meredith and Serge fill my head with all sorts of things. They even tried to make me believe *you* had killed Papa. But I came across the letter earlier. When I read it, I knew you were innocent. Papa couldn't have been coerced into writing that."

McCloud scanned it, then returned it to her, his eyes warm. "I knew he had more faith in me than I had in myself."

He stood and went to the window. "There's something else."

She closed her eyes and held her breath. Now he would tell her he was leaving.

"I have a twin brother, Julia."

Her eyes flew open. "A brother? Oh, dear. Did she ... did she try to kill him, too?"

"No." He paused, and Julia wondered if he would continue. "Her mother sold him."

"Rosa Columbo *sold* a baby?"

"She couldn't bring herself to bury both of us. I guess that's a point in her favor." The hard edge of irony laced his pain.

Julia's emotions were saturated. "You mean Grandmama Rosa actually—" She couldn't finish the thought, much less the sentence. It was too difficult to picture that sweet old woman trying to hurt anyone.

"Yes. Meredith ordered her to get rid of both of us."

"Do you know where he is?"

McCloud stared outside. "No, but I have to find him." He turned, looking at her with such intensity, Julia felt a nibble of fear. "Do you understand, Julia? I *have* to find him."

Marymae began to fuss, and Julia tended the child, grateful for the interruption. *Now* he would tell her he was leaving.

He flung himself from the window and paced beside the bed. "I know I can't just up and leave, like I used to. And if you don't want me to go, I won't."

She gaped at him. "You're asking me?"

"Of course. This is a marriage, Julia. An equal partnership. You have as many rights as I do. If you don't want me to go, I won't," he repeated. "But if I *do* go, it'll be hard on you. My old friend Baptiste can come and do the chores." He looked sheepish. "I've already sent word to him, and he's replied."

"Baptiste? The trapper you lived with? The one who taught you—" She recalled their talk the day she and Marymae visited him at the site of his cabin. Her face flooded at the memory.

McCloud smiled, the first she'd seen in days, and it spread warmth into her chest and around her heart.

"So, you remember. I think we can convince him to help us for about a month. Maybe more. He'll stay as long as we need him. He's not a bad sort, Julia. Just a bit rough around the edges."

That part didn't bother her at all. But Lord in heaven, could she stand to be separated from McCloud for a whole month? Maybe longer? "You mean . . . you mean you'd come back?"

"You'll have to trust me, Julia. Maybe this brother of mine is impossible to find. I don't know. But I have to try. I know he isn't dead." He brought his fist to his heart. "In here, I *know* he's alive."

She sat up and hugged her knees. He hadn't said whether or not he'd be back. "Have you any clues?"

"Just one. He was sold to a family by the name of Fletcher."

"Fletcher," she repeated. "It doesn't ring a bell with me." She took Marymae into her arms and scooted off the bed. "How will you begin?" She went into the kitchen to get the baby a bottle.

He followed her. "I'm going to examine courthouse records from here to the Oregon border, if I have to."

The idea of him leaving for any length of time suddenly hit her. One night apart had been bad enough.

She'd slept very little at Meredith's, worrying that McCloud wouldn't return from Martinez. Worrying that he'd have an accident. Just plain worrying. She'd been cold, even with the heated foot warmer Meredith had brought her. She'd missed having McCloud to curl up with. Missed his firm, hairy calves on which she could warm her cold toes. She'd missed the passion that had been theirs. She'd missed waking up and finding him beside her, gazing down at her.

She pulled a bottle from the dark pantry, then sat at the table and fed the baby. "I'm going to miss you, McCloud."

He sat across from her and caught her eye. "You wouldn't have said that yesterday," he reminded her.

She swallowed the sob that closed her throat. *Oh, but I would have, my handsome husband. No matter what had happened, I would have missed you.*

"When will you leave?" She felt the tears, and blinked furiously to keep them at bay.

He came around the table and stood behind her, gently massaging her shoulders. She squeezed her eyes shut and pressed her lips together, working hard not to let the sob that had closed her throat escape. When he placed a hand on her shoulder, she briefly captured it against her cheek.

"At first light." His fingers grazed her chin, then her neck, working their way to her braid.

"I want to make love to you, Julia."

"Oh, McCloud," she said, her body responding, "I want that, too."

He bent and kissed her neck, sending waves of longing through her.

"Let me put the baby down for her nap."

Eager with anticipation, she put the sleeping child to bed. When she came out of the bedroom, McCloud was waiting for her. She stood on her tiptoes and kissed him, loving the stubble that chafed her mouth, loving his sensual lips. One day, if—no, when—he came back, and if she had the nerve, she wanted to suck on them.

They stood together, and Julia pushed thoughts of tomorrow from her mind. At least they would have tonight, and she would selfishly hold that memory near her heart.

Suddenly McCloud raised his head.

"What is it?"

He gazed intently at the window. "Someone's coming."

Disappointed that they had to postpone their love-making, Julia took his hand and they went to the front door, stepping out onto the porch.

"Woo-hoo! Julia!"

"It's my aunt Mattie, Papa's sister." Julia smiled and raised her hand in greeting, relieved that she wouldn't be alone when McCloud left. Then she saw who sat beside her in the buggy, and her heart dropped. "And Josette."

❧ 16 ❧

With increasing distress, Julia watched the buggy approach. Josette. Her sister's name alone filled her with dread. Her brave talk about not letting Josette take control crumbled around her like so much rubble. Somehow, Julia had convinced herself that Josette wouldn't come home. It had been a fanciful sort of wish, one she would never have wasted time on before she'd fallen in love with McCloud.

Turning, she saw the muscles working in his jaw. He didn't take his gaze off the buggy. Not because of any curiosity about Aunt Mattie, Julia was sure; the source of his interest was Josette, for he stared at her. Julia would almost have made a pact with the devil to know what he was thinking. Almost.

"Mr. McCloud!" Josette's familiar, high-pitched voice burst like shattering glass through Julia's fragile state of mind.

Her sister stepped from the buggy and hurried toward them, lifting her skirts with dainty fingers. Julia's stomach dropped farther. It probably wasn't noticeable to McCloud, but she saw it. Josette's voluptuous breasts strained at the bodice of her gown. Her elevated waistline hid an expanding waist and growing stomach. One of her conversations with McCloud returned, haunting Julia, casting poison upon her dreams:

And I suppose if she came back with another child for you to take care of, you'd take on that responsibility, too?

Josette rushed up the steps and threw herself at him. "Oh, Mr. McCloud, I'm so *happy* you're here."

McCloud reached out to hold her—to keep from tumbling backward at the impact, Julia told herself. She held her breath, knowing with certainty that she didn't want to read his mind even if she could.

"Of course I'm here. I live here."

Josette drew back, her eyes bright with carefully unshed tears. "You mean it's true? You married *Julia?*" Her shock and dismay were evident. "How could you! Oh, how *could* you!"

Without giving her an answer or even acknowledging her distress, he put Josette away from him and turned to Julia. "I don't think I'll wait until morning. I'm leaving now." His voice was gruff, angry.

Confused, she nodded and turned to study the buggy, hoping to hide her turbulent feelings. A moment ago she hadn't wanted him to leave. Now, because of the arrival of her sister, she was anxious to see him go.

"Just a minute, young man." Aunt Mattie's bossy voice stabbed the air. She hopped down from the buggy with the energy of a woman half her age and bustled toward them, her step spry and her spine straight. She was forty-five years old, but she was tiny and her golden hair had very little gray. "Carry in our baggage before you go gallivanting off to the Good Lord knows where."

McCloud shot Julia a brief look, in which she was certain she saw amusement, then went to do Mattie's bidding.

"Come here, dear," Mattie ordered, pulling Julia into her arms.

Julia clung to her aunt. She smelled of camphor and lilacs. Julia was so pleased she'd come, she felt like crying. "I'm glad to see you, Aunt Mattie."

They hugged, swaying back and forth in each other's arms.

"I miss Papa so much," Julia said in a hushed tone.

"I know, I know," Mattie soothed. "I'm sorry I wasn't here when they put him in the ground. I should never have stayed away so long, and I shouldn't have let you take on everything alone."

They stood together until Josette's shrill voice interrupted them.

"Are you two going to stand out here all day? I'm hungry. When's dinner, Julia? I want something to eat." She swished past them and went into the house.

Julia and her aunt exchanged knowing looks. "She's only been gone a few months, dear. You didn't really expect her to change that quickly, did you?"

"There's always hope," Julia said on an exaggerated sigh. Before following Josette inside, Julia caught her aunt's arm. "She's pregnant again, isn't she?"

Mattie lifted a tawny, disdainful brow. "I'd say she's about five months along, going on six."

"That much." Julia felt her world teeter on the brink of disaster. McCloud had been hired in September and was with them through October. Plenty of time. Oh, God ... plenty of time. "So she got pregnant even before she left."

Mattie attempted to brush the dust from her black silk full-length cape. "Seems likely."

There was a spinning in the pit of Julia's stomach, and she hated to go inside, even though she knew Josette was in there alone with McCloud. "When did she arrive at your place?"

Mattie uttered an indelicate snort. "About a month ago, I'd wager. The man she was living with kicked her out when he discovered she was with child, and someone else's, to boot."

Julia expelled a weary sigh and rubbed her neck, trying to ignore the little voices in her head that told her the baby was McCloud's.

"My boarders even got tired of her whining. At first, of course, they were enchanted with her and coddled her something awful, but," Mattie added with a sigh, "she *does* grate on a person after a while."

"Who's taking care of your place while you're here?"

"A lady friend of mine. She's down on her luck, poor thing. Watching after the boarders takes her mind off her troubles."

Speaking of troubles ... Having Josette home was a burden, but Julia quietly chastised herself. After all, it was Josette's home, too.

"Come on, dear. We'd best get inside and rescue that husband of yours. Ever since I told your sister you'd married him, she's talked of nothing else. I expect she's jealous, carrying on like she is," Mattie observed. "She's certainly mucked up her life, now I expect she wants to muck up yours."

If misery had been water, Julia would have drowned.

As usual, Mattie took the lead. Julia followed her into the house, dreading her sister's homecoming, and feeling guilty because of it. In spite of everything, they *were* sisters.

Once inside, neither McCloud nor Josette were anywhere to be seen. That sickened Julia even more.

Mattie went directly to the pie safe and studied its contents. "Did that man of yours say he was leaving?"

"Yes. He'll be gone for a month, maybe more." She was sure he'd be back, now that Josette was home.

"I'll fix him something to take with him." Mattie disappeared into the dark pantry.

"Thank you, Mattie, he'll appreciate that." She wanted to march to McCloud's room and find out what, if anything, was going on in there, but it would have made her appear distrustful of him, and she didn't want him to think that. And, she wanted to drag her sister out by her ear. Instead of doing either, she went into her bedroom and checked on Marymae, who napped peacefully, innocent of the upheaval.

Julia left her room just as McCloud was leaving his. He carried the small leather case she knew held most of what he owned in the world.

She attempted to scurry away, but he stopped her. "Julia."

Her heart vaulted at his touch. "Aunt Mattie is fixing you something to take with you."

"To hell with food, Julia, look at me."

She compiled. Confusion sprang inside her like wildflowers after a summer rain, for his eyes were warm and intense. Oh, Lord in heaven, no matter what he had or not had done, she would miss him, and love him until her dying day.

"Now that you know the circumstances of my birth, you must know how I feel about your sister."

Deep down inside she knew what he meant, and that knowledge lifted some of the heaviness from around her heart. She knew that no man who had been abandoned by his mother could care for a woman who had done something similar to a child of her own.

She wanted to fling herself into his arms, thank him for alleviating some of her fears. "McCloud, I—"

He pressed a finger over her lips, then bent to kiss her, sending vibrating waves of longing through her. "For everything else that's happened, I'm sorry," he said softly, his face expressively sad.

"Sorry?" What did he have to be sorry about? About leaving? About fathering Josette's baby? About having to dash all of her foolish, feminine dreams? *Tell me, damn you, tell me!* Even though she wanted to say those things, she couldn't. Something deep inside her refused to hear the answers.

"Baptiste will be here sometime tomorrow afternoon." He traced her features with a callused finger, then moved his hands to her shoulders.

She hid her feelings at best she could, and tried to pull away, but he wouldn't release her. She memorized the sensation of his hands cupping her shoulders, knowing that she would long for those hands every waking minute of every day until he returned. "It would be best if you just left, McCloud. I don't think I can—"

"Mr. McCloud," Josette said, buttoning the last button on her bodice as she sashayed from his room. "I—" She stopped when she saw Julia, a look of satisfaction on her face. "Oh, I'm so sorry," she said, not sounding the least bit apologetic. "Did I interrupt something?"

Julia glared at her sister, attempting to ignore the queasiness that spread into her chest and stomach. She knew her sister. Josette was capable of attempting seduction with any woman's husband, including hers.

What she didn't want to believe and refused to accept was that Josette could have been successful with McCloud, no matter what history they may or may not have shared.

Gathering her courage, Julia stood on tiptoe and brushed her mouth over her husband's. He caught her lips with his and gave her a hard, deep kiss. Her blood thickened like warm honey. When he finally released her, she gave him a wavering smile, took his arm and walked toward the kitchen, leaving Josette behind.

"You'd better go if you want to get to Martinez before dark," Julia advised. And she wanted him gone. She'd despised McCloud last fall when she thought he was carrying on with Josette behind her back, but it hadn't been personal, or at least she'd told herself it wasn't. She'd convinced herself she'd been trying to protect her sister. But now, Julia loathed the rivalry that sprang up between her and Josette because of him.

"Yeah," he muttered. "I guess I'd better go. Kiss the baby for me." He picked up his lunch and his leather bag, then left the house without looking back.

"I will," she promised.

Josette swept past her and followed McCloud outside. Julia knew she should go after her. Instead she went to the window and watched.

Josette ran after McCloud and grabbed his arm. He stopped, but Julia couldn't see his face. She could, however, see Josette's. It was pinched, pained, and Julia saw the tears streaming down her sister's cheeks. Icy nausea sprang to the back of Julia's throat. She hurried to the door, flinging it open.

"McCloud?" She kept her voice from showing her concern.

He turned, Josette clinging to his arm, and studied her.

Julia swallowed, biting back the words of love, fear, and doubt that welled into her throat. "Take care of yourself."

Giving her a brief smile, he crossed to the paddock.

Josette sidled up and stood beside her. Both women watched him leave.

"He was stupid to marry you, Julia. I don't know what you did to convince him, but you must have done something. He wouldn't have done it unless there had been a reason." Josette's voice was laced with deep-seated anger.

"It was in Papa's will," Julia answered, immediately sorry she'd mentioned it.

Josette snorted. "That's reason enough for any man. Of course," she added, a slyness in her tone, "that doesn't mean he'll be faithful."

Julia had enough difficulty clinging to her dreams without hearing those words. McCloud had seemed happy with her, and he'd as much as said that Josette no longer interested him. He appeared to be settling into life on the ranch, but she wondered how long it would last. Once he'd tasted his freedom, would he want it again? She was sure he'd been faithful during their brief time together, but she wondered, too, if that would continue when he came home. She wanted to believe it would.

Lengthy silence hung between the sisters. Finally, Josette announced, "He would have married me if I'd been here, Julia. Papa would have seen to it."

Papa. She wondered if Papa's will had been drawn after Josette left. If so, *would* he have insisted that McCloud marry Josette?

At times Julia cursed her vivid memory. And now,

as pictures of Josette and McCloud going off in the buggy to gather gooseberries bloomed in her head, was no exception. "Would Papa have had reason to?"

Josette rubbed both hands over her abdomen. "We'll know soon, won't we?"

Julia felt beaten, but she worked through it, refusing to let Josette get the upper hand. She couldn't afford to let her. "Perhaps. But I wouldn't exactly call that proof. And don't you forget that he married me, Josette. Whatever the reason, McCloud is an honorable man." Brave talk from a woman whose entire life wavered like a house of cards. Josette smirked and, with a tapered finger, twirled one long, loopy, sunshine-drenched curl. "It'll be here when he returns, Julia dearest," she reminded her. "Then we'll see just how honorable he is."

Leaving Josette standing outside, Julia went into the house and stood by the window. The only evidence McCloud had been there was the lingering dust kicked up by his stallion. Julia's dreams of happiness dissipated as permanently as that dust in the wind.

"Ju-lee-a!" Josette's hands were over her ears. "Can't you do something about that squalling child?"

With a wailing Marymae in her arms, Julia went into the dark pantry and retrieved a rusk. When she emerged, she removed McCloud's clever contraption from the entry, put the baby in it, and hoisted it onto her back, fastening the straps across her chest.

"What in the world is that?" Josette's question was filled with ridicule.

Julia handed the baby the dried toast over her shoulder, then went about stirring the cooked fruit for jam. Marymae quieted immediately. "It's a carrier. McCloud made it."

Josette snorted. "Probably because he couldn't stand to hear her caterwaul, either."

It had been two weeks since McCloud had left, and Julia decided she wasn't going to supply Josette with any ammunition about their marriage. She would neither defend nor defile him. Her restraint frustrated Josette further.

Mattie poured boiling water over the glass canning jars and lids. "If you ask me, it's a clever invention. He must have been a pretty handy man to have around, Julia."

Julia lifted the kettle of cooked fruit off the fire and set it on the counter to cool. Mattie talked of him in the past tense, as if he were never coming back. As the days passed, Julia began to wonder if she might be right. Her nights had been cold and empty, her days full of Josette's whiny demands and suggestive innuendoes about her relationship with McCloud. And always, there were Mattie's probing questions. There were times when Julia had to physically stop herself from running into the woods, screaming.

Mattie glanced out the window, her expression turning sour. "Here comes that . . . that filthy little Frenchman your husband hired."

If nothing else, Baptiste's presence lightened Julia's mood. "Mattie," she scolded in a soft tone. "Baptiste has been wonderful, and you know it."

Pursing her lips, Mattie took the tongs and removed the scalded glassware from the dishpan. "I have *never* encountered such a foul-minded man, and believe you me, in my business, I've met all kinds. Everything I say, he appears to misunderstand, finding—well, you know, an inappropriate meaning behind it."

Quietly, Julia agreed. But Baptiste didn't offend her. His banter with Mattie reminded her of her early days with McCloud. And in spite of everything, she found the Frenchman charming. She had to admit, however, that he was an odd little man, relishing the way the women blushed at his off-color comments.

"I find him repulsive." Josette munched on what Julia suspected was her fifth cinnamon bun. Her lips were slick with butter as she licked it off her fingers.

Julia hid a caustic smile. Of course she did. Baptiste hadn't fawned and drooled over Josette as she'd expected him to. For that reason alone, Julia liked him, sensing there was an intelligent, honorable man buried somewhere beneath the layers of bawdy behavior.

Again, rather like McCloud. She pushed back her memories, for they made her yearn for him.

Baptiste stepped inside, the ever-present mocking smile showing beneath his drooping black mustache. "Ah, *mon chou,*" he said, crossing to Mattie and giving her a familiar swat on the buttocks.

Mattie gasped and turned, her neck stained red as she threatened him with a wooden spoon.

"Without you," Baptiste went on, ignoring her angry stance, "my life has no meaning. Without you, I am only an earthworm." He pressed the offending hand to his heart.

Mattie narrowed her gaze at him, the wooden spoon held battle-ready. "Don't hornswaggle me, you odious man. I wasn't born in the woods to be scared by an owl."

He laughed, the booming sound filling the room as he poured himself coffee and helped himself to a warm bun. "You think I am not serious, eh? You think you are not a desirable woman, eh?"

"What I think—" With a huff, she pursed her lips and shook the spoon in his direction. "What I think, Mr. Baptiste, is that the Good Lord will see that you spend your fair share of time burning in the fires of purgatory. That's what I think," she announced, turning back to her task with a flourish.

Unscathed by Mattie's statement, his gaze fell on Julia, and she felt herself blush. His intimate glances were never suggestive. "And you, *ma cocotte,*" he said around a smile. "How are you this fine morning?"

"I'm fine, Baptiste. Thank you for asking."

"And the *bébé?* She is good?"

"She's teething. Thank goodness for this carrier McCloud made. When she's in it, she's not nearly as cross as she would otherwise be." Julia found it amusing that he called Mattie his "cabbage" and her his "hen." She assumed they were words of endearment, but she found neither particular complimentary. He didn't refer to Josette with any form of endearment at all. In fact, he avoided her. But then, Josette had become increasingly peevish as her pregnancy progressed, and no one relished being around her at all.

"Oui," he answered around a mouthful of bun. "Wolfgang was always clever with his hands, eh?" He wiggled his eyebrows at her, causing Julia's blush to race to the roots of her hair.

Josette finished her sweet roll then paced in front of the window, her hand massaging the small of her back. "I'm so *bored,*" she complained. "I'd forgotten that there's nothing to do out here in the sticks."

Julia continued to work at the counter. "The jam jars need filling," she suggested.

Her sister made an impatient sound in her throat as she stared outside. "That's *not* what I had in mind."

Julia wished she could hide her impatience. "Then why didn't you stay in the city, Josette? You've never liked it here, anyway."

Josette flounced from the window, toying with the

ribbon at her expanding waistline. "I had my reasons."
She tossed Julia a knowing look.

I'll just bet you did. Julia had refused to ask Josette
who had fathered her baby. Knowing her sister as well
as she did, she wasn't sure she could trust her to tell
the truth, anyway. That being the case, she decided
the question didn't require asking.

Julia wanted McCloud to return, but she dreaded
it. Confrontation was inevitable. While he was gone,
both Mattie and Baptiste defused her anger toward
her sister merely by being supportive. She found their
banter amusing and surprisingly relaxing. It was her
buffer against Josette.

The clock in the other room struck ten, reminding
Julia that she was going to Walnut Hill to the jail to
see Serge. She'd been putting it off, but knew she had
to face him, find out why he'd done what he'd done,
knowing that any answer he gave would hurt her.

Marymae's head bobbed on Julia's shoulder. She
carefully extricated herself from the carrier and went
into the bedroom, taking Marymae out and putting
her in bed.

With a heavy sigh, she went to her wardrobe and
wondered what a person wore to visit a jailbird.

Meredith gazed at her son through the bars. It
broke her heart to have to visit him here, in this
dreadful, dirty, smelly place. Until today, she had
avoided asking him his reasons for doing what he did.
Until today, she couldn't have accepted his answer.
But she could avoid it no longer; she had to know.

Serge's clothes were disheveled and soiled, and he
hadn't shaved in days. The thick, dark stubble gave
him a manly look, and for a moment Meredith was

reminded of her father, a man whom she'd loved, perhaps more than she'd loved her own husband.

"Well, if it isn't my dear mother." Serge's voice was laced with sarcasm. "To what do I owe this honor?" He languidly pulled himself to a sitting position.

Meredith brought her handkerchief to her nose, hoping to filter out some of the stench. "The lawyer I've secured will be here sometime this afternoon."

Her son turned from her and studied the brick wall. "It's about time, don't you think? I've been rotting in this hellhole for two weeks."

Meredith stifled her apology for allowing him to languish in jail. "Why did you do it, Serge?"

He rounded on her. "You believe everyone but me, don't you?"

She pressed her handkerchief against her eyes. "You were outfoxed, Serge. By your own half brother." Her secret, she knew, had been discovered by Serge.

He clamped his jaw shut and refused to answer.

"Serge, dear, the sheriff took me out to the sites of the ditches." Her heart ached for her lost dreams of an empire.

"Tell me, Mother," he said, his mouth curled into a snarl. "What else was I to do? How could I compete with someone like Wolf McCloud, even though he *is* a breed? He's as much your son as I am. He even took the woman you wanted me to marry."

"It would have been a mistake. Unfair to both of you. You know that as well as I."

He snorted a nasty laugh. "You never let me forget it."

Meredith's knees gave way and she dropped into a chair by the cell. "He means nothing to me, Serge.

Nothing. And I never wanted you to know about ...
about what happened." Her voice was a mere whisper.

"Oh, I knew about it. I read all about it in Grandmama's journal."

Meredith sat up, surprised. "Her journal? She wrote about it in her journal?"

"Yes, Mother. In great length. I read every sordid word. By the way, thank you for forcing me to learn Italian."

Everything had come apart, and Meredith didn't know how to knit it together. The entire fabric of her life had become frayed, weakened by her own greed.

"The day he came to call on you, I had a hunch it was him. Your response when I offered to get rid of him was proof enough for me." Serge drew closer to the bars, gripping them so hard his knuckles were white. "Everything I did, even before I knew about him, was for you, Mother. *Everything.*"

She gave him a look that spoke of the pain in her heart. "But I will never claim him, Serge. *You're* the only son I want."

He gave her a disparaging laugh. "Am I? Am I really?" He shook his head with disbelief. "I've never been the son you wanted. I've never been anything you've wanted."

Meredith felt beaten, for his words held the clanging ring of truth. "Why did you have poor Amos killed?"

He pressed his face against the bars. "I did it for *you,* Mother. Don't you see? He found out what we were doing. I had no choice. God," he said on a gasp of breath. "I just wanted you to be proud of me. Just once I wanted to do something to make you proud." His words were punctuated with his own pain.

For the first time in her life, Meredith began to understand what she'd done to her son. In her quest for power and perfection, she'd completely denied Serge the option of being who he was, and not who she wanted him to be.

Julia studied the exterior of the jail, noting that the boards needed a fresh coat of paint. Wild oats, taller than she was, grew in abundance on the south side of the building, the breeze brushing it erratically against the windows. Taking a deep breath, she opened the door and stepped inside. Cigar smoke hung in the air, and underlying that odor was the distinct smell of dirt, tobacco, and urine. Years of it, clinging to the walls and the corners of the ceiling and the floor.

The deputy, a gaunt young man with a hawk nose and a shock of unruly mud-colored hair, traced a Wanted poster with his finger.

"I'm here to see Serge Henley," Julia announced.

He gave her a brief nod. "He's in there, ma'am. He's already got a visitor."

"Can I see him?" At his indifferent shrug, Julia went into the room where the prisoners were kept. Glancing at the first cell, she saw Frank Barnes lounging on his cot. Before she could move on, he saw her.

He greeted her with a lascivious smile that made her flesh crawl. "Miss Julia."

Nodding politely, she walked on by, but like a bolt of lightning he was at the bars, gripping her arm.

"Not so fast, there." He smelled of whiskey, and she briefly wondered how he'd gotten it.

"What do you want, Frank?" She discovered that she had no feelings for him at all. He wasn't even worth the effort to hate. In spite of everything, he'd planted the seed that had given her Marymae, the joy of her life.

"Why'd you take on the brat's care, Miss Julia?"

The question surprised her. "That's no concern of yours."

His fingers pinched her skin. "Ah, but it is. The brat's mine, too."

She tugged her arm from his grip and glared at him. "I'll forgive the baby for that. She's not responsible for her disgusting parentage."

He laughed quietly, but his eyes were hard. "Such big words. Always such big words, Miss Julia. It's no wonder I couldn't get inside them drawers of yours. You prob'ly didn't understand what I was tryin' to do."

Julia could taste the bitter bile that rose into her throat. "I understood you perfectly, Frank. People like you aren't capable of insinuation."

He continued to grin. "I don't give a shit what that means, Miss Julia, but I'll tell you what I think. I think you're carin' for that baby 'cause it's part of me."

Julia almost laughed out loud. "You go right ahead and think what you like. It makes no difference to me. I'm just happy I can love a child whose parents are so completely despicable."

Not getting the response he'd hoped for, Frank Barnes scowled and returned to his filthy cot.

Julia stepped to the next cell. Meredith sat slumped over, looking sad and defeated. She stood as Julia approached.

"Julia, my dear." She held out her arms.

Julia stopped, avoiding Meredith's embrace. "How could you blame McCloud for something Serge did, Meredith? How *could* you?"

Meredith's arms fell to her sides. She took a deep breath and turned away. "I didn't know. I wanted to believe it was him," she added, turning an intent gaze on Julia. "In my heart, I *had* to believe it. His appearance in my life was a threat to all I'd worked for. And I was angry that he was everything my Serge was not."

"I can almost understand abandonment, Meredith. I couldn't have done it, but most white women would have. But to have the baby killed . . ." She shuddered to think what her life would have been like without McCloud.

"No one can imagine what I felt when I discovered he was alive." Meredith's voice was wistful. "He stood before me . . . strong, proud, virile." She laughed, a choking sound that tore from her throat. "He'd survived despite what I'd done to him. And," she added, giving Julia a plaintive look, "he had you.

"Isn't it ironic? Since you and Serge were children, I'd purposely blinded myself to his faults and failings, hoping one day Amos and I could bring the two of you together. And what happens? You marry my son anyway. The son I'd ordered my poor mother to get rid of."

Julia wanted to be angry with Meredith. On some level she was, but she also felt sorry for her. "You didn't know about Serge's involvement in Papa's death?"

"She didn't know, Julia," Serge interjected.

She turned toward the cell, shocked at Serge's unkempt appearance. "And you," she said, hoping to keep the pain from her voice. "How could you have had Papa killed? Papa loved you Serge. He *loved* you! You were the son he'd never had."

Serge rammed his fists into the pockets of his coat and presented both women his back.

A wave of weakness attacked Julia, and she leaned against the bars. She shouldn't have come, but she'd had to. She'd had to find out for herself what had happened, and now she knew.

"Serge," she said, her voice soft, "would that sedative have killed me?"

He swung around, his face etched with an agony of his own. "Of course not! Jesus Christ, Julia, I've loved you like a sister for so long, I can't remember a time when you weren't in my life."

Julia swallowed the knot of tears. "But you could kill Papa."

He gazed at the floor, appearing unwilling to look at her. "I had to please Mother. I did it for her. I'd even promised to kill your precious husband, but Mother wouldn't let me. So instead I sent him a warning."

Shocked, Julia asked, "What warning?"

"I tied a calf inside one of the caves he always rode by on his way home from his cabin. Then I created a landslide, making sure he had a devil of a time digging his way out."

"You did that?" Julia remembered how McCloud had tried to make light of the cave-in, but now she knew he'd only done that so she wouldn't worry. Or ask too many questions. He must have known it was a trap, and he probably knew it was for him.

"How could you be so sure it would be McCloud who entered the cave?" she asked.

"Because I knew his routine. I did that, Julia, and I'm not sorry. I wish he'd suffocated in there." His eyes burned with a hatred she'd never seen before.

Julia turned, anxious to leave, wondering just how much worse things could get.

❖ 17 ❖

Wolf allowed Baptiste to pick his way over the patches of crusty snow, following a path that led up through the brush. Although the ground was still frozen, most of the snow had melted. The air felt cold, but the sun was warm.

He'd had difficulty finding the family name, for records had been destroyed in so many counties. He'd hoped to be on his way home by now, not just arriving at his destination. He worried about Julia. Not because of the day-to-day chores that he had to trust Baptiste to do, but because of the burden of having her sister underfoot.

As he'd begun to pack that day, Josette had sashayed into his room and tried to seduce him. He let out a snort of disgust. She'd nearly bared her bosom right there in front of him, as if she were taking up where she'd left off. She was a woman to be pitied; had his own circumstances been different, he might have yielded to that. Despite feeling like a coward for leaving Julia with such a handful, he found himself unable to get out of there fast enough.

Julia. Emotion caught in his gut as it did every time he thought about her, and he almost doubled over. Julia, with her sharp, intelligent wit and her pouty mouth. Julia, with her prim, tight hairdo and her deep, hot passion. Julia, with her taut look of disapproval and her hearty, earthy laugh. Julia. Julia. Julia. He loved her. Holy double hell, he loved her! It was an emotion he'd never felt, never expected to experience in his lifetime.

As his mount stopped at the edge of the pines, Wolf felt an urgency to turn and hurry back to this woman who was his wife. But he'd come this far, and he was anxious to discover whether this man, this Tristan Fletcher, was, indeed, the other part of him. That part he'd been missing for so many years.

Wolf studied the big stone house. Two hundred miles north of Walnut Hill, it sat in a valley on the western slopes of the Sierra Nevadas, Wolf guessed about twenty-five hundred feet above sea level, for he'd been climbing since he left Sacramento.

He'd stopped in Hatter's Horn, the tiny village down the road, and discovered the Fletcher ranch was not far away. He'd also discovered that "old man" Fletcher had died years ago, and his wife, "the bitch of three counties," had followed him more recently.

The house appeared to loom into the light from the gloomy historical past. Wolf's courage flagged. He'd grown up expecting disappointment. He wanted to believe his search was over, as it seemed it was, but the feeling of terminal frustration was still there. Tristan, the old man at the bar had called him. "Yep, he's a breed. Looks just like you as a matter of fact," the old barkeep had said.

Tristan Fletcher and Wolfgang Amadeus Morning Cloud. Wolf's mouth twisted into a mocking smile.

They had been throwaway children, unwanted and un-loved by the woman who bore them, yet each sur-vived, and each had carved out a place for himself in a world that pitied and pampered no one.

"Yep," the saloon keeper had told him over a shot of bad whiskey, "he come home from New York right after his ma died. Been gone about six months. I heared tell the will brung him back. Prob'ly the money and the land. O'course, coulda been the sister. She's a strange one, let me tell ya. He ain't been able to keep a nurse, 'cause they ain't willin' to put up with her temper or her carryin's on." He'd touched a dirty, gnarled finger to his temple. "She ain't right up here, if ya know what I'm sayin'. A woman full-growed what acts like a child."

Wolf gave Baptiste a quiet command, and the ani-mal forged ahead, through the thin layer of snow. Wolf's heart surged in anticipation as a stallion, black as his own, pranced from the barn. Baptiste jibbed beneath him, moving restlessly.

Wolf let his gaze rest on the rider. Dressed in buck-skins and a flowing black greatcoat that covered his mount's rump, he reined in the animal and returned Wolf's perusal from across the wide, green, snow-spattered yard.

They approached each other. When they were a few feet apart, Wolf's heart clattered in his chest, for it was like looking into a mirror.

"Whether I knew it or not," Wolf said without pre-amble, "I've spent most of my life searching for you."

His brother's mouth lifted into a half grin. "And I, you."

Julia churned butter on the porch, anxious to escape Josette's whining. Marymae napped beside the churn in a wooden cradle Baptiste had built because she'd outgrown the old one. The night before, in front of the fire, Marymae had slithered to Baptiste on her belly—her first attempt at crawling.

Julia raised her face to the sun. It was warm; it felt good. Meredith's men had recently finished the new barn from lumber McCloud had purchased before he left. It had been two months. A lifetime.

She touched her abdomen. Not an hour went by that she didn't think about him. Miss him. Want to tell him her news. Carrying his child should have brought her more joy. In some ways she was happy to have a part of him with her. In others, she wondered how she would manage—with Marymae, her own child, and the one Josette was carrying—if McCloud didn't return. And even if he did return, she didn't know what to expect from him.

She sucked in a breath of spicy spring air, which was filled with the tang of the incense cedar needles and the budding bay laurels. Warm chinook winds rustled the new leaves of the cottonwood trees, and the flowering mustard on the slopes of Devil Mountain was slowly being replaced with purple lupine, yellow meadow daisies, and circular clumps of magenta red maids. The bountiful colors and smells of spring stole her breath away.

Julia's reverie was interrupted by a shriek from inside the house, followed by the sharp slamming of a door. She closed her eyes and tried to ignore the impatience that clamored over her skin.

Mattie bustled outside, her arms heavy with rugs. She dumped all but one on the floor, then shook the rag rug over the railing, onto the grass. Bits of dust sifted through the air, fluttering to the ground.

"What's her problem now?" Julia asked.

With a cluck of her tongue, Mattie dropped the rug and picked up another, shaking it as she'd done the first. "She's having a conniption fit because she has nothing to wear that doesn't cut her off at the middle. Her back hurts no matter how she sits, and she has an eruption on her forehead. Probably from the sweets she's been eating, but you can't tell her that."

Julia swallowed her impatience. "In other words, just an ordinary day in the tragic life of Josette Larson."

Mattie's answer was a grim smile. "She has over two months until her time." She clucked her tongue again. "If she lasts, I'll be surprised."

"What are her choices?"

They exchanged glances. Julia didn't trust Josette not to try something stupid.

Mattie looked away, and Julia followed her gaze to her burgeoning flower garden. "Your crocuses and daffodils are coming in," Mattie said.

"I know," Julia answered on a sigh. "The rock roses are budding, too." A new season had begun, and McCloud was gone. She ached for him daily.

Mattie picked up the rugs and opened the door. "My, it is nice out here, isn't it? I think while the stew is cooking and the bread is baking, I'll get my knitting and join you."

With a smile and a nod, Julia waited for her aunt to return. It had been a blessing to have her around. She'd forgotten just what a good companion Mattie was. She and Papa had not gotten on well, especially since Mattie's way of life was not to Papa's liking. He'd groused that Josette was Mattie all over again, but Julia knew that wasn't so. True, Mattie had never married and had run a boardinghouse near the San Francisco docks for years, taking in all sorts of dregs and derelicts. And Julia had secretly wondered if Mattie might have had a lover or two in her past. That, of course, was never mentioned in their household. And the scandal of Mattie not being conventional was something they hadn't been allowed to talk about in front of Papa.

But Mattie was nothing like Josette. Mattie was savvy and smart. And had a good heart in spite of her often biting tongue. In that respect, Julia guessed she and Mattie were alike. Not that she herself claimed to have such a good, generous heart, but Julia knew her words were often strident.

Mattie poked her head outside. "You seen my knitting needles?"

"No. Aren't they in your sewing basket?"

Mattie's tawny brows were pinched together. "No, and not two hours ago I was rummaging through my basket, searching for thread to mend that Frenchman's shirt, and they were there then."

"They didn't fall out and land on the floor, did they?"

Mattie shook her head. "I've looked everywhere. Even under the sofa pillows."

Julia's hand stilled on the churn. "Is Josette in the bedroom with the door shut?"

At Mattie's impatient nod, something cold clutched at Julia's heart. "You don't suppose—"

Mattie put a hand to her bosom. "I can't imagine—"

Julia leaped to her feet and followed Mattie into the house, running toward the bedroom her aunt shared with Josette. Mattie grabbed the doorknob. It turned, but the door didn't open.

"Josette!"

The coldness around Julia's heart spread into her

stomach. She pounded on the door. "Josette, open this door!"

Both women were quiet for a moment, their ears to the door, listening for sounds from the room. Julia heard high-pitched whimpering.

"Oh, dear Lord, Mattie, do you think she's—"

"Josette Larson, open this door or I'll come in the window!" Mattie shouted.

Mattie turned to leave, but Julia stopped her. "You stay here. I'll go."

Julia lifted her skirts and ran through the house, out the back door, and to the bedroom window. She dragged a crate beneath the sill and stood on it, standing on her tiptoes to see inside.

One hand flew to her mouth, for her sister was lying on the bed, her skirt up around her hips and her legs spread apart. She clutched two knitting needles in her fist and was trying to—

Julia's shock caused her to tumble from the crate and she landed flat on her bottom on the grass. Scrambling to her feet, she put the crate on its end, stood on it again and forced the window open. She dragged herself through the opening and slid to the floor.

She struggled to her feet and threw herself across the bed, grabbing her sister's arm, holding it down until she could twist the knitting needles from her grip.

Mattie pounded on the door. "Josette? Julia? What's happening in there?"

Julia's heart was in her throat, beating so hard it threatened to come out her ears. She crossed to the door, pulled the chair out from under the knob and opened it. Mattie stumbled inside.

"What was she trying to do?"

Julia raised the needles in her direction.

Mattie hurried to the bed, yanked Josette to a sitting position and slapped her on the cheek. With a whimpering cry, Josette cowered against the headboard, one hand covering the cheek Mattie had hit. Her eyes, filled with fear, never left her aunt's face.

"How *dare* you try such a stunt!"

Julia discovered she was clutching the needles so tightly, her knuckles were white.

"Did she get them inside?"

Julia continued to examine them. "I don't think so. There's no blood."

"Please, Aunt Mattie," Josette whined. "Don't hit me anymore."

Mattie grasped her by the shoulders and shook her. "I should slap you senseless," she threatened. "I know what you were trying to do, you spoiled girl, but do you know you could have *killed* yourself? Do you?"

Fat tears tracked Josette's blotchy cheeks. "I don't care. I hate this. I *hate* being this way!"

Mattie flung Josette away from her and stood, planting her fists on her hips. "And you think ramming a knitting needle up inside you is the answer? Hell, no," she swore soundly. "The answer, my girl, is not to get yourself in this condition in the first place."

Josette rolled her head and pouted, the tears coming. "It's too late now, isn't it?" she spat at her aunt.

Mattie heaved a sigh. "Yes, it certainly is."

"I don't want to go through this again. It *hurts*," Josette blubbered.

"And you don't think it would hurt if you jabbed those needles into your body? Not only would that baby come before it's due, and probably die, but you could do all kinds of permanent damage, you fool."

Josette didn't answer, but her tears continued.

"There's no way that baby can get out *without* hurting. What you were trying to do would just make it worse."

Julia stepped to the bed, angry with her sister for attempting such a stupid thing, but feeling a pinch of pity for her as well. Being the source of Mattie's anger wasn't a pleasant position to find yourself in.

"Aunt Mattie is right, Josette," Julia chided. "You've got to learn how to keep this from happening. You've just *got* to."

Crying in earnest now, Josette rolled to her side and clutched at her stomach. "Don't you yell at me, too, Julia, dearest. I don't feel good. I feel awful."

"Lie on your back," Mattie ordered. When Josette complied, Mattie pushed her skirt farther up her hips and yanked her knees apart. "Let me see if you've done any damage."

Josette clamped her legs together.

"Oh, for the sake of the Good Lord," Mattie muttered, "you spread 'em for everyone else, spread 'em for me."

Even Julia blushed at Mattie's blunt words. Josette turned her face to the wall and allowed her aunt to examine her.

Julia studied her sister's legs, now swollen so badly she couldn't make out her delicate anklebones. Moving closer, she bent and touched her, leaving a thumbprint in the puffy skin above her ankle. Her alarm was immediate.

"Mattie?"

Her aunt followed Julia's gaze to the lowest part of Josette's calf. Neither said a word for fear of adding to Josette's hysteria.

Mattie pulled Josette's dress down then felt her forehead. Julia could tell she was concerned, but she said, "I don't think she hurt anything. I guess time will tell."

It made Julia ill to think that Josette purposely wanted to get rid of the baby. And if the baby happened to be McCloud's, it made it that much worse. Julia placed a protective hand over her own stomach, silently assuring the baby that grew there that no matter what, she would love it beyond measure.

Julia and Mattie turned to leave, but Josette grabbed Julia's hand.

"Stay with me a minute, please?"

The plea came as such a surprise, Julia could only nod.

After Mattie had gone, Julia sat down on the bed. Her sister's swollen, tearstained face tugged at something inside her.

"Julia, I'm so scared," Josette admitted, her lower lip trembling.

Julia stroked her sister's arm. "I'm sure you are, Josie, but trying to get rid of the baby is no solution. Better to have it come out naturally."

Josette expelled a watery sigh. "It's not just that. There's something wrong; I can tell." She lifted her skirt, exposing her ankles. "Look at them, Julia. They didn't swell like that the last time."

Julia nodded in agreement, and realized this was the first actual conversation they'd had in years. Josette was truly frightened.

"You'd better stay off your feet." Julia expected she would anyway.

"But there's nothing to *do*. And when I just lie here, I start to think, and I *hate* it, Julia."

Julia swallowed a smile. Of course she did, poor Josie. She'd never really gotten the hang of it.

"I suppose Mattie could teach you to knit, but I don't think she'd trust you with the needles."

Josette blushed. "I noticed you're making a quilt. Could I help you stitch the squares together?"

It was the first time in Julia's memory that Josette had ever offered to do anything. She couldn't turn her down. "Of course. I'll get things together for you."

"Do you miss Mr. McCloud, Julia?"

Caution made Julia hesitate. "Why do you ask?"

"Because I do," Josette said on a sigh. "He was such a fun person, wasn't he?"

Julia straightened the bedding, then fluffed her sister's pillow. "Yes. He was."

Julia missed him so much. Often at night she would sit bolt upright in bed, her heart hammering her ribs as the nightmare returned to haunt her. The nightmare of him calling to her from some deep, dark place from which he couldn't get free. When morning came, she would think about it and wonder why she would dream of McCloud's fears when she had so many of her own.

And now, as she stared into her sister's pitiful face, she admitted to herself that Josette could very well be carrying McCloud's baby, but even if she was, there was nothing she could do about it. What was done, was done. Julia loved McCloud with a desperation that bordered on quiet panic, and if he'd lain with her sister those many months ago, she would have to learn to live with it.

Her stomach churned, and she continued to rub it, binding herself forever to the child growing in her womb. Yes, she'd accept Josette's baby if it were McCloud's, and would love it as if it were her own. But that didn't mean she wouldn't have trouble getting used to the idea.

✹ 18 ✹

Wolf sat in front of the large, stone fireplace. The fire blazed, hypnotizing him. His brother's Swedish housekeeper had treated him like a long-lost son, and Wolf had felt at home, in spite of the grand surroundings. He missed Julia, wished she were here to share this time with him.

"You look lost in a world of your own." Tristan took the seat across from him and handed him a snifter of brandy.

Wolf accepted the warm glass, swirling it before bringing it to his lips. "I was thinking about my wife."

Tristan's mouth curved into a dry smile. "Wife. That's a foreign word to me."

"It was to me, too. I'd never considered myself the type of man to have a wife, much less be faithful to her. I've lived a damned hard life. Thought I'd drink myself to death or die in a whore's bed." He laughed. "Maybe both, if I was lucky."

"You said she had a child. How do you feel about that."

301

Wolf saw his reflection in the amber liquid at the bottom of his glass. Outside he was the same. Inside, he'd changed so much he hardly recognized himself. "When I learned what had happened to us, I decided I'd never refuse to care for an unwanted child, no matter whose it was."

He'd filled his brother in on their mother and half brother over dinner. Tristan had been interested, but admitted that he hadn't felt the same urgency to find his mother. Unlike Wolf, he hadn't honed the sixth sense they shared. He'd known it was there; he shared his twin's intuition, certain there was a part of himself missing, but didn't take the time to delve into it. But the minute Wolf had ridden up, Tristan had admitted he felt gooseflesh.

Tristan grimaced. "You're way too noble."

"Hell, I'm not noble. What you do, caring for a grown woman with the mind of a child, is an honorable thing, Tris."

Tristan sipped his brandy. "I've never known anything else. Besides, Emily was more of a mother to me than my own." He shot Wolf an embarrassed smile. "You know what I mean."

"She's very sweet." It was unusual to watch a woman who was in her middle thirties act like a child not yet in her teens. There was an attachment between them that Wolf didn't understand, but he sensed Emily was jealous of anyone who encroached on her brother's time. Tristan had hired a nurse recently, but Wolf didn't give her much of a future with them, for she appeared to have little patience with Emily.

"We confused the hell out of her, but she loved it."

They laughed together.

"So, tell me about this wife of yours," Tristan said.

"Julia." The sound of her name, along with the brandy, made Wolf feel warm inside. "She's the best thing that's ever happened to me."

Tristan shifted in his chair. "Sounds serious."

One corner of Wolf's mouth lifted. "That's what marriage is, brother. Serious."

"You couldn't prove it by me. I was engaged once, but ..." Tristan shrugged, draining his glass.

"I sense more behind it than that."

His brother stared into the fire, his empty snifter dangling from his fingers. "I thought so, too. A funny thing happens to rich, well-bred white women when they get around a breed. You ever notice that?"

Wolf mentally counted the white women, well-bred and not, whom he bedded. "Yes, I've noticed."

"We're a stud service, that's all."

"You've had a different life from mine. There weren't too many well-bred women of any color where I grew up."

"I found mine in New York. Can't say any of them were memorable, including my ex-fiancée."

Wolf heard the bitterness in his brother's voice. "I got lucky with Julia. I still don't think I deserve her, but I'm working on it."

"Is she pretty?"

"She's beautiful. Smart. Witty. Funny. Loving. Giving. Compassionate. Passionate."

Tristan chuckled. He rose and placed his empty snifter on the mantel. "None of those attributes describe what she looks like, brother."

Julia's sweet face floated before him. "No, but they all describe what she is." He was leaving in the morning, anxious to get home. Anxious to resume his marriage. His life.

* * *

Julia stretched and rubbed the small of her back. Washing windows was one of her least hated chores, for at least she could be outside. Meredith sat on the porch, sipping a cup of tea. She'd stopped on her way from the jail, and Julia had vowed to be indifferent to her, but couldn't. Meredith had become pathetic. Impeccably groomed and dressed in the past, she was now untidy, as if the mere act of doing her hair was a chore. Julia felt sorry for her in spite of what she'd done.

"I keep asking myself if I would have lived my life differently if I'd known the outcome."

Julia dropped into a chair beside her. "What's your answer?"

Meredith shook her head. "I don't know." She gave Julia a wan smile. "You must think I'm terrible, considering what I've done."

Julia sighed. "I don't understand, Meredith. I couldn't abandon a child, much less tell someone else to kill it for me." She couldn't forgive Meredith for that.

"It's no excuse, Julia, but I was young. Very young and very wild." Her hands shook as she took a sip of tea. She put the cup on her knee and wrapped her hands around it.

"Part of the reason we came west was because of me," she admitted, her voice filled with shame. "My papa said it would tame me. He was ashamed of how I acted. In the eyes of his friends, he was a failure because of me." She smirked, the wrinkles around her mouth accentuating her age. "No good, little Italian girl would act so brazen, he would say, his voice filled with quiet shame. I loved my father, but I didn't care. It was the only way to get his attention."

She studied her tea. "Now, it pains me to say it,

but I see similarities in my relationship with Serge. I'm responsible for his behavior, but ... am I also responsible for, you know, the way he is? The choices he's made?"

At the mention of Serge's sexual preference, Julia thawed, for she wondered if anything could be harder for a parent to accept than that. "I don't know. But if it's any consolation, I don't think Serge did it to hurt you. I can't imagine why anyone would ... be that way by choice."

Meredith's eyes were filled with cautious hope. "You don't think so?"

"McCloud had never met Serge before, yet he knew. Lord, Meredith, I'm one of the most innocent women in the world, but even *I* knew that Serge was different, even if I couldn't put my finger on what it was that singled him out."

Meredith took a shuddering breath. "I've made a mess of my life. I don't confess this to many people, but I wasn't raped by that savage."

Julia's hand went to her chest. "What happened?"

"I went with him of my own free will. Your husband is the spitting image of him." She made a croaking sound, one that Julia assumed was supposed to be a laugh.

"I was sure I couldn't conjure up an image of him in my mind. Then your husband turned up at my house. Lord, the past roared at me with the speed of a bullet." She rubbed her temples. "I was certain I'd put it all behind me, and there he was, big as life and twice as dangerous to everything I'd worked so hard for, and to everything I'd tried so hard to forget."

There was nothing to say. "You tried to kill him," Julia reminded her.

"No. I didn't want him dead, I—"

"Why not?" Julia pushed. "You wanted him dead when he was just a baby and had done nothing. I can't believe you didn't want him dead after he showed up, threatening everything you'd worked for."

Meredith put her cup on the floor. "Maybe I did. You don't understand, Julia. Once things started going wrong for me, I couldn't stop them. Any means to get what I wanted seemed all right."

Julia felt a hitch in her throat. "Even the death of your son."

"Yes," Meredith added on a whisper. "Even that. Because he was a stranger to me."

Shocked to hear her admit it, Julia stood, grabbing the chair to keep it from clattering to the floor. "Why did you stop here today?"

"I've come to make amends."

If the entire situation hadn't been so serious, Julia might have laughed. "You should talk to McCloud, not me."

"He wouldn't listen to me and you know it."

Julia pulled in a shaky breath. "What makes you think I will?"

"A woman's heart is more forgiving." Her voice held the quiet ring of hope.

Julia walked to the edge of the porch. "What do you want to do?"

"I want to leave my land to your heirs."

Julia spun around and caught Meredith's gaze. "Your land?" Her heart surged with hope. All those wonderful fertile acres ... Then she remembered the proud man she married.

"McCloud would never accept it. I know he wouldn't."

"Then you'd better find a way to make him listen, Julia, because either I leave my land to him and his

306

heirs, and he accepts it, or I sell it to the first person who wants it. And I can't believe that husband of yours is so prideful and stubborn that he'd let that land slip through his fingers."

She rose and went down the porch steps. "Mother and I are moving to Martinez. The trial will be there, I guess. Whatever Serge is, he's the only thing I have left, and I *will* be there for him."

She took Julia's hand in hers. "You have one month to contact Earl Williams and tell him yea or nay. After that, he'll sell it."

Julia watched her leave, wondering if McCloud would even be home in a month. If he wasn't, did she dare agree to accept the land on his behalf, knowing how he felt about his mother?

Wolf tied the horses to the hitching post and stepped into the jail. It was hard not to tell his half brother to go straight to hell, then wipe him from his mind forever. After all, he was so close to home, he could almost smell the sweet scent of his wife. But he needed to know the man better. Find out why Serge hated him so much. What made him tick.

He went inside, walked passed the empty desk and into the room that held the cells. Barnes snored on his cot. Serge was reading the paper.

"Hello, Serge."

Serge put the paper on the cot and stood, wiping his palms on his trousers. "What do you want?"

"Some answers."

Serge approached the bars, his steps leery. "What else is there to know? You've got everything you want. I've got nothing."

Wolf's reaction was to ask him whose fault that was,

but he refrained. Despite everything that had happened, he felt sorry for the man.

"Who burned down my barn and my cabin, Serge?"

"Frank. On my orders."

Wolf felt as if there were a weight on his chest. "Did you hate me that much?"

"I hated what you were." Serge dragged his fingers through his long, disheveled hair. "Do you have any idea what it feels like to be me?" There was a hint of panic in his voice.

"No, I don't."

Serge pounded his fist on the bars. "At least you didn't tell me you understood. God, but I hate that. No one understands unless they're inside my skin."

"I am sorry about one thing, though."

"Yeah? What's that?" He sounded defensive, as if expecting an insult.

"That we didn't get to know each other."

Serge snorted. "And why would you want to get to know your Nancy-boy brother, huh?"

Shame crept into Wolf's face. Even though he'd used the term as part of his act when he and Crawford set the trap for Barnes, he'd also used it when talking with Julia. "I apologize for that. It was cruel and uncalled for."

"Yes. It was. I was never a threat to you, you must have known that."

"I knew it immediately. I should have been more sensitive, Serge. If anyone understands what it's like to be an outcast, it's me."

Serge swung away. "I'd like you to do me a favor."

"Name it."

"I want you to keep an eye on Mother."

"The *hell* I will—"

"That's all I ask, McCloud. She doesn't need

money, she doesn't need friends. She's got plenty of both. But I'd like to know that you aren't holding a grudge against her for something she did twenty-six years ago. Haven't you ever done anything you regret?"

He pushed the right buttons, didn't he? Wolf thought. He took a deep breath and dug his hands into his back pockets. "All right. I'll see what I can do."

Tears pooled in Serge's eyes and he blinked. "That's all I ask."

Wolf stuck his hand through the bars, Serge hesitated, then took it. His grip was firm. Serge had done a lot of terrible things, but Wolf pitied him just the same. His life in prison would be miserable, especially if Barnes were there to tell everyone Serge's inclination.

Josette's limbs continued to swell. Mattie had drawn Julia aside the day they'd discovered her trying to abort and told her that Josette had a fever, and Mattie was concerned. The doctor was called to examine her, and his diagnosis wasn't good. He feared Josette had poison in her blood, and if that were the case, there was nothing anyone could do but wait.

She got out of bed only to relieve herself, and needed help to do so. She was petulant, listless, and slept a great deal. When she was awake and alert, she worked on the quilt. Her stitches were not as clean and even as Julia's, but Julia didn't care. The fact that Josette was willing to do *something* made it worthwhile.

The sisters had formed a quiet truce. Josette had even apologized for all of the things she'd done to Julia in the past. But that had been weeks ago. Now,

Josette was having trouble with her memory, sometimes even becoming delirious.

Julia stopped at her sister's room on her way outside to hang laundry. Josette's face bore the ravages of her disease. Her once sunny-blond hair was dull and stringy. Her eyes were flat and her mouth in a perpetual frown. Julia still hadn't gotten up the nerve to ask about the baby.

Smiling at her sister, she sat on the bed. "How are you this morning?"

Josette cringed. "I feel terrible."

Julia brushed her sister's hair off her forehead, uncovering a mass of reddened blotches. "How about if I fix your hair today?"

Josette's answer was a bloodless shrug. "What difference does it make what I look like? I'm fat and swollen and I feel like a cow."

Josette's fingers were puffy and almost lifeless as Julia clasped them in hers. "You're still the prettiest Larson girl around," she encouraged.

"If you say so, Julia."

Julia continued to hold Josette's hand. "Josie, I want to ask you something. I think I deserve the truth."

Josette gave her a puzzled look. "What is it?"

"Who's the father of your baby?" Julia held her breath.

Josette grimaced and frowned, rubbing her forehead with her free hand. "You mean Frank?"

Julia's hopes soared. "Frank is the father of the baby you're carrying?"

Josette shook her head. "Frank is Marymae's father. You know that."

Trying not to sound impatient, she pressed on. "But who fathered the one you're carrying? Frank?"

"No," Josette whined. "I *told* you, Frank is Marymae's father."

Julia took a deep breath and said a quick prayer. "Is it McCloud?"

"Mr. McCloud?" Her smile was almost grotesque as her dry lips stretched over her teeth. "He's such a nice man, isn't he, Julia?"

Julia dredged up more patience. "Yes, he's a nice man. Is he the father of your baby?"

Josette stretched, her eyes dreamy. "He always took me berry picking. Remember, Julia? He was so nice. And handsome. Wasn't he handsome, Julia?"

Julia examined Josette carefully, looking for signs of pretense. She found none. Her escape into a safer place happened more and more often. Julia's heart ached for her.

"Yes, Josie. He was a handsome man." She patted her sister's hand and stood. She wouldn't get an answer out of her today.

She hurried outside. Mattie was already hanging wash on the rope that was pulled tight between two oak trees. Julia took the other end of a sheet Mattie had picked out of the basket and drew it along the line. The wind was strong, whipping the laundry into their faces as they worked.

"With this wind, I'd expect these things to dry in no time," Mattie announced as she picked up one of Baptiste's shirts and pinned it to the line.

Mattie had already patched that shirt. Julia also recalled the rest of his clothes, which were as sparse and worn as McCloud's. She thought about the three new shirts she had sewn her husband, something to keep her fingers busy during the nights when she couldn't sleep. Or when Josette was restless and kept her awake. She wondered if he would ever return and wear them. As the weeks went by, she wondered if he'd return at all.

"That Frenchman doesn't have a pot to pee in," Mattie exclaimed, poking her fingers through a hole in the knee of a pair of Baptiste's trousers.

Julia smiled. "Maybe he just doesn't like to spend his money on clothes."

Mattie made an indelicate sound in her throat as she examined the other knee. "Not spending money on clothes is one thing. Walking around looking poor as a hind-tit calf is another."

"I'm surprised. McCloud told me Baptiste was living with his fourth wife. I'd expect her to at least keep his clothes patched."

Mattie snorted again. "He made some comment to me the other day about how his squaw left and returned to her people. Can't say I blame her, poor thing. He's not an easy man to get along with."

Julia had noticed that in spite of Mattie's harsh words, she had softened considerably toward the Frenchman. "Maybe all he needs is a good woman to keep him in line."

"Don't go getting any ideas, Julia McCloud. I'd sooner live with a pack of wolves."

Julia McCloud. Julia's heart swelled with pride. She was Julia McCloud, Wolf McCloud's wife, pregnant with his child, and no matter what happened, no one could take that from her. "No, you wouldn't. Why not take him to San Francisco with you?"

Mattie stopped working and stared at Julia as if she were insane. "What? Like a pet rooster or something? Excuse the cussing, dear, but hell and damnation! What would I do with the likes of him? What's any man good for, anyway?"

Julia enjoyed teasing her aunt, for the woman

blushed like a bride when she was befuddled. "They're good for warming your feet at night." *Your feet are colder than a witch's tit.* She shook away the quiet voice in her head, for the memory of that night in McCloud's bed was one she tucked in a safe place, fearing that if she dwelled on it, it would dissipate like smoke on the wind.

"Well," Mattie groused, "I expect you got one of the last good ones, dear." She patted Julia's stomach. "How have you been feeling?"

Mattie had guessed Julia's condition early on. They hadn't mentioned it in front of Josette, however.

"I'm fine. Really, I'm fine." She'd be better if her husband returned.

She pinned another sheet to the line, her gaze going to the barn. She hoped McCloud wouldn't be upset when he learned Meredith's men finished it.

"You're thinking about that man of yours, aren't you?" Mattie clipped pins in the center of the sheet to keep it from dragging on the ground.

"I think of little else, if you want to know the truth."

"Are you concerned that Josette is carrying his baby?"

Julia's heart lurched. "Why would you say that? I don't think I've ever mentioned it."

"You didn't have to, dear. I've heard Josette's snide remarks and I've seen the concern on your face."

Julia stopped working. "When Papa first hired him, he was with Josette a lot. She'd beg Papa to let McCloud take her out to 'pick gooseberries,' or some such excuse."

"How do you know that's not what they were doing?"

"Oh, Mattie." She wasn't able to hold back her disbelief. "They may have come home with gooseberries, but I can't believe that's all they did."

"You don't trust your Mr. McCloud?"

"I certainly didn't trust him *then*. He gave me no reason to. He was brash, impertinent, and an outrageous flirt."

"Hmmmm. I see your point."

"I've nearly convinced myself that it won't matter to me if the baby *is* McCloud's. What good would it do? What's done is done." She hoped she sounded more convincing than she felt.

Stooping to the basket, Mattie pulled out some diapers and clipped them to the line. "Who is Marymae's father?"

The wind blew a strand of hair into Julia's face, and she brushed it off. "He was one of the hands. Papa fired him after he discovered Josette's condition, but he didn't go far. He was working at the ranch over the hill."

"Was?" Mattie picked up the empty basket and they started toward the house.

"He's in jail." She swallowed her revulsion. "He killed Papa."

Mattie's sharp intake of breath was followed by, "The bastard deserves to rot there."

Julia rubbed her arms as they walked. "Personally, I'd sooner see him hanged."

"By his you-know-whats, if it were up to me," Mattie interjected. "Pardon me, dear, but men so often think with their balls, let them die by them since they find them so all-fired precious."

Julia laughed, surprised she didn't blush. "And here I thought you were my sweet old Aunt Mattie."

"Nothing sweet about me." They reached the porch

and she stopped. "Is there any chance that the bastard is also the father of this baby?"

A squiggle of hope burgeoned in Julia's chest. "I don't know. It's possible, I guess."

Mattie clucked her tongue. "No doubt you've spent all your time worrying about your man and Josette."

Julia gave her a cynical smile. "No doubt."

The wind picked up the sound of approaching horses, and both women turned, shading their eyes against the sharp morning sun.

In a heartbeat Julia knew it was McCloud. But it wasn't until she saw him, his thighs clutching his stallion's belly, that she knew just how much she'd missed him, and how embedded the longing was in her soul.

⚡ 19 ⚡

With shaky fingers, Julia hastily tucked the wild ends of her hair into her chignon. She wished she'd known he was coming, for she would have changed her clothes. Her apron was permanently stained with berry juice from canning, and wet with gray wash water.

He dismounted, his eyes never leaving her. Only then did she notice the other horse. It looked very much like Sally. But Julia's gaze traveled back to her husband. She stared at him, wanting to see hope, love, and joy, for that's what she felt in her heart.

He tied both his black and the Morgan to the short hitching post near the porch and strode to her, devouring her with his gaze.

They stood, mere inches apart, and Julia felt longing and hunger, both of which she knew were mirrored in her eyes.

"You came home." She wanted to touch him, trace his features with her fingers, throw herself at his hard chest.

He studied her, as if trying to remember every nuance of her. She wished she'd been prepared for his homecoming, but if she'd known he was coming, she would have been a wreck.

"Yes, Julia. I've come *home.*"

The sound of his voice made her weak, the memory of it washing over her like nectar heated by the sun. She rushed into his embrace. He held her so tightly, she could hardly breathe, but she didn't care. It seemed the most natural place in the world to be, for she'd dreamed of it, hoped for it, wanted it more than she'd wanted anything else for a very long time.

She couldn't speak; words were inadequate to explain how she felt. She breathed in his smell, trapping it in her lungs as she rubbed her face over his shirt. She traced his scars with her fingertips, remembering each groove, wishing again she could heal him.

"My lands," Mattie interrupted from somewhere behind her. "I couldn't separate the two of you with a spatula."

Julia laughed. "Oh, McCloud, I'm so glad you're home."

She heard faint yelping coming from one of the horses. Standing on tiptoe, Julia peered over McCloud's shoulder at the Morgan and saw two fluffy heads poking out of the saddlebag.

"What do we have here?"

His grin was sheepish, boyish. "I was sure you said we needed a dog."

She went to the saddlebag and bit back the urge to laugh. "Oh, they're adorable."

At being noticed, the pups yipped and wiggled as they tried to get out of the bag. Julia lifted them out, and they immediately went for her face, licking and nipping.

"But McCloud," she said between bouts of laughter, "why two of them?" She put them on the ground and they wrestled and tugged at one another, tumbling around, happy to be free.

He knelt and played with them. "Well, they were brothers." He shrugged. "I just couldn't see separating them."

Julia forced back tears of understanding. "Of course you couldn't," she answered on a quiet breath.

Mattie cleared her throat. "I can see you two want to be alone." She lifted the puppies into the laundry basket. "I'll just take these rascals and put them on the porch."

Julia heard her, but didn't respond. She knew tears of happiness seeped from the corners of her eyes, but she didn't care. McCloud was home. Her husband, her lover, the father of the child now thriving in her womb. She returned to his arms and clung to him.

He claimed her lips. The kiss was hard. Fierce. Open-mouthed. He possessed her tongue, darting around it, circling it, demanding more.

He tasted sweet. Hot. Familiar. She felt the intimate explosion of biting, pinching hunger. Raising one knee, she swung it around to the back of his leg, dragging him closer.

His breath came hard as he raised his head. His eyes were dark with desire and he inhaled deeply.

"I've missed you, Julia. I've missed everything about you. Your smell," he added, bending to nuzzle her hair. "God, but I've missed it. There's nothing more arousing to me than the way you smell, like fresh air and the hot, secret aroma of woman. *My* woman." He dragged his face over hers, his stubble scraping her skin. She caught his mouth when it moved close, and they exchanged wet kisses.

He shuddered against her ear. "I knew a long time ago that if I were thrown blindfolded into a roomful of women, I could pick you out with no trouble at all."

His earthy words thrilled her. She arched her neck, allowing him to lick her there. He moved to her ear, where he drew her lobe into his mouth, biting down gently. She shivered as her desire deepened, and when he returned to her neck and sucked on it, she thought she would splinter into a million sparkly pieces.

He pressed against her, allowing her to feel him. "See?" he whispered against her ear. "I'm horny as a tomcat on a back alley fence, woman."

Her answer was a warm chuckle. "Oh, McCloud, how I've missed your sweet-talkin' ways."

His chest shook with laughter. Pulling her to him, he lifted her skirts and wrapped her legs around his back. She felt the long, hard heat of him at the juncture of her thighs. She bit back a sound of pleasure and rested her head on his shoulder.

"I've never been much of a sweet talker, Julia, you know that. But I like the hot words. The ones that make you blush." He bent and made a growling noise on her neck.

It tickled, and she laughed again, then stared up into his sultry eyes. "Oh, McCloud, I do love you so."

The words were barely out of her mouth before she realized she must have said them out loud. She'd hoped she hadn't, but one look at his face assured her that she had.

He released her, and her legs swung to the ground. They stood and stared at each other, Julia wishing she could take the words back. Not because they weren't true, but because she was afraid they would frighten her husband off.

There was confusion in his eyes, but he said nothing.

He just took her hand and pulled her toward the Morgan.

"This," he said, rubbing the animal's nose, "is for you."

She didn't want presents; she wanted his love. But she gave him a wide, pleased smile. "For me?"

"A gift from my brother."

"You found him! Oh, I'm so glad."

She stroked the mare's nose. "I want you to tell me all about your trip. Was it what you'd expected?"

McCloud touched the mare, too, his fingers a hairbreadth from hers. "It was. We're alike in many ways, Julia, but different, too. He has money and power. I have you."

She wanted to believe that meant McCloud was the luckier man, but after nearly scaring him off with her words of love, she couldn't be sure.

"She's pregnant. By his black Arabian." He expelled a sound of disbelief. "Christ, Julia, we even own the same kind of horse."

Julia pressed her nose to the mare's forehead, sensing an immediate bond. But she couldn't tell McCloud about their baby ... not yet. She felt she'd already shocked him enough for one day. And maybe ... just maybe, she was afraid of his reaction.

She dug into her apron pocket and pulled out a partly eaten apple, lifting it to the animal's mouth. "She's beautiful, McCloud." And she was. As the mare daintily took the treat, Julia studied her, a familiar ache giving her a flash of sadness. She was very much like her sweet Sally.

"What's her name?" The mare nuzzled Julia's hand, searching for another treat.

"He called her Weeko."

"Weeko," Julia repeated, pleased when the animal's ears perked up. "What does it mean?"

"It's an Indian name for 'pretty.' "

Julia continued to stroke the mare. "When is she due to foal?"

"About the same time Sally would have."

Julia thought about Sally's death and the loss of the barn, and everything they'd gone through since. "She's a wonderful gift, McCloud. Thank you."

"It's sort of a peace offering for being gone so long." He tipped her face to his. "Has Baptiste given you trouble?"

"Oh, no," she said swiftly. "He's been very kind." She found herself smiling. "In fact, I've gotten rather used to having him around."

His fingers still stroked her chin. "So the old reprobate didn't embarrass you too much?"

She cocked her head. "Actually, he reminds me a lot of you."

His grin was full and heart-stopping. "So, he *did* embarrass you."

She returned his smile. "I think he's after Mattie."

"I hope she can give as good as she gets." His gaze wandered toward the barn.

"She's perfectly capable of holding her own, McCloud."

His fingers stroked her neck. "Rather like you, I'd expect." He appeared distracted as he continued to study the newly built structure. "I see you got someone to finish the barn."

"Meredith's men did, McCloud."

A muscle tightened in his jaw.

"I know what you're thinking."

He quirked a sexy black eyebrow at her. "What am I thinking, Julia?"

She put her arm around his waist and drew him toward the barn. "You're thinking that you can do your own work, and that you don't want help from her."

He gave a rakish smile. "That's exactly what I'm thinking. I told her the first time I saw her that I didn't want a damn thing from her, and I meant it. She could offer me the moon and I'd tell her to blow it out her ass."

She had to tell him what his mother wanted to do. But ... not yet.

"I'm also a practical man," he continued. "I'm grateful the barn is done, even if it was her workmen who did it. But then, since I discovered they were the ones who burned it down in the first place, it evens out. I don't owe her a damned thing, Julia."

Julia let out a quiet whoosh of air. She could see Meredith's land slipping through her fingers. She understood McCloud's feelings, but she wanted that land. For their children. And their children's children. She'd become greedy now that she was pregnant with a child of her own.

They entered the barn. The smell of new wood lingered with the smell of hay. Dust particles danced in the filtering light from a window.

"It smells lusty," he declared.

Julia sniffed the air. "Lusty? How can a barn smell lusty, McCloud? Musty, maybe, or dusty, but—"

He drew her to him, his eyes dark and smoky. "Where is everyone?"

Her heartbeat accelerated. "Baptiste went into Walnut Hill." She shook with desire. "Mattie's in the house; Marymae is asleep." She didn't mention Josette, and he didn't ask.

He dragged her to a dark, hay-filled corner. "I've

wanted a roll in the hay with you for a long time. I don't want it to be quick, but damnit, Julia, I don't know how long I can wait." He took her hand and pressed it against his fly. He was thick and hard, and Julia rubbed him with her palm.

With nimble fingers he unbuttoned his jeans and drew her hand inside. Weak with hunger, Julia fondled him, reaching low and caressing the warm sac, then moved her fingers to his shaft again. Small amounts of his seed oozed from the slippery tip, and Julia had the insane urge to take him into her mouth.

He gripped her fingers. "No more, sweetheart, or I'll spend all over your hand."

She reached under her skirt and untied her drawers, letting them fall to her ankles, then stepped out of them. His hands were on her immediately, his thumbs nudging at her cleft. Evidence of her hunger ran down the insides of her thighs, and she was unable to stand, for her knees would not hold her.

He pressed her gently to the hay, flinging her skirt up and devouring her with his greedy gaze. She squirmed, anxious for him. "McCloud." Her voice was a pleading whisper.

He spread her legs and came between them, then lowered his head and kissed her *there*. She bucked, the sensation of his mouth on her nether parts so exquisite, she thought she would splinter into a million pieces and die from the pleasure.

Grabbing at his hair, she held him there, feeling the kernel of pleasure expand into a roaring climax as she trapped him with her thighs.

When he moved up and claimed her mouth, she tasted herself on his lips. He entered her, driving deep, then rocked with her until she felt his explosion inside her.

They clung to one another, the only sounds those of their mingled breathing as they tried to catch their breath.

Julia threaded her fingers through his hair, a languid sense of surrender making her unwilling to move. "I've missed you, McCloud. I—" She wanted to explain her love for him, assure him that she didn't want to trap him. "I don't—"

He pressed one hand over her mouth; the other went beneath her skirt. "Someone's coming," he whispered close to her ear.

She almost giggled. What difference did it make? They were married, for heaven's sake. She glanced at him. His jeans were down around his knees, his dark, muscular thighs pressed to her naked hip. His fingers found her, and she bit her lip to keep from moaning her pleasure.

"Those stupid geldings. They are no better than camels," Baptiste muttered as he entered the barn.

Julia slapped McCloud's hand away from between her legs, but it came back, stroking deep. She grabbed his hair, but had no desire to push him away. He rubbed himself against her hip and she felt him harden, suddenly realizing he enjoyed the game they played.

She reached down and stroked him. He laughed quietly, then stuck his tongue in her ear.

Baptiste's footsteps scuffed louder, and Julia had a wild feeling that they would be discovered. And suddenly she didn't care, because McCloud's fingers were working their magic and she felt ready to erupt again.

But she couldn't lose control, not with Baptiste just a few feet away! She pushed on McCloud's chest, but he rolled over and entered her, and she clung to him, relieved when his mouth covered hers, for had it not, her cries of completion would not only have brought Baptiste to their hideaway, but would have undoubtedly brought Mattie running from the house with the shotgun.

When they could breathe again, Julia listened for Baptiste.

"He's gone," McCloud said, and kissed her again.

She drove her fist into his shoulder. "That was a dirty trick. What if he'd seen us? What then?"

He gave her a expansive smile. "But he didn't. At least, I don't think he did." He rolled off her and brought her with him. "But wasn't it exciting? Didn't you get all hot and horny wondering if he'd find us?"

She couldn't help but laugh. "You are terrible. Do you always get your thrills in the midst of danger?"

He no longer smiled, but his eyes were warm. "Not always."

His serious side befuddled her. She reached for her drawers, but he stopped her.

"Don't put them on, Julia."

"McCloud," she scolded, "we are not alone. Remember?"

He cursed. "Oh, yeah. It's all coming back to me now."

She scrambled into her underwear, tying it hastily at her waist before straightening her skirts. Her eyes drifted to her husband and she shivered. He was ready for her again.

"Shameful man," she murmured around a smile. "Make yourself decent."

With an exaggerated sigh, he hiked up his jeans. "An impossible task, m'love. Are you up to it?"

She turned away before he could see the longing in her eyes. "It's a tempting offer. I'll think about it," she answered lightly. As she ambled toward the door, she added, "However, I actually prefer you the way you are. Irreverently *in*decent."

His laughter followed her as she left the barn. She was grinning herself—as she ran smack dab into Baptiste. A blush started at her neck and ended as it sank into her scalp.

"So, Wolfgang is home, eh?"

She brushed the hay off her skirt and gave him a sick smile as she hurried toward the house.

The Frenchman laughed, the bawdy sound intensifying Julia's embarrassment. He wandered into the barn, singing a tune in French that Julia was certain she wouldn't want him to translate.

"So, *mon ami*," Baptiste said around a huge, lusty grin, "I see you take care of the important things first, eh?"

Feeling no remorse, Wolf returned the grin and stuffed his shirt into his jeans. "Thanks for being here for me."

"I am glad you are back. Not that I haven't enjoyed the change," Baptiste added, "but I think you are definitely needed here."

"Anything serious?" With Serge and Frank Barnes in jail, he didn't worry about that threat.

"Just the pregnant one," he said with disgust. "She is like poison, making remarks about you and her in front of the sweet one."

"The sweet one?" They left the barn and went to tend the horses.

"Of course. The one you married. She is the sweet one."

Wolf chuckled. "So that's how you see her? Sweet?"

"*Oui.* She puts up with much from the other one."

"Yeah. I was kind of hoping 'the other one' would be gone when I got home."

"No. The pregnancy is not going well. The *bébé* may even be in danger. She tried to kill it."

Wolf swatted the black on the rump and closed the paddock gate. "I guess I'll have to face the situation sooner or later." He handed the mare's reins to his friend. "Put her in the barn, would you?"

Baptiste led the mare into the barn. Wolf pulled in a fortified sigh and headed for the house.

Josette had been watching for him, because when he passed her room, she called to him.

Stopping at the door, Wolf looked in. Josette was on the bed, resting against the headboard. At least, he thought it must be her, but God almighty, she looked nothing like the woman he remembered.

"I want to talk to you," she announced.

Wolf was careful not to stare at her face, now swollen and covered with red blotches. He stepped inside and went to the foot of the bed. "What do you want?"

"You can look at me, Mr. McCloud. The expression on your face won't shock me. I know what I look like."

He raised his eyes, surprised at her tone. This was not the flighty, spoiled Josette that he remembered.

She straightened the quilt she was stitching over her stomach. "I've had a lot of time to think since I've been home." She uttered a humorless laugh. "Everyone assumes I don't think at all, but I've had nothing else to do, and the truth to tell, I find the process quite boring."

She linked her swollen fingers together. "They tell me that sometimes I'm out of my head. Since I'm not right now, I have to ask a favor."

Wolf felt an urgent need to be with Julia. "What

do you want from me?" He was impatient and didn't care if Josette knew it. He'd never cared much for her type, but when he discovered what she'd done to Marymae, what feelings he'd had for her disappeared. Now he felt only pity.

"I know about Papa's will, Mr. McCloud. I know you married my sister so you could have the land."

He had no intentions of explaining his feelings for Julia. "And if I did?"

"It's my land, too. I don't even want anything for myself, which may be hard for everyone to understand, since I spent most of my life wanting *everything* for myself. You see," she continued, blotting her forehead with a crumpled linen square, "I know I'm dying."

Her bluntness shocked Wolf, and he didn't know what to say.

"What I want from you is some assurance that my children—Marymae and the one I'm carrying, should it survive and I don't—will be well cared for. I don't want them left out in the cold when you have your own children, Mr. McCloud."

"What makes you think Julia would allow such a thing?"

"Women who think they're in love do stupid things. I should know." She sniggered a skeptical laugh. "She'd do anything you asked. If you should happen to not want my babies, she'd pawn them off on someone else."

Wolf couldn't believe what he was hearing. "She wouldn't do that."

"Why not? I did."

Wolf made a fist, then stuffed it into his pocket to keep from sending it through the wall. "She'd give her *life* for your children. And I would never ask her to choose."

"What of your heirs, Mr. McCloud? How do I know you won't force her to change her mind once you have children of your own?"

"I wouldn't abandon a child because it wasn't mine." He had the urge to tell her why, but decided he wouldn't waste the energy. He heard the pups' noisy play, and was glad he hadn't separated them.

"I'm surprised you didn't learn more from Julia," he said. "I've known her only months, and she's taught me more about love and honor than I knew existed."

"How noble." The words were strained. "That's your answer, then?" She was sweating and in some distress.

"That's my answer. They'll be cared for and loved. I wouldn't have it any other way."

Anxious to leave her, he was out the door when she emitted a high-pitched scream.

❋ 20 ❋

Josette's scream sent Julia running from her own room. She found McCloud on his knees by the bed.

"McCloud? What is it?"

"I don't know. We were talking, and all of a sudden she cried out."

Julia willed herself not to panic. "Get Mattie, will you, please? Tell her to hurry."

McCloud left the room, and Julia turned to her sister, noting the vacant look in her eyes.

"Josie?" She tapped her sister's cheek. She got no response, then all of a sudden Josette stiffened and cried out again.

Julia whipped the covers off and looked at her sister's pelvis. Fear sprang to the back of her throat. Josette was in labor.

Mattie bustled into the room. "What is it? What's happened?"

"She's in labor, Mattie. I don't think there's time to get the doctor."

Mattie took charge. "Send one of the men for him,

anyway. It'll give them something to do and keep them out of our hair."

McCloud poked his head around the corner. "What do you want me to do?"

Julia hoped he saw her gratitude. "Would you ride to Walnut Hill and get the doctor? Tell him it's Josette's time. And McCloud . . . ?"

He reappeared in the doorway. "Yes?"

"Be careful, but . . . please hurry." At his quick nod, she turned back to the bed.

She'd been present at Josette's last birth, but so had the doctor. Her job had been to keep him supplied with whatever he needed.

"Julia." Mattie clapped her hands to get Julia's attention. "If you faint, you'll be as helpful to me as tits on a bull. Now go get me some clean bedding. Put my sewing scissors in hot water, then bring some water and soft cloths and keep your sister comfortable."

"Yes. That's what I was going to do, Mattie." Julia hurried to gather what they would need, and prayed for both her sister and the unborn child.

Julia pinched back tears and pressed her fingers to her quivering lips as they lowered Josette's casket into the ground. McCloud carried Marymae, and Mattie kept the tiny newborn baby girl wrapped like a mummy, even though there was no wind and the sun was warm. It was almost in passing that Julia noticed the baby's white-blond hair and fair skin. So much had happened so quickly, the baby's father had become the least important issue.

Grass and wildflowers grew over Papa's grave, which lay a few feet away, and it gave Julia solace to know that Josette's wouldn't be a patch of bare earth for long.

Julia listened to the preacher's prayers and accepted condolences from neighbors, but heard nothing. All she could think about was her poor sister, unable to find happiness in life. She hoped Josette would find it in death.

"She gave us two beautiful daughters, sweetheart."

Julia gave her husband a wavery smile. "I know. I'll miss her, and I'm so sorry she's gone, but she wasn't happy, Mac. And she wasn't well." She'd begun to shorten his name during the chaos of Josette's birthing, and somehow it felt right. In her quiet musings, she would continue to think of Wolf as that wild, dangerous, disreputable breed who stole her heart. But Mac was the man she loved. And the man she'd tamed.

He led her to the buggy, helped her in, and handed her Marymae. Mattie was already there with the new baby, whose cries sounded like those of a newborn calf.

"We've got to name her, Julia." Mattie's voice was soft, as if she didn't want to startle her.

"I know. I'd like to name her Bethany. When we were children, Josette had an old rag doll that she dragged everywhere. She'd called her Bethany."

They rode home in silence, Julia leaning on McCloud's shoulder. Everything had happened so fast, she hadn't had time to tell him about her pregnancy or his mother's land offer.

Later that night, when everyone else was finally asleep, Julia cuddled close to her husband's chest. "Your mother wants to leave us her land."

"I don't want it."

She made a face in the darkness. "Don't be selfish and stubborn. Think of the children. I don't care if you don't want it. I do. It's a windfall. It's the children's future we have to worry about, not ours. Although, with three children under the age of three, we could use it, too."

His hand stopped on her buttocks. "I wondered when you were going to tell me."

She rose up on her elbow. "You knew?"

"When my wife's perky breasts start to fill out the bodice of her gown, I get suspicious."

"We're going to have quite a houseful," she warned.

"I guess we'll have to consider taking Meredith up on her offer, won't we?"

Julia lay her head on his arm and breathed a sigh of relief. "I guess we will."

"Julia?"

"Yes?" She kissed his shoulder.

"From the first moment I saw you, I knew you were a woman out of my reach. I thought to myself, 'What could I do to deserve her?' I couldn't think of a damned thing. You were smart and witty. Noble and brave. And a whole passel of exciting contradictions I've only begun to understand."

If he meant to compliment her, he was going about it the wrong way. "Is this leading up to something I don't want to hear?"

"I don't think so. I want to tell you all of this, so be patient with me. The first night you invited me into your bed, I could tell that you were offering out of a sense of duty. I wanted fire. Passion." He bent and kissed her, the familiarity of his mouth provocative foreplay.

"I knew I wouldn't find it that night, and I honestly didn't know if I'd ever find it with you. Hell, how could a woman like you possibly give yourself to a man like me? I didn't deserve you, and I don't feel worthy. You say you love me. That's not an easy thing for me to accept."

She turned in his arms. "And why not?"

"Because you're not getting nearly the man you deserve." He rubbed his lips against her forehead.

"Do you love me, Wolfgang McCloud?"

"I love you, and I'm happy you're my wife. I got a better deal out of this than you."

Relieved, she nestled closer. "That's your opinion. Do you know what you've done for me?"

"This I've got to hear."

"You've made me feel beautiful. You've brought passion and love into my life, and I never believed it would happen to me. And you're an honorable, decent man, Mac."

"Hell, I'm not that decent. I'd thought about you naked long before I believed I'd actually see you that way."

Laughing, she thumped his shoulder with her fist.

"Julia," he began, "I'm going to say this once, then we never have to mention it again. . . ."

She waited.

"I love Marymae, and I'll love Bethany, too. I plan on telling them often, because when they learn about things, they'll need to know that they *are* loved. They're luckier than my brother and me. From the very beginning, they've had you. They can't be blamed for the circumstances of their births any more than I should be blamed for the circumstances of mine. I never want them to feel second best. I never want them to think that just because we aren't their natural parents, we can't love them as much as we do our own."

Julia felt tears slide down her cheeks. "I'd like to

meet your brother one day, although I can tell without seeing him that I got the pick of the litter."

He smiled against her hair. "Speaking of litters, what'll we name those two rascals I brought home?"

"Do you think Papa and Angus would be offended if we named the puppies after them?"

"Angus and Amos. They sound a lot alike, so they'll both come running when one is called. Hell," he said with a laugh, "it works for me." He bent and claimed her mouth.

Love, ripe with tenderness and passion, spilled from Julia's heart, cleansing her soul. Life would not be easy, but with Wolf McCloud by her side, she knew she would never be lonely. And loneliness was a far harder burden to bear, because one bore it alone.

❖ Epilogue ❖

The McCloud ranch,
late July, 1882

Marymae held Weeko's bit with one hand and waved at her father with the other. Her sun-bleached golden braid bobbed slightly as she jogged in a circle. "Papa! Look! Sammy's riding!"

Wolf stood in the yard and returned the wave, amazed that all of his children loved to ride. Sam, their three-year-old son, had taken to horses as quickly as his four older sisters. Now, his chubby fingers gripped the reins and his dark brows were shoved down over his eyes as he concentrated on the task of staying in the saddle.

The lovable mutts, Amos and Angus, lolled in the shade like a couple of comfortable old bachelors, while the newest McCloud puppy, one Baptiste had brought home from a neighboring ranch, frolicked nearby. The children hadn't agreed upon a name for it. Wolf had suggested "Dizzy," because it ran in circles all the time, but his girls wouldn't go for it. He wondered if four independent-spirited young women could decide on a name before the poor dog was old and arthritic and ready for the boneyard.

Bethany, the spitting image of her older sister, rode into the yard on Weeko's filly, Sally Too, sired by Wolf's stallion, Baptiste. The colt Weeko had been carrying when Wolf had brought her home was now a gelding, and he grazed in the pasture with the other horses. All of the children had ridden him, and Baptiste had promptly named him Diable Noir, which everyone shortened to "Devil," since he wasn't entirely black, anyway.

Beth stopped to study her brother's progress. "Don't sit so stiff in the saddle, Sammy," she instructed, her voice a little bossy. "Move with it."

"Don't talk to me while I'm ridin'!" Sam scolded, his intense scowl deepening.

Marymae's disposition was sunny and sweet. She happily wore dresses when she wasn't helping with the animals. Beth's was a bit more like Julia's. She took charge, and Marymae let her. And she was completely at home in a pair of pants. Her favorite perch was high up in an oak tree where she had a good view of the mountain. Neither girl had the selfish, petulant qualities of their natural mother.

Wolf's gaze went to the wide, closed-in porch as Julia stepped outside. His heart expanded with emotion at the sight of her. Even after having given birth to three children, she was trim and beautiful. In his opinion, she got lovelier every day, and he counted himself among the luckiest men in the world.

She strolled out to meet him, the breeze pressing her dress against her body. The familiar curves warmed him.

Rising to her toes, she accepted his kiss. "You taste good, Mr. McCloud," she said around a smile.

He licked his lips. "Not as good as you. *You* taste like cinnamon and sugar."

"Joanna and Joy are in the kitchen with Mattie, learning how to bake bread. I whipped up a coffee cake just so I could stay around and hear the lesson."

The older girls did their cooking chores with Mattie's supervision, but neither was as enthusiastic about them as the twins. They'd taken to it from the time they were old enough to pull a chair up to the counter. Marymae and Beth preferred spending all their time with the horses. They were good workers, for they understood that if you want to ride, you must learn to care for the animals. It wasn't all fun.

Wolf gave her a wry smile. "Well, at least two of my children enjoy being in the kitchen."

"Don't forget Sam," she reminded him. "He *loves* to help when we make strawberry jam."

Wolf drew in a heavy sigh. "I don't want my son to be a sissy, Julia."

She smacked his shoulder. "Shame on you, Wolf McCloud. If your daughters can ride as good as a man, there's no reason why your son can't learn to cook. Why, I remember how pleased I was when I discovered you could make oatmeal." She gave him a skeptical smile. "Of course, I didn't know that it was the *only* thing you could make."

"All right, all right," he said, bending to claim her mouth. "I see your point." He'd never had much luck arguing with his wife, and over the years, he'd discovered she was usually right, anyway.

"Beth and Marymae were studying that old photograph of Josette and me again this morning. Marymae finally asked me to tell her about their mother."

"What did you say?" He watched his fair-haired girls, love welling up inside him.

"Oh, among other things, I told them that their

mother was véry pretty, and that she'd loved them very much."

He smiled, though it didn't reach his eyes. "True enough, I guess. As far as I'm concerned, they never have to know the details."

Julia stretched and planted a kiss on his chin. "They won't hear it from me, darling. That reminds me." She looped her arm through his. "Baptiste heard they've transferred Frank Barnes to that new prison up the coast."

"Good riddance." He'd actually felt sorry for Meredith the day she learned Serge had been killed in prison. And what was worse, it had been an accident.

"Mattie's baking up a storm in there. She's got great plans for Marymae's birthday cake, too."

"Is everyone coming?"

"I've invited Meredith," she said with caution.

"I know." He'd attempted to come to terms with his feelings for his mother, without complete success.

"And you know your brother can't come. They're expecting that baby any day now. But we got a letter from Susannah and Nathan this morning, and they think they'll all be able to make it. Except for Jackson. He's off in Mexico or South America somewhere, fighting one government or another."

"Yeah, and I'll bet he doesn't make jam, either," Wolf murmured.

Julia glared at him. "Listen to me," she warned, pulling on his earlobe. "Don't think about Serge. Ever since Sam was born, you've had this . . . this foolish fear that just because he's a boy, he's going to be different."

"What if he is?"

"What if he isn't?" She planted her fists on her hips. "My father liked to make doughnuts. He loved to watch them rise to the top and sputter in the lard. Figure that one out. He was just a man who happened to like to make and eat doughnuts. It didn't make him a sissy. Sam adores strawberry jam. It's the *only* time he's in the kitchen to help." She shook her head in wonder. "And he spreads it on everything from bread to apricots to escalloped potatoes. I've even seen him dip cucumber pickles into it."

She made such incredible sense, Wolf thought. "I know you're right," he said, "but every now and then those thoughts creep in anyway."

"Thinking about it one way or the other isn't going to change anything. You'll just use perfectly good energy worrying about something that doesn't deserve it. He'll be fine," she assured him, squeezing his arm. "Let him be what he'll be. Just because Marymae and Beth haven't taken to cooking like the other two girls, will you toss them out of the house?"

Wolf's guilt ran deep. If Samuel Amadeus McCloud was like his half brother, Serge Henley, Wolf thought, he would never forgive himself. He would love his son no matter what, but he wouldn't forgive himself for causing him to be different. "Of course not."

"All right, then," she said softly. "Don't worry about things before they even happen. Chances are, you'll be worrying for nothing." She put her arm around his waist and hugged him. "Let's just love them all."

He felt foolish. "I do, honey."

One of the twins opened the door and poked her head out. "Mama?"

Julia turned, shading her eyes. "Yes, Joanna?"

That was another marvel about his wife. From the beginning, she could tell the twins apart. He'd had to work at it a bit.

"Aunt Mattie wants to know if you want one of us to ride over to the little house and ask Uncle Baptiste if he'll take the buggy to town and pick up the 'you-know-what,' " she finished, tossing a quick glance at her oldest sister.

Wolf smiled. The "you-know-what" was Marymae's birthday present: a new saddle for her English riding lessons.

He gazed at Joanna, remembering how surprised he'd been that both she and her sister were so much darker than the older girls. Of course, he shouldn't have been. He was just an ignorant father who was so much in love with the mother of his children that he expected all of them to look like her.

The twins and Sam had dusky skin that turned a beautiful honey-brown in the summer, and their hair, though dark, bleached to a streaked, sunny-lemon color. Marymae's and Bethany's hair bleached to white.

"Tell Aunt Mattie that it would be wonderful if Uncle Baptiste could pick up the 'you-know-what,' darling."

The day Julia's aunt told them she was selling her boardinghouse and staying to help with the children was a day they all rejoiced. Having four girls under the age of two years could have been a nightmare. As it was, Mattie had run the household with an iron fist encased in velvet. In Wolf's own quiet prayers, after he'd thanked the powers that be for giving him the opportunity to have the wonderful life he had, he thanked Mattie for her decision.

After Sam was born, Mattie and Baptiste had sneaked into Martinez and gotten married. Wolf had been glad. The marriage seemed to agree with both of them. Baptiste had taken over the fruit-drying business and had added vineyards of his own. Both were thriving.

The decision to move onto Meredith's ranch and let Mattie and Baptiste have theirs hadn't been an easy one. Wolf imagined old ghosts would haunt him, but Julia and Mattie had redecorated, and he felt comfortable living here.

He'd kept his promise to Serge, too, making sure Meredith wanted for nothing—except his complete forgiveness. Since Rosa's death the year before, she was alone. Julia invited Meredith to visit the children now and then, and when she came, he usually found a way to keep busy and out of sight.

Forgiveness was a difficult concept for him when it came to his mother. At least Josette had wanted to make things right for her children before she died. Maybe that's what Meredith was doing, too. Julia kept reminding him that his mother was alone.

In some ways, he was grateful to her. Had she not abandoned him, he would not have searched for her. And if he hadn't searched for her, he wouldn't have found Julia. And if he hadn't found Julia, his life would have been worth nothing.

Julia leaned against him. "What's got you so deep in thought, darling?"

"I'm quietly giving thanks."

"Hmmm. I'm not sure how I feel about this new, serious Wolf McCloud. He'll have to be evaluated." She tilted her chin and smiled at him.

"Kiss her, Papa! Kiss her!" Beth shouted from her perch on the corral gate.

"Beth, leave them alone," Marymae chided, more sensitive to the tender feelings between her parents than her younger, wilder sister.

Wolf smiled into Julia's hair, breathing in, never

tiring of her scent, then bent and kissed her soundly, bringing cheers from both Beth and Sam.

With reluctance, he left her mouth. "Don't worry about it, love. I haven't changed that much. My fondest moments are those during which you're naked."

She gave him a wry smile. "If only your children could hear the way you talk to their mother. Which reminds me," she added, her hands meandering down his back to his own walkaways. "Have we got the reservations at the hotel?"

She squeezed, and he felt the stirrings of desire. "Greedy wench, aren't you? Of course we have." Mattie and Baptiste had made reservations for the two of them to spend two nights at the hotel that had been built on top of Devil Mountain; they did it every year after Marymae's birthday party, and each year, Wolf swore they enjoyed it more. There was precious little time to be alone with this woman who had given him the kind of life he'd only dreamed about.

"Have I told you that I love you today?" He loved her lively blue eyes.

Her smile was warm, her lips the most sensual he'd ever known. "Not since very early this morning. Right before Sam crawled in and disturbed us," she added, her smile turning wary.

He chuckled. "We've got to get that boy to sleep a little later. At least until dawn."

Just then, Sam ran across the yard toward them. "Pa! Pa! Did you see me? Did you see?" He barreled into Wolf's arms and was immediately raised to his father's shoulders.

"I sure did. You were a real cowhand on that horse, son."

"I don't think I've seen such a handsome man on

horseback since the first time I saw your father, Sammy," Julia complimented, smiling up at her son.

"I'm gonna be like Pa when I grow up, Mama." He grabbed his father's hair and held on as they strolled toward the house.

"Oh," she said, disappointed. "You mean you aren't going to be your Mama's big boy anymore?"

He shook his head. "Nope. I'm gonna be Pa's boy."

Wolf's heart expanded and his fears disappeared. He pressed his lips to his son's chunky calf and made a sputtering sound, sending Sam into peals of laughter.

Everything was going to be fine, he decided. Whatever happened, it would be fine. How else could it be with a wife like Julia and children like theirs?